“You kn

sex is . . . a sleep aid.

“Seriously?” Zoe asked.

“Seriously,” Tyler said. “It releases endorphins and—”

“No, I mean… You’re seriously using that as a pick-up line?”

Tyler’s grin widened. “Not working, huh?” His smile made the desire in his eyes intensify. “It was a shot in the dark. I’ve never been very good at it.”

She suddenly found his humor contagious. “Never good at sex?”

He let loose a laugh. It fell on her like a soft and welcome rain.

“Not good at pick-up lines.” He moved in a few steps. “I’m actually really good at sex. I studied—”

“Enough,” Zoe said.

Still grinning, Tyler brushed her hair from her shoulder. She felt his breath against her cheek and his lips started moving lower.

“Really good at it,” he whispered…

Praise for
Only in Texas

"5 Stars! An entertaining tale with delightful, fully formed characters and an intriguing mystery."

—*RT Book Reviews*

"I lost count of the number of times I laughed out loud... Craig [has a] wonderful ability to write comedic dialogue, appealing characters, tender sentiments, and sexy love scenes... I'm not sure how I missed Ms. Craig's books... Now that I know what is inside the covers, I won't make that mistake again."

—All About Romance (LikesBooks.com)

"Fun... [a] caper-filled story... a good madcap-type romance. I look forward to Tyler and Austin's stories."

—TheRomanceReader.com

"Steamy... Craig seems to have a real knack for writing fun little romantic romps... There is an almost tongue-in-cheek quality to them that just makes them fun to read... I know all I need to do is just sit back and enjoy the ride... Be sure to check out *Only in Texas*."

—TopRomanceNovels.com

"Absolutely a delight to read. Christie Craig has hit a home run with *Only in Texas*. I laughed, teared up, laughed, sighed, laughed, blushed, laughed and laughed, and finally finished the last page with a bit of sadness because I did not want this book to end. It made for a great weekend of reading pleasure."

—GoodReads.com

"Craig offers up another well-written and nicely plotted story...[She] always delivers enjoyable, light romantic mysteries—add *Only in Texas* to the list."

—BookLoons.com

Acclaim for Christie Craig

"Funny, hot, and suspenseful, Craig's writing has it all. She's the newest addition to my list of have-to-read authors. Warning: Definitely addictive."

—Nina Bangs, *New York Times* bestselling author

"Craig is the jewel of my finds when it comes to new authors to add to my favorites list. Her characters draw you in immediately, make you care about them in no time flat, and her humor is to die for."

—GoodBadandUnread.com

"Christie Craig writes delicious sexy romances that are as addictive as a can of Pringles; once you start, you can't stop! Hilarious, romantic...entertaining from start to finish."

—NightOwlRomance.com

"Craig is like chocolate: addicting and good for you. I dare you to dive in and not get a good laugh."

—BookBitch.com

Also by Christie Craig

Only in Texas

Blame It on Texas

CHRISTIE CRAIG

FOREVER

NEW YORK BOSTON

This book is a work of fiction. Names, characters, places, and incidents are the product of the author's imagination or are used fictitiously. Any resemblance to actual events, locales, or persons, living or dead, is coincidental.

Forever
Hachette Book Group
237 Park Avenue
New York, NY 10017

www.HachetteBookGroup.com

Printed in the United States of America

First Edition: August 2012
10 9 8 7 6 5 4 3 2 1

OPM

Forever is an imprint of Grand Central Publishing.
The Forever name and logo are trademarks of Hachette Book Group, Inc.

To my real-life hero, Steve, whose love, support, and humor not only helped me achieve all my career dreams but who is my best friend.

Acknowledgments

To my editor, Michele Bidelspach, who helps make me the best I can be. To my agent, Kim Lionetti, who keeps me on the right path. To my writing buddies and friends: you know who you are and how important you are to me. Thanks so much for the critiques and friendship. And finally to all my readers who took the time to send me an e-mail to say they enjoyed my books. Those kind words feed my inspiration. Thank you, all.

Blame It on Texas

CHAPTER ONE

"WHY ARE YOU SO SAD, *Tio*?"

Tyler Lopez looked down at his six-year-old niece. Her brown eyes were so warm they could... They could persuade a grown man to make a complete idiot out of himself.

Pinching the red ball rubber-banded to his face, Tyler dropped his clown-suited ass on the picnic bench beside the birthday girl. When the real clown canceled late last night, his twin sister, Samantha, had called him in desperation. *Anna will be so disappointed.* Tyler adored all his nieces and nephews, but there was something about Anna—quiet and a bookworm like himself—that made her his favorite. And that made the thought of disappointing her impossible.

"I'm a clown. Clowns aren't sad." He looked out at the twenty or so family members mingling together at the other picnic tables in his sister's backyard. Two of his brothers were pointing and laughing at him. If Anna wasn't sitting right in front of him, he'd have shot them the bird. The Texas humidity, almost unbearable even in September, made the clown suit cling to his skin. The sudden pain in his right leg didn't help his disposition.

"Da...dang it!" he muttered, and scooped up the little orange kitten who had mistaken his leg for a climbing post. Bringing the spirited, blood-drawing feline on top of the table, he knew he couldn't complain too loudly or Anna's mother would be over here to give him hell. Especially since he'd given the kitten to his niece last month as an early birthday present. And according to his sister, the animal was a reincarnated demon. Hence the kitten's name, Damien.

"Some clowns are sad," Anna said. She closed the book she'd been reading and gave Damien a purr-inducing scratch behind the ear.

"Not this clown." He told himself it wasn't a lie. Tyler gave the cat an under-chin rub. That led to the kitten jumping into Tyler's lap and curling up. No doubt the feline remembered who'd snatched him up from the middle of I-10 before he got smeared on the freeway. And he'd better remember it—Tyler had almost become an oil spot in the road himself in the process.

"You remember my friend, Austin?" Tyler asked Anna. "Well, this is his suit, and he specifically told me it was a happy clown." Austin, one of the partners at their private detective agency, had purchased the costume to do an undercover gig. As fate would have it, he hadn't gotten around to tossing it out yet.

"But when you walked in, Mama told *Tia* Lola, 'Here comes the sad man behind the clown face.' "

Tyler inwardly flinched but continued to smile. It was something he'd gotten good at doing—putting up a front. A skill he'd mastered during his year and a half in prison.

"Do you believe everything your mama says?" he asked in a teasing voice to hide his frustration. He loved his seven siblings, but a big family came with a big price. Having them poke around in his personal business was part of that price.

"I do." Anna's dark brown pigtails, tied with bright red ribbons, bounced around her face as she bobbed her head up and down. "Mama doesn't lie. She says it's a sin."

Okay, that hadn't been the right thing to say. "I think she was just joking."

"She wasn't laughing. Then *Tia* Lola said you were sad because you missed Lisa."

Tyler's chest tightened. He didn't miss Lisa. How could he miss someone who turned her back on him when he needed her the most? Someone who—

"And then," Anna continued, "Leo walked into the room and said it was probably because you picked up a bar of soap in prison." Her tiny brows pulled in confusion at the same time Tyler's gut pulled with fury. "I don't understand that, *Tio*."

"Leo's full of..." Tyler caught himself just in time.

"Full of what?" Anna asked, a half smile pulling at her lips.

Tyler's gaze shot to the piñata hanging above the tree. "Full of candy."

Anna snickered. "Mama said he was full of shit."

Tyler grinned. "Well, like you just said, your mama doesn't lie. But... we all have... excrement in our insides."

"Excrement?" He could see the child figuring out the word's meaning and filing it away in her knowledge-hungry brain. "That's gross."

"I agree." Tyler's smile came easier.

"Almost as gross as how babies are made," she said.

That little announcement came out of left field, and Tyler's jaw fell open.

Anna stared at him with the same face she'd made at dinner a few weeks ago when her mom made her eat a bite of broccoli. "I read a book about it."

"What book?" he managed to ask.

"The one Mama bought me after I told her I didn't believe the stork brought my baby brother."

"Oh," he said, not sure what else to say. But his smile lingered as he thought about his sister dealing with her inquisitive daughter. He smiled until he saw Anna's full-of-shit stepfather walk out of the patio door and snag a beer from one of the coolers.

Leo Medina, his twin sister's second husband, was a jerkwad, right up there with Anna's deadbeat daddy. While Tyler tried to overlook his sister's ghastly taste in husbands, ignoring Leo was hard. And for damn good reasons, too. First and foremost, Tyler didn't like the way Leo treated his sister and ignored Anna. Then there were the other reasons, or suspected reasons.

"Did you and Lisa want to have a baby?" Anna asked.

Tyler swallowed, searching for words. "We... we weren't married."

She made another funny face. "I'm not getting married."

"Me, either," he told her honestly. After living with the result of his parents' dysfunctional relationship, he'd always had reservations. Lisa had made him throw caution to the wind. Unfortunately, that wind blew up a hell of a lot of heartache. Thankfully, he was smart enough to avoid that mistake again.

"I liked Lisa," Anna said. "She was pretty. She told

me I was going to get to be the flower girl in her wedding. Why are you and her not getting married anymore? Is it because you think making babies is gross, too?"

He nearly swallowed his tongue. "Lisa married someone else."

"Maybe if you told her you were sorry, she would get a divorce like Mama did with my daddy. Then Lisa could marry you."

Sorry for what? For being framed for a crime he didn't commit? "I don't think so."

"Saying you're sorry works. It worked on Mom when Leo hit her. And she was mad."

"What?" Tyler felt like his blood pressure shot up a good twenty points. He hadn't needed another reason to dislike Leo, but damn if he didn't have one. "Leo hit your mom? Are you sure?"

"Yeah, but he said he was sorry. So if you apologize to Lisa—"

"Excuse me, Anna, but I need to... I have to do something." He passed Anna her cat and gave the girl's pigtail a teasing yank, hoping his rage didn't show through his painted clown face.

"Okay." The innocence on her face was the opposite of everything Tyler felt.

He stood up and looked around for Samantha. When he spotted his twin sister setting food out on a table, he realized her large sunglasses meant something other than protection from the glare. It meant protecting her son-of-a-bitch husband.

Moving in, Tyler gently caught her by the arm. "We need to talk."

"I'm getting the food out," she protested. Her long

black hair shifted around her shoulders. While they shared their light olive skin and dark hair—both inherited from their Hispanic mother—Anna had also taken her mom's petite build. Tyler's six-foot frame came directly from his father. He hoped to God it was the only trait he'd inherited from the SOB.

"Food can wait." He pulled off his multicolored wig and his red ball nose, and he walked her inside the house and guided her past the kitchen, not stopping until they stood in the enclosed laundry room, which smelled like clean clothes.

"What the hell is up with you?" She snapped her hands on her hips. Her movement reminded him of their mom so much. His chest tightened. While his mother had been dead for four years, he still missed her—and it always made family get-togethers bittersweet.

"Take your sunglasses off, Sis."

"What?"

"You heard me."

She frowned. Carefully, he removed the shades. He held his breath, afraid of how bad it was. Thankfully, it wasn't as bad as he feared. As an ex-cop, he'd seen women so battered that he'd puked. But it was his childhood memories that were the worst. Sam hadn't just inherited their mother's build and coloring; she'd inherited their mother's knack for choosing losers. Staring into his twin's face, there was no mistaking the light bruise under her left eye. Then he remembered she'd missed the family's mandatory Sunday breakfast last week. The bruise had had time to fade, which meant it must have been nasty when it was fresh.

He touched his sister's cheek under the evidence. "Leo do this?"

"No," she snapped, proving her daughter wrong. Sam did lie. She just wasn't good at it.

But holy hell, why did she put up with this crap? The answer rolled over him like an overloaded concrete truck. Because their no-good father had treated their mom the same way. Tyler had studied it in college.

Statistically, the odds of her choosing men just like dear ol' Dad were great. The odds of him becoming his dad were greater. And considering the rage he felt now for Leo, the odds might be right.

He turned to leave, and Sam caught his arm. "Don't do it, Tyler. I beg you."

He gently cupped her face in his palm. "If you knew someone was hurting me, would you stand by and let it happen?"

"No, but..." Tears filled her eyes, and seeing those watery eyes did something to his gut.

"He was drunk," she continued.

"Isn't that what they said about dear ol' Dad?" That crowd of emotion in his gut shifted up into his chest and formed a knot—a knot of anger, hurt, and an unrelenting need to protect his sister the way he'd needed to protect his mom all those times.

"Please," she muttered.

"I love you, Sam. I know you're going to be pissed at me, but he needs to know he can't do this."

He didn't stay around long enough to hear her pleas or to see the tears slip from her lashes onto her cheeks. That would have broken his heart, and Tyler wasn't sure his heart could take any more breaking. So, he plopped his wig and rubber nose back on, and shuffled his clown ass out to teach his brother-in-law a lesson about hitting girls.

* * *

Hesitating in the kitchen for a minute to collect himself, Tyler stepped outside. He went to the cooler, figuring Leo wouldn't be too far from the alcohol. He pulled out two beers, uncapped one and drank half of it in one swig, then looked around for Leo. He spotted him chatting with Tyler's oldest brother's wife. And damn if he didn't see the man eye his sister-in-law's breasts when she wasn't looking.

"Leo?" Tyler held up the two beers as if to say, "Come join me." When Tyler saw the man coming, he stepped through the backyard gate and moved between Sam's house and the neighbor's. He heard the gate shift behind him.

"What's up?" Leo asked.

Setting the two beers on top of an air conditioner that hummed as it cooled his sister's house, Tyler faced Leo, who stood so close that the man's beer-laden breath filled Tyler's airspace. He didn't waste any time getting to the point. "You hit her."

Leo stepped back, or he started to. "It was just a tap." But before his foot hit the ground, Tyler's fist punched the man's nose and knocked him flat on his ass.

"Christ!" Leo reached for his nose.

"It was just a tap," Tyler growled, but he knew Leo's nose had to be hurting like hell because Tyler's fist did. And he saw his knuckles bleeding where he'd obviously loosened a couple of teeth.

"You fucking jailbird clown! You broke my nose!"

Jailbird was the word that almost did Tyler in.

Leo started to get up, no doubt to give what he'd gotten, and Tyler almost let him. Almost chose to let go and enjoy this. But taking a deep breath, he pulled his emotions back and moved in to tower over his slimeball of a brother-in-law.

"Don't do it, Leo. If you get up, I'm going to hit you again. I know you think you want to hit me back. It's only fair, right? But it wasn't fair when you hit Sam. And I'm not planning on fighting fair now."

He rubbed his fist in his other hand and continued, "If you get up, and if you even get one punch in, I'm going to yell for my four brothers, and when I tell them what you did, every one of them will help me beat your ass to a pulp. Consider yourself lucky you faced only me this time."

Leo wiped his bloody nose and stared up with hatred in his eyes. But the man was smarter than Tyler gave him credit for. He didn't get up.

A damn shame, too. "Oh," he added, "if I see one bruise, one little bruise, on my sister, I won't come alone next time." Pulling off the red rubber nose, he tossed it at Leo. "Since I broke yours, have this one."

"Spiders. Definitely spiders."

"Don't forget snakes."

"Trust me, it's clowns." Zoe Adams removed her waitress apron and added her two cents to the conversation the other waitresses of Cookie's Café were having about their biggest fears. She plopped down on one of the stools lining the breakfast counter and pulled out her tips to count. She hoped she had enough to pay the rent. Looking up at the other diner employees, she added, "And considering my regular gig is that of kindergarten teacher, I've had to face that fear more times than I care to admit."

"I'd take a clown over a spider any day," said Jamie. Like Zoe, she was in her mid-twenties.

"I can step on a spider," Zoe said, looking at the other waitresses she'd worked with for two weeks. Crazy how in just two weeks she'd felt a part of something. A part of Cookie's Café.

"Clowns are too big for my size sixes." She held up her foot. "I don't know what it is, but I see one and it's like I hear scary music and my mind starts flashing *Friday the 13th* images." In truth, clowns weren't her biggest fear. Small, dark places scared Zoe more than anything. Not that she'd share that with her co-workers, or anyone else for that matter.

Some things Zoe didn't talk about. Especially the things she didn't understand. And for the last three weeks, her life was filled with a lot of those things. Crazy how watching that episode of the TV series *Unsolved Mystery Hunters* had turned her life upside down, and brought her from Alabama to Texas in search of the truth.

"Flying roaches. I hate 'em," Dixie Talbot said, joining in on the conversation. In her sixties, Dixie was the matriarchal cook, waitress, and part-owner of Cookie's Café. "Years ago, I stood right over there by Booth Two, and one of those nasty creatures flew into my shirt."

Zoe stopped counting her money and laughed. "Yeah, Fred told me about the striptease you pulled, too."

"Honey, he'd better be glad that roach flew off my right boob once the top came off, or I swear to everything holy I'd have been standing there naked as a jaybird."

"Was that the day he proposed to you?" Zoe asked.

They laughed. It was the laughter, the camaraderie of Dixie and the other diner employees, that kept Zoe from looking for a higher paying gig while she was here. God knew she could use the money. Kindergarten teachers didn't rake in the big bucks.

Oh, it was enough to get by, but not enough to fund this research trip to Miller, Texas, when she had to pay for two apartments. Not to mention the entire month off from work—a month she only got because the principal had been friends with her mom. But more than money, Zoe needed companionship. When her mama died two years ago, Zoe had not only lost her last living relative, she'd lost her best companion. Then, last year when her live-in boyfriend had decided he'd rather date a stripper than a kindergarten teacher, Zoe had spent too much time alone.

And lonely.

Hey, maybe she should get Dixie to teach her a few moves. Not that Zoe wanted Chris back. Nope. For four years, she'd given her heart and soul to that man. She'd already had names picked out for the two kids they'd have together, thinking any day he'd pop the question. And he had popped one. It just wasn't the question she'd expected. *"Do you mind if I bring home my stripper girlfriend to live here until you can find another place?"*

Okay, he hadn't actually worded it like that, but he might as well have. He'd taken Zoe's heart and returned it, along with her self-esteem, in a big mangled mess. Not so much of a mess that she hadn't reminded him that she'd been the one to rent the apartment, and he could just grab his stuff and get the hell out. Oh, he'd accused her of being so unfair. Didn't she realize it wasn't his fault he'd fallen in love with someone else?

What she understood was that she'd been played for a fool—paying most of the bills, being his personal housecleaner, trying to be the perfect housewife. Even a year later, it still stung like a paper cut right across her heart.

Zoe's cell phone rang. Considering she'd gotten only two calls in the two weeks she'd been in Texas—one from her principal back in Alabama confirming she'd be at work on September 25, and the other a wrong number—a call was a big thing. Zoe checked the number. Unknown Caller.

"Hello?" Zoe answered. While she hated it, there was a part of her that hoped it would be Chris, wanting her back, telling her he'd screwed up. Not that she'd take him back, but it would be nice to know he missed her.

She heard someone breathing, but nothing else. "Hello?"

"Leave," the whispery voice said.

CHAPTER TWO

"WHAT?" ZOE SAID, unsure if she'd heard correctly.

Click.

"You okay?" Dixie asked.

"Yeah. Wrong number." Stashing her phone in her apron, she looked up at Dixie. "Can I use your computer?"

"You betcha. Just stay off those porn sites," Dixie teased.

"Just can't help myself." Zoe scooted her butt off the stool. "It's been a month of Sundays since I've known bliss."

"I could remedy that," offered Juan, the fry cook.

"I'll consider it as soon as you get written permission from your wife." She shot him a smile, knowing he was only kidding because she'd seen him light up when his pregnant wife stopped by earlier.

"Heck," Juan said, grinning back. "I was only offering to make you some French toast."

While all the employees snickered, Zoe grabbed her bag that held a change of clothes and went to the office.

Ten minutes later, Dixie brought two big bowls of

chicken and dumplings into the office and set one in front of Zoe on the oversized and time-worn oak desk. "Eat before you go."

Zoe smiled. It had been forever since she'd had anyone looking out for her. She was going to miss Dixie when she left.

"Thanks. I've smelled these cooking all morning." She dished a spoonful into her mouth and moaned as the savory taste exploded on her tongue. "My mama used to make these."

"Mine are better," Dixie teased, and dropped into the desk chair beside Zoe and started eating. After a minute of silence, Dixie asked, "You miss her—your mama?"

"Like the dickens. She was special." But if Zoe's suspicions were true, her mama wasn't the person Zoe had always thought she was. In the pro/con list Zoe had made before she decided to actually come to Texas, uncovering any ugly secrets about her parents had been the only con.

Dixie's gaze shifted to the computer monitor.

Zoe reached for the mouse to delete the screen. Quickly realizing it would be rude, she moved her hand and spooned another dumpling into her mouth. Besides, Dixie had already gotten a peek at Zoe's research last week when she'd gone for a potty break and forgot to close the screen. When she'd returned, Dixie was reading the article Zoe had found at the library and had downloaded onto a flash drive.

"The Bradfords again?" Dixie asked. "Is there a reason you're so intrigued with that rich family?"

Zoe glanced at the screen. She couldn't divulge everything. People would think she was crazy—hell, sometimes she considered the possibility herself. But she could tell Dixie part of it. "There was a story about them on that *Unsolved Mystery Hunters* show three weeks ago. I guess I love a good puzzle."

"About the murder of that kid?" Dixie asked.

Zoe nodded and her chest constricted.

"I remember that. They never did find out who killed her. Sad stuff."

"Yeah." Zoe spooned another bite into her mouth and stared at the picture of Thomas Bradford. It was as if Zoe felt by staring at the man, she could discover the truth. But no such discovery came.

"I heard that old man isn't doing so well. The kids and grandkids are fighting over his inheritance. Lucky for me, all I've got is this run-down café, and neither of my kids wants it."

"It's not run-down," Zoe said. "Best food in town." She spooned a big chunk of stewed chicken into her mouth.

Dixie chuckled. "That's because you're not a citified gal like my kids. My son ran off to California to learn to talk like they do on the six o'clock news. Works for a radio station out there. Boy's ashamed of his southern roots. And my daughter—you wouldn't catch a dumpling within six feet of her lips. Says she's allergic to carbs."

Zoe frowned. "I haven't met a carb I haven't loved. Guess it shows, too. I'll bet I've gained five pounds since I started working here."

"And you're wearing it well, too, honey. You should see the guys checking out your butt." Dixie looked back at the computer screen. "If you're real curious about the Bradfords, you should ask those PIs who come in for my chili cheeseburgers on Tuesdays. They do work for the Bradfords, I think."

Zoe's interest was piqued. "What PIs?" She didn't have money to hire a private investigator, but if they had knowledge about the Bradfords, she could at least ask them some questions. How much would they charge just to talk to her? Nothing, she hoped.

"Those three hunk-a-hunk men, two dark haired and one blond. All of them drool-worthy. They own that PI agency, Only in Texas." Dixie shook her head. "Are you seriously telling me you haven't noticed them?"

Zoe tried to think. "They only come in on Tuesdays?" While she didn't recall them, she mentally stored away the agency's title.

Dixie dropped her spoon in her bowl. "Girl, you are either blind or a lesbian not to have noticed them."

"Neither. Self-preservation. Just mending a broken heart," Zoe said. "I'm not sure men are worth the risk, so I've trained myself not to notice things like sexy bedroom eyes or broad shoulders." But she was getting a little breathless just thinking about it. Maybe she should reconsider dating again. If for no other reason than to have someone call her, and make her cell phone worth its monthly charge.

"Oh, honey, those boys would be worth it. Then again, 'cause I like ya, if you noticed them too much I'd reel you in so fast you'd leave skid marks on my linoleum."

"What's wrong with them?" Zoe tried to feign only a mild curiosity while she pushed another dumpling around her bowl. But on the inside she felt her excitement growing by leaps and bounds. This might be her big break. The one that answered the questions Zoe had been looking for all her life.

God knew all of her other plans had seemed to fail

these days. Phone calls to the Bradford businesses, and even a couple of drop-in visits to the mansion—not that she'd gotten past the security gate. The last time, she'd been told by one security guard that if he saw her there again, he was calling the cops.

Heck, last week, she'd even tried following the limo when they'd left the house, and got herself a nice little ticket for running a red light that she didn't run. The cop who gave her the ticket suggested she go find another old fart to seduce because Mr. Bradford wasn't in the market for an Anna Nicole.

"Nothing wrong with those three guys if you like suspected murderers." Dixie arched her painted brow.

"They're murderers?" Zoe asked.

"I said 'suspected.' They used to be cops. Supposedly, they got involved in some seedy drug deals, and then they got arrested for brutally murdering this couple. Practically decapitated the woman." She ran a finger across her neck. "Then they got convicted and went to jail."

Zoe touched her neck. "And what? They escape every Tuesday just for your chili cheeseburgers?"

Dixie laughed. "Hey, my cooking's that good. But actually, they got let go."

"So, they're not guilty?" Zoe hoped that was the case. If she was going to look them up, and you could bet she was, she'd like it if they weren't murderers.

"Well, that depends on who you talk to. You know small towns—folks around here get one thing in their mind, and changing it is about as easy as chewing glass. My neighbor has a son-in-law who works for the Glencoe Police Department where they worked. According to him, they had those three down and dirty. But then they got themselves...What do you call it when the governor lets someone go?"

"Pardoned?" Zoe asked.

"No, the other word. Exonerated. That's it."

"Dixie," someone called from out front. "Getting busy."

"Guess I'm on again." Dixie stood up and pressed a hand on Zoe's shoulder. "Don't know why, kid, but only after a couple of weeks I decided I like you. I know you said you were only here for a month to say you'd done Texas, but I really wish you'd stick around and become a full-fledged Texan."

Emotion filled Zoe's chest. Reaching back, Zoe put her hand on top of Dixie's. "I like you, too. But I've got a job and a life waiting for me in Alabama." *A lonely life.* The thought whispered across her heart.

"Well, if you change your mind. You got friends here." With a wink, Dixie walked out of the room.

Zoe sat there a few minutes, savoring that wonderful feeling of hearing Dixie's words. Nothing like feeling someone cared about you.

Shifting her mental gears, she wondered if she should wait until Tuesday and hope the PI threesome showed up, or if she should take matters into her own hands. Impatience stirred inside her; she had less than a month before she was expected to be back at work. She hit the Google search engine. Typing in the agency name, she whispered, "Come to Mama." Then she touched her neck again, hoping her impatience didn't lead to her losing her head. Figuratively, of course.

Less than thirty minutes later, Zoe parked in front of the Only in Texas office. The sign in the window read they were open. The fact that her Google search informed her that until recently their place of business had housed a funeral home almost seemed absurd. Convicted—albeit exonerated—murderers had bought an old funeral home to house their business. Was there not something slightly off about that? Maybe three angry ex-cops making a point to the townsfolk who'd judged them unfairly?

But angry men or not, she wanted answers. She grabbed her purse, climbed out of her silver Chevy Cobalt, and went to see if she could wrangle herself up some answers. Stopping at the large redbrick building door, she released her shoulder-length auburn hair from her ponytail and shook it out. Her hair, a tad too thick and too curly, usually caught a man's eye. And if it took letting her hair down for a bit to encourage one of these men to talk with her, she wasn't above doing it.

All she had to figure out was how much to tell the PIs. Sooner or later, she was going to have to trust someone. She just wasn't sure who or when. Stepping inside the business, leaving the bright sunshine for a dark room, she allowed her eyes a second to adjust. And when they did, her gaze caught on the only piece of "furniture"—if you could call it that—in the room. She took a quick step back. A coffin, yup, an honest-to-goodness coffin with a raised lid, bracketed the back wall.

"Hello?" she muttered in the dead silence. And it did feel dead. Like a funeral home felt. She'd been in too many already in her life. First her dad when she was sixteen, her best friend who'd been killed in a car accident their senior year of high school, and then her mom. Personally, she preferred to never visit another one.

A noise, a slight moan, echoed from the room. No

wait…not from the room, from the casket. *Shit!* Her heart started racing. Her eyes shot back to the casket, and her hands jerked behind her, feeling for the doorknob. Then another snortlike noise came from the coffin. Suddenly, a big canine face popped up and rested its round head on the coffin's wooden edge.

Zoe chuckled. "A vampire dog, huh?"

The dog stretched its neck—what little neck it had—and leaped out of the casket and came sniffing around her feet.

"So, you're the official door greeter?" She knelt to pet the English bulldog as it started sniffing her up and down. "You smell Lucky on me? Or is it the Slam Dunk, Three-Egg Dollar Ninety-Nine special you smell?" It took two or three shampoos every night to get the smell of bacon from her hair. After a couple of seconds of giving the animal attention, she stood up.

"Hello?" she called again.

And again no one answered. She walked down the hall. The dog followed, his paws clicking on the wood floor, but the lack of noise filtering into the building seemed louder than the clickity-clack of his paws. The first door to the left was a large office. Three unmanned desks filled the room. She stepped inside.

A sign hanging from the front desk said, "If no one is here, press the button."

Zoe looked for the button. Various files and papers covered the desk. Was the button under those? Moving in, she looked around the desk. She lifted a big pile of files when a name on one of the folders caught her eye. Bradford.

The same Bradford?

Zoe reached for the file, then pulled her hand back as if it might bite. Then she reached for it again and pulled back just as quickly. Yanking her purse higher on her shoulder, she stood there while her conscience played tug-of-war with her desire for answers. She gave the room a good look-see for anyone who might tattle if she…took a small peek.

Looking down at the dog, she asked, "You wouldn't tell on me, would you?"

When he shook his head back and forth, she laughed.

Finally, her desire for answers won out. She flipped open the file. Less than a dozen sheets of paper resided there. The first one looked like a resume. She picked it up to read it, when the sound of a door opening filled the quiet office.

The dog barked and took off running.

She dropped the papers back on the desk and slapped the file closed. She stepped away from behind the desk, but in her haste, her purse knocked the folder off, and the file and all dozen or so papers scattered on the floor.

"Damn." She dropped to the floor on her hands and knees to gather the evidence of her wrongdoing. She heard footsteps moving closer, and her heart pounded.

Snagging the folder and papers, she threw them on the desk and was about to stand up when she heard those footsteps enter the room, followed by the sounds of clicking paws.

Friggin' great.

Now all she had to explain was why she was down on all fours behind someone's desk. Her heart did another flip-flop when she remembered she was possibly dealing with angry ex-cops, now ex-cons, who'd been accused of murder.

The dog pranced around the desk and licked her right on the lips, then started sniffing her bacon-scented hair. Those footsteps moved closer still, and her mind raced right along with her heart.

The deep masculine sound of a man clearing his throat came from behind her. “Nice view.”

“Oh, I was just...” She looked back over her shoulder, praying she’d come up with a good excuse for being in this ridiculous position. But the moment her gaze landed on the clown, the only thing she came up with was a scream. A loud one.

CHAPTER THREE

DIOS. TYLER WATCHED the shapely jeans-covered butt disappear around the desk. He did a side step so as not to lose the view and watched her crawling at an amazing speed toward the door. It wasn't every day he found a woman on her hands and knees behind his desk. So he jumped into action and planted his clown feet in front of the door.

The woman, long red hair hanging free and swishing around her arms, came to a dead stop about a foot from him. She raised her face. Her blue eyes, wide with what looked like panic, stared up at him. As soon as he got over the sheer terror he saw in her eyes, he realized the view from this side was just as nice as the one from her backside. Maybe even better. Her green scooped-neck T-shirt hung low, providing a nice view of her tan, lacy bra and ample breasts. Damn, she was hot.

"Hello," he said. Then, somehow sensing the costume might have something to do with her fear, he yanked off the wig and without meaning to, his gaze shot back to her bra, or rather at the size Cs that were close to falling out of it.

Clearly seeing where his gaze had fallen, she slapped a hand to her chest. Balancing on one hand and two knees, she attempted to stand up. Apparently still shaken, she almost fell. He reached for her, but she lurched back. When she was finally on her feet, he summed up the package. Maybe five-four or -five in height, ample breasts, and a round ass.

"Nice," he said without meaning to. ". . . to meet you."

Alarm remained clear on her face—a face that would have been appealing if not for the fear. A face that stirred a slight flash of recognition, too.

"Do I know you?" He ran his hand over his swollen and bloody knuckles.

"I was . . ." She swallowed. "The . . . my purse hit it. I was . . ." She stopped jabbering and gazed at his injured hand.

He stopped trying to make sense of her mumbo-jumbo and shrugged. "Had to teach someone a lesson."

She drew in a breath and stepped away from him as if thinking she might be next in line.

"He deserved it." He studied her face again. "Who are you?" And just like that, he remembered Dallas saying he'd hired a receptionist. He looked back at the stack of files on his desk, then at her.

"My contact . . ." She slammed one eye closed. "My contact fell out."

"You're the new receptionist," he said, and let himself give her another glance up and down. "Nice . . . to meet you," he said again, but sexy, hot, and stacked were the words that came to mind.

Damn, he could kiss Dallas. She'd make a breath-taking addition to the office. Of course, it was going to be hard to focus on anything but her. *Hard* being the key word. And a certain southern part of his anatomy had already twitched its approval. Which was a bit bothersome. He usually had better control. Thank goodness he had room in the costume.

"I'm Tyler." She didn't answer, just stared.

He frowned. "You don't like clowns, do you?"

"No." She gasped, trying to get oxygen down her lungs.

He hid his battered hand behind him. "Don't worry, I'm a friendly clown. And I don't run around in costumes all the time." And he could get really friendly if she was so inclined. "My niece's clown canceled and—"

"Contact." She blurted out again, as if she hadn't been listening. Then she slammed her left eye shut and opened again. "I lost it. Got some extras in my car." She started forward, stopped, and backed up, as if scared to get close.

He stepped back, giving her room to pass. With only one eye open, she stared at the small space, then back at him. He took another step back and she scooted past—quickly, too. For a second, he could swear he got a whiff of bacon, but that couldn't be right. Stepping through the doorway, he watched her hotfoot it down the hall.

"When you get back, let's introduce ourselves," he said. Her hips swayed back and forth with her quick steps. Things below the belt did another twitch and almost gave her a standing ovation as she passed through the front door.

Still smiling, opening and closing his swollen fist—and mentally preparing a list of questions about the new receptionist—he remembered he had a change of clothes in his car. Moving down the hall, he walked out the front door just in time to see a silver Cobalt with Alabama tags speeding out of the parking lot.

He stared after her. Hadn't she said she had contacts in her car? So, why was she—?

"Hey," Dallas O'Connor said from behind him. "I thought I heard someone come in. You're back early. How did the party go?"

Tyler turned around and scratched his head. "She left."

"Who left?"

"The new receptionist." Tyler ran his left hand over his swollen knuckles again.

"Ellen was here?" Dallas asked. "She said it would be around three."

"Is that her name?" Tyler asked.

"Yeah, it's Ellen Wise. You met her. Nikki's friend. The one who was stabbed at the gallery."

"Not the blonde?" Tyler asked.

"Yeah. She needed a job and we needed a receptionist. But I'm telling both you and Austin that she's off limits. No screwing with—"

"That wasn't Ellen," Tyler interrupted.

"Who wasn't Ellen?"

"The sexy redheaded chick I found on her hands and knees under my desk."

Dallas laughed. "You must have been dreaming."

"Seriously, she was . . ." Tyler walked back to the office with Dallas and his dog Bud following. Stopping at the office door, Tyler looked at his desk. "She was there." He noticed a piece of paper on the floor and picked it up. It was one of the resumes they'd taken to fill the new position for the Bradford security job. He dropped it on the desk and continued to rub his fist.

"What happened to your knuckles?" Dallas asked from the doorway.

Tyler looked up. "My brother-in-law's teeth got in the way when I broke his nose."

"So the party went that well, did it?"

"Yeah." Tyler glanced away, not wanting to think about Leo or how pissed his sister was at him. Or the fact that he might have ruined Anna's party. So instead, he remembered the redhead's face. Remembered how she'd looked familiar.

"How bad is your hand?" Dallas asked.

"Not as bad as his nose," Tyler answered.

"Did you confront him about the glass with your prints that the cops found at the crime scene?"

Tyler tightened his sore fist. Funny how he'd forgotten all about his suspicions that Leo had been one of the people who had framed him and his partners until now. His suspicions hadn't gone away—his sister was just more important. But now he knew how low Leo could go, and Tyler's suspicions grew even stronger. His prints had gotten to the crime scene somehow. The fact that they had been found on a glass just like the one his sister owned made him wonder. No way in hell would Tyler ever suspect anyone in his family; but Leo? Oh, yeah.

"No, I confronted him about hitting my sister."

Dallas frowned. "And you didn't break his neck?"

"That's next time," Tyler said. "She was going through our files."

"Your sister?"

"The redhead."

"What files?" Dallas asked.

"The Bradford file, I think."

"You're serious? There really was someone here?"

He looked up at Dallas. "Yes, a redhead."

"On her hands and knees behind your desk?" Dallas asked.

Tyler nodded.

Dallas picked up the file and thumbed through it. "She couldn't have been here long. I was in the apartment less than five minutes." He looked around. "Maybe she was just some mixed-up kid looking for change."

"She wasn't a kid. She was full grown." Tyler held out his hands in front of his chest and flinched when he tried to move his right fist.

Dallas chuckled. "Then maybe she was looking for Austin."

"I don't think so."

"Why not?" Dallas chuckled. "Wasn't she hot enough?"

"Hot, yes, but she didn't look slutty enough," he said, suddenly feeling annoyed. Annoyed that Austin got all the action, annoyed he couldn't bring himself to play the game the way Austin did. And the way Dallas had played it before he'd met Nikki.

Dallas grinned. "He does like 'em cheap and dumb, doesn't he?"

"Yeah," Tyler said, still unable to laugh. The fact that his body had reacted so strongly to the mysterious guest meant one thing: He needed to get laid.

Getting laid wasn't the problem. Finding someone who would keep it as simple as he wanted it kept was the issue. When his last three "simple" relationships turned complicated and ended badly, he decided to cease and desist until he figured out what he was doing wrong. If Austin and Dallas could do this, he could do it, too.

Tyler was smart enough to see patterns, and as soon as

he figured out what mistake he kept making, he'd fix it. But it looked as if he needed to fix it fast.

"You actually caught her going through this file?" Dallas asked.

"Not exactly. I think she got scared and hid behind the desk when I walked in."

Dallas looked up from the file. "There's nothing in here but resumes. You sure it was this file?"

"Not sure of anything." His mind created the image of her again, both the rear view and the front view. "Except…"

"Except what?"

I need to get laid. He didn't answer.

"Did you get a look at her car and the license number?" Dallas asked.

The sound of her voice tiptoed through his memory. Even her voice had been familiar. "It was a silver Chevy Cobalt. I didn't get the number. But it was an Alabama tag. And I know her."

"From where?"

"Not sure. But it'll come to me. Sooner or later." And he wasn't going to have a moment of peace until it did.

"Shoot!" Why hadn't she just admitted the truth? Why hadn't she just told him? Maybe he'd have given her some information or gotten her in contact with the Bradfords. Why had she acted like a scared, guilty rabbit?

She white-knuckled the steering wheel and kept checking her rearview mirror for a car driven by a broad-shouldered clown with chocolate brown eyes and black hair.

Why had she run? The question bounced around her

head again, but this time the answers spurted back from her still panicked brain. *You ran because of the clown suit, because the clown had admitted to "teaching someone a lesson" with his fists. Because... because he might have decided to teach you a lesson for snooping. Because he'd been ogling your girls as they were about to fall out of your bra.*

It could have been worse. He could have been staring at her neck. *You ran because you were a scared, guilty rabbit snooping through his files.*

Stopping at a red light, concentrating on not hyperventilating, Zoe's cell phone rang. She dug it out from her purse and looked for the number. Unknown caller. "Crap!" Was it the clown? He was a private detective. He found people for a living.

It couldn't be. He couldn't have found her that fast. Could he?

No. Plus, she'd already had a call earlier from Mr. Unknown Caller. She remembered the whispered voice, *Leave*. Just a wrong number. "Hello."

Just like the earlier call, she heard only breathing.

"At least ask me what color my underwear is," she snapped at the same time her patience did.

The whisper came on the line again. "Get the hell away before it's too late."

"Too late for what?" Her question was answered by the silence of a dead line.

"That's just rude," she muttered as the ominous click from the phone seeped into her chest.

She tossed the phone in the passenger seat and went back to white-knuckling the steering wheel. Just a wrong number. Why would someone threaten her? Unless...

unless someone had figured out the reason she was here. But why? Who? How? She hadn't told anyone... yet.

Maybe she should. Tell someone, that is. But who could she trust?

Certainly not a clown who used his fists to teach people lessons.

Tyler stared at his recently written list of questions. List making was his slightly obsessive/compulsive way of organizing his thoughts. Not that he really liked admitting he was slightly OCD, because he wasn't... well, not really.

Six of the questions related to redheads he'd met in the last couple of months, three related to his sister Sam, and one on why he couldn't find the right kind of woman to have casual sex with. When he heard the front door to the office open, his gaze shot up. While he knew it was unlikely to be her, he sat there, hoping a sexy redhead would appear in the doorway. That would take care of at least seven of his questions.

The footsteps neared and a figure appeared.

Not the redhead. Just Rick Clark, a detective with the Miller PD, and a recent part-time security guard they'd hired to secure the Bradford place.

While security wasn't really the agency's gig, after a recent break-in at the Bradford mansion that appeared to be an inside job, Mr. Bradford's lawyer had hired them to find the culprits. They had, and then he requested they handle hiring the replacements for the three guilty guards.

When Tyler had recommended hiring Rick—who had a great resume and came recommended by Dallas's brother Tony—Dallas hadn't been thrilled.

Supposedly, there was some grudge between Dallas

and Rick, but Dallas had conceded that it had nothing to do with his work ability and had backed down. So Rick got the Bradford job.

While penning his list of questions to be answered, Tyler realized Rick might have some info on the redhead. It was a long shot, but Tyler had discovered most answers stemmed from long shots, so he generally looked there first. Especially since no matter how hard he tried to remember where he'd run across the sexy redhead, he'd come up empty. And he wasn't used to that.

"What's up?" Rick said.

Tyler motioned to a chair. "How's the Bradford gig going?"

"Boring, why?" His brows tightened. "Someone complain about me? Fuck, I don't need this job that bad."

"No, you got a thumbs-up. I was just...curious if you've hit any snags."

"Snags?"

Tyler considered how to answer and then just said it. "Sexy redheads?"

"My kind of snags." Rick laughed. "But you know, someone did mention having to run a pretty redhead off at the gate."

Tyler jotted down the question: *Who was the redhead at Bradford's place?* "Did they get any info on her?"

"All I was told was that they thought she was an Anna Nicole wannabe, thinking if she screwed Old Man Bradford a few times before he passed, she might get her greedy hands on his money. You know women, they think what they got between their legs is—"

A loud clearing of a throat echoed from the office door. Tyler looked up.

Ellen Wise, their new receptionist, stood there. She held her hands over the ears of a little blond girl who looked to be around the same age as Tyler's niece, Anna.

"Sorry," Tyler and Rick said at the same time, and Tyler realized they would probably have to clean up their act a bit once Ellen came on board. Not that it hadn't already been polished with Nikki hanging around.

"I swung by to pick up the paperwork I needed to fill out," Ellen said.

The little girl pulled her mother's hands from over her ears. "I've heard bad words before. Yesterday at school, Mark got put in time-out for telling the teacher she had the face of a puckered butthole."

"And if you repeat it again, you'll get a time-out." Ellen sounded every bit like a mother.

Tyler bit his cheek to keep from smiling. "Ellen, this is Rick Clark. He's—"

"We've met." Rick grinned at Ellen.

Ellen tilted her head as if confused. "We have?"

"I worked with Tony O'Connor on your case." He smiled. "Saw you at the hospital."

Ellen's face brightened to a shade of embarrassed pink. "You're not one of the guys I..."—she covered the girl's ears again—"'propositioned,' are you?"

"You mean I wasn't the only one?" He slapped his hand over his heart. "Now, I'm offended."

"It was the drugs talking," she said, and then her eyes widened as if she realized what she'd said. "Not drug drugs. The morphine they gave me after the surgery when I was stabbed."

The little girl pulled her mother's hands from her ears again. "Why can grown-ups say dirty words but kids can't?"

"I didn't say a dirty word," Ellen said. "It was a grown-up word."

"What's a grown-up word?" the girl asked.

"I'll tell you when you're a grown-up," Ellen said.

Tyler stood, found the papers on Dallas's desk, and handed them to Ellen. Then he held out his hand to the little girl. "I don't think we've met. My name's Tyler."

"My name is Britney Wise. I'm six," she said with pride. She took his hand and gave it a good shake. Then her eyes went to Rick. "My mama was stabbed."

"Yes, I know," Rick said. "That was awful, wasn't it?"

"Not really." Britney looked back up at Tyler. "She got to eat a lot of ice cream."

Rick laughed. "I'll bet she shared it with you."

"Some," Britney said.

Tyler chuckled. "I have a niece who turned six today," he said, but his smile had to be forced when he thought about Anna and her mother and the possibility that they were both pissed at him. He needed to call his sister and let her tell him what a terrible brother and uncle he was. Let her get mad so she could start getting over it. And she would get over it. But probably not in time for him to attend breakfast tomorrow. Which meant, he couldn't go. But being a no-show to the family breakfast was a criminal offense.

"Thank you." Ellen held up the papers, making Tyler realize he'd gotten lost in his thoughts again—a bad habit of his. "I'll see you on Monday."

"I look forward to it," Tyler said, and he did. Ellen was attractive, but he'd been a lot happier when he'd thought their new receptionist was the redhead.

Tyler watched Ellen gaze toward Rick. "Nice to meet you... again."

"You, too. Oh, I'll see you around. I'm in and out of here," Rick said, and Tyler didn't miss the way he said it with interest. Ellen nodded and walked out. Rick wheeled his chair to the door to watch her move down the hall. When he looked back at Tyler, he grinned. "Damn, I'm gonna have to take her up on her original offer."

"She's a mother," Tyler said. For some reason, women with kids were off limits for him. He liked kids too much and could remember with detail how he felt about the boyfriends who'd come calling for his mom.

Without warning, Tyler found himself hoping the sexy redhead didn't have a kid.

"And how do you think she got to be a mother?" Rick asked.

Tyler frowned. "Word of warning. She's friends with Dallas's fiancée. I'd be careful."

"I'm always careful." Rick grinned.

Tyler suspected his warning had fallen on deaf ears.

Rick's cell rang, and he pulled it out and looked at the number. "Damn."

"You need to take it?" Tyler asked.

"No, I'll deal with it later." Frowning, Rick tucked the phone back in his pocket.

"About the redhead. Can you ask around and see if anyone's got anything on her?"

Curiosity sparked in Rick's green eyes. "I can, but why?"

Tyler debated telling Rick, but remembered Dallas's brother vouching for the man. "Don't mention it, but I found a redhead snooping around the office, and it appeared as if she might have been interested in the Bradford file."

Rick leaned in. "What was in the file?"

"Nothing. That's why I don't want you mentioning it. I'm just curious. And seriously, keep it low key, if you know what I mean." Tyler didn't want to stir up anyone's suspicions, especially when he wasn't a hundred percent sure the redhead had anything to do with the Bradfords.

"I'm working second shift this evening. I'll ask around."

"Thanks."

The redhead's face filled his head again and so did the certainty that he knew her. He wanted answers, and he wanted them now.

"They were nice." Britney skipped out into the parking lot.

"Yes, they were," Ellen answered, and ran a hand over her daughter's soft blond hair. But she was having second thoughts about accepting the job. Noel would give her hell. She could already hear his list of reasons ringing in her ear.

Do you know what kind of people walk into a PI office?

What kind of mother works in a place like that?

You're working for a bunch of ex-cons. Are you trying to get yourself stabbed again?

How Noel could blame her for getting stabbed was beyond her. But being a lawyer, and one that seldom lost a case, he had a way of twisting things to work in his favor. He'd twisted her, hadn't he? Like a pretzel, leaving her heart mangled.

Then again, Noel would give her hell no matter what job she took. And she was tired of making life choices just to avoid pissing him off. However, the price of pissing him off could be too great.

She glanced at Britney. While her daughter looked more like her, she could see Noel in her, too. The dimple in her chin, the way her smile was a bit crooked. Funny how the biggest mistake in her life had given her the best thing in the world.

"I thought we were going to see Nikki," Britney said as they got into their car.

"I said we might. She must still be helping Mr. O'Connor pack up his things. But we'll see her later." Ellen started the car.

"Can I have my book now? Pleeeasssse."

"Sure." Ellen looked in the backseat.

"You put the bag in the trunk." Britney made a pleading face.

A sucker for her daughter's "pleases," Ellen cut the engine off, then popped the trunk. Moving to the back of the Honda, she reached for the bag that had slid deep into the trunk. Leaning her knee on the back of the car, she half-crawled into the trunk.

"Can I help you?" a deep voice asked.

Ellen shot up so fast she banged her head on the trunk lid. "Ouch!"

"Sorry, I didn't mean to startle you." A deep chuckle followed the words.

Looking over her shoulder, she saw Rick Clark, the man whom supposedly she'd begged to have sex with her. Ellen blamed it on the morphine, but even now she felt herself being lured by his sexy laugh. She also felt his gaze on her extending ass.

"Just getting Britney's book." Snatching the bag, she crawled out and smiled cautiously. LeAnn, whose husband was Rick's partner, had warned Ellen that Rick was a bit of a player. Not that Ellen would have been tempted to carry through with her proposition.

Meeting the man's soft green eyes, she amended her last thought. She might have been tempted, but she wouldn't go there. She'd been played by a player once. Never again.

When she closed the trunk, the bag holding the books split in two, and the contents hit the pavement by her sandals.

Rick knelt down and picked up Britney's books. "Is she reading already? How old is she?"

"She's six and already a bit of a bookworm."

"Like her mom?" he asked, eyeing the books.

"Guilty." She shot up.

He stood up, too. "What age do kids start reading?"

For a second she believed he was interested, but wasn't that what players did? Pretend to be interested in something you liked? Get you thinking they were a nice guy so they could sleep with you, get you pregnant, and then tell you they were married? Or was that just Noel's mode of operation?

"Six. I should... go."

"Did you encourage her to read?" He thumbed through the book and then smiled up at her.

She had to reach deep to remember not to be fooled by smiling sexy eyes. "I read to her." She motioned to the books he held, hoping she didn't come off rude, but she didn't want to encourage him.

"Later." He handed her the books.

She turned away, applauding herself for escaping before he did something like...

"Would you like to do dinner sometime?" he asked before she got the door open.

She looked back. "Uh...I kind of got a lot on my plate right now."

"Seeing someone else, huh?"

"Sorry." It was easier to lie. Or to let him assume.

"He's a lucky guy." He didn't seem offended. She gave him credit for making it easy.

"Thanks," she said.

"Take care." He started backing away.

"You, too." Oddly enough she wondered about LeAnn's assessment of him. Not that it mattered. Romance was out of the question right now.

CHAPTER FOUR

TYLER WOKE UP at his usual six a.m. time for Sunday morning and debated pulling the covers back over his head. He'd tossed and turned most of the night, trying to remember how he knew the redhead. Not that it hadn't been fun at times. He'd played mental paper dolls, where he stripped the redhead naked and dressed her in different uniforms, hoping it would help him remember where he'd met her. He'd tried a nurse's uniform, a sexy cocktail waitress getup, and a prim and proper librarian outfit.

Though his mental exercises hadn't solved the puzzle of the redhead's identity, it might have answered part of his relationship problems.

As Dallas had pointed out yesterday, Austin liked his women cheap and probably not college educated.

Of all the outfits Tyler had mentally dressed the redhead in, the one that landed him in the shower at one this morning had been the librarian. He obviously had a thing for women with IQs larger than their breast size.

He was smart enough to know that when a person repeated a mistake, it meant they were following a pattern.

And since he'd found himself with someone who wanted more than he did and things had ended badly a few times now, he had to accept that his pattern must be falling for the wrong kind of woman. Apparently, exceptionally smart women were less likely to participate in casual affairs.

So all he had to do was change the type of woman he asked out. And perhaps, he'd already gotten a head start. The redhead hadn't made a lick of sense, and he'd certainly appreciated her other assets.

Five minutes later, Tyler walked to the kitchen of his two-bedroom apartment and poured himself a cup of coffee. After a couple of sips, he looked at the clock. He'd told Dallas he would meet him at his dad's house around ten thirty to help move his dad's things into his new place. Dallas's dad had finally decided that remaining in his old home was making it hard to move past the loss of his wife. So he was moving into the adult retirement community where Nikki's grandmother lived, and Dallas and Nikki were going to move into Dallas's dad's house. Which meant the apartment at the office was going to be empty. And since Tyler practically lived there already, moving in just made sense.

Looking at the empty boxes he'd gathered a week ago, he wondered why he kept postponing the packing. It wasn't that he didn't want to move.

Hell...maybe the move would shake him out of his rut. A new place to live. A new type of woman to fall for—one that just wanted to have some fun. A better attitude so his family would stop thinking he was depressed.

Taking another sip of coffee, Tyler opened the refrigerator as if food might magically appear there. It didn't.

What he wouldn't give for a plate of *huevos rancheros*—the kind being served in about thirty minutes at his sister's place. But when Sam wouldn't take his calls last night, he'd left a message and said he was skipping breakfast. If Sam was mad, and she obviously was, he knew she wouldn't go if she thought he was going. With a new baby and an asshole of a husband, she needed the family more than he did. So he'd give her a week to get over being pissed.

Shutting the fridge, Tyler tried to recall if he'd ever seen *huevos rancheros* on the menu at Cookie's Café. But instead of envisioning the menu, his mind produced an image of the pretty waitress who...

"That's it!" He abandoned his coffee and grabbed his keys, remembering how it pissed him off that the waitress would never make direct eye contact. Not that she lacked service skills, but because she was pretty enough that a man wanted her full attention.

The thrill of seeing her again, and making direct eye contact this time, surged through his blood. He told himself the thrill was all about solving the puzzle of her identity, and not about the instant lust she'd brought out in him, but when he almost left the apartment without his shoes on, he called himself a liar. Only lust made him forget clothing items.

When Tyler spotted the silver Cobalt with Alabama tags parked around the back of the diner, the thrill shot through him again. Pulling out his phone, he typed in her license plate number and then e-mailed it to his cousin who was a Texas Highway Patrol officer.

After parking, Tyler took a minute to figure out how

best to approach her. Finally, he decided to play it by ear. Inside, he immediately spotted her waiting on an elderly couple. As he took his first step inside, his phone rang.

He checked the number. Ramon, his oldest brother—no doubt calling to give him an ass-chewing for not showing up for breakfast. And it wasn't as if Tyler could explain. If Ramon knew Leo had hit Sam, shit would hit the fan.

"Hi, brother," Tyler said.

"Hey," Ramon said. "You wanna explain why you aren't here? You and Sam are both missing. We made a pact, brother. You don't miss our family breakfasts."

"Sam's not there?" Tyler asked. "Have you called her?"

"She says the baby's running a little fever. Lola went over to check on him. What's your excuse?"

"It's work." He watched Red taking an elderly couple's order. She laughed at something the old man said.

"Work comes before family? That's bullshit."

Ramon was a hardass about keeping the family together, but Tyler couldn't blame him. Ten years Tyler's senior, Ramon had quit college and gone to work in construction to keep the family together after their father had died. In so many ways, Ramon had taken over as head of the household.

"We all got together yesterday at Anna's birthday."

"You left early and didn't even say good-bye. What the hell was up with that?"

"You know me, I had something on my mind and was halfway down the road before I realized I hadn't said good-bye. Besides, I'm doing what I can," Tyler said.

"Well, do more." Ramon hung up.

Tyler looked up at the redheaded waitress. Her hair was up in a tight bun, which explained why he hadn't recognized her. Her dark auburn hair was her best feature, but pulled up in that tight bun, her hair almost appeared brown.

His gaze did a quick up and down of her shapely body. She filled out the white skirt and top to perfection, and he almost conceded that her hair came in second. Not that her face was bad. He watched her smile and make direct eye contact with the couple. So she didn't avoid eye contact with everyone. Maybe it was just men she deprived of her attention.

"Have a seat anywhere," the elderly waitress said as she passed with a tray of food balanced on one hand.

He nodded, then, after studying the table setup, he surmised which tables would be Red's. When she moved to a dirty table, pocketed the tip, and started stacking dishes, he moved forward.

"Mind if I sit here?" He waited for her to look at him, anticipating her reaction.

"No problem." She barely glanced at him as she cleaned the table. "I'll have it cleaned in a sec." Her soft southern drawl came through.

He remembered he'd been wearing the clown costume the previous afternoon and had to bite back a smile. When she leaned over to clean the far end of the table, his gaze shifted to her ass and he recalled watching her crawl across his office floor.

"Coffee?" She gave the table two more swipes, her hips moving with the circular motion.

"That would be fine." When she straightened from wiping the table, he sat down. "Thanks."

He waited to see if she'd meet his gaze. Clown costume or not, he hoped for a flash of recognition, but like in the past, she didn't look at him directly. He watched her step away. She snagged a cup and filled it with coffee. As she started away from the counter, a bell rang. She turned back and placed the coffee on a tray loaded down with three plates of food.

She moved toward him and set the coffee on his table while balancing the tray with her other hand.

"Got some cream?" He continued to stare at her.

"Yup." She dug into her apron and pulled out a few creamers.

As she set the creamer down, he asked, "So you found your contact lens?"

Her gaze shot to his face, and her blue eyes finally widened with recognition.

He grinned and winked, enjoying it a tad too much.

She didn't move, but one of the plates on her tray did. She adjusted the hand holding the tray as if trying to prevent the disaster, but it was too late. Tyler saw it happening, but there was nothing he could do to stop it. The white plate flew off the tray, heading right at his head. He dodged the plate, but the warm grits and scrambled eggs made a direct hit with his face.

"Shit," she muttered as the plate crashed to the floor.

He knocked a blob of butter from his cheek and looked at her. She jumped back as if afraid he might hit her. Her quick retreat sent the second and third plate racing across the tray, and, once again, he was the finish line. The next plate to hit had a couple of sunny-side-up eggs, wheat toast with extra butter, and what he thought was hash browns. The food came so fast he wasn't completely sure.

Well, not sure until several forkfuls of shredded potatoes, accompanied by the half-cooked eggs, plopped right in his lap.

Somehow, he'd managed to catch one plate before it hit the floor, but the other plate bounced off the table, hit the linoleum, and shattered. As a thick glob of grits fell from the end of his nose, laughter exploded from the other diner patrons.

"I..." She stared at him.

He scooted his chair back from the table and stared down at himself. She dropped the tray on the edge of his table, grabbed his napkin, and started wiping globs of still warm grits off his chest. She kept wiping, following the trail of food down to his lap. She attempted to flop one half-cooked egg from his crotch. But the yoke burst and he watched it run between his legs.

Finally, she raised her head, met his gaze, and froze. He stared into her beautiful blue eyes and the sweetest mouth he could ever remember seeing. Appearing almost as mesmerized by his gaze as he was by hers, her hand with the napkin slipped deeper between his legs. Her gentle touch came in direct contact with sensitive body parts and felt pretty damn good, too. She jumped back as if suddenly realizing where her hand was.

A smile pulled at his mouth, but, seeing panic in her eyes, he bit it back. "It's okay."

She continued to stare. "Sorry. Really sorry."

She stepped back and must have stepped on a part of the broken plate, because her right foot slipped out from under her and she plopped down on her ass. The chorus of laughter filling the diner grew louder. For the first time, he frowned at the crowd.

"You okay?" He jumped up and reached out his hand—a hand partially covered in scrambled eggs.

She didn't take his hand. "I'm fine." She eked out the words.

Then her wide blue eyes blinked, and she covered her mouth with her palm. He didn't know if she was crying or laughing, but then humor shone through her eyes. And damn if she wasn't pretty with her eyes lit up like that, too.

"You're a mess," she said.

He glanced down at the front of his shirt, where he wore an array of breakfast foods. Chuckling, he removed a piece of buttered toast glued to his chest and other remnants of scrambled eggs from his shoulder. Then he wiped what he thought was a pat of butter from the side of his ear.

"Here." The older waitress showed up and pushed a damp towel into his hands. When she looked at him, she cracked a smile, too.

He used the towel to remove what he suspected was congealed hash browns from the side of his face and watched as Red got to her feet. She pushed herself up, and he checked out her calves to make sure she hadn't been cut by the shattered plates. No blood, but really nice legs.

When he raised his eyes to her face, a frown replaced her smile. She went to the counter and started calling out orders to the cooks. Not that they were listening. They were too busy laughing and peering out the open service window at him.

He sat down on the other side of the table and tried to get most of the grits off his chest with the towel, but he didn't take his eyes off the redhead. Just in case she tried to run. Though, why she would duck out was beyond him. He still didn't have a clue why she'd been rummaging around his desk the previous day.

The older waitress followed Red behind the counter, and they whispered back and forth. Once Red looked back and met his eyes again. But she quickly turned away.

Was she going to run again? He wasn't sure, but he wasn't about to let her get away this time. He pushed back his chair, just in case he had to dart after her.

Recalling what Rick said about Red being an Anna Nicole wannabe, he frowned. Then his eyes went to her curvy backside, and he had to admit she probably had what it took to follow in the late woman's footsteps. But for some reason, he didn't believe it.

He reached for his coffee but saw it had eggs in it, and he pushed it away. Suddenly, another cup was set in front of him. Looking up, he stared at the older waitress.

"Breakfast's on me this morning," she said.

He arched a brow at her and smiled. "I could swear it was on me." He glanced down at his chest, still speckled with grits and eggs.

She grinned. Suddenly realizing that she blocked his view, and afraid she was a decoy, he rose from his seat to make sure Red was still at the counter. She was.

As if she knew what he'd been checking on, the older waitress's grin faded. "You eat and then you leave."

He remembered hearing someone calling the woman by her name. "Dixie, right?"

"Yup."

"Well, Dixie, I have a little problem. I need to speak to . . . Red before I go."

She set one hand on her hip, and he could see attitude all over her. "Red's busy working."

"It's okay." Red appeared beside Dixie. She dropped a couple of creams beside his coffee. "I'll take care of this, Dixie. Thanks."

Dixie looked at Red and then back at him. "You see that barrel-chested man behind the counter, there?"

Tyler nodded, and she continued, "That's my Fred. He packs heat and he's not scared to use it."

CHAPTER FIVE

"I DON'T THINK HE'LL NEED TO." Tyler chose not to tell her that he packed heat as well. Hell, if she wanted to check with Internal Affairs of the Glencoe police, located just down the road, they'd tell her that he wasn't afraid to use it, either. Three times he'd had to use his weapon. Three times he'd been investigated, and three times it had been judged a good shoot. He didn't take shooting someone lightly, but he didn't dillydally when someone was about to shoot him, either.

Dixie took off. Red, towel in her hand, started cleaning the mess off his table. She paused after a couple of swipes and raised her face to stare at him. "What is it you want?"

"I think I should be asking you that."

"I suppose that's fair." She bit her lip, and he could see her trying to figure out what to say. What he didn't know was if she planned on lying. "I…I was going to talk to you guys about a case."

"What kind of case?" he asked.

"A…" She lowered her voice. "A difficult one."

He reached for the cream she'd given him, pulled the

tab off one, and poured it into his cup. "And how does it involve Mr. Bradford?" He decided to give her a little nudge so they could get to the truth quicker. "Heard you've been hanging out at the Bradford place, too."

She looked surprised. Glancing around the diner as if worried others might be listening, she leaned in. "Can we talk later? After I get off work?"

"And give you a chance to run away again?" He pulled his cup to his lips and studied her reaction.

"No. To give us some privacy."

As crazy as it was, his mind went to the private fantasies he'd had about her last night. He pushed those thoughts away and studied her expression again. If she was lying, she didn't give the regular twitches. But he'd been wrong before. "Don't you get a break?"

She frowned and did a visual sweep around the room. "Let the breakfast crowd leave and...I'll see if I can't take a few minutes."

He nodded and thought she would walk away. She didn't. Their eyes met and held. "What do you want?" she asked again.

You dressed like a prim and proper librarian. Or maybe just to see a laugh light up your eyes again. "I figured that was clear. Answers," he said.

"I mean for breakfast."

He obviously was not at the top of his game. "You serve *huevos rancheros*?"

She nodded.

"Can you serve them on a plate so I can eat them instead of wear them?" He grinned, hoping to coax another smile out of her.

Almost. He saw a flash of a smile touch her eyes, but

something held her back. And he guessed what it was, too. She didn't trust him, and that was okay—he didn't trust her, either.

"*Huevos rancheros* on a plate coming up." She started to walk away.

"One more thing," he said.

She turned around.

"What's your name?"

"Zoe," she said.

"Last name?"

Her expression told him she wasn't thrilled about giving it to him.

"Adams. Zoe Adams."

He stretched out his hand. "Nice to meet you, Zoe. I'm Tyler Lopez."

She hesitated, but he didn't drop his hand. As he hoped, after a long second, she felt forced to comply. She slipped her palm in his. Her hand was soft, small, and felt nice against his. Somehow he knew last night's fantasy hadn't done her justice.

A surge of desire shot straight to his gut and then went lower. So sweet was her touch that he didn't want to release her hand, but he felt her pull away. To hold on would have intimidated her, so he forced himself to let that soft-as-silk palm slip from his.

Reining in his thoughts, he asked, "Where in Alabama are you from, Zoe?"

"How did you…"

"Your license plate."

"Oh." She hesitated. "Beaverville."

He tried not to laugh, but it seeped out. "I understand your hesitation."

Her eyes tightened. "For a guy who's wearing eggs, grits, hash browns, and half a pat of butter in his hair, you sure are quick to poke fun at others."

He bit back his smile. "I wasn't poking fun at anyone. Just the name of a town." He ran a hand through his hair, and sure as hell, a couple of forkfuls of breakfast fell to the table.

She swiped it up and then looked at him. "But it's my town." Then rolling her eyes, she took the towel and wiped his temple. The nubby feel of cotton moved over his brow, and he saw her staring, probably at his scar. The scar that would forever remind him of his stint in prison and how people and an entire justice system could let one down.

When she continued to stare, he was suddenly self-conscious. But not so concerned that he didn't appreciate how gentle her touch felt. Damn, had it been that long since he'd been touched?

"And I don't like people poking fun at it," she finished, dropping her hand from his brow.

"In that case, I apologize," he said, trying to keep his voice even. "But let me remind you that the reason I've turned into a human breakfast buffet is because of you."

Her lips twitched as if she wanted to smile, but she stopped again. "For which I've already apologized," she countered, then twisted on the heels of her white tennis shoes and sashayed away. And she looked really good doing it, too.

As soon as he was able to take his eyes off her, he pulled out his smartphone. First, he checked to see if his cousin had gotten back to him on her license plate number. When he didn't find an e-mail from Pablo, Tyler pulled up Google. He typed in her name and Beaverville, Alabama. Hopefully, by the time she took a break, he'd know enough about Zoe Adams that if she tried to lie to him, he'd be able to call her on it.

"He's watching you like a hawk," Jamie, one of the waitresses, said.

"Don't care," Zoe said, but it was a lie. She cared. And not only that, she'd found herself watching him as well. What was he doing on that smartphone? She sensed he was looking up information on her. Several times when she'd let herself get a glimpse of him, she found him watching her. Her heart had been thumping like a trapped bird since she'd shaken his hand. She'd been so nervous that she'd asked Jamie to do all the refreshing of his coffee.

"Not a problem." Jamie immediately refreshed her lipstick. Zoe regretted asking the man-hungry waitress to do it.

Zoe wished she could believe the emotional storm stirring inside her was from fear over chatting with an ex-con with anger issues who liked to teach lessons with his fists. But nope. She wasn't the slightest bit afraid of Tyler Lopez.

The man hadn't shown an ounce of anger when she dropped three hot plates of food on him. A real rageaholic wouldn't be that understanding. Then she tried to convince herself that her heart palpitations were a residual effect from the clown outfit he'd worn yesterday, but nope.

It wasn't fear making her heart thump around in her chest. It was something more primal. It was his sexy bedroom eyes, his wide, thick shoulders, and the kiss-me smile he'd shot at her several times now. It was the desire to run her fingers over the scar that lined his left brow and ask him how he got it. It was basic, to the core, uncontrollable, old-fashioned lust. And she hadn't been hit with this in a very long time.

She was so screwed. And Lord have mercy on her, she prayed she hadn't meant that literally.

"There's a gun in my desk drawer. If he makes an unwanted pass, or gets out of hand, just let him know you're armed," Dixie told her after she asked if she and Tyler could go into her office to chat.

"I'm not going to shoot him," she assured Dixie.

"Maybe not, but I'm not letting anything happen to you on my watch, girly."

"I'll be fine." And Zoe actually felt guilty that she was about to tell a strange man something she'd been unable to confide in Dixie—a woman who'd been nothing but nice to her. A woman who trusted Zoe with the keys to the cash register and made sure she ate before she left every shift.

Then again, maybe that was why she could tell Tyler Lopez her secret and not Dixie. She might be in lust with him, but she didn't care if he thought she was a nut job. If Dixie started thinking Zoe needed to check herself in for a mental evaluation, well, that would hurt.

Taking a deep breath, she poured herself some coffee, grabbed her purse, and went to get this over with. When she stepped away from the counter, she felt that hollow feeling in the pit of her stomach.

This feeling was fear. But not of Tyler Lopez. Was she afraid that he'd think she was crazy? Or was she afraid to discover her suspicions were all true? She pushed that thought aside in her mind. Who wanted to learn that everything you believed to be true about yourself was a lie?

But darn it, she hadn't come all the way to Texas, taken time off from work, to chicken out now. She wanted answers.

When she got to the table, he was reading his phone screen and laughing.

"What's so funny?" she asked.

He actually jumped. "Uh . . . nothing."

She knew he was lying. She also knew that whatever caused his laughter had something to do with her. Her gaze shot to the screen on his phone and, while she inwardly flinched, gave herself credit for being right.

"You still have grits in your hair, you know."

He laughed again. "Yeah, but . . . I haven't ever won a pageant and been given the title of Queen Beaver." Gesturing toward his phone, he shook his head. "Why in hell would you have ever entered that contest?"

She didn't know why, but she told him the truth. "Because the woman running that pageant was doing it in honor of her daughter—my best friend—who'd been killed by a drunk driver six weeks before. The proceeds went to fund MADD—Mothers Against Drunk Drivers."

His smile vanished, and regret flashed in his brown eyes. She almost felt guilty for being brutally honest. He wasn't the first one to tease her about the title. Heck, even Jay Leno had posted the headline on the *Tonight Show*, practically making her a celebrity in Beaverville.

Tyler touched his phone screen and made the article disappear. "Okay, I apologize for the second time in less than thirty minutes. Which is a record for me, by the way."

She swallowed the nervous tickle down her throat. "Dixie agreed to let us use the office to talk." While she didn't want to tell him, she gave him credit for apologizing.

"Okay." As he followed her to the office, she felt him

lean close to her ear and whisper, "I'm serious, I didn't mean to—"

"It's okay. It *is* funny." She pushed open the door and motioned to one of the chairs. Her pulse raced when he moved past her and his shoulder brushed against hers. Her palms started feeling clammy as she shut the door and sat in the chair beside him. His knee bumped up against hers, and the butterflies in her stomach started playing bumper cars. Had the office always been this small?

"Where do I start?" she muttered.

He didn't say anything, just waited, staring at her with his sexy brown eyes.

Taking a deep breath, she slipped her purse off her shoulder, set it in her lap, then pulled out a photocopy of the article she'd found in the local library's microfiche. The article contained a picture of Caroline Bradford sitting in a tire swing. Then she pulled out her wallet and retrieved the school picture of herself in first grade.

Hesitating, she handed both items to him.

He glanced at them, then back at her as if he preferred she explain what she'd attempted to make him read.

"That's a picture of Caroline Bradford taken a week before she went missing." She tapped the photocopied article. "She was almost four in the picture."

He nodded.

"And that's a picture of me right before my sixth birthday."

He looked down, studied the pictures, then glanced back up. His brows tightened as if his brain chewed on bits of information. Then he held up a hand and shook his head. "Please. Please tell me that you aren't saying you think you're Caroline Bradford?"

CHAPTER SIX

Zoe pointed to the pictures. "You don't see the resemblance?"

His brow pinched tighter. He looked back at the pictures and then up again. "It's two redheaded girls."

"Or is it the same girl?" she asked. "Can't you see it's the same girl?"

He shook his head. "You seriously don't think..." A piece of egg fell into his lap. "She was murdered. They recovered her body."

"Look at the pictures," she insisted, desperation rising in her throat and stinging her sinuses.

He put the photocopied article and her picture on the desk and studied them. Then he crossed his arms and stared at her. "What I see are two redheaded girls."

She shook her head, wishing she'd never told him. A part of her knew people would think she was crazy. She grabbed hold of what he said and went on the defensive. "So you're saying all redheads look alike? That's insulting."

"It's not an insult. I happen to like redheads."

Her throat tightened. When her vision got blurry,

she blinked a couple of times. Then somehow she found another stash of courage. "It's me. They're both me."

He inhaled. "Okay, I admit the pictures look alike, but we all look like somebody. Just because you..." He stopped talking, and his expression took on the appearance of suspicion. "You saw this on that TV show that aired a couple months ago, didn't you?"

"Yes, I saw the show, but—"

"Is that why you're here? Why you came to Texas?"

"Yes, but—"

He rolled his eyes, as if he was thinking she was a total fruitcake. "You came all the way to Texas because you looked like a millionaire's kidnapped grandchild? What? Did you not hear the part about her body being found?"

"I heard it, but—"

"But you still thought you might be able to sweet-talk the old man out of some money. That's what you want, isn't it?"

"No!" She jumped up from the chair. "I want the truth. I want answers. That's what I want. Then I'm going back to Alabama."

He stood there staring at her as if she was lacking both a brain and any morality. "Don't you realize that all it takes is a simple DNA test to prove you aren't the old man's granddaughter? He's not going to hand you money—"

"I know that. I'm not stupid."

"What a shame," he said.

She didn't understand what he meant, but she continued. "Why would anyone take my word when there's a simple test? All I want you to do is ask if he would be willing to do the test. I'll figure out how to pay for it myself."

He started to walk out but then turned around. "Do you realize how stupid I would look going to this man and telling him that I have a girl who thinks she might be his murdered grandchild? Never mind that the police are certain that they found the body."

"They didn't have DNA then," she blurted out. "I've read the reports—they never said anything about checking dental records. The only evidence they had was the child's size, her clothing, and a stuffed bear that belonged to... to Caroline. Those things could have been planted."

He ran a palm over his face. "You really believe this?"

She nodded, hesitant to admit it verbally, but she'd already crossed the line of no return.

"Why? I mean, I see the pictures, but unless you're really a whack job, you've got to have more reasons than the fact that you look like the dead girl."

She wavered on telling him more; he already thought she was crazy. But then she reminded herself she didn't care what he thought. He wasn't important to her. She glanced down at the picture.

"The swing. I remember it. I've always had this vision of a tire swing and someone with long red hair pushing me on it. And the house. A big white house. Inside, there's one room that has bookcases floor to ceiling; I remember that, too. And when I was young I called my mother, Mother Two. As if there was another mother somewhere. There are no pictures of me as an infant. None."

"Were you adopted?" he asked.

She shook her head. "No. My parents would never admit anything, but I didn't look like either of them. And I asked, but my mother said I looked like my great-aunt, but she didn't have a picture of my great-aunt. And then..."

"Then what?" he asked.

This was her trump card. If he didn't see this as evidence of what she felt was true, she would never convince him. "And then when my mother died, I found my birth certificate."

"And?"

"She never told me that I was born in Texas. I've always thought I was born in Alabama."

"So you have a birth certificate?" he asked.

"Yes, but she never told me I was born in Texas."

He shook his head and in a bad, "can't believe this shit" kind of way. "Okay, so she didn't tell you where you were born, but you have the birth certificate. So you should know you're not Caroline Bradford."

"Why would they lie about where I was born? And that's not all. There are a lot of little things that never added up about my childhood. Don't get me wrong, I loved my parents, but they've lied to me about so many things from my childhood. And if they lied about that, then what else did they lie about?"

He shook his head. "I don't know, but this... This can't be true. I... It's absurd, Zoe."

"Absurd maybe, but possible. The absurd is the essential concept and the first truth."

He cocked his head. "Albert Camus."

"I know who said it. My point is that he's right. I could be right."

Tyler shook his head. "But you have a birth certificate. That should prove you—"

"And you've never heard of forged documents? Please, you're a PI."

He just stared.

"Admit it," Zoe said. "There is a possibility that I'm right. And now someone is telling me to leave."

His eyes tightened with what appeared to be genuine concern. "Who's telling you to leave?"

"I don't know. Someone called me, and his exact words were, 'Leave. Get the hell away before it's too late.' "

"Too late for what?"

"I asked the same question," she said.

"And . . . ?"

"He hung up."

"Okay, so who else have you told this story to?" he asked.

She took a deep breath. "No one."

He rolled his eyes again. "No one?"

"Not a soul."

The look was back in his eyes. As if he was worried she'd honestly lost her mind. "That doesn't make sense. If no one knows what you're doing here, how and why would they warn you to leave?"

"I don't know. I guess it could have been a wrong number."

"So this person only called once?"

Okay, now he really didn't believe her. "I got one hang-up and then that call."

"From the same number?"

"Don't know. My phone listed both as an unknown caller."

He raked a hand through his hair, and a couple more pieces of scrambled eggs rained down.

"You're not going to help me, are you?" she asked.

He closed his eyes for a second. "Do you have your birth certificate?"

"Yes. I was going to go to the library later and..." She saw from his expression he really didn't care what she'd been going to do. She pulled her birth certificate from her purse and handed it to him.

He studied it. "I'll check and see if this is the real thing. But that's all. I'm not going to Mr. Bradford. I can't."

He started out, but she blurted out, "How much?"

Looking back, he asked, "How much what?"

"How much is this going to cost me?"

He hesitated, and when his gaze met hers, she saw that flash of something in his eyes, something she hadn't seen for a long time. Old-fashioned male interest.

"Nothing," he said. "It'll only take a phone call."

"You think I'm crazy, don't you?"

He tapped the birth certificate against his jean-covered thigh. "I think the idea of you being Caroline Bradford is crazy. I haven't made my mind up about you." He looked at his watch. "I need to be somewhere." He pulled out his smartphone. "Give me your cell number. I'll call when and if I find something. Probably tomorrow or Tuesday."

She called out her number. He typed it into his phone.

"Stay away from the Bradfords' place. They could have you arrested next time."

She nodded. "Thank you."

"Don't thank me yet."

Zoe watched him leave, and even though she knew he wasn't promising anything, she felt more hopeful than she ever had.

Rick Clark arrived at the Bradford security gate five minutes late for his ten o'clock shift. He wouldn't have been late if Western Union had lived up to the tagline:

"Send money in minutes." It had taken almost an hour to get the money wired to New Orleans. He could have hopped on a plane and given it to her in person almost as fast. Not that he was eager to see Candy.

Seeing Ricky was another matter.

Rick's gut knotted. He wasn't going for father of the year; truth was, he didn't know how to be a father, considering his own had died before he started school, but it had been three months since he'd seen the boy, and two before that. Not that he hadn't tried to see Ricky. He had. Would his own son even remember him at this point?

And if he did remember him, would he even want to see Rick again? He'd tried everything—gifts, candy. How, Rick wondered, did a father convince a kid to love him when the kid's mom seemed determined to keep them apart?

Was Ricky reading yet? Probably not. He'd probably never seen his mom pick up a book the way that Ellen Wise did. Maybe for his son's next birthday he'd send a few books. Would Candy read them to him? The answer rolling around his head made the anger swelling in his chest grow a little bigger.

But damn, he was a cop and he was tired of playing by the rules. Rules Candy didn't follow and then manipulated for her own good. No, not even for her good. He didn't have proof, but everything in his gut said Candy had fallen off the wagon again. If the court didn't see his side this time, he'd start playing by his own damn rules. Somehow he'd get Ricky away from her. No friggin' wonder fathers were kidnapping their own kids—the messed-up justice system automatically sided with mothers. As if having breasts made them better parents.

Parking his car, he sat there white-knuckling the steering wheel and trying to talk his blood pressure down. A knock hit the window, and he almost reached for his gun. When he saw it was Windsor, the head honcho of the guard, he frowned and got out.

"You're late," Windsor snapped.

"Seven minutes." Rick bit back his attitude. In spite of what he'd told Tyler, he needed this gig. Between paying child support, the lawyer, and the emergency money Candy constantly needed, he could barely get by. "Sorry."

Windsor nodded and started back to the office, obviously to clock out. Bradford, the owner of the estate, was older than dirt and still used the old punch card method of keeping track of employees' hours. Remembering Tyler's request to get the scoop on the mysterious redhead, Rick caught up with Windsor.

"Boring day?" Rick asked.

"No more than usual." Windsor rubbed a hand over his old-man belly. He wasn't much younger than the boss and bragged he'd been with Bradford from the very beginning. If anyone knew something about the redhead, this was the man.

"So that redhead gave up trying to seduce the old man?"

"What redhead?" Windsor kept walking.

"One of the guards mentioned a redhead."

"Yeah. I'm sure she's off chasing some other rich ol' man by now."

"Did you guys get a license plate and check her out?"

"Didn't see much need in it."

"Well, if she shows up again, get me a license number and I'll run it."

"I have a feeling she's moved on," Windsor said.

Rick's phone rang, and he pulled it out and eyed the number. "I'll be right up."

He hung back. "Hey, Jeff." Rick's gut tightened, knowing his friend and lawyer working the custody case was going to fly off the handle with the news.

"Tell me this call is about inviting me out for a beer and not the case."

Rick frowned. "I just wired Candy another two hundred."

"I told you to stop that shit. You pay child support; you're not her money bag."

"She said they were out of groceries."

"And you believed her."

Rick gritted his teeth. "I don't know, but I'm not gonna let my boy go hungry."

"Jesus, Rick. You told me yourself you thought she's drinking or using again. You're supporting her habit."

"Then get my son away from her, Jeff. Do it, or I'll do it myself."

"Sorry, I'm late," Tyler said thirty minutes later when Dallas opened his father's door.

"No problem. I appreciate you helping." Tyler walked into the house that was filled with wall-to-wall boxes and people.

"Hi, Tyler." Nikki ran up to him and gave him a hug.

"Hey, gorgeous."

"Watch it," Dallas said.

"You just better be glad she chose you to puke on," Tyler said. The first time Dallas and Nikki met had been at a murder scene, and she'd gotten sick all over him. It was a little something Tyler and Austin didn't let Dallas forget.

"Is that egg in your hair?" Nikki asked.

Tyler ran another hand through his hair. "I thought I got it all out."

"You got egged?" She grinned.

"Sort of." He nodded when Ellen Wise, Nikki's friend and their new receptionist, walked into the room.

"Hi, Tyler," she said.

"I hope you don't work too hard today, because I've got tons of filing for you to do tomorrow."

"Don't worry. I'm ready to get that office whipped into shape." She smiled, and Tyler realized again how pretty she was—not that she compared to Zoe. But he'd bet she wasn't crazy, either.

"You got more egg on your collar." Nikki brushed it off.

"Yeah, I had an accident at the diner."

"Nikki?" LeAnn, Dallas's sister-in-law, popped into the room. "Did you want those lamps in the extra bedroom?" The women took off to deal with lamp business.

Tyler looked at Dallas. "I remembered where I knew the redhead from."

Dallas's eyes rounded. "Where?"

"Cookie's Café. She's a waitress."

"Did you go over there yet?" Dallas asked.

"That's why I'm late."

"And she egged you?" Dallas half-grinned.

"Not on purpose," he said.

"Did you find out why she was snooping around our office?"

"Yeah." He sighed. "It's crazy."

"Let me guess. She was looking for Austin?"

"No. I was right. She was looking through the Bradford files."

"Why?"

"She thinks she's the Bradford child who was kidnapped."

Footsteps sounded behind Dallas, and Tyler looked up. Mr. O'Connor walked into the room. "Did you say Bradford kid? You know, I went to school with that girl's mama. She was a pretty thing."

Tyler nodded at Dallas's dad. "Hello, old man."

"Who you calling old?" Mr. O'Connor said. "I'll bet you fight like a girl."

Tyler grinned.

"Wait," Dallas said. "The kid who was kidnapped... They found her body."

"I know," Tyler said. "I tried explaining it to her."

"So she's a whacko, huh?"

"No. Maybe." He stopped himself from defending her. "She believes they identified the body wrong."

"They said the mom was whacko for a while," Mr. O'Connor said. "She was actually a suspect, too. I didn't believe it. Nancy Bright was a nonconformist in high school, but she wasn't the type who'd hurt a fly. Smart, sweet, and built in all the right places." He held his hands out from his chest.

"She died, right?" Tyler asked. "Both her and her husband, right?" He'd been trying to remember everything he knew about the Bradfords on the drive here.

"Yeah. They were killed in that plane crash only weeks after the kid was kidnapped. I asked her to the Junior Prom. That's before I started dating Dallas's mom.

But Nancy had already been asked by a football player. Not that I wasn't a catch." He chuckled. "As a matter of fact... Where did I put that box?"

He walked across the room and flipped open a box and pulled a book. "Here." He turned a few pages. "Tell me I wasn't every woman's dream." He handed the book to Dallas.

Dallas laughed. "Damn, Dad, you looked like Tony."

"He couldn't have been that good looking." Tony, Dallas's brother, walked in from the bedroom with a box in his hands and continued toward the front door. "Are we going to load furniture and boxes today, or are we gonna stand around and shoot the shit? You see that's the difference between PIs and cops. We actually do the work."

"Kiss my ass." Dallas laughed and passed the book to Tyler.

Tyler looked at the picture. "Actually, I think you look like Dallas, too."

Mr. O'Connor reached in and flipped a couple of pages, and put his finger on a face. "There's Nancy Bright. Soon to be Nancy Bradford. Pretty thing."

When Mr. O'Connor's finger shifted away, Tyler's breath caught. Holy hell, but it was as if he was looking at Zoe Adams.

"Damn," he muttered.

"What?" Mr. O'Connor asked.

"That's... her. I mean, that looks like the waitress."

Dallas walked over and glanced at the picture. "Maybe it's because they're both redheads."

"No. The eyes, the mouth, everything." *The breasts.*

"Don't tell me you're actually thinking she might be this Bradford kid," Dallas said. "That's crazy."

"And absurd." Tyler remembered Zoe saying, *Admit it. There is a possibility that I'm right.* "The absurd is the essential concept and the first truth. Albert Camus." Tyler looked back at the picture. "The resemblance is uncanny."

Tyler looked back at Mr. O'Connor. "Can I borrow this?"

"Sure." The old man pointed a finger at him. "I know where you work if you don't return it."

Tyler remembered something else Zoe had said. *And now someone is telling me to leave.*

It hadn't made a bit of sense, especially when she admitted she hadn't told anyone why she was here in Texas. But...if anyone knew her mother, and took one look at Zoe, they wouldn't have to be told.

Did that mean someone really had been threatening Zoe Adams?

He set the book down on the bar. "Let me help you guys load a few things, and then I'd better head out."

"We're going to end up taking her case, aren't we?" Dallas asked.

"Maybe," Tyler said. The look Zoe had sent him when she told him thank you flashed in his head. "Show me some furniture that needs carrying out. You aren't going to have me long."

Zoe sat at her kitchen table with her lunch—a bag of carrots and a bowl of ranch dressing—and her computer in front of her. She leaned her elbow on the table, and it wobbled. Looking under the table, she toe-kicked the piece of folded newspaper back under the table's right leg.

Not that she expected much from the prefurnished one-bedroom rental. She'd been fortunate to find one at all. Still the bland, run-down place and furniture did make her long for her own apartment. Her place in Alabama wasn't anything grand, but it was cozy, colorful, and filled with things that belonged to her. She'd never thought of herself as materialistic, but she missed her things. Stupid things, like the bright red throw pillows her mother had made her, her favorite frying pan, and her microwave that had the perfect popcorn setting on it.

Glancing over at the stain-spotted sofa, she frowned. She never sat on the piece of furniture because it looked… filthy, and for some reason every time she looked at it, she imagined some hairy, heavyset couch potato stretched out with half his dinner spilled on the sofa. Hence the stains.

Refocusing on the computer, she finished reading another article on Tyler Lopez and frowned. "How could they do that to him?" Zoe muttered, feeling angry at a system that could have convicted someone for something they didn't do. He'd been a cop, and it sounded like the whole police force had turned their backs on him and his two partners.

As soon as Tyler had left, Zoe got on Dixie's computer and downloaded all the files she could find about Tyler Lopez and his case. Hey, he'd Googled her, so it was only fair. Only difference was, she wasn't laughing at what she read. Just the opposite—her heart hurt for the man.

She reached for a carrot and dipped it in dressing. "Seriously. I hope he sued the state." Her cat meowed at her feet as if certain Zoe had been talking to him. And hey, it was probably better than the idea of her rambling on to herself.

The feline leaped up onto the table, something that he seldom did. "Can you believe that even after all that, he's still a nice guy?" She munched on the carrot and watched Lucky poke his face into the dressing.

He yanked his orange face back, squinted his one eye, and stuck his tongue half out, making a comment about what he thought of her menu.

She grinned and gave him a scratch behind his bobbed ear. "I told you it wasn't ice cream." Lucky moved in, sniffed her half-eaten carrot, and then rubbed his face against her cheek. "I'll share if you really want it." She sighed and leaned into his soft affection. Considering he was all she had, she treated him more like a family member than a pet. Perhaps it wasn't completely emotionally healthy, but she suspected she wasn't the only person in the world whose pets were their best friends. Besides, how could she not love such a brave little fighter?

When she'd seen the news about the kitten that had been trapped in a burning building, and was severely burned but refused to die, she'd been one of about ten cat lovers who'd showed up at the vet offering to help pay his vet bills.

Within a year, Zoe had lost her mother, her boyfriend, and her twenty-one-year-old cat Henry, and had discovered her birth certificate, causing her to question everything she knew about herself and her parents. The kitten's spirit had been just what Zoe needed to focus on. And after visiting the cat almost three times a week for two months, Dr. Shoemaker had asked her if she wanted to take Lucky, a name given to the kitten by local press, home. Zoe had jumped at the offer. She'd been lucky to get Lucky.

"I have one more article to look at and I'll get your paté," she told the feline as she dipped her carrot into the dressing again.

The last article had a picture of Tyler. His warm brown eyes stared from the computer screen, and Zoe remembered how her heart had taken flight when she'd shaken his hand. The crazy thing was that she actually thought she'd seen some of the same feeling in his expression. Not that anything could ever come of it.

She had a microwave waiting for her in Alabama.

Her heart did a small lurch when her cell phone rang. She couldn't help but think that it might be Tyler. Then again, he'd said it would be Monday or Tuesday. Still she didn't waste any time answering the call.

"Hello?" Something akin to giddiness sounded in her voice.

Silence reigned for a moment, and then...

"Let me spell it out for you," a gravelly voice said. "Leave town now or die, bitch!"

CHAPTER SEVEN

TYLER HELPED CART OUT the larger pieces of furniture to the moving van. While everyone joked and laughed, his mind stayed on Zoe Adams. And not just on how sexy she looked, or how he'd been so damn eager to make her smile. He started listing questions in his head about her possible case. Was someone really threatening her to force her to leave town? Why? Was it someone in the Bradford family who didn't want to share the old man's inheritance? Or did the threat stem from someone who was involved with the kidnapping?

Then came the big question. If the girl they found dead all those years ago wasn't Caroline Bradford, who was she? Had the same person who kidnapped Caroline killed the other kid? Supposing of course that Zoe was Caroline Bradford, instead of an eerie lookalike.

The more he thought about why someone might want to get rid of Zoe, the more eager he was to get back to her. Then he tried to recall what he had learned in the ten minutes he'd watched of the damn show that started it all. The child's body had been burned according to the authorities. Cause of death had been listed as violent. It hadn't been pretty. Remembering he had Zoe's cell number, relief went straight to his solar plexus. He took a break and gave her a call.

The phone rang four times and then went to voice mail. He left a message and asked her to call him back. When his phone didn't immediately ring with her return call, he grew more concerned.

Looking up the diner's number, he called and asked to speak to her. He was informed that Zoe had left work an hour ago. He gave his name and was about to ask for Zoe's home address when the waitress said she couldn't talk. She hung up.

Shit!

He dialed back, but no one answered. After a quick, almost-rude good-bye to Dallas and the others, Tyler headed back to the diner. As he drove, Zoe's smile flashed in his head again, and he found himself pushing the speed limit. He just hoped the knot in his gut was the *huevos rancheros* and not a foreshadowing of something bad.

When he got to the diner, the parking lot was full, so he had to park on the street. He walked inside and sought out Dixie.

"Hey." He stopped beside her and a table of three women. "Can I talk to you for a second?"

She gestured to her customers. "I'm kind of busy here."

"Yeah, but I promise only to take a minute."

"Let me get this order," she said.

He looked over at the table where Zoe had spilled a tray full of food on him, and her smile filled his mind. Looking back at Dixie casually conversing with her customers, his patience snapped.

"Okay, I've waited long enough," he said. "I need to know Zoe's home address. Now."

Her eyes widened, and she led him away from the table. "Why would you think I'd give it to you? That girl never dropped a French fry until you showed up. You walk in and say something to her, make her so nervous that she slings plates of food everywhere."

"I'll pay for the expense," he said.

"I don't give a crap about the money—it's her I'm worried about."

"That makes two of us."

Dixie's expression grew hard. "Look here, buster. I know all about you and what some people think you did."

Tyler felt the punch straight to his gut. He ought to be used to people's reaction by now, but it still surprised him. "Then you also know I was exonerated. Look, she's not answering her phone and I'm worried about her."

"Maybe she doesn't want to talk to you."

"I think she would. She trusted me enough to talk to me this morning."

Another waitress walked by. "Zoe seems to be the popular girl of the day," she said as if she'd been listening in on the conversation. "She's had two people calling for her."

"I called once," Tyler said. "Who was the other person?"

"He didn't say. But he hung up as soon as I told him she would be getting off in an hour."

"Does she usually have anyone calling for her?" Tyler looked to Dixie.

"No." Worry made the wrinkles in the older woman's face deepen. "The girl's a loner. She doesn't know anyone in town."

His gut tightened even more. Logic told him he might be overreacting, but instinct told him differently. His stomach clenched harder. It definitely wasn't the *huevos rancheros.* "I want her address and I want it now."

Tyler called Zoe at least four more times while he drove, all of which went to voice mail. It only made him drive faster. He knew where the high-ticketed spots were for the Glencoe PD, and he avoided them. Getting closer to the address Dixie had given him, he recognized the neighborhood as one that had the highest crime rates on this side of town. Why was Zoe living here? Was she hoping to become a statistic? *Gorgeous redheaded Alabamian falls prey to Texas crime.*

He turned onto her street and slammed on his brakes when he caught an address. Half a block dowh the road he found it. Her place was actually a run-down house turned into run-down apartments. He actually remembered a suspect he'd investigated once who lived here a few years back. The place had been a pigsty then.

He parked in the street, and the tightness in his chest lessened when he saw her car. But the hair on the back of his neck stood up as if someone was watching him. Looking around, he reached into his shirt and released his shoulder holster.

He got to her door and knocked. No one answered. Leaning close, he called out. "Zoe? It's Tyler."

He waited about fifteen seconds before his patience wore out. He moved to the window. Instead of a curtain, there was a sheer piece of fabric. He could see right through it. Perfect for a Peeping Tom... or worse.

His gaze shifted from the emptiness to the few items

filling the room. The thread-worn and stained sofa looked like someone had picked it up from somebody else's curb. The carpet had bald spots, and, while it looked like it used to be orange, it now matched the dirty brown sofa.

Unsure how to proceed, he moved back to the door and knocked with enthusiasm. Finally, he reached for the knob and turned it. It actually opened. A frown tightened his mouth. She lived in the gutter of town and didn't bother to lock her door?

He stepped inside. "Zoe?"

No one answered. He stuck his hand under his shirt and gripped his gun, tempted to bring it out, but he didn't want to stumble across her and scare her. Assuming she was here.

His gaze shifted left to right, looking for signs of a struggle. Nothing looked out of place. He took a few more steps.

"Zoe?" he called again, and then moved to the table. A laptop sat on it. Giving it a glance, he then looked into the tiny kitchen. As much of a dump as the place was, there wasn't a crumb on the faded Formica counter or a dirty dish in the sink.

He moved back to the table and noticed the laptop was on. He touched it and the screen woke up. It took about a second for him to recognize the article. "Great." She knew all his dirty little secrets. The knowledge stung, although he wasn't sure why. The whole damn world knew. And half of them still considered him a dirty cop, like Dixie at the diner.

Beside the laptop was a half-empty bag of baby carrots, a bowl of what looked like dressing, and her cell phone. He touched the bowl to see if it was still cold.

Nope. He started to step away from the table, when he saw her purse on a kitchen chair.

If her car and purse were here, where the hell was she?

He looked back to the hall. It obviously led to the bedroom and bath. A fear that he'd catch her stepping out of the shower had a vision filling his head. The fear quickly changed to something completely different. To cover his ass, he called her name as he moved down the hall.

The bathroom door, halfway down the hall, stood open. A new shower curtain—a bright red and green checkered pattern—hung from a shower rod. Somehow he knew Zoe had added that little furnishing. The bathroom smelled like a clean woman. Stationed at different places in the bathroom, he saw the feminine-smelling soap, some newish-looking towels, and a few small bottles of skin care products. What the bathroom didn't contain was the very moist, fresh-smelling, and naked Zoe he'd been envisioning.

He started into the bedroom. The thought hit that she might be asleep and hadn't heard him. In which case, she'd probably be upset that he'd invited himself in. His gaze shot straight to the bed when he stepped in the room.

Empty. A blanket was stretched out on top of the bed. Not so neatly in place that one could consider the bed made, but enough to say someone had given it a little effort. A stack of library books stood on the floor beside the bed.

Tyler moved in to see her reading taste.

He found a nonfiction book titled *Jump-Start Your Brain;* a romance novel with a shirtless hunk on the cover; a biography of Helen Keller, that he'd read; and another book on social psychology, that he'd read as well. The woman had eclectic taste. He frowned. Zoe Adams wasn't going to fit into his new class of datable women. As crazy as it seemed, he wondered if he'd instinctively known it and if that was why he'd found her so attractive. His same pattern—his romance mistake—shining through.

He noticed a litter box in the corner. Funny, he hadn't seen a cat. "Kitty? Kitty," he said. No creature darted out from under the bed.

His gaze shifted, and he found her waitress uniform, accompanied by some silky looking underwear, in a basket at the foot of the bed. So she'd come home and changed clothes. And then what?

His mind created images he didn't like, such as someone forcing her to go with them. But wouldn't she have fought them, caused a sign of struggle? For some reason, she didn't seem the type who'd go down easy. He stood there, trying to figure out what he planned to do next. And that's when he heard it—footsteps. Someone was in the apartment.

He had his gun out in a matter of seconds.

Taking a deep breath, he moved toward the door, his gun held out and ready to shoot.

Zoe walked into her place and realized she hadn't even locked the door. She mentally gave herself a good scolding. Considering the reason she'd left in the first place was because of a threatening phone call, you'd think she'd have taken care to lock up.

Then again, maybe she should take it easy on herself. This was all new for her. It was the first time she'd ever had someone threaten to kill her. Or was it?

The vague memory whispered into her mind—the one she'd had forever and the one she contributed to her fear of small, dark places. A mental video played in her head, the one of her in a dark closet. Alone. And terrified.

Her breath caught. It suddenly hit her that whoever was calling her could be the same person who put her in that closet—if it really happened.

Okay, she was definitely going to lock the door from now on.

Stopping only a few feet inside her apartment, Zoe looked around for Lucky, her official door greeter. He wasn't there, running figure eights between her legs, begging to be picked up.

Chills crawled up her spine, but she shook her head. She was overreacting. It was the middle of the day. Who in their right mind would break into an apartment? Right?

Right, she answered herself. It was tonight she should be worried about.

And she would be.

Holding tight to the plate of leftovers her elderly neighbor had made her bring home, Zoe moved down the hall, thinking any minute the cat would come bolting out of the bedroom. She hadn't wanted to be alone after the threatening phone call. So when Mrs. Hernandez knocked on her door and invited Zoe to her apartment to celebrate her granddaughter's birthday, Zoe had slipped twenty dollars from her grocery money account into an envelope and ran out.

And she'd actually had fun, too, though she'd spent most of her time trying to remember the Spanish she'd learned in high school. Everyone seemed to love hearing her try her best to speak, mangling their language. Zoe had loved being in the midst of company.

With a heavy plate of the best Mexican food she'd ever

tasted, well worth the twenty she'd given as a gift, she got almost to the entrance of her bedroom when she heard it. Someone was in there. Before she saw the person, she saw the gun.

She didn't have time to think.

Didn't have time to run.

So she did the only thing she could. With everything she had, she tossed the heavy ceramic plate loaded with Spanish rice and chicken enchiladas at the intruder and let out a scream.

The plate no sooner left her fingertips than Zoe recognized the man.

With his right hand occupied with the gun, he used his left arm to block the plate. Unfortunately, the food found its way around his attempted block. And for the second time in one day, she'd showered Tyler Lopez with food.

"You have to be kidding me." He looked down at his chest, now covered in bits of rice, tiny cubes of tomatoes, and big chunks of enchiladas smothered in a warm, creamy cilantro sauce. Amazingly, his tone didn't sound furious, more like surprised.

She was much closer to the furious mark. "I was going to eat on that for two days." And considering she'd given her grocery money as a gift, she'd really been happy.

A blob of enchilada, sauce included, literally rolled down his forehead to his mouth. She saw his tongue swipe across his lips.

"Damn, that's good. I haven't eaten since breakfast." He smiled, and then, reaching into his food-splattered shirt, he slipped his gun inside.

She almost found his smile contagious. Almost. "What are you doing in my house?"

Guilt flashed in his eyes. "I...knocked."

"And I obviously didn't answer."

"No, you didn't. But I saw your car and was worried, so I...came in to make sure you were okay."

"And how is that *not* trespassing?"

He licked his lips again, to catch another swipe of sauce. "I didn't say it wasn't." His brow creased. He pointed a finger at her. "But you should have locked the door. Then you'd have me on breaking and entering." He didn't smile now, but humor brightened his brown eyes.

"I was next door." She knew it didn't excuse her, but it was all she had right now.

"Doesn't matter." The humor faded from his eyes. "Especially in this neighborhood."

She rolled her eyes. "I haven't had a problem with intruders until now."

They stood and stared at each other. Why was he here?

"Did you find out something about my birth certificate?" she asked, telling herself that had to be why he was here. That or he'd somehow guessed how attracted she was to him and how easy it would be to get her in the sack.

"No," he said.

"No, what?" she asked, her mind still on her getting in the sack with him.

"No, I didn't find out anything on your birth certificate. But I ran across something else."

"What?"

"It's in my car." He pointed down to his shirt. "Can I use your bathroom to clean up?"

She nodded, and he stepped inside the bathroom. He didn't shut the door. She heard the water turn on. The pipes started groaning as they always did.

"Do you want me to rinse out your shirt so the sauce won't stain?"

He looked at her as she stepped inside the door. "No, it's okay."

"I don't mind." She eyed the short-sleeve button-down, a solid colored light blue that looked really good on him. "It looks like a nice shirt, and I'm betting it will be ruined if you don't rinse it out."

"Okay." When he started unbuttoning his shirt, slowly, one button at a time, the awkwardness level in the room shot up way past the normal range and flew right into the "I wish I could fade into the nineteen-eighties' washed out yellow and green wallpaper" range.

Too late, she remembered how it had felt to be with him in Dixie's small office. She shouldn't be this close; shouldn't be watching him remove his clothes. She looked away and hoped he didn't see the embarrassment tiptoeing up her neck and cheeks. God, it wasn't like she was a virgin or anything. Granted, it had been a long time. But she'd lived with Chris for three years—she was no stranger to sex. Before Chris, she'd been with three other guys. Of course, one was so bad she was hard-pressed to count him as the real deal. It had happened so fast, she wasn't sure if Tab A had ever made it into Slot B.

"Here," he said.

Forced to look up, her mind somehow stuck on slots and tabs, she took the shirt from his hands. Her first illogical thought was that as good as the shirt had looked on him, it looked even better off.

Thankfully, he had on one of those ribbed fitted T-shirts—wife-beaters someone had dubbed them. Not that the clingy piece of cotton hid anything, or caused any sort of a negative emotion. Nope. How could there be anything negative about all that bare, warm, olive-colored skin that was sculpted with masculine ripples and muscles? But damn, the man had a nice chest and abs. Even the sight of the gun strapped around him didn't take away from the awesome shoot-me-now view.

Chin held high, desperately trying to appear unaffected, she gracefully turned and started out. She might have been more successful in portraying the poised role of an experienced woman who didn't melt at the sight of a man's half-naked chest, if she hadn't missed the door and run right into the door frame... with a loud thud.

She probably looked like a total geek. Okay, not probably, it was more like definitely, but it was the sound of his laugh, deep and sexy, that had a moan slipping from her lips.

CHAPTER EIGHT

WHEN THE MAN STEPPED into the kitchen a minute later, Zoe had finished taking her frustration out on his innocent shirt and he'd apparently finished laughing. She wrung out the shirt one more time to get out the excess water. From the corner of her eye, she saw him drop his shoulder holster with his gun down on one end of the table, before he turned toward her.

"There," she said, and shook it open. "Good as new." Then, forcing herself to face him, vowing not to look below his chin, she said, "I'll just grab a hanger so it can dry."

"Thanks," he said as she brushed past him. And she actually had to brush against him to get past. Not that it was his fault, the kitchen was that small.

She moved down the hall, attempting not to step into the food or the broken plate. She hoped it wasn't one of Mrs. Hernandez's favorite dishes.

Stepping inside the bedroom, she spotted Lucky now resting on top of the bed. Obviously he'd gotten past his phobia over having a stranger in the house, but not so much that he felt ready to come out and meet their houseguest.

She didn't altogether blame him, either. Tyler Lopez made her feel jumpy, too. Probably not for the same reasons as Lucky, but she could still relate. The lyrics from some song, *too sexy for your shirt*, echoed in her head.

She moved closer to the bed, leaned her knee on the mattress, and gave Lucky a gentle scratch under the chin. "It's gonna be okay," she whispered. Then she went to the closet and snagged a hanger—something that, as a child, she hadn't been able to do.

Yup, closets rated right up there with clowns. Her psychologist back then had called it auchloclaustrophobia, derived from the fear of small places and the fear of the dark. She'd been so relieved to have a name for what bothered her that she'd learned to spell it at the ripe young age of six.

But from where the actual fear derived was a mystery. Oh, she told the doc and her parents about the nightmare. "Just a bad dream," they had all said.

And she'd believed them. Or at least she'd convinced herself she had. She'd moved on, lived her life with just a few hang-ups. But all that changed when less than three weeks ago she saw her picture on the television show. That was the day when she knew she had to find the truth, even if the truth wasn't pretty. That was the day she'd made her plan to come to Texas. After all, according to her birth certificate, she'd been born here.

"Just a dream, my ass!" she muttered, thinking about the phone calls, and had to push back the residual anger at her parents again. All those years. All those lies.

Stepping into the living room, she hung the shirt on the doorknob before facing him.

He stood just outside the kitchen, staring at her. She felt

the awkward sensation return, but not because she stood too close to him this time. No, this time it was probably because she was trying so hard not to look at his chest.

"Are you okay?" he asked.

"Fine," she said, knowing it was a lie but saying it anyway.

A slight smile pulled his lips to the right. Do I make you nervous?"

"A little," she answered, and then wished she hadn't.

His smile widened. "Is it because I'm not wearing a shirt?"

Embarrassment prickled. Just because it was the truth didn't mean she had to admit it. Her gaze caught on his gun on the table. "Probably has more to do with the fact that you pointed a gun at me."

The humor in his eyes faded. His gaze shifted back to the kitchen table. "You do know I didn't do it, right?"

Confusion stirred in her chest. "Do what?"

He frowned. "I saw what you were reading," he said, and she saw something, too.

She saw something that looked like pain in his eyes. She could only guess how much it had hurt to be accused and to be found guilty of something so ugly. Had people he cared about turned their backs on him? Maybe even his family? If so, that had to hurt. Her own parents had never turned their backs on her, but their dishonesty felt like a betrayal.

"I don't…I don't wash shirts for people I think are killers." She tried to make light of it, but the humor seemed to fall flat.

He glanced back at the computer screen as if thinking. He didn't look happy.

"You Googled me," she said.

"I know." He gazed back at her. "I don't care. I just didn't want you to think..."

"I don't...think anything." Her gaze fell to his chest. "I'm not nervous because I'm afraid of you."

He continued to stare at her, and when her eyes betrayed her and lowered to his chest again, the humor returned to his eyes. "Is my missing shirt making you nervous?"

She rolled her eyes. "Please, I've seen tons of naked guys." *Did I really just say that?*

His grin widened. "I'm not naked."

"Okay, I've seen tons of half-naked guys." She really needed to just shut up.

"Tons?" His grin widened. "Lucky guys."

"Oh, I didn't mean..." Time to shut up. She concentrated on not blushing. Then she realized what she should be talking about instead of half-naked guys. He'd come here for a reason and not to stand around and flirt with her. "What is it you have to show me?"

He nodded. "Let me get it."

When the door closed, she moved to the kitchen table and closed her computer. Okay, she was so going to get hold of herself now. Act her age. What was it about this guy that made her feel like a giddy thirteen-year-old girl? Probably pure lust. Then again, maybe it wasn't only the attraction. Maybe it was partly because he was the first person she'd ever confessed her Bradford story to.

Yeah, she felt better attributing some of her anxiety to that. Heading to the kitchen, she grabbed supplies and got busy cleaning up the mess on the hall floor.

She was almost finished when he walked in. He didn't

knock, not that it mattered. She just noticed it, and for some reason it seemed to mean something—as if they had moved past the stranger stage and on to a new stage. But new stages could be dangerous.

He had a book in his hands.

"Here, let me help you." He dropped the book on the table and came over and held the dustpan while she swept the last of the mess into the pan.

"There," she said. "I can mop later." She looked toward the table and grabbed the trash can. "Show me what you brought."

He took the trash from her and started walking down the hall beside her. His bare shoulder brushed against hers, and she pretended not to notice.

He moved into the kitchen area and set the trash can next to the refrigerator. She sat at the table and pulled the book over. She ran her thumb over the gold emblem on the front cover of what looked like an old high school yearbook.

"Have you seen any pictures of Nancy Bradford?" He pulled out a chair and sat beside her.

She looked over at him. "She died."

"I know," he said. "I'm sorry."

Why was he apologizing? Had he changed his mind and now believed her?

She told him the little she knew. "One article I read said she didn't care much for all the press that came with being married to a millionaire. The only picture I found of her was from her obituary in the newspaper, and it wasn't very clear." She glanced back at the book. "Is this her high school yearbook?"

"It's her high school. Not her book." He picked up the book and started flipping through the pages.

Zoe's heart raced as she watched him leaf through the book. The next thing she knew, tears filled her eyes and her lips began to tremble. "Does she look like me? Is that why you brought this?"

He raised his gaze and obviously saw her tears because his expression filled with empathy. "Yes." He flipped a few more pages and then pushed the yearbook to her.

She had to blink to get the watery sheen from her eyes, but when she saw the picture, her eyes filled with more tears. Of course, she had suspected. She'd even worked on accepting it as the truth. But seeing the evidence with her own eyes made all the suppressed hurt and anger rain down on her like pitchforks. She pressed a hand over her lips. When the tears flowed harder, and she couldn't seem to catch her breath, she pushed away from the table, brought her legs up on the chair, and rested her forehead on her bent knees.

After a few seconds, he asked, "Are you okay?"

She forced a shaky breath into her lungs, looked up, and swatted at her cheeks. "No, I'm not okay. I'm madder than hell right now! How could they have done this?"

"Who could have done what?"

"My parents. They lied to me. I told them about the nightmares about...about the things I remembered, and they always said I was imagining things. They sent me to a shrink and lied to him that I was just a confused kid. Other kids called me crazy because I saw a shrink. How could they have done that?" She gave her cheeks another swiping to get rid of the tears.

He started to say something, stopped, and then started again. "I don't know." He paused again. "I know how it looks right now, but it could still turn out to be some freak coincidence. We don't know for certain if this means anything."

"It's not a coincidence. I know," she said, sounding harsher than she intended. "There's a part of me that has always known. But I believed my parents. I loved them. I loved them all my life, and now I don't even know who they were. What kind of people kidnap a kid and lie to her?"

"I don't know." He sounded honestly concerned as he brushed a strand of hair from her face. "But I'll get to the bottom of this. I already told one of my partners that we're taking your case."

His words took a few laps around her addled brain, and she tried to figure out why it bothered her. She finally figured it out. "No. I can't. I mean, I can't pay you."

"Then you're lucky that we don't charge for our services."

She did one more wipe of her cheeks. "You don't charge?" She arched a brow in disbelief. "That's not good business sense."

He grinned. "We charge for some cases, but we do a lot of pro bono work." He nodded toward the laptop. "Let's just say that, considering how the justice system screwed the three of us, we kind of like making sure it doesn't screw over someone else."

"But this doesn't really involve the justice system."

His brow tightened as if he hadn't considered that point. "It's close enough."

She tried to wrap her mind around that and couldn't. "I don't like being a charity case."

"Okay, we'll bill you and you can pay as little as you want when you can."

She considered his offer and couldn't find a downside to it. Nodding, she lowered her feet to the floor. "I can live with that." Too late she realized how close he was, and how close she was to him. Her legs came between his, her right knee brushing the inside of his lower thigh. The feeling of being "too close" swelled in her chest.

"Good." His voice sounded deeper. His warm brown eyes met hers. He reached up and brushed another strand of hair that clung to her tear-dampened cheeks.

She wasn't a hundred percent positive, but the moment felt like that part in the movies when romantic music started playing and someone was about to get kissed.

Something told her that giving in to that temptation wouldn't be a good idea. And for more than one reason.

Vulnerability: She simply wasn't in the best emotional place to start a relationship.

Geographical undesirability: She had to go home. In a few weeks she was back to 'Bama.

Trust issues: She had no problem believing that Tyler hadn't killed anyone. But that didn't mean someone who looked like him didn't crush hearts. People hurt people. People lie. Even good people. Even people she loved. People like her parents. She blinked, and when she opened her eyes, his mouth was even closer.

She jumped up. Fast. Toppled over the chair in the process, too. It hit the frayed carpet with a thud.

Unsure what to say, she reached down to her knee and faked a moan. "Leg cramp."

Doubt filled his eyes. Faking had never been her strong point.

Suddenly, she heard an odd kind of crack and then a strange clunk. The crack came again, only this time it was followed by some peculiar pings.

"Shit! Get down!" Tyler yelled.

The next thing she knew, he bolted from the chair and charged right at her. She landed, flat on her back, so hard that the impact knocked the wind out of her lungs. And when he landed on top of her, what little air she had left spilled out of her lips in a rush.

She tried to push him off.

"Stop! Someone is shooting at you!" he growled.

Another crack sounded, followed by more crunchlike noises. His words hadn't completely sunk in when Zoe saw a puff of dusty white Sheetrock rain down from the wall, leaving a round hole in the drywall.

She stopped trying to get him off her. Not so much because he'd asked her to, or because it was the smart thing to do, but because sheer panic prevented her from moving. Someone was shooting at her. A scream lodged in her throat.

He adjusted his weight so that it didn't feel so smothering. She managed to suck air into her lungs. "Shit!" The one word eked out.

"I already said that." He looked back at the table. "I'm going for my gun. You stay down."

"No!" She flung her arms around him, pulled his chest flush against hers, and even locked one leg around his waist. "I don't like that idea. Come up with another one."

He frowned. "You're safe if you stay down."

"But what about you?" She tightened her hold on him and flung her other leg around his waist, tightening her thighs around him.

He stared into her eyes. "Careful or I'm gonna think you like this position."

She scowled at him. "Seriously? You can think about sex right now?"

"I guess I like the position, too." He bounced off her and ran for the gun, just as more cracking noises filled the air.

Tyler heard the shots and got two steps away from his gun when something hit him. Not a damn bullet but a five-foot-five redhead. Some part of her made a direct hit on the back of his knee, and he fell. On his way down, he turned and grabbed her to get her away from the window. When he hit the floor, she came down on top of him. Hard.

"I told you to stay down!" he growled.

She raised her head and rested her chin on his chest. "And I told you I didn't like that idea!" Her voice quavered, and she had tears in her eyes again.

It was the tears that took the edge off his anger. Growing up with three sisters, he should be immune to feminine tears, but something about hers cut right to his emotional quick.

"I need to get my gun," he said.

"No," she snapped. "Because then you're gonna want to look out the window—and in the movies, that's when someone always gets shot."

"I'm not going to get shot," he said calmly, recognizing the irrational fear in her wide-eyed gaze. He could feel her shaking, but she tightened her grip on him. As much as he wished he could patiently talk her down from the panic ledge, he didn't have time. So he'd have to try another tactic to get her to release him.

"I like this position, too." His words encouraged her to loosen her hold on him. But when he considered she might get up, he came up with Plan B. He rolled her over, closer to the table, and, while pinning her to the floor, he reached for his gun. Once he had it in his hands, he felt better.

Brushing a thick curtain of dark red hair from her eyes, he looked at her. "Now, stay down. It's okay. You understand?"

She nodded. But when he went to move, she tightened her arms around him again. "Zoe, let go or I swear to God I'm going to kiss you." He wasn't exactly sure how he knew it would work, but the fact that she'd jumped halfway across the room and faked a leg cramp when he'd gotten close to her face probably clued him in.

She let go. He crawled over to the window and peered out. He didn't see anyone. Seconds later, he figured out why. The screech of a car speeding off sounded nearby.

"Damn," he muttered. By the time he got out front, they'd be gone. His best hope was that someone had seen the car.

On automatic, forgetting he'd taken off his shoulder holster, he tried to put away his gun. That's when he saw the blood.

Blood?

He did a quick mental search for pain in his body and found none. He even pulled up his T-shirt to make sure. Nothing. It wasn't his blood. "Shit." He turned to Zoe.

CHAPTER NINE

ZOE LAY STILL, her eyes closed, her hand pressed over her arm. It was nothing more than a big scratch—she'd checked—but it burned like the dickens, and the thought that she'd been shot was enough to make her have a meltdown. Okay, another meltdown. She'd already lost it when she'd seen the picture of her... mom. This was turning out to be a pretty piss-poor, meltdown kind of day.

"Zoe. Talk to me." She heard his voice at the same time she felt him lifting her shirt.

She grabbed her shirt to stop him from pulling it up over her bra—she hadn't even worn her best one—and opened her eyes.

"Let me see!" he growled.

She had her mind on her bra, but she realized he meant her wound. At least she hoped he did. "It's here." She looked at her arm and saw the blood and put her hand over it.

He set the gun down on the floor and carefully moved her hand and peeled up her bloody sleeve. "I'll get you to the hospital."

"Hospital?" She lifted up on her elbow and looked at

her arm. Maybe she had missed something. But nope. It was still just a scratch, not that it felt like it at this point.

"It wouldn't even take a stitch."

"You were shot."

"I was scratched by a bullet. There's a difference." Hearing herself put it like that made her feel better. Her pulse seemed to inch down a notch, too.

"You're bleeding," he said.

"I think you bleed when you're scratched by a bullet," she said. "Seriously, it's just a scratch."

He stared at her arm and then back at her face as if debating whether to throw her over his shoulder and cart her out. Hoping to prove she was okay, she sat up.

"Are you afraid of doctors?" he asked.

"No, that's not on my phobia list. Not that I don't have a few...but at this moment, I'm afraid of my two-hundred-dollar deductible."

He gave her one of those girls-are-so-dumb looks that would have been more appropriate on a young boy. "I'll take care of it."

"I don't think so." When he didn't look convinced, she added, "I'm fine. It feels more like a burn than a scratch. I have some antibiotic cream and Band-Aids." She looked at the window and her concern shifted. "Are they gone?"

"I think so." He continued to stare at her arm. "But I believe you need to be checked by a doctor."

"And I believe I'm fine. It's only going to take one Band-Aid and not even the biggest one in the pack."

"LeAnn," he said.

"My name's Zoe," she countered.

"I know. LeAnn's a nurse, and she can look at it and tell us if you need to be seen by a doctor."

Before she could argue, he pulled out his phone and dialed. "Is LeAnn with you guys?"

Pause.

"Good." Tyler kept it brief and told the barest of details. Address, bullets, her being shot, needing to be checked. "Tell her I'll kiss her for it."

Who was LeAnn? His wife?

Her gaze darted to his left hand. No ring.

He continued, "Yeah. I heard him drive off. See you in about twenty." He hung up and looked at her. "I know that hurts."

"I can hardly feel it." And it wasn't as big of a lie as it had been earlier. The scratch had stopped burning like hell and was now only burning like purgatory. Not that she knew a heck of a lot about purgatory; she'd been raised Baptist. Then again, she'd also been raised to believe she was the daughter of Mildred and Ralph Adams. The thought that they had lied to her rang another painful bell inside her heart.

She took a deep breath. "I guess he really meant it, huh?"

"Who meant what?" he asked.

She grimaced. "I got another phone call. They said I had to leave or I'd die. Not that I'm dead... yet." This was so not a good day.

His brows tightened. "Why the hell didn't you tell me this before?"

She wasn't fond of being scolded. "Between finding you pointing a gun at me, to"—she motioned to the book on the table—"seeing the picture, then being shot at, it sort of slipped my mind."

There was also the whole God-he-looks-sexy-without-his-shirt issue, but she decided to let that one go unsaid.

Because it wasn't going to be an issue. He had LeAnn. And she had a list of reasons not to let herself consider getting involved with the opposite sex.

"It shouldn't have slipped your mind," he growled.

"Live and learn," she said.

"Or die and wish you had," he snapped. "What else did he say?"

"That pretty much covers it." She frowned.

He frowned back at her. "I need to go outside and check to see if anyone saw anything. Then we're going to go see LeAnn. Are you okay for a few minutes alone?"

"I'm fine." She stood up to show him she meant it. Alone wasn't a problem. She'd been alone for a long time. Well, not completely alone. She had Lucky. Glancing back, she saw the cat standing in the bedroom doorway, hesitant to come out. Then she glanced again at the windows, and her pulse started to race a little faster. She could have been killed. "I'm good," she lied.

"We'll leave in a few minutes. Get anything you might need for a few days. Austin will be here in about ten minutes, and we'll call the cops to come out and do a report."

She barely heard anything he said past... "A few days?"

"You can't stay here," he said. "Unless you want whoever did this to come back and finish what he started."

"But..."

"I have a place you can stay. A safe house," he added rather quickly. Too quickly.

What was he not telling her? The need to be logical battled with her need to just give in to the fear swelling in her chest. "Is it covered in the cost of your regular services? Or is it extra? Because I'm definitely going with the basic, low-budget PI package here."

"It's included."

Her gaze went to the shot-up windows; fear fluttered in her stomach like birds needing to escape, and she decided not to argue. "Okay, but I have a cat."

"The cat can come." He gave her hand a squeeze. "I'll just be outside, so don't panic."

"I'm not panicking." She saw his disbelief. "Not anymore."

He nodded and left—bloody T-shirt and all.

She darted to the bathroom to swallow three extra-strength pain relievers. "I'm fine," she said to herself. And then she bit down on her lip and stared at her image in the bathroom mirror. Now that she didn't have anyone to put up a front for, she could admit that being scratched by a bullet wasn't for wimps. And right now, she was feeling a tad wimpy.

Tyler checked out the street—empty. He replayed in his mind those seconds before the bullets had ricocheted through Zoe's apartment.

There hadn't been a blast. The first thing he'd heard was the shattering of glass.

Someone used a silencer.

He added a few more inquiries to his mental list of questions and then got busy trying to find someone who could answer a few of them.

Four apartments later, he approached the last door. Most of the neighbors, possible criminals themselves, had nothing to report. Two were pissed that Tyler interrupted their Sunday siestas.

But at the last apartment, a Hispanic grandmotherly type opened the door. He gave her the spiel about Apartment

Four having been sprayed with bullets. The woman's breath caught. Her gaze lowered to the front of his T-shirt. *"Dios."* She crossed herself. "Are you okay? Is Zoe okay? I can call nine-one-one."

"Everything is fine." The mouthwatering aromas wafting from behind the door told Tyler that the plate of food that Zoe had tossed at him had come from here. "Loved the chicken enchiladas," he said.

The fear faded from her aged eyes. "You are someone special to Zoe?"

He considered it for about a fraction of a second. *"Sí."* He was someone special. He was the one who was going to make sure whoever tried to hurt her didn't succeed.

A couple of minutes later, he stood on Zoe's front porch, staring at the holes in her windows when he saw Austin walk up.

"What kind of shit did you fall into?" he asked.

"You got here fast," Tyler said.

"I was just off of I-Ten when Dallas called. What's up?" His partner's eyes dropped to the front of his T-shirt, and he flinched. "You okay?"

"Yeah, I wasn't the one hit."

"The redhead?" Austin grimaced.

"Yeah, just grazed. I'm taking her to see LeAnn. Dallas told you about her?"

"Yeah, it's not every day that a man finds a redhead on her hands and knees under his desk." He grinned with a spark of interest in his eyes.

That spark pissed Tyler off. The words *she's mine* almost slipped from his lips, but he held them back, knowing they sounded juvenile. "Did Dallas tell you what it's about?" he asked.

"Yeah. Do you really think she's the Bradford kid risen from the dead?"

"I think she looks so much like Nancy Bradford that she could be her twin. She's been getting threatening phone calls telling her to leave town, and now this. Somebody doesn't want her here."

Austin considered him for a moment and then grinned. "You must be in hog heaven."

"Why?" Tyler asked, thinking it had to do with Zoe being beautiful.

"You always love a mystery. I'll bet you've already got a list of questions going."

"And it's getting longer." He pointed to the holes in the glass again. "Do you think they were aiming that high for a reason?"

"Could be they weren't looking to kill her," Austin said. "Just shake her up."

"They succeeded." A surge of protectiveness stiffened Tyler's shoulders.

"You didn't see the shooter?"

"No." He'd been too busy rolling around on the floor with her. He remembered how she'd felt stretched out on top of him, too. The way her hair had shifted like silk across his chest. Then he thought about the way he'd felt on top of her, with her legs wrapped around his waist and the way he'd fit so well between her legs.

"Neighbors see anyone?" Austin asked.

Tyler pushed the beginning of his physical awareness from his mind. "The shooter used a silencer. Doesn't mean someone couldn't have seen him, though. I've checked these four units. Got nothing."

"Has it been called in yet?"

"Not unless the neighbors did it." Tyler looked back toward the street. "I'd kind of like to get her out of here so she doesn't have to be interrogated just yet. I'm not sure I want any of the details leaked to the press yet."

Austin looked around. "Chances are no one called. From the looks of things, a little gunfire is not that uncommon around here."

"Do you want to call it in?" Austin asked.

Tyler contemplated it. "Yeah, we might need it on the record."

Austin nodded. "Why is a pretty redhead living in a dump like this anyway?"

"I think she's low on cash."

"She could lose more than cash living here," Austin said, confirming exactly what Tyler had thought. "I can call it in and hang out until they show up if you want to skip out with her."

Tyler nodded. "Thanks." He looked in the window to see if he could spot Zoe to make sure she wasn't panicking. She must have been in the bedroom.

He recalled how upset she'd been seeing Nancy Bradford's picture, and then being shot at and hit by a stray bullet. Hell, it was amazing she hadn't locked herself in a closet and cried her eyes out. That was what his sisters did when they had a bad day.

"I'm not doing it for you," Austin said. "I just love showing myself to all our fellow officers who looked the other way when they let the system take us down."

Tyler glanced at Austin. "Don't go starting trouble."

"Hey . . . dishing out a little comeuppance is good for the soul."

Tyler completely understood. There were still a few

guys on the Glencoe force to whom he'd like to offer some comeuppance. Cops and co-workers he'd considered friends, who as soon at the rumors had started flying wouldn't look him in the eye. Even after having his life back for over a year, the sting of their betrayal hadn't gone away.

He doubted it ever would.

"How are we playing it?" Austin asked. "We're keeping the Bradfords completely out of it now, right?"

"For now." Tyler looked back in the window and saw Zoe walking the hall into the bedroom.

Austin spotted her, too. "Damn. No wonder we're taking the case."

Tyler's frown came from deep in his gut. "Back off," he said, no longer caring if he sounded juvenile.

"You ready?"

Zoe jumped at the sound of his voice. With the water pipes playing their groan-and-moan song, she hadn't heard him approach the door. Now with a toothbrush working on her back molars, a mouthful of minty-tasting toothpaste foaming out the corners of her mouth and dripping onto her chin, she answered, "Juss bout." She talked around the brush, but did a poor job of it.

She pulled the toothbrush out of her mouth, spit, rinsed, and then wiped toothpaste dribble from her face. She'd never considered brushing her teeth as intimate, but it felt that way as he leaned his sexy self against the door frame, watching her. The feeling reminded her of a morning-after kind of thing. Problem was she hadn't gotten to enjoy the night. Of course, they'd rolled around on the floor while he conversed about positions. She cut her eyes to the clean shirt she'd put on to make sure she hadn't bled out from under the Band-Aid. She hadn't.

Looking up, she caught her reflection in the mirror and noticed her hair flipping in about six different directions. She grabbed a clip from the drawer. With a quick twist through her hair, she fastened it on her head.

When she glanced at him, he frowned. "I like it down better."

A retort lingered on the tip of her tongue, but she swallowed it. He was helping her find the answers she'd been seeking all her life. What's more, he was willing to work out a payment plan—even let her stay at the company's safe house. It sounded too good to be true. And that scared her.

Just trust him, she told herself. *It's blind trust*, her inner voice warned.

"I need to grab a couple of things." She waited for him to move back.

He took one small step, and she squeezed past him, then ducked into her bedroom. Grabbing her overnight bag in one hand, her purse in the other.

"Is your arm hurting?" he asked.

She looked back. He stood leaning against the door frame, watching her.

"Barely know it's there." She looked back at the cat cage, the bag of litter, and the emptied litter box pushed up beside the bed. She saw Lucky peering out from behind the bars, eyeing their visitor with his one eye. Taking a step closer to the bed, she dropped her purse on the mattress, planning to slip it in with her clothes.

Realizing she'd have to ask Tyler for a hand, she looked back. "Do you want to get Lucky?"

His eyes widened. "Now?"

"Yeah." Hadn't he said she could bring her cat?

They stood staring at each other.

Finally he said, "I'm not sure now is the right time."

It took her a second to make sense of what he meant, or rather what he thought she meant. She laughed. He stared at her like she was nuts.

She bit back her laugh. "No, I mean... my cat, Lucky." She pointed to the cat carrier.

"Oh, you didn't mean..." He reached up and brushed his finger over his chin as he stared at her and then the cat carrier. "Your... cat's named Lucky?"

Were his cheeks really turning pink? "Yes." She grinned. "I meant, did you want to get... the cat?"

His smile spread across his face, and the self-conscious look faded a tad. "I can do that, too."

Maybe it was his half-embarrassed, half-amused expression. Maybe it was just that she had so much stress bottled up inside her. Whatever it was, she started laughing again and couldn't stop.

He continued to lean against the door frame, smiling. Her laughter finally faded. Their gazes met and held. The humorous mood slipped into something... different. Different like one of those "romantic music playing in the background" moments again.

"I'm ready," she said.

He moved in, set the bag of litter in the litter box, picked it up and held it with one arm, and then carefully, as if not wanting to alarm Lucky, picked up the cat cage. He looked back at her. "You do that well." He started out.

"Do what well?" She followed him down the hall.

"Laugh."

As silly as it sounded, she sensed he meant it as a real compliment. "Thank you."

At four, Rick was looking for his card in the Bradfords' office to punch out when Michael Warren, a police officer for Glencoe and a part-time guard, came to clock in.

"How's it going?" Michael asked.

"Same old shit, different day," Rick said. "Be warned. Mrs. Daniels, Bradford's daughter, is here, and she's in a talkative mood. I now know more about her problems with her ex, her yoga instructor, her trip to the shooting range, and her latest charity dilemmas than I care to know."

Michael chuckled. "She was here last week. My head hurt from listening to her. But she did give me a bonus for doing her a favor."

"You slept with her?" Rick teased, but in truth a couple of times he'd caught the fifty-year-old woman watching him with cougar eyes. He found his punch card and clocked out.

"Hell no. But if she paid me enough." Michael laughed. "She gave me a fifty-dollar bonus for pulling over the redhead who was following her dad's limo."

Rick looked back. "I thought she'd stopped hanging around."

"She did after I pulled her over and gave her a ticket and told her to stay away."

Rick had thought it was odd that Windsor hadn't gotten any more info on the redhead, and now he was a tad suspicious. He almost asked if Windsor knew about this, but decided not to show his cards yet. He had no idea what he was dealing with.

"When did this happen?" He slid his time card into the slot.

"Last Monday, I think. Mrs. Daniels saw the redhead had followed Mr. Bradford's limo and gave me a call to see if I could put a stop to it. She hasn't been back since."

"Did you run a check on her?" Rick asked.

"Nah, I gave the information to Mrs. Daniels. I figured she got Windsor or one of you guys to run the plates."

"Was her name Kathy?" He tossed out the first thing that came to him in hopes of getting more information.

"No. Her first name started with Z and the last name was Adams. She had an Alabama license plate. It was Zoe."

"Oh," he said, pretending it was no big deal, but he repeated the info in his head so he wouldn't forget it.

Michael moved in and stuck his card into the time clock machine. "She was a hottie, too. The redhead, I mean. Hard to believe that a girl like that wanted to sleep with the old fart. Even with little blue pills, I don't think he can get it up."

"That's probably what she's hoping for," Rick said. "There's not much a woman won't do for money." For some reason, he remembered Ellen Wise. Okay, so maybe there were one or two decent women out there. A few who actually cared about their kids, bought them books—even read to them at night. "Have a good one." Rick walked out of the house, his curiosity piqued about what was going on with the mystery redhead. Had Windsor lied to him about getting info on her? Or had the old man's daughter even told Windsor she got Michael involved? Who was hiding something and who wasn't? More important, why?

Yup, his curiosity was piqued, all right. Getting into

his car, he decided he wasn't playing in the dark anymore. If they wanted his help, they had to fill him in. He pulled out his phone and saw he'd missed a call. From Candy again.

"No fucking way." He tossed the phone in the passenger seat.

CHAPTER TEN

TEN MINUTES LATER, Zoe parked beside Tyler at the Only in Texas office. She'd been so off her game from everything that happened, she hadn't even bothered to ask where they were going. He'd said, "Follow me," and like a lost puppy she'd done it.

Blind faith. Scary stuff. If there was anything to be learned from this whole Bradford issue, it was that trusting someone was risky business. She spotted a beat-up Saturn parked in the back of the lot. The sight brought the memory of her sixteenth birthday tiptoeing across her heart before she could stop it. Her parents had taken her out and bought her a slightly more than used Saturn with plenty of dings and dents in it. Then, they'd all piled in her very first car and went to eat at an expensive steak restaurant. It had been her best birthday, and the last one she'd celebrated with her dad. He'd died three days later from a heart attack. No one had called her princess since.

Questions bounced around in her head like Ping-Pong balls. How could her mom and dad have sat there celebrating her birthday and pretending to be her parents?

Why had they kidnapped her? How could they have lied to her all those years? Had their love been a lie, too?

Tears filled her eyes when she realized that now even her memories were tainted.

She took a deep breath, getting oxygen to her brain, and told herself to get a grip. Told herself she would get through this. That she would survive. She was a survivor.

"Like you." She glanced over her shoulder. Lucky sat in the carrying case with his salmon-colored nose pressed against the metal bars. Unlike most cats, Lucky didn't mind being confined in small spaces. He'd spent so much time in a small cage at the vet's office healing from his burns that even now, she regularly found him sleeping in the pet carrier.

A tap at her window had her opening the car door. Tyler stood there. She'd handed him his shirt when they walked out of her apartment, but he hadn't put it on. It was probably still damp, but wasn't that better than running around in a wife-beater T-shirt with her blood on it? Someone was bound to start wondering how he'd gotten her blood all over him. Someone like LeAnn. And what was he going to tell her? Oh, we were just trying out different positions.

Realistically, she knew his main objective had been to keep her down, but he'd put a sexual slant on the whole situation. And now she couldn't seem to forget it.

She stepped out of the car. "Can I bring Lucky in here, or are we going to just be here a few minutes?"

He hesitated. "Bring him in. But we may have to close him in one room because of Bud."

"Bud?"

Tyler opened the rear car door to get the carrier out. "The dog. I'm not sure if he's cat-friendly."

Tyler pulled the carrier to the edge of the seat and leaned down to peek inside. Lucky had his back to the cage's front.

"He's shy," Zoe said.

"Not like his master," he said.

While Zoe tried to figure out if that was a compliment or an insult, Tyler picked up the cage. Without a shirt, his biceps bulged slightly with that little bit of weight. When they passed Tyler's car, she saw his shirt hanging in his backseat.

She slowed down. "Shouldn't you put on your shirt?"

"It's still wet." He kept walking.

She moved in step with him. "It might be better than trying to explain." She pointed to his shirt. "The blood."

His brows pinched in puzzlement. "They know you were shot. LeAnn's going to check you out, remember?"

"I know, but..." She waved at the stain again.

He put his hand over the dark red smear on his shirt. "I didn't realize it bothered you. I have a shirt in the office."

"It doesn't bother me, but it might bother LeAnn."

He shot her another puzzled look. "She's a nurse. She sees blood all the time."

"But it's my blood and it's on you."

He paused in front of the door and gazed at her. "Why? Oh, you think that...LeAnn's..."

"I'll tell you what LeAnn is. LeAnn's pissed." The beautiful brunette standing at the door did look upset.

Zoe shot Tyler an I-told-you-so look. And while she knew she had no right, none whatsoever, she felt a bit of jealousy. Then that unjustified emotion turned to another equally unjustified emotion. Anger. While Tyler hadn't actually crossed a line, he'd done his share of flirting.

Enough that she hadn't thought he was otherwise committed. Enough that if there hadn't been bullets flying around, she might have even responded to some of that flirting.

"You call up and say someone is shot and you'll be here in fifteen minutes, and it's been almost thirty!" Her gaze dropped to Tyler's shirt. "You aren't hit, are you?"

"No." Tyler pointed at Zoe.

LeAnn faced Zoe. "Where are you shot?"

"Arm," she and Tyler said at the same time.

"Come on." LeAnn grabbed Zoe by the hand and led her inside.

"It's not bad," Zoe said as she was being pulled past the casket and down the hall. It still freaked her out a bit to see it.

"I got supplies set out in here." LeAnn took Zoe past the office and into another room with a large conference table. "Sit down and let me see."

"It's just a scratch." Zoe looked over her shoulder to see if Tyler had followed her. He had, and he smiled at her as if he had some inside joke.

When he moved into the room, he shut the door and sat the cat carrier down in the corner. Everyone just stared at each other for a second, and the silence seemed long.

"I should probably introduce you two," Tyler said. "LeAnn, this is Zoe, our new client. And Zoe, this is Mrs. LeAnn O'Connor—wife of Tony O'Connor. Dallas's brother."

She wasn't sure who Tony or Dallas were, but the way Tyler said, "Mrs." and "wife" told Zoe he knew she'd misread the whole LeAnn situation. And yeah, she'd misread it. But in her defense, he hadn't actually made it clear.

"Let me see the wound," LeAnn said, drawing Zoe's attention.

Zoe pulled up her sleeve.

"Does she need to be seen by a doctor?" Tyler asked.

Zoe rolled her eyes. "It's a scratch."

"I'm warning you now," Tyler said to LeAnn. "She's going to fight you if you say she needs to see a doctor. She's stubborn."

Zoe's mouth dropped open. LeAnn glanced back at Tyler. "No name calling." Then she looked back at Zoe. "Do you want him to leave? I'm good at getting rid of men."

Though LeAnn appeared to be joking, it was Tyler's frown that made Zoe smile. "No. He's fine."

LeAnn gawked at the Band-Aid. "Where did all that blood come from?"

"This is it," Zoe said, and shot Tyler an I-told-you-so look.

LeAnn looked back at Tyler. "You said she was shot."

"She was," Tyler said. "And it was bleeding a lot." He motioned to the front of his shirt. "And she was hurting like hell."

"It didn't hurt *that* bad," Zoe said.

"You were gritting your teeth."

"I was panicked. I'd never been shot before. Or had a gun pointed at me." She cut him a hard stare, so he understood she was referring to him and his gun.

"Which is a miracle considering that neighborhood," Tyler countered.

"It's not that bad of a neighborhood," Zoe said.

"Do you want me to print the list of crimes that happened there just last week?"

"Don't argue with my patient." LeAnn slipped on a pair of rubber gloves and pulled off the bandage.

Zoe flinched when the Band-Aid pulled across the wound and a stream of blood started streaming down her arm.

LeAnn eyed the wound. "It is pretty deep."

"Told you," Tyler said.

"But," LeAnn continued, "it's not bad enough for a stitch. If we wash it and put some antibiotic cream on it, it should be fine."

Zoe shot Tyler another smirk, then focused on LeAnn. "I already did that."

"Okay. But let's do it one more time. If you don't mind." LeAnn waited for Zoe to agree. "I am a professional."

"That's fine," Zoe said.

"Great. But if it does start looking infected, you need to go and see a doctor."

"We will." Tyler moved closer to the table.

We? Zoe wondered, and even LeAnn looked back at him puzzled.

Suddenly, the door behind Tyler opened and in walked a dark-haired man, early thirties, with a beer in his hand. He nodded a quick hello at Zoe. Zoe nodded a quick hello back. He was attractive, but he didn't hold a candle to Tyler. Without realizing it, her gaze went back to him and she admired his abs. Again.

Surprising herself by her wayward thoughts, she felt her cheeks grow warm. Why was she thinking about looks when... Had she lost a lot more blood than she realized?

"Tyler, I didn't know you guys got here," the newcomer said as another dark-haired man—roughly the same age and bearing a striking resemblance to the first—came through the same door. They had to be brothers, Zoe decided. Maybe even twins. The second brother nodded another quick hello at Zoe, and she did the same again.

She recalled Tyler saying something about Tony, LeAnn's husband, and his brother.

LeAnn tossed a warm smile toward the last one to walk into the room. Zoe got the feeling that was LeAnn's husband, Tony.

"Does she need to go to the hospital?" Tony asked LeAnn.

"Nah," answered Tyler, the same time Zoe chimed in with the same answer.

LeAnn started to introduce them when an older man, who looked like the two younger men, pushed his way into the room. The brothers moved around to accommodate the growing crowd. And the crowd kept growing—two blond women in their late twenties, an older lady, probably well into her sixties if not beyond, and a young African American man who looked all of eighteen joined the group. The room was big, but with this horde of people it felt small, and Zoe felt as if she was on center stage in a crowd of strangers.

Zoe wasn't shy, but with everyone staring at her, she got a nervous tickle in her stomach that reminded her how she'd felt the first days of teaching. Though she had to admit these people were a tad scarier than a room full of five-year-olds. And she didn't think singing "Bunny Foo Foo" would put everyone at ease.

Her gaze again shifted to Tyler, the one familiar person in the room. She could swear she saw an apology in his eyes. Did he know she felt ready to jump out of her skin?

Tyler's frowned deepened. "Maybe we should introduce—"

"She does look like Nancy," the older man interrupted.

Zoe's breath caught. Did he know about the Bradfords? Did everyone?

"What?" the youngest of the men in the room asked. "You think she looks like me?"

"Not you, Eddie. I said she looks like Nancy, not Nance."

"Nancy who?" asked the older woman, telling Zoe that not everyone knew.

"Nancy Bradford," the old man answered. "She thinks she's the kid who went missing all those years ago."

Zoe bit down on her lip. Well, they knew now.

"Hey," Tyler started to talk again, but was cut off by the older woman.

"Wasn't that kid found dead?" The older woman looked at Zoe with sympathy. "Sorry. I mean, you're obviously not dead."

"Nana," one of the blondes said. "We're being rude."

"She looks pretty good for a dead person," the one named Eddie said with a snicker.

Insecurities built in Zoe's chest. Was everyone going to think she was a few fries short of a Happy Meal? She hadn't been ready to announce this to the world. She'd told Tyler, but…

LeAnn looked at Zoe. "Nikki's right. We're being rude. Normally, we behave ourselves. But first let me finish this." She smiled and then looked back at Zoe's wound. "This might sting," LeAnn said as she dabbed some cream on Zoe's wound.

What stung more was realizing that everyone knew her

best-kept secret and were probably thinking she needed to rush over to the nearest mental institute and commit herself. She looked at Tyler again.

Her emotions must have been apparent because the apology in his eyes seemed more prevalent.

"Look," Tyler said, louder this time. He glanced at the crowd. "We'd kind of like it if the whole Bradford thing didn't leak out right now."

"He's right," the brother who Zoe thought was named Dallas said. "This doesn't get repeated."

"Not a word," said the older man.

"Lips sealed," said the old lady.

Eddie spoke up next. "Would it be rude for me to ask exactly what the Bradford thing is so I'll know what I'm not supposed to leak out?"

"I'd like to know, too," said an unfamiliar male voice at the door. Everyone looked up as another man walked in the room.

"Shit," Tyler said, frowning harder.

"Rick? What the hell?" Tony said. "I thought you had to work. Your lazy ass just didn't want to help me move my dad!"

Zoe's eyes moved from one person to the next, and she felt slightly relieved that everyone wasn't focused on her anymore.

"No, I just got off. And part of the reason I'm here is to see if you could still use a hand." Rick—Zoe assumed that was the newcomer's name—moved into the crowded room. His gaze found Zoe's, and everyone else in the room followed his lead. "The other reason is you," he said. "You must be the mystery redhead everybody is talking about."

Her stomach got that first-day-at-teaching quiver again. She opened her mouth to speak but decided to just nod instead. Everyone continued to stare at her, and she stopped feeling so much like a nervous teacher and more like a toad about to be dissected in a science class.

"Almost done," said LeAnn, looking at Zoe with empathy. Zoe wasn't sure if the empathy came from the wound, the situation, or the fact that the woman thought Zoe was about to be carted off to the loony bin.

"What happened to your arm?" Eddie asked Zoe.

LeAnn answered as she put a bandage on Zoe's arm. "She got shot."

"Shot?" Eddie looked at Tyler. "You didn't shoot her, did you?"

"No," Tyler said.

"But you didn't protect her, and that's almost as bad," said the old man, and chuckled. "And you call yourself a good PI."

"I told her to stay down," Tyler said as if he didn't appreciate the joke.

"He did tell me," she said. They were her first words since the crowd had arrived, and everyone's gazes shot back to her. "I was trying to protect him."

"Someone has to," the old man said, and everyone laughed.

Tyler's frown deepened.

"Who shot you?" asked Rick, completely serious.

"We don't know," Tyler said.

"Why is it that bad shit is always happening to the people who hang around you guys?" asked the grandmother.

"You got that wrong," Tyler said. "They come to us after bad shit happens."

"And you guys fix it." Eddie met Zoe's gaze. "Whatever is going on, they'll fix it. They saved my ass. And I'm not nearly as good looking as you are." Everyone chuckled again.

Tony looked at Tyler. "I hope you guys reported the shooting."

"Austin was calling it in when we left," Tyler said.

"Would someone like to fill me in on what's going on?" Rick asked.

She saw Tyler's jaw clamp down, but he motioned for Rick to follow him out the door. Before he walked out, he glanced over his shoulder at Zoe as if to say he'd be right back. "Maybe someone could introduce themselves and stop treating her like she's a science experiment?"

Funny how he'd practically used the same analogy she'd come up with.

"I'm sorry, we did storm in here," said one of the blond women. "I'm Nikki, Dallas's fiancée." She nodded toward the other brother. "Dallas is one of Tyler's partners. This is Ellen." Nikki waved at the other blonde standing beside her. "She's a friend and the new receptionist at the agency."

Ellen smiled. Nikki continued to introduce everyone else. From Dallas's brother, Tony, who was a homicide detective and LeAnn's husband, and the brothers' father Mr. O'Connor, to Nikki's grandmother whom everyone called Nana, and Eddie Nance, who was a former client and now worked for Nikki in her art gallery.

Mentally trying to sort out who was who, she almost missed what Eddie said. "Did it hurt getting shot?"

"Not too terribly," Zoe said.

"You barely feel a thing," said Tony. He pulled the collar of his shirt back and showed off a scar. "I took one."

"Barely felt it, my butt." LeAnn snickered. "You were cussing like a sailor. You even threw a urinal at one doc."

"Getting shot didn't hurt. Letting you guys poke and prod me with needles was the killer." A grin spread across Tony's face. "But I mostly did it to just get your attention. Every time I misbehaved they sent you in to talk to me." He looked at Zoe. "That's when I met her. Getting shot was the best day of my life."

"So does that mean getting puked on was the best day of Dallas's life?" asked Mr. O'Connor, who snorted with laughter.

"It was." Dallas hooked an arm around Nikki. "She was feeling a little green the first time I met her. One look at her and I wanted her heart. Instead she gave me everything in her stomach."

Everyone laughed.

"But getting shot beats getting puked on," said Tony. "You don't even have a scar."

"Please, that tiny scar you got is nothing," said Dallas. "Look at this." Dallas pulled up his jeans to show off a scar above his ankle. "Sixteen stitches."

"You fell off a bicycle," Tony countered.

"A scar's a scar," Dallas said. "Besides, you're the one who pushed me off the bike."

"A scar from a bullet trumps any other scar," Tony said.

"Getting shot can't be as bad as falling off of a roof and landing on a shovel," the older O'Connor said, and pulled up the sleeve of his T-shirt. "Thirty stitches. To the bone."

"I can beat that," Eddie said. "I got gored by a Long Horn." He pulled up his shirt and showed off a jagged scar on his abdomen. "Me and a couple friends of mine decided to play rodeo clowns. I don't recommend it."

"I'm glad he got you coming and not going, or I'd have had to cover my eyes," said Nana.

"That's nothing," said Mr. O'Connor. He pulled up his shirt.

Zoe's eyes moved from one scar to the next on various body parts, feeling as if she was trapped in some kind of a wacky sitcom.

LeAnn, still standing next to Zoe, rolled her eyes. "Men and their scars. Have you ever seen a woman show off her scars?"

"We hide them and buy expensive creams to make them fade away," said Nikki.

"True." Ellen, the other blonde, pressed a hand against her abdomen. She looked at the men in the crowd. "Believe me, if I wanted to, I could put all you men to shame."

Zoe couldn't help but wonder what had happened to Ellen.

"See, women don't show off scars as if they are trophies." LeAnn gave her husband a jab with her elbow.

"We earned these. What's the use of getting a scar if we can't brag a bit?" Tony leaned in and kissed his wife. "Besides, I thought you said it was sexy."

"It is, but you don't have to tell everyone." LeAnn grinned.

Zoe realized that any thought of being judged by this group had vanished sometime between the laughter and the scar exhibit. How could they think she was the mental one, when it was so obvious they were crazy? Nevertheless, even as over-the-top as all these people were, the shared camaraderie was so vibrant that her life seemed dull and a little lonely.

She watched Tony wrap his arm around his wife's waist. Maybe a lot lonely, Zoe conceded. It had been a long time since she felt treasured, loved, even touched. Well, excluding her and Tyler's little position tryout on the floor while being shot at.

"Hey," Dallas said. "There's pizza in the apartment if getting shot didn't ruin your appetite."

Zoe grinned. "Thanks, I always plan ahead. I ate right before I got shot."

Tyler walked into the office. "What's up?" he asked Rick.

"That's what I want to know." Rick dropped into a chair. "What's the deal with the redhead?"

"Did you find something else out?" Tyler walked to the back of the room and opened a closet where he kept some extra clothes.

"I might have."

"Like what?"

"Uh-uh," Rick said. "You first."

Tyler pulled off the bloody T-shirt and slipped on a clean blue tee. He heard laughter coming from down the hall, and he hoped it wasn't at Zoe's expense. The riff-raff crowd that hung around here these days was great but could be a handful.

For a minute there, Zoe had looked like she'd wanted to bolt. He remembered that look on her face when he'd found her crouched behind his desk.

Tucking in his shirt, Tyler looked at Rick. "It doesn't go any further."

Rick nodded. Tyler sat down and told Rick everything, from the picture of a young Zoe that looked like Caroline Bradford to the picture of Nancy Bradford.

Rick shook his head. "Just because she looks like someone doesn't mean—"

"Right," Tyler interrupted. "Then you tell me why someone is shooting at her."

Rick paused. "I see why you might be checking into it, but—"

"There you guys are." Dallas walked into the office, followed by Tony. Dallas had three beers in his hands and passed one to Tyler and one to Rick. Tony had a folded piece of pizza in his hand and was busy eating.

Dallas glanced from Rick to Tyler. "What's wrong?"

"I asked Rick to see if he could find anything out about Zoe's visits to the Bradford place," Tyler explained.

"And you got something?" Dallas leaned against his desk.

"I found her name and knew she drove a car with an Alabama license. But you got her." Rick pulled the beer to his lips. "And she's quite a prize." He arched an eyebrow. "Is she single?"

Tyler frowned. "Keep your dick in your pants, would you?"

Rick grinned. "It is. I know because it moved when I looked at Red. But, hey, I don't poach on another guy's territory, so just tell me to back off and I'll back off."

"I thought you had something to tell me," Tyler said. He didn't want to defend his position on Zoe Adams. Especially when he hadn't decided what that position was. Was he interested in her? Hell, yeah, but considering he didn't want anything serious—and would run from it if it came to that—he didn't feel his position was worth defending.

Not yet anyway. Tyler got up and was almost out the door when he heard Rick's comeback.

"I do have something," Rick said. "The real question is, do you want to hear it or not?"

CHAPTER ELEVEN

TYLER TURNED AND faced Rick Clark. "Talk," he said.

"Remember when I told you I mentioned the redhead to the head honcho of security and he said she just disappeared?"

"Yeah."

"Well, it seemed kind of strange that Windsor hadn't run a check on her or anything. Then today I find out that Bradford's daughter, Mrs. Daniels, had one of the guards who works for Glencoe PD follow Red—"

"Her name is Zoe," Tyler cut in.

"Fine. Zoe. Anyway, Mrs. Daniels had the guy warn her off. Supposedly, Red—I mean, Zoe—was following Mr. Bradford's limo."

"So you're saying Windsor lied?" Tyler said.

"I'm not sure. I guess Mrs. Daniels could have done this without telling Windsor. But why? As a matter of fact, I'm not sure why she'd get involved to start with."

"That's interesting." Tyler pulled his pad over and jotted down another question.

"Wait a minute." Tony spoke around pizza in his mouth.

"You think someone in the Bradford family could have been behind the kidnapping?" He shook his head. "But if Zoe is the kidnapped Bradford kid, then we have a dead girl who was misidentified. That shit doesn't happen."

"I know it's unlikely," Tyler said. "I did some Internet searches and read that the clothes and a toy of the kid's were identified by the parents as belonging to Caroline Bradford. It never said anything about dental records, and DNA matches weren't standard then."

"So you think someone planted those things to make it look like the dead girl was Caroline Bradford?" Dallas took another swig of his beer.

"I don't know," Tyler said. "Until I saw the likeness between Zoe and Nancy Bradford, I believed Zoe was half-delusional. Hearing about the threatening calls she'd been getting—"

"What phone calls?" Dallas asked.

"Somebody keeps calling her cell phone, telling her to leave town while she still can. By itself, it means nothing. But when someone shot up her apartment, I changed my mind. Now, I'm betting there's something to what she says."

"Or..." Rick said, "she set this whole thing up to convince you guys to help her get to the old man."

Tyler scowled.

"He has a point," Tony said. "She could be playing you."

"She didn't know I'd be at her place this afternoon," Tyler said. "And did I forget to mention she got shot? Besides, she... she's not like that."

"Why? Because she's beautiful?" Rick shook his head. "Believe me, the prettier the woman, the more conniving she can be. They lure us in with sex and use and abuse us."

Tony and Dallas both cleared their throats as if in a warning not to talk ill of all women.

Rick looked at the three of them, frowned, and held up his hands in defeat. "Fine, I'll admit it. You two," he pointed to Dallas and Tony, "found the two in that tiny percentage of women who are the exceptions to the rule, but I'm talking generalities. You guys friggin' lucked out and found decent women."

"We didn't luck out, you fucked up," Tony said. "I know Candy did a real bad number on you, but you can't go blaming all women."

Rick frowned. "I'm not talking about Candy. I'm talking about Red."

"Yeah," Tyler said. "There's some bad ones out there. But I'm telling you, Zoe isn't like that."

"Fine, I just wanted to point out all possible angles here," Rick conceded again.

They all took a few sips of beer. Tyler looked back at Rick. "Can you feel around and see if you get anything else? I'm sure we can compensate you for the added trouble."

"You got me the job," Rick said. "You don't have to add to it. Doing a little undercover makes babysitting an old man's mansion less boring." Rick looked at Tony. "Is there more of that pizza left? I'm starved."

"In the kitchen. But I don't know if you deserve any. You didn't move one finger to help me move my dad," Tony said, and they walked out together.

When Tyler started to follow, Dallas motioned for him to hang back. "What's your plan?" he asked.

"I'm still working on it. Got a lot of questions to answer." Tyler decided to voice some of his thoughts. "I got her birth certificate."

Dallas looked perplexed. "She has a birth certificate as Zoe Adams? But why do you think she's...I don't get it."

"She'd never seen it until a few years ago. After her mom died. Her dad died earlier. They had told her that she was born in Alabama. But the certificate says she was born in Texas. I figured I'd check it out tomorrow."

Dallas ran a finger over his chin, which he did a lot when trying to wrap his head around something. No doubt the birth certificate caused Dallas to doubt Zoe's claim. Tyler couldn't blame Dallas for questioning it; he'd felt the same way when he first learned about the birth certificate. But even before someone had started shooting at her, there was something about Zoe that had made him feel differently. And it wasn't just how she'd felt under him, or on top of him. He felt a tightening down south and questioned if it was all her, or if he was just that long overdue for some female company.

Dallas cleared his throat.

Tyler looked at him. "What?"

"I asked you if you wanted to just take this to the old man and see what he says."

"Oh, I considered that," Tyler said. "But if his daughter had something to do with the shootings, it might put Zoe in more danger. And there's also the possibility that the old man will pull his security contract."

"I don't care about the contract," Dallas said. "It's a lot of money, but we can get by without it."

"True, but if he fires us, he'll probably fire the men we hired. A few of them need the job. And I think having Rick inside might help us. The longer we can keep our name out of this, the better."

Dallas nodded. "This is fucked up," he said. "We're investigating one of our own clients."

"I know," Tyler said. "My head's firing questions faster than I can take them down." He moved to his desk and jotted down another one: *What was Nancy Bradford's relationship with her sister-in-law?*

"And you're loving it," Dallas said. "Nothing makes you happier than a good puzzle."

"Which makes me good at my job." And it did. When he was younger, Tyler had been teased for his love of questions and solving puzzles. His brain just worked differently than everybody else's. His questions were the best way to keep him from obsessing on some other, less important angle. He looked back at his list of questions. "Obviously the first order of business is making sure she's out of harm's way. The second is finding out for sure if Zoe is or isn't a Bradford."

"Which means a DNA test," Dallas said.

An idea occurred to Tyler. "If Rick is as good as your brother says, maybe he can get us some DNA on the sly without the old man knowing."

Dallas nodded. "But first let's check out the birth certificate. We should follow the paper route until we have something else to go on."

Tyler fought the need to insist Zoe's claim was valid. Why he was so hyped on defending her, he didn't know. He jotted that question down, too.

When he looked up, Dallas had started to walk out. "Oh, one other thing." Tyler spoke low in case anyone walked in. "I sort of lied about having a safe house she could stay at."

Dallas shrugged as if it was no big deal. "Just take her home with you."

"That had been my original plan, but I think she'd take it as me trying to... you know, get her to my place and into my bed or something, instead of an offer to help her."

Humor flashed in his partner's eyes. "What's wrong? You don't want her in your bed?"

When Tyler didn't answer, Dallas's grin faded, and he added, "Just get her a hotel room."

"She has financial issues and I think she'd frown on that, too. She wouldn't accept our help gratis. I had to agree to a payment plan."

Dallas made a face. "Nikki was the same way. What is it with women who can't accept a helping hand? I mean, someone wants to do something for me, I'm all for it."

"I think they're scared we'll want some of it paid back in trade."

"That would have been okay with me, too. With Nikki, of course." Dallas laughed.

Tyler grinned, but didn't say anything about Zoe. He did, however, remember almost kissing her. Chasing that image from his mind, he finally moved to the question he wanted to ask. "Didn't you tell me that you and Nikki were already staying at your new place?"

"Yeah." The reason for the question must have hit him for he said, "Oh, hell yeah. Just let her stay here. We've already moved the few pieces of furniture that we're taking with us. So it's mostly still furnished. We bought mostly new stuff. I was going to see if you wanted the bedroom suite and pink sofa, or I was gonna donate it to Goodwill."

"I have my own stuff when I move in, but hold off donating. I'll let Zoe stay here for a while."

"Is she going to stay here alone?" Dallas asked.

"Not alone," Tyler said, thinking Dallas was worried

about having a stranger in the office. They could lock the office door, but still…

"I didn't think so." Dallas's chuckle let Tyler know he'd been wrong about the motives behind Dallas's question. "Who knows? She might change her mind about the trade."

"It's not *exactly* like that." Tyler wasn't ready to publicly announce his interest in Zoe. Not that he wasn't interested; he just needed to answer a few more questions. And go over the pro and con list growing in his mind. Zoe Adams was smart, unlike the type of woman he'd just decided to go after. She came across as the type who didn't go for uncommitted flings. Then again, she'd mentioned something about just being here temporarily. The temporary status was a pro. A big pro, right?

When Tyler looked up, he found Dallas studying him.

"Define 'exactly,'" Dallas said.

Tyler shrugged. "You already said it. I'm mostly in it for the puzzle."

"Then you're *mostly* an idiot," Dallas said. "She's hot, and I saw the way you looked at her. So a word of warning. If you keep playing it cool like you just did with Rick, she's going to have guys like him and Austin all over her." He walked out of the office.

"I'm not an idiot," Tyler muttered. As a matter of fact, he was so smart that he took Dallas's warning right to heart. Sure, she was the same type of woman he always fell for, and as he'd finally realized that probably had led to his issues in the past, but she wasn't planning on staying in Texas so…That's when he made up his mind. There was no logical reason why he and Zoe couldn't enjoy her time in Texas.

If she was interested.

A smile welled up inside him when he remembered how nervous she'd gotten when he took off his shirt. How her eyes had kept going to his chest. How her pupils had dilated and she'd become jittery. She'd even run into the wall.

The smile led to a light chuckle. He wasn't laughing at her, more like relating to her. Because, damn, if she'd taken off some article of clothing, he might have been the one running into walls.

Recognizing attraction was something he knew about. As a geeky sixteen-year-old interested in getting laid, he'd done the only thing he knew how to do—research it. He'd read every book the library had on physical attraction—how to spot it and how to encourage it. A few of his friends, who thought sex education only meant eyeballing Marco's dad's *Playboy* magazines, had laughed their asses off at him. Until they realized Tyler wasn't meeting them on Friday movie/magazine night because he had better things to do. Things that didn't involve magazines.

So he was pretty damn certain Zoe Adams was interested. On second thought, he grabbed his phone, surfed over to Amazon, found a few books on the psychology and social culture of interpersonal attraction, and downloaded two. He was up for some light reading anyway.

He was about to walk out to find Zoe when his phone rang. Hoping it was Austin calling him back, he looked at the caller ID. He'd tried earlier and Austin hadn't answered his phone. Tyler frowned. It was his big sister, probably phoning to chastise him for not showing up for breakfast.

"At least grab something to drink," Nikki said to Zoe as everyone drifted out of the room.

"Thanks." Zoe motioned to the cat carrier by the door. "I just need to get some things out of the car for my cat."

"Oh," Nikki said. "I didn't realize you brought someone with you." She started to walk to the cat carrier.

"He's a little skittish," Zoe said.

"Oh, well let him out in the room. Just shut the door. Bud's in the backyard. We have to keep him there when a lot of people come over or he gets excited and makes happy sprinkles everywhere."

"Happy sprinkles?"

"Pees everywhere." Nikki smiled. "Just keep the door closed, in case someone accidentally lets him in. I'm not sure he's a cat lover."

"Thanks," Zoe said.

While she was nice, Zoe could see the questions in her eyes. Who was the strange redhead who claimed to be a kidnapped kid who'd supposedly been found murdered?

Nikki started out and then looked back. "Seriously, whatever is going on with you, Only in Texas will take care of it. Dallas and the guys are that good."

"Thanks," Zoe said again, and she meant it.

When Nikki left and shut the door, Zoe knelt down and tapped on the metal bars of the carrying case. "Hey, guy... you okay?"

Lucky meowed and rubbed his forehead against the back of her fingers. Amazingly, he didn't appear freaked out. The cat continued to prove his resilience. Maybe even more than she had, considering how she'd felt like a fish out of water in the crowd.

She almost unlatched the carrier, but decided she should get a litter box set up first. "I'll be right back." She wiggled her finger against the side of his face.

The door to the office swung open and Mr. O'Connor stood in the doorway. Beside him stood Nikki's grandmother. "Us old folks are out of here," said Mr. O'Connor. "It was nice to meet ya. I'm sure my son and his friends are gonna make things right." He paused. "You do look just like your mom, you know?"

Zoe's chest tightened at his words. She wanted to ask him questions about Nancy Bradford, but she couldn't seem to get them out. She wasn't even sure what kind of questions to ask. "Thanks."

Nana waved. "The boys are good guys. You can trust them."

Trust? The word hung in her heart. But Zoe nodded.

Pulling the keys from her pocket, she walked outside. Texas heat radiated from the concrete. For a second, she wanted to get in her car, get on I-10, and drive as fast as she could to Alabama—to throw herself into teaching, sing "Little Bunny Foo Foo" for a bunch of kindergarten kids, and forget everything.

"Do you think she's the Bradford kid?" Ellen asked, following Nikki into the kitchen.

"I don't know." Nikki filled a glass with white wine. "But Mr. O'Connor said she looks like Nancy Bradford. He went to school with her."

LeAnn moved into the kitchen. "Can you imagine how she must feel? I wonder if she remembers anything."

"Were the people who raised her abusive to her?" Ellen's chest tightened at the thought of any child being abused, even when the child was now an adult.

Nikki shrugged. "I don't know. I think the only one who knows anything is Tyler."

LeAnn grinned. "I think Tyler's got the hots for Zoe."

"Really?" Nikki asked. "I was beginning to worry about that guy. I've never heard him mention a girlfriend. When I asked Dallas about him, he said Tyler still was hung up over his fiancée who dumped him when they got arrested."

LeAnn grinned. "You know when a couple is bantering back and forth and you can feel the sexual friction in the air, that's what it was like."

Ellen sighed inwardly. It had been a long time since she'd felt any kind of sexual friction. Physical or airborne.

She sipped her wine and looked out the kitchen window to the backyard where the men were chatting. Her gaze landed on Rick Clark. His brown hair looked windblown, and he laughed at something one of the other guys had said. He had a nice laugh, the kind that made one want to laugh along with him.

She started noticing other things about the green-eyed devil, like how broad his shoulders were, and how he carried himself with a certain confidence that she found appealing. She saw him reach down and give Bud a hearty pat on his side, and then he tossed the Frisbee for the dog. Leave it to her to always be attracted to the bad boy. Not that she'd personally picked up on that vibe from him. Oh, he had the looks; she just didn't get the too cocky vibe. But when she'd told Nikki about how he'd asked her out, her friend had repeated the "he's a bad boy" warning.

Several times since he'd shown up, she'd caught him studying her. Not inappropriately so. The first time, he'd nodded as if to acknowledge her. But when he came into the apartment with Tony to snag some pizza he'd met her gaze again, and she thought he meant to come over and talk to her.

She'd ducked out, then ran to the bathroom to avoid him and any awkwardness. She'd considered snagging her purse and leaving when she got out. But then she realized that she had to get over it. Obviously, the man did side jobs for Only in Texas, which meant he'd be in and out of the office. She'd just have to suck it up.

They were adults. He'd asked her out; she said no. End of story.

So why was she admiring how the man pressed a beer to his lips? She was so caught up watching those lips press against the bottle that she hadn't realized his gaze had shifted from the dog and was now staring right at the window. Or rather staring right at her as she gaped at him like forbidden candy in a glass case.

Swinging around, she almost spilled her wine, and she noticed Nikki studying her. Maybe Ellen shouldn't have told Nikki about him asking her out, especially when Nikki took one look at her and said, *Oh, hell, you're still attracted to him.*

She'd denied it, but Nikki saw right through her the way girlfriends do.

Nikki sighed. "You may want to run to the bathroom again; it looks like he's coming inside."

"Shit!" Ellen started to dart off.

"Wait. Tony stopped him," LeAnn said, looking out the window. "That's my man. Put the guy in his place. Thump him in the balls."

Ellen's curiosity got the best of her. "Is he *that* bad?"

LeAnn rolled her eyes. "To be honest, the guy would take a bullet for my husband, and I *love* him for that, but…" She paused, took another sip of her wine, and made a face.

"Dallas is not crazy about the guy, either," Nikki jumped in.

"It's the women he dates." LeAnn set the wine down. "It's apparent he's after one thing. And as soon as he gets it, he moves on to another one. Or at least he did. In his defense, I haven't heard about any of his new conquests in a while." She looked at her wine. "Tony says he's just bitter about his breakup. But from where I'm standing, I'm not sure he just didn't get a taste of his own medicine. Speaking of tastes...Is it me, or does this wine—"

"Hey," a male voice interrupted. Tyler stood in the kitchen doorway. "Where's Zoe?"

"She said she had to grab something from her car," Nikki answered.

"Oh," he said, and then his eyes rounded and his expression changed. "Not again." He took off so fast, he tripped over the coffee table, nearly fell on his face, but didn't even slow down.

Nikki chuckled and glanced at LeAnn. "Yup, I see the tension you were talking about." Then her gaze settled back on Ellen. "Which sort of ruins my plans."

"What plans?" asked Ellen in a serious tone.

"I was kind of hoping that you and Tyler might...hit it off."

Ellen shook her head. "Oh, please."

"Why not?" Nikki asked. "Unlike someone else"—she motioned to the window—"Tyler comes with my blessing."

"I'm not interested in Rick. I'm not looking for any tension." The fact that she missed it was another matter.

Nikki made a face and looked at LeAnn. "This from a girl who threatened to sign me up to an Internet dating site."

"That's different," Ellen said.

"How's it different?" both LeAnn and Nikki asked at the same time.

"Please. I have a kid."

Nikki shook her head. "Having a kid doesn't mean you lose the itch."

It does when your kid's father is a super high-profile lawyer and is looking for a reason to take your kid away. "I have too much on my plate. Between my parents, work, and Britney, I have no energy to give to men. And we all know they take a lot of energy."

"But the good kind." LeAnn grinned. "And since your morphine-induced confession, we know you miss it."

"Don't worry." Ellen laughed. "Since my morphine confession, I've taken care of that problem. I now have BOB."

"Bob?" Nikki grabbed her elbow. "You met someone and you haven't told me? How could you not tell me?"

Ellen grinned and leaned in. "BOB . . . B. O. B. My battery-operated boyfriend. He fulfills my every desire."

LeAnn and Nikki laughed. "Please," said Nikki. "The real thing is better."

Yeah, Ellen thought. But the real thing came with a price tag she wasn't willing to pay.

CHAPTER TWELVE

ZOE HAD FILLED the small plastic box with kitty litter in the car and was just about to reach for the office door when it swung open. Tyler barreled out and ran right into her. She managed not to drop the box, but the jolt had litter flying up and raining down on her. A couple of pieces found their way down her shirt.

Lucky for her, it was clean litter.

"I'm sorry," Tyler said.

Zoe grinned. "Trying to get even for the food spills?"

"No, I thought..." His eyes lowered to her chest. "You've got kitty litter in your cleavage."

Zoe laughed and removed the litter.

Tyler grinned. "I was afraid you were trying to bolt again."

"Why would I do that?" she asked, not wanting to admit that the thought had occurred to her.

He shrugged. "You already did it once."

"But you were dressed as a clown," she said, only half-teasing.

He returned her smile and brushed off her shoulder.

Several pebbles of litter fell to the pavement. The aroma of clean fresh-scented litter swirled around them. Their gazes met and held.

"So, it had nothing to do with the fact that you were snooping in our files?" he asked, still teasing.

"Maybe a little." She cringed. "I was looking for the button to push to call someone—like the note that hung from the desk said—and just happened to see the file."

"There is no button," he said. "A bad joke, I guess."

"Probably." She looked down at the litter box. "I was getting a litter box for Lucky. That is if we have time. But if we're leaving now..." She almost hoped he'd say they were leaving so she could be alone and filter through everything that had happened.

"No, it's fine." He paused as if chewing on his next words. "Here, let me." He took the cat box from her.

His hand touching hers sent a bolt of warm emotion through her. But damn, she must be pretty pathetic when just a casual brushing of a man's hand against hers sparked an emotional rush. Or maybe she was just an emotional wreck.

He continued to stare. "I'm sorry about how things went in there. The way everyone just stormed in. They can be overwhelming." He started for the door, and she fell in step beside him.

"They seemed nice, though," she said. Her gaze went to the scar when he pulled the litter box against him and reached for the door with his free hand. She sort of wished he'd been in the room when the guys had been participating in the game of show-and-tell about their scars. She'd like to know how he got his.

"They are." He stepped back for her to enter. "Doesn't

mean they aren't hard to take, especially when they're all together. It's a zoo."

"Most families are that way," Zoe said, and her gaze caught on the casket again. And for a brief second she thought of everyone she'd lost.

"They aren't my family," he said behind her.

"I meant makeshift family, you know, the friends in your life."

"Oh. I guess you could say they are sort of like a family to each other." He nodded.

"But not you?" she asked, finding his answer odd.

"Well, no... I mean, I'm close to my partners."

She wondered if Tyler's real family had turned their backs on him when he'd been accused of murder. "Are you close to your real family?"

He nodded. "Yeah. I'm afraid they're crazier than the bunch you just met."

"It's still nice to have them." She recalled how all her life she'd felt as if she'd been a part of something bigger and had lost it. Then she wondered how her real family would feel about her now? Her heart gripped at how awkward this was going to be.

"You okay?" Tyler asked.

She realized she'd stopped and just stood in the middle of the entryway. "Fine." She started down the hall to the room where she'd left Lucky.

"What about you?" he asked as he followed her into the room. "You got any other family members?" He sat the box down near the carrier.

She knelt and opened the carrier's door. "I've got Lucky." She reached in and gently pulled out the cat. "No aunts or uncles?" he asked.

She shook her head. "Both my parents were only children, and..." A wave of fresh hurt filled her chest, and she pushed it back. "They said they had me late in life. So no family." But who knows, maybe they lied about that, too?

With Lucky snuggled against her chest, she stood up. She saw the look on Tyler's face when he got his first really good look at the feline.

"Christ," Tyler said, and took a step back.

His reaction wasn't that uncommon, but it still stung. With Lucky's one eye sewn up, half his ear missing, his missing left foot, and the scar on his neck, she knew the cat wasn't the prettiest thing to look at. Which only made Zoe love him more. She snuggled the feline closer, instinctively wanting to protect him from any negative vibes he might pick up.

She knew the cat didn't feel them, but she felt them for him.

"What happened to him?" To Tyler's credit, he didn't look as appalled as most people.

"He survived a fire and a chemical explosion. Hence the name, Lucky."

Tyler continued to stare. "Tell me he still has testicles, because that's the only way I'm going to consider him lucky."

Zoe laughed. "Sorry. He had those removed before the accident."

He looked again at the cat, only now he didn't look as repulsed as he did sympathetic. "Then you might need to rename him."

She rubbed Lucky under his chin, and he started to purr. "Hey, sweetie," she said. "I got your litter box."

Kneeling, she set him down. The cat moved around the room, his missing foot barely causing a limp.

When she stood up, Tyler was watching the cat. "At least he gets around good," he said as if trying to find something positive to say.

To Tyler's credit, when Lucky moved over and started rubbing himself against Tyler's leg, he didn't pull away. Most people didn't want to touch the cat, as if they feared his disfigurement might be contagious.

"He wouldn't die," Zoe said. "The firemen found him three days after the explosion when they were doing their investigation. The press was there, and they actually got it all on tape. They took him to a vet. At first the vet was going to just put him down, but six people called and said they'd help pay for the bills if they'd try to save him."

"And you were one of them." He squatted down and offered Lucky his hand. The cat moved in cautiously and rubbed his face against Tyler's fingers. Which was odd; Lucky didn't usually take to people that quickly. Even rarer, people usually didn't take to him. Her admiration for Tyler shot up a few notches.

"Yup. He lived at the vet's for two months, and Dr. Shoemaker drew names to see which of his financial supporters was going to get to take him home. The press covered it and everything. You could say I got lucky and got Lucky." She grinned, remembering Tyler's misunderstanding earlier.

Tyler looked up at her. "Something tells me it might have been rigged."

Zoe shrugged, still feeling a tinge of guilt. "It was. Dr. Shoemaker said of all the contributors, I was the only one who came to see him when the press wasn't going to be there. So he said he made sure I got him. I felt bad, but I wanted Lucky so badly that I kept my mouth shut."

Tyler stood up. "You visited a sick cat at the vet?"

"The vet was on my way home from work. So, I'd stop by. It's not like I went out of my way or anything."

"Unbelievable," he said. Lucky started doing figure eights around Tyler's legs.

"Not really. You can do a search on the Internet about him. He's sort of a celebrity in Beaverville. He even had several cat magazines do stories on him. Took pictures and everything."

She picked up the cat to prevent him from shedding all over Tyler's jeans. Lucky started rubbing his face against her breasts.

Tyler stared, to the point Zoe felt self-conscious.

"Okay," he muttered, his voice a little deeper than normal. "I guess he is lucky."

"Damn!" Ellen looked down at the black tire track on her white T-shirt.

When she'd left the office, she'd found she had a flat tire. She'd been tempted to run inside and pretend to be the weak little woman and ask one of the guys for help, but she wasn't a weak little woman. She could change a tire as good as a man.

Better than most.

Her father had made sure of it. Her first job, and the only one she'd worked at until she started college, was in one of his auto repair shops. It had taken awhile, but soon she'd earned the respect of most of her father's mechanics.

That said, she obviously couldn't change a tire wearing white clothes.

"Christ, let me do that."

Ellen turned and faced Rick Clark. Freaking great! Couldn't it have been any of the other guys?

He pushed up the sleeves of his light blue oxford shirt, exposing his super-toned forearms, which were lightly dusted with dark hair. She frowned when she realized that even the man's arm hair did something to her.

"Why didn't you ask for help?" He reached for the tire.

She latched on to her spare and took a few steps back. "I got this," she said. Forgetting about black streaks, she pulled the tire closer and wished he wasn't so close. Was that clean spicy scent his aftershave? Or just him?

His brows tightened. "I can have it changed in no time flat."

She frowned. His tone threw her back to having to prove herself when she worked at her dad's shop. "So can I."

His gaze lowered to the tire. "You're getting tire tracks all over your shirt."

"I didn't like this shirt anyway," she said.

"Seriously, let me do it."

"*Seriously*, I can handle it." She knew she sounded unappreciative, but she couldn't help it. Not only was she annoyed that she found him so damn attractive, but she'd never liked it when a man, any man, treated her like a weakling.

"Just give me the tire," he said, "and I'll be happy to do it."

She stiffened. "You got problems with your hearing, Detective?"

The puzzlement left his eyes, replaced with an almost accusing tightness. He held up his hands and took a step back, making it clear he thought she was rude.

And maybe it was for the best; let him think she was a bitch. Fix it so he never even thought about asking her out again.

She moved over to the back tire and dropped the spare and then went back to the trunk to get the lug wrench and jack. She practically had to crawl into the trunk to get the wrench, and she felt him staring.

Once she had what she needed, she went back to the flat. She knelt down and took a deep breath. He stood there, arms crossed, staring at her. She popped off her hubcap and let it fall to the parking lot with a loud bang.

"So, you're one of those, huh?"

She glared back at him over her shoulder. "One of what?"

"I-am-woman-hear-me-roar types," he said, frowning.

"Really? You get that because I can change my own tire?" She didn't wait for him to answer. She turned back to the flat, listened for him to walk away, and picked up her lug wrench. No receding footsteps filled her ears. Did he plan to stand there and watch?

Fine. Let him! She'd show him. *Hear me roar, my ass!*

Lug wrench on, she secured her footing so she could put her weight into loosening the nuts. Then, feeling his eyes boring down her back, hoping it would fuel her strength, she gave it everything she had.

And it didn't budge. Neither did she.

She kept pushing and pushing, putting every bit of strength she had into the job. Her strength leaked out of her in the form of sweat. One rather large drip rolled down her brow and hung on to the very end of her nose. Finally, she released her hold on the wrench and relaxed her stance.

She waited for his sarcastic remark. She even looked forward to it, hoping it would get her adrenaline up.

He didn't say a word.

Staring at the lug nut as if it were the enemy, she recalled her father had taken her car in to get her last new tire and some idiot had probably used an impact wrench on the dang nuts.

But she wasn't giving up yet. Wiping her hands on her jeans, she grabbed the lug wrench and went back in for the kill.

She gave it everything she had.

Her all.

And then some.

It still wasn't enough. She released the wrench and almost released some unladylike language she'd learned while working at the shop.

She waited for him to say something sarcastic.

Not a word.

Counting to five, she wiped the sweat from her cheek and looked back at him.

He stood there, arms crossed over his wide chest, smiling at her.

"You're enjoying this, aren't you?"

His smile widened. "Yeah. Actually, I am."

She stood up. "You don't have to be a smartass."

"And you didn't have to be an old battle-ax like my sixth-grade teacher, either, but it didn't stop you."

Somewhere between trying to come up with a retort that would put him in his place and mentally berating whoever had changed her tires, she came to her senses.

He was right. She'd been rude.

"Okay, I admit I was . . . not being nice."

He raised an eyebrow. "Is that the same as being an old battle-ax?"

She let go of a deep breath and a big chunk of her pride. "Yes, it is. I'm sorry."

He looked back at her tire and then up at her. "Well, I guess I'll see you." He turned away.

"Seriously?" she muttered before she could stop herself.

He turned around and had another big smile on his face. "Nah, I was just giving you a hard time." Pushing up his sleeves again, he knelt in front of the tire.

He removed the lug wrench hanging from the tire, repositioned it, and put muscle into the job. Lots of muscle. She knew because she saw his biceps bulging under his shirt. She was so caught up in watching his muscles shifting under the light blue cotton, it took her a second to realize he wasn't having any more luck than she'd had.

She regained some of her damaged pride. "Not so easy, is it?"

He released his hold and looked up at her. "I'm just pretending it's difficult to make you feel better." He smiled.

"Right," she said, knowing he was lying through his teeth.

He reattached the lug wrench, and this time, the nut gave way. He glanced up again. "See."

She rolled her eyes, and he got busy loosening the other nuts.

When he finished that, the temptation to tell him she could handle it from there was strong. But she was afraid she would come off as being bitchy again, so she bit her lip.

A couple of times during the process, he looked up at her, but he didn't say anything and neither did she. When the spare tire was in place and the lug nuts tightened, he stood up. "That spare isn't meant to be driven long. You should get a new tire soon. If you're nervous about driving on it, I could drive up to get a new tire and put it on for you."

"I'm fine," she said, and then, realizing that might have sounded rude, she added, "My dad owns several auto repair shops. I'm not trying to roar, but if the lug nuts hadn't been on so tight, I could have taken care of it. I worked there for four years before I went to college. I really can change a tire, the oil, and even rebuild a transmission."

He grinned and reared back on the heels of his shoes. "The woman really can roar. I'm impressed."

"You'd have been more impressed if someone hadn't used an impact wrench to tighten my lug nuts." She grinned. After the smile they shared went a fraction of a second long, she added, "Thanks for your help."

"You're welcome." He loaded everything back into her trunk. When he faced her again, he studied her. Then he touched his cheek. "You've got some grease on your face. Not that it doesn't look good on you. Nothing hotter than a woman who can work on cars." His green eyes sparkled with sexual innuendo.

Not good, she thought as she reached up and ran her fingers over her cheek.

"It's still there," he said. Then, as if reading her nervousness, he waved to his car. "I guess...I should be going. Don't be running any curbs with that spare." He held up his hands and shrugged. "Not that you don't already know that."

She watched him walk away, and then she turned to her car. She had to give the guy credit for not hitting on her harder. He could have asked her out again, knowing she'd feel too guilty to refuse this time after he'd helped her.

Then she heard footsteps coming behind her. "I forgot to ask."

Right. She should have expected it. This was just how he'd done it before—walk away and then come back and catch her by surprise. As she turned to face him, her stomach knotted at the thought of having to turn him down. She ignored the slightest undercurrent of temptation to say yes. But it just wasn't worth the hassle. Definitely not worth the risk.

"You know that book you had for your daughter—*Dogs to the Rescue*—is it for girls and boys, or just girls?"

She was so set on hearing him ask her out a second time, that it took her a minute to wrap her head around his question.

She nodded. "It could appeal to both."

"Thanks." His cell phone rang. He took it out of his shirt pocket and looked at the screen. He muttered something under his breath and jabbed his phone off. Still scowling, he snapped his gaze up at her. "Sorry." He turned and left.

She got in her car and made it down the block before she couldn't resist any longer. She reached for her phone and dialed Nikki.

"Hey," Nikki said.

Ellen bit into her bottom lip. "Don't think anything of this, but...I was wondering does Rick Clark have kids?"

"Not that I've ever heard of. Why?"

"Because...he keeps asking me about kids' books."

"Oh, God," Nikki said. "He'll say anything to get in your pants. Don't give him the time of day."

"I'm not," Ellen said. But she frowned, not liking how everyone accused him of being one thing but she kept seeing a different side of him. Not that he couldn't be putting on the front for a reason. Players did that kind of thing, didn't they?

"Did he ask you out again? You're not dating him, Ellen. He's bad news."

"He didn't ask me out. And remember, I told you not to make anything of it. Okay, I'm driving, I shouldn't be talking." She hung up before Nikki started handing out even more relationship advice. Nikki wasn't one to talk about relationships. She'd had her own issues and had almost blown things with Dallas because of her fear of getting hurt.

Not that her own situation with Rick had any similarities to Nikki's. Nikki had been stubborn, but Ellen was... well, she was being smart. Huge difference.

Ellen tightened her fingers around the wheel. "I'm not giving him the time of day," she muttered, but she couldn't stop thinking about how good he looked changing her tire.

She thought about him all the way home. Right up until she saw Noel's car parked in her driveway.

Oh, hell. Not again!

CHAPTER THIRTEEN

As TEMPTING AS it was to stomp her foot on the gas and squeal away, Ellen didn't. She parked her Honda on the street, not wanting anything to prevent Noel from leaving. Before she could take her key out of the ignition, Noel got out of his car.

She watched his six-foot-plus frame move toward her. She felt tightness in her gut, not anything like she felt when she'd seen Rick approach. This one came from something akin to hatred. The thought that she'd once believed she'd loved the man made her feel sick.

When she'd gone to him with news of her pregnancy, insecure but believing they were in love, his confession that he was already married had stunned her. But his willingness—some might say eagerness—to pay for the abortion had crushed her.

Hurt and humiliated, she told him she'd take care of it. And she had. She'd packed her bags and went to live in Florida with her aunt. Only when her dad had his heart attack did she move back to Texas.

It was time to come home, too. Britney was three and

was missing out on seeing her grandparents. And her parents needed Ellen. For the first six months, being home had been good. But then she'd run into Noel and his wife at the mall. Noel had taken one look at Britney and knew.

The next day, he'd shown up at her parents' house, furious. "Let me get this straight," she'd said. "You're angry because I didn't kill my child?"

They had argued. She told him to get lost. He did. For six months.

Ellen gripped the steering wheel, and when she looked down she saw her daughter's book on the passenger seat. Her daughter. It took more than a sperm donation to make a man a father.

After that six months, Noel showed up and insisted on being a part of Britney's life. He even apologized. He said he and his wife were talking divorce, and he didn't want her to use his daughter against him. So it might take a while before he could see Britney regularly.

Ellen wasn't sure she had a right to keep Britney from him, so she agreed. She didn't like the fact that he planned to keep Britney from his wife. But considering Ellen had wanted nothing to do with him emotionally, she hadn't argued.

After a few visits, Noel made it clear that it wasn't just Britney he wanted. She'd put the brakes on that idea fast and hard. At first, Noel played by her rules. Things changed when she met James. James, a divorced plumber who'd worked on her parents' house, was fun, sexy, and, while it wasn't serious, Ellen had hopes. But Noel had come unglued. *If you're going to date, couldn't you find a guy who didn't unstop toilets for a living?*

At the memory, Ellen inhaled and stared at Noel's car. A nice, *rich* car. A real shame that money didn't buy class.

Noel might have insisted she stay away from James, but she wasn't about to let Noel control her life, so she continued to see James.

A month later, Noel showed up with pictures of her and James having sex in her hot tub. The pictures made two people making love look like something out of a porn movie. Noel made it clear that James had to go, or he was suing for custody of Britney. Noel said he'd told his wife about Britney and she was willing to help him raise her.

Ellen didn't know if Noel had really told his wife; she hadn't cared. What mattered was that he threatened to take her daughter away. She went to James with the problem. She thought if Noel used the pictures, James would stand beside her in court proving it hadn't been a sleazy affair. Instead, James had been upset that she'd had an affair with a married man. Because his ex had cheated on him, he considered Ellen just as bad. It didn't seem to matter that she hadn't known Noel was married. James ended their relationship, and she went to see a family friend who was also a lawyer. He'd been brutally honest. If Noel hadn't been a high-powered attorney, her friend could have guaranteed Ellen that the most Noel could get was joint custody. But with Noel's power, money, and friends—friends who wore robes and sat on benches—anything was possible.

His threat and the possibility of losing Britney almost had her returning to Florida. But she had refused to abandon her parents. So she told herself that Noel hadn't won. And for almost three years now, she'd lived her life without seeking his permission. However, whenever she found herself tempted to rejoin the dating game, she'd remember how well her last two attempts had ended up and then realize that no man was worth the possibility of her losing Britney.

Lost in thought, she looked up and was startled to see Noel now standing outside her car; she got out to face him.

"Where have you been?" he asked.

"Helping a friend move," she said. "Not that it's any of your business."

"What do you have all over your clothes and face?" He frowned as if seeing her dirty disgusted him. Oh, how she wished he'd known her when she worked at her dad's shop.

"I had a flat tire."

He looked at the car. "Couldn't you have gotten someone else to change it?"

I did. "I managed."

"Where's Britney?" he asked.

"My parents took her to the beach."

"You know I see her on Sundays."

She glared at him. "You didn't come the last two weeks. And she waited for you." As much as Ellen secretly resented it, Britney loved Noel and the attention he gave her for those few hours a week.

"I couldn't get away," he said.

"Well, Britney wanted to go to the beach with her grandparents, and I couldn't tell her no."

"Don't be a bitch," he snapped.

"When it comes to Britney, I'm allowed. I don't have to play fair."

"Fair? You think this is fair to Britney?" He waved toward the house. "You could be living somewhere nice instead of this slum if you'd let me help you. Let me get you a place in Houston. I could see you guys three times as much."

"It's called suburban middle-class." She waved at the house. And I've already told you, put the money in a savings account and give it to her when she's eighteen. And come back later if you want to see her." She started for the front porch.

"It doesn't have to be like this between us," he called out. "We were good together once. It could be good again."

"I don't want your money." She continued walking and muttered, "And I certainly don't want you."

Tyler's grandfather believed he could predict an oncoming storm. Tyler may not know anything about the weather, but he could sense a woman's scorn faster than anyone else. Probably a learned skill from living with three sisters. And from the way Zoe looked at him, his scorn meter was telling him to duck for cover.

"This is the safe house?" Zoe followed Tyler into the small kitchen the instant Nikki and Dallas had left.

So that was what this was about.

The four of them had spent the last hour visiting. Things had gone fine. But when he and Dallas had come inside from tossing the ball to Bud, Zoe's mood had changed from tired to somehow ticked-off. And he hadn't been completely sure why.

He nodded. "This is it." He'd been thinking about coming clean about that and explaining his reasons for not being completely honest.

"Really?" Her tone, coupled with her body language,

warned him that it might be too late. She wasn't happy. How did that translate for him? How did Zoe Adams deal with unhappiness?

"Yeah." He opened the fridge and stared inside it, working on a game plan.

"But I thought..." She paused.

"Thought what?" He continued to stare at the mostly empty fridge. They were going to have to make a food run. His mind gravitated to any subject other than the one making him feel uncomfortable. He'd lied to her. Sort of. Not that he'd had much option at the time.

"Nikki and Dallas just moved out of here," she said.

"Yes." He glanced up and didn't have a clue how to deal with her. She was an unknown to him. He'd never met anyone quite like her.

She stared at him. Her blue eyes tightened, giving her even more of that woman-scorned look.

"And I could swear something was said about you moving in." Her tone was edgier now.

He ducked back down into the refrigerator and pulled out two beers. He held out one to her, hoping it might be viewed as a peace offering.

"No."

That look in her eyes pulled at his conscience. He returned one of the bottles to the shelf and shut the door.

"You don't have a safe house, do you?" she asked.

"More like a safe apartment." He tossed a little humor at the situation, hoping that would soothe her. Then he faced her. She didn't look soothed.

It was a stupid move, but he tried a change of subject. "We need to run to my place and pick up some pots and pans and stuff."

She turned and hotfooted it out of the kitchen, leaving a wake of fury like only a pissed-off woman could leave.

Okay...so this was how Zoe dealt with anger. Running away wasn't a good method.

It could be worse. She could be a screamer like Lola. Or a crier like Sam.

He debated the wisdom of letting her be alone and took a swig of beer. Then he remembered they'd left the apartment door open, hoping Lucky would venture in. The thought that she could be collecting her cat to leave had him tearing out of the kitchen. He shot into the living room and came to an awkward halt when he spotted her. Just sitting on the sofa—hands folded tightly in her lap.

He waited for her to look at him. She didn't. The uncomfortable feeling in his chest grew. He'd dealt with and placated irate and scorned sisters most of his life; this should be a piece of cake.

It wasn't.

It even felt different from his few arguments with Lisa. But why? He jotted that question in his memory bank and refocused on Zoe.

I know I lied to you, he almost said, but decided the direct approach might be too much.

"You okay?" he asked.

"Fine," she snapped.

He opened his mouth to say something but didn't know what he should say. Words came out before he had a chance to consider them. "Did you know tone can tell a person more than the words?"

She glanced at him, but didn't speak.

His need to clarify surged forth. "You said 'fine' in an irritated tone. You're either using Socratic irony or..."

"Socratic irony?" she asked.

"It means—"

"I know what it means. I wasn't..." She shook her head. "Have you considered that maybe after realizing my entire freaking life has been a lie, I don't appreciate it when someone else *lies* to me?"

Guilt settled in his chest. "I guess that could explain the tone, too."

"I know you're helping me." She pressed her hands against the pink leather of the sofa. "But is it too much to ask that you not lie to me?"

He sat in the brown leather chair across from the sofa, rolled the cold beer in his hands, and tried to figure out how to deal with this. He decided on the truth. Risky, but he'd give it a shot.

"When I told you that we had a safe house, I was trying to placate you to agree to our help. You're right—it was a bad judgment call. But it seemed like the only way to get you out of your apartment before whoever shot at you returned and tried again."

"You suck at apologies." She gripped her hands in her lap again.

He nodded. "I'll concede that as well. When I'm nervous, I always overthink things and words escape the brain and hence... sucky apologies."

She released her hands, a sign of a less hostile disposition. *Fast to anger, yet quick to forgive.* He stored that fact with the others he'd collected about the woman. Most of them involved paradoxes.

Stubborn, tenacious enough to go through somebody's files, and yet considerate enough that she visited sick cats at a vet. Freaked at being shot at, but brave enough to put herself in danger to protect someone else—even someone she barely knew. Worried about money, but willing to pay vet bills for a cat that wasn't hers. Lived in a dump, but kept the worn and stained space spotless. Logical, but still emotional. (Of course, she was female, which made that almost understandable.) Intelligent enough to be anything she'd liked, but instead she taught kids the alphabet. Naturally classy, but not a hint of pretentiousness.

"What are you nervous about?" she asked.

The question upped his nervous quotient. He started to overthink his answer and then just spit it out. "I don't want you upset at me."

Her shoulders relaxed as if she'd lost more of her bad mood. "I'm not upset, I'm... Okay, I was upset."

Her honestly appealed to him.

He saw her eyes grow moist, and she looked to be at her breaking point. Not that he blamed her. She'd had a ball-busting kind of day. He cautiously moved to the sofa and sat next to her.

She blinked. "I shouldn't have come here."

"The apartment?" he asked, afraid she might insist on leaving.

"Texas."

"You really can't blame it on Texas."

"I know." Her voice trembled.

He felt that slight quiver in his gut.

She shifted in her seat. "Perhaps I should just forget all this and go back to Alabama."

"You can't do that because..." His reasoning didn't make itself clear.

"You can't put the toothpaste back in the tube," he said.

She looked at him.

He explained, "My sister says that all the time."

"It's a good analogy, but..."

"But...what?"

"But...I know I told you all this...I just hadn't told anyone else."

He knew she was referring to his friends and business partners. "You're upset—"

"Not really upset, it's just people are going to think I'm...crazy."

"I don't think you're crazy."

"You did at first."

"Look, it doesn't matter what people think. What matters is getting to the truth and making sure whoever is trying to hurt you is caught and stopped." There. Those were the reasons she couldn't leave Texas that he couldn't think of earlier.

She shifted. Her leg brushed against his. "But I don't want your friends to think..."

"My friends are the last people who would judge you. Nikki found her ex-husband's body in the trunk of her car and was the prime suspect for his murder. Ellen got stabbed when the same person who took out Nikki's ex mistook Ellen for Nikki. When Ellen was in the hospital, stoned out of her mind on painkillers, she propositioned every single guy who came into her room."

When that didn't seem enough to convince her, he continued, "Eddie Nance nearly went down for a robbery he didn't commit. Tony and LeAnn were separated, and Tony came up with some ludicrous story about bedbugs taking over his apartment so he could move back in with her and win her back. Don't even get me started about Nikki's crazy grandmother and Dallas and Tony's dad.

Point is, all of us have found ourselves in crazy situations. They aren't going to judge you."

She took a deep breath, and those wet, beautiful eyes looked up at him. Gone was the anger he'd spotted earlier, replaced by . . .

"Thank you," she said. "You might suck at apologies, but you rock at pep talks."

Something warm swelled inside his chest. "I'll make sure to put that on my resume."

"You do that," she said. "I'll even offer a reference if need be."

Their gazes met, and all he could think about was kissing her.

Tasting her mouth.

Touching her.

The feel of her leg pressing against his felt nice. Really nice.

There were half a dozen logical reasons why kissing her wasn't a good idea. She was too upset. It was too soon. She'd just gotten over being angry. She'd been shot. And . . .

He always listened to logic.

But not now.

He didn't move. Except to shift closer. To lower his head. To dip his chin down a few inches.

He brushed his mouth against hers.

Slow.

Easy.

Giving her ample time to pull back. This had to be mutual. He knew that.

She didn't pull back. It *was* mutual.

And he was so damn glad he hadn't listened to logic.

She tasted like wine to his beer. Her lips were soft to his firm. She closed her eyes, and there was something so sexy watching her eyelids flutter closed. So sexy feeling her moist lips slip against his. So sexy when she tilted her face to the right so her mouth fit better against his.

He deepened the kiss, and her tongue swept against his, inviting him to move deeper. And there wasn't a part of him that didn't embrace the invitation. His body hummed with pleasure. His blood found its way down south at a very fast rate.

Any resemblance to logic evaporated in the heat of the moment.

Slipping one arm between her and the pink sofa, he drew her a bit closer. But he wanted more.

As if she'd read his mind, she swung around, sat on his lap with her knees straddling him. He moaned with pleasure when her sweet bottom pressed against the top of his thighs.

Her hand moved to his shoulders and pulled him closer. Closer was good. Her breasts came against his chest, and nothing had ever felt so right.

"Is anyone here?"

Austin's voice sent Zoe and Tyler jerking apart, just like two kids who'd gotten busted making out on her parents' sofa. She climbed off of him, fast, and landed on the very edge of the sofa cushion and slid off the pink leather. He wasn't even sure she landed before she popped up and plopped her butt back down on the seat.

Tyler's gaze shot to the door where Austin stood.

"Bad timing, huh?"

Zoe opened her mouth as if to answer, but then closed it.

"Okay. I... I'm gonna go now." Austin took a step back. His gaze shifted to Zoe. "We'll worry about introductions later."

"I'm going to kill him." Tyler started to get up. "Slowly."

"Don't!" Zoe grabbed his arm. She released it extra fast, and he knew she'd felt it, too—that warm zing from their touch.

He looked into her eyes and tried to read her, but all he could see was embarrassment. His brain went from anger at Austin to the need to go back in for another kiss. But with the door open and Austin lurking close by, logic prevailed this time.

Brushing a strand of hair from her bright red cheek, he said, "Fine. I'll forgo killing him and just hurt him a little." He smiled, but she didn't smile back.

He looked at the door and back at her. "I do need to talk with him before he runs off."

She nodded.

He stood, still tasting her mouth on the tip of his tongue and still feeling the effect of their kiss in his tight jeans.

Almost out the door, he looked back. She sat, gnawing on her bottom lip, eyes closed as if repenting from some terrible sin. He got a bad feeling that she wasn't nearly as thrilled about the new development in their relationship as he was.

Not that he was going to let that completely ruin his mood. Whatever reservations she had about pursuing their attraction, he'd deal with them. He took off to find Austin.

CHAPTER FOURTEEN

DAMN! DAMN! DAMN!

Zoe tried to breathe slowly. What the hell had she done? He might have started it, but she'd climbed aboard the fast-moving ride, called shotgun seat, and went along with the thrill like an adrenaline junky. Lord help her, but she should have more willpower than that.

She was still trying to figure out this little issue called her whole freaking life: who she was, who she wasn't, and who was trying to kill her. What the hell was she thinking? Jumping aboard another potential disaster in the making. As nice as Tyler was—to look at, to kiss—she'd be an idiot to let this happen.

And she wouldn't.

She wouldn't let it happen.

Not again.

She closed her eyes tighter and could hear her mama say, *"Zoe Girl, everything that glitters isn't gold. Just because you want something doesn't mean you need it. Just because someone says they have your best interests at heart, doesn't mean they won't break your heart in the end."*

The words of wisdom echoed in her mind. She couldn't help but wonder if her mama had included herself and her dad in the people who could possibly break Zoe's heart. Because they had definitely broken her heart. And now, more than ever, she took her mama's warning seriously.

Not that it stopped her from occasionally trying to conjure up a reason her parents could have justified what they'd done. But it came back to the fact that they'd lied to her. Lied to her in spite of the fact that she'd had suspicions, questions, and nightmares. Lied to her even knowing how crazy it made her feel not to understand these things.

The fact that she sat here not two minutes after she'd been kissed silly, feeling angry at her parents instead of thinking about that kiss, drove home her point.

She needed to stay focused on getting her life back together—not doing something that could bring more pain on top of what she already had. She'd be heading back to Alabama very soon; she'd like to go without leaving bits and pieces of her broken self behind.

"Goddamn, mother . . . !"

Tyler heard Austin belt out a string of curses. He hurried his steps. When Austin cursed in a tone that wasn't underlined with humor, he had a reason. And his reason was usually bad.

Tyler cut the corner into the office and saw the reason. Cowering in one corner of the office sat Lucky. Cowering in the opposite corner was Austin.

Austin looked up. "Get the broom and get that thing out of here. Damn stray must have snuck in when I walked in and I didn't see him."

"He's not a stray," Tyler said. "He's Zoe's cat."

Austin gaped at him with a look of sheer horror. "But . . . it's been mutilated."

"It was in an accident."

"Ran over?" Austin made a face of disgust.

"Blown up."

"I believe it." He hesitated. "It hissed at me."

"Probably after you yelled at him."

Austin shook his head. "I don't like cats."

"I don't think he likes you, either."

Austin frowned. "But I'm better looking and have all my limbs and body parts."

"The better looking part of that statement is debatable." Tyler watched Austin cautiously move out of the corner.

"Look, it's not that I don't feel for the cat, but can you please get him out of here?" Austin waved his hand toward the helpless feline.

If Tyler wasn't still pissed at the man for breaking up his kiss—the first one of many Tyler hoped—he'd have laughed. "Really? Romeo has a kryptonite? You're an ailurophobe?"

"I'm a what?" Austin's gaze shot back to Lucky as the cat shifted.

"You have a phobia of cats?"

"There's a name for that? How the hell do you know that shit?"

"I read. You should try it sometime," Tyler said.

"I read."

Tyler smirked. "I don't mean condom boxes."

Lucky meowed. Austin flinched. Tyler finally laughed.

"I'm not scared," Austin said. "I just don't like them."

Right. Tyler picked Lucky up. "When were you bitten?"

"I didn't say I was," Austin said.

Tyler just looked at him.

"Fine, I was six. But I'm not scared. I'm just cautious."

The cat reared his head up and rubbed his face against Tyler's chest. "Well, I don't think Lucky is an attack cat."

Setting the feline down carefully in the hall, he shut the office door and faced Austin. "What happened at Zoe's and why the hell didn't you answer your damn phone when I called?"

Austin dropped into his desk chair.

Austin's smile widened. "I wasn't aware that you even knew how to put the moves on. But it looked like you were doing pretty good. If you need any tips, I'm your man."

Tyler respected Austin, but sometimes the guy didn't know when to shut the hell up. "Drop it."

Austin's shit-eating grin vanished. "It took an hour for the cops to show up. I was leaving when they got there."

"What did you tell them?"

"That I was combing the neighborhood, working on one of our cases, when I heard shots and called them."

"Did they buy it?" Tyler asked.

"Hell, no. Cops are all suspicious bastards. They assume everyone's lying."

"You *were* lying." Tyler ignored the fact that they used to be the suspicious bastards. And in some ways still were. PIs or cops, it was their job to be suspicious.

"They didn't know I was lying."

Tyler shook his head. "So what happened?"

"They wanted to take me down to the station and ask some questions."

"And?" Tyler asked.

"I told them to go screw themselves. That I'd called it in, I didn't do the shooting. Unfortunately, someone found a spot of blood on her floor. And it got more serious."

"Shit," Tyler said. "I should have cleaned that up."

"Yeah, well, thankfully they chatted with the neighbors who said they'd seen Zoe drive off. When I left they were trying to reach the landlord. If the landlord has her cell number, she can expect a call from Glencoe's not so finest. Remember that grumpy Thompson?"

"Hell." Tyler frowned. He needed to get to Zoe. Not to restart what they'd had going, either. They needed to talk about the best way to deal with the police when they found her.

He opened the door and was almost out when Austin spoke up.

"Hell, what?" asked Austin.

Tyler turned around. "If she talks to the cops, the whole Bradford thing will get leaked."

"Have her tell them she wasn't there when the shooting took place. I didn't give them a specific time when it happened. Say it's a drive-by shooting. In that neighborhood it makes sense. They don't have to know about the Bradfords until we're ready for them to know."

"I don't see her lying very well."

"Then tell her not to answer her phone. If you want, I can show her how that's done." He smiled.

Tyler ignored Austin's attempt at humor, his mind calculating the pros and cons of Zoe not taking the call. He couldn't find a downside. Of course, the cops would end up learning where she worked, and people at the diner knew of Zoe's connection to him, and that would lead them here. But maybe they wouldn't go that far? And if they did, it would still buy them time.

"Yeah, that's what I'll do," he said to Austin.

"It's too late," the soft voice said behind him.

Tyler swung around. Zoe stood in the doorway, her phone in her hands. Her lips were still wet, maybe even from their kiss. Damn she was pretty. However, she didn't look any happier now than when he'd left her.

"Too late for what?" He hoped like hell that she didn't mean them. They barely knew each other. How could it be too late?

"A Sergeant Thompson from the Glencoe police just called. He wants me to come to the station immediately."

"You ready?" Tyler asked Zoe, who hadn't said a word during the fifteen-minute ride to the police station. He'd tried to prepare her for what lay head. He'd also given her their alternatives. Stay put, and risk the cops looking for her. Go and tell them the whole truth, and risk him not getting information out of the Bradfords. Or go and offer limited information—leave the Bradfords completely out of it, and don't even mention the threatening phone calls. He recommended option three.

She went with it, too, but that didn't mean she was happy about it. He wasn't happy seeing her unhappy. She hadn't smiled once since their kiss, and until this moment, he'd had to work to keep from smiling. He hoped to alter Zoe's mood as soon as he got this behind them.

"I hate doing this." Her blue eyes rounded with concern.

"I know." *So do I.* The giddiness he'd felt since he'd kissed Zoe had lingered until he pulled up at the police station. For eight years he'd come here, given his all to the force, even believed the force was his family. Only to have that family turn its back on him. And when Lisa jumped ship like everyone on the force, it was like the damn piece of straw that did the camel in. It made him realize that caring for people, really caring, could do him in, too.

They got out of the car. He met Zoe at the front of the car and tried to put his complete focus on her and not the knots in his gut.

Logically, it shouldn't bother him. It was history. It should even bring a bit of pride to walk back and show his face to the nonbelievers.

He hadn't come back here since they brought him in and stripped him of his gun, his badge, and his belief in justice.

Since he'd been released, he'd bought himself several guns, didn't want the damn badge, but his belief in the justice system had forever been changed. Oh, he still believed in justice, he just now knew you couldn't count on it...or the people who swore by it.

Opening the door, he guided her to the front desk, which was manned by a woman in her mid-fifties who had her nose buried in a book. He recognized the title of the latest *New York Times* bestseller. And he recognized the woman behind the novel, too.

His chest tightened. "This is Zoe Adams, and we're here to see Officer Thompson."

The woman looked up, and her eyes widened with recognition.

Lois MacDonald had a passion for the written word, which meant they'd always had something to talk about. He wouldn't call what they had friendship, but it was close.

"Tyler? I... wondered if I'd ever see you again." She blushed as if embarrassed.

"I'm like a bad penny. Just keep showing up," he said. "Is Thompson in?"

He knew Larry Thompson, too. Unlike Mrs. MacDonald, he hadn't cared for the guy then, and something told Tyler he was going to like the guy even less now. But to get Zoe out of here without any trouble, he'd behave. "I'll give him a call." She paused and then started to speak again.

And damn it, he knew before she opened her mouth what she planned on saying.

"I'm sorry. For what happened. It shouldn't have happened."

Emotion tightened his gut. When he was first released, he couldn't wait to hear someone say it. Now, he hated it. What do you say to people who you actually considered one of your tribe, people who you would have defended to the end, but people who turned their back on you before you even got a chance to tell your side of the story?

He couldn't say it was all right, because it wasn't. He couldn't say he forgave them, because he hadn't forgiven anyone. He could tell them to go fuck themselves, and part of him wanted to, but he didn't want them to know he still cared what they thought. And he didn't care. Well, not as much as he used to.

"It really shouldn't have happened," she repeated.

"No, it shouldn't have." He touched Zoe's elbow to motion her forward.

They got several feet when Zoe leaned in. "I'm sorry. I read the story but it didn't click that this was the same station." She stopped and caught his arm. "Let's go. You shouldn't have to be here."

"It's fine. Let's just—"

"No, it's not." She looked at him, as if she could read every emotion running through him. And if she could, so could everyone else. He didn't like that.

"I've known you only a couple of days, and I already know you couldn't have done what they accused you of doing. How could they . . . ?"

He'd asked himself that question. And answered it, but it didn't make it right. Still he told her, "There was a lot of evidence."

"But they knew you," she insisted.

He met her gaze, and there was something in her eyes that touched his soul. He wasn't even sure what it was, but it lifted the heaviness in his chest. Suddenly, he didn't care about Lois MacDonald or all the other jerks here.

"It doesn't matter." He smiled, not knowing exactly why he was smiling, but—

"Goddamn it! I knew he was lying to me." A male voice boomed.

Tyler recognized the voice, and he knew the meeting wasn't going to go well.

Tyler looked at Larry Thompson. He took a deep breath and reminded himself that this was about Zoe. He flashed a smile he didn't really feel. "Zoe Adams, this is Detective Thompson. I think you spoke on the phone."

Zoe forced a smile and nodded. He'd warned Zoe that Thompson could be uncouth. And now more than ever, he worried Zoe might not be able to do this.

Thompson, an old-school kind of guy, wore a tie to work every day as if that made up for his lack of manners in every other department. Truth was, he didn't have any manners. Even worse was the fact that his tie usually carried evidence of the man's last meal. Possibly yesterday's as well. Tyler's gaze shifted down to the stained piece of silk resting against the man's gut.

Zoe nodded again. "You said you needed to see me."

"What the hell is going on?" Thompson asked Tyler, ignoring Zoe's attempt at politeness. "I swear they'd have done the world a favor if they'd have kept your asses locked up."

Anger stirred in Tyler's gut, but he bit it back. "You called Miss Adams. You tell us."

"Your partner lied through his teeth to me."

"He didn't lie," Zoe said, and stiffened her shoulders. "I believe he told you that he was in the neighborhood investigating a case when the shooting occurred."

"And somehow you just happened to get your apartment shot up, right? And you just happen to show up here with his partner. And it's all a coincidence. I'm not supposed to believe any of this is connected. Look, whatever is going on you'd better trust us and not those fruitcakes."

Tyler watched Zoe's expression harden. "I hear these shootings happen all the time in my neighborhood," she said, surprising Tyler. He'd told her what to say, but he hadn't expected her to say it so convincingly.

"I should have checked the neighborhood out closer before I moved in," she continued, ad-libbing now. "Then again, I was under the assumption that I could have faith in this police department. Sadly, I was mistaken."

"Do I look like an idiot to you?" Thompson snapped, not surprising Tyler with his abruptness. Without thinking, he moved between the asshole and Zoe.

Tyler had a retort on the tip of his tongue, but Zoe shot around him and let loose first.

"I'm going to assume that's a rhetorical question and you really don't care to hear my opinion."

Zoe's comment was so close to the words resting on the tip of his tongue, Tyler almost laughed. Of course, he'd have pointed out the gravy on the man's tie and used a bit more colorful language. She did it in her Alabama, almost ladylike, drawl, and he had to admit he liked that drawl.

"But just in case I'm mistaken in my assumption, Detective, my answer would be dependent upon whether or not you were part of the asinine group who sat back and did nothing when three of their own men were arrested for a crime they didn't commit."

Tyler smiled. Oh, yeah, he liked everything about her. He couldn't remember liking this much about a person, so fast, in . . . a very long time.

Thompson opened his mouth as if to speak, then shut it. "If all this is a coincidence, how do you two know each other?" Thompson's words came out like an accusation.

"We met at the diner where Zoe works," Tyler said. "She dropped a couple of plates of food on me, and we've been inseparable ever since." For good measure, he looped his arm around Zoe and slipped his palm in the soft curve of her waist.

His hand fit perfectly there—as if it had been made to fit in that sweet spot. Zoe leaned into him. His heart got another shot of adrenaline when the side of her breast brushed up against his rib cage. Oh yeah, he could get used to this.

CHAPTER FIFTEEN

Ten minutes later, Tyler and Zoe walked out of the Glencoe PD. He still had his arm around her, his hand still warm in the curve of her waist.

He leaned down and whispered, "You did great."

She frowned as they continued to the car. "I don't think he believed a word I said."

"Doesn't matter what he believes. You didn't say anything that gave him a reason to doubt you or to think you're into something criminal. He'll let it go."

Arriving at his car, he needed to move his hand from around her to retrieve his keys from his pocket. But damn, he didn't want to let her go. Not now, and maybe not for a very long time. But he couldn't just stand here in the parking lot with her snug against him.

Accepting the inevitable, he slipped his hand around her back and went to fish out his keys. As he feared, the moment his hand left her waist, she stepped back. He figured he'd have to work hard to get that close to her again. Not that it wouldn't be worth the effort.

He unlocked the car and opened her door. She slipped

into the front seat and looked up. Her frown deepened. "I lied."

"For a good reason." *Just like I did*, he thought but didn't say it. He fought the urge to lean down and kiss the frown from her lips.

"Doesn't make it right," she said.

"I think it does." He shut her door.

When he climbed in through the driver's side door and their gazes met, he spotted the whispering of pain in her eyes. "It's not the same thing," he said, knowing she was thinking of her parents.

"Isn't it?" The pain in her eyes became more evident. "You want to know what's awful? I'm almost hoping that I learn my biological parents were abusive to me so I can justify why the Adamses would have done it. Maybe the Bradfords gave me to them. But even then, why couldn't they have told me the truth?"

The questions he needed to ask her bubbled to the surface. He almost didn't want to ask, afraid she wouldn't welcome the questions, but he needed to know the answers. "Your parents...the Adamses, they never..." His gut tightened at the thought of anyone hurting her. "Did they abuse you?"

Her eyes widened. "No. Never."

"Your dad...he never..."

"Oh, God, no!" She paused. "Don't you see, that's what makes this so hard? I always thought they were the perfect parents and I was the imperfect child. We didn't have a lot of money, but they paid for me to see a shrink all those years. If they were guilty of anything, it was of loving me too much. Giving in to my every whim. I said I wanted to play guitar, and my dad went out and bought me a guitar."

A sheen of tears filled her eyes. "I changed to the trumpet midstream, and when he couldn't afford to buy one, he rented one. He paid for ballet lessons because I was certain I wanted to be a ballerina when I grew up."

One tear slipped from her lashes, and she wiped it away. "When I turned sixteen they bought me a used Saturn—even though my dad's truck was on its last leg. They never missed a school event, even in high school when none of the other parents went. And when Dad died, Mom pulled herself together and continued to be Supermom."

Tyler saw her struggle to keep it together even as her emotions were too close to the surface.

"She started tutoring kids to pay for my college education. Only after she died did I learn she'd mortgaged the house to pay off my college loans. But now I look back, and I...I can't help but wonder if how they acted wasn't all a lie. Did they really not love me but were just trying to make up for kidnapping me?"

He brushed the back of his hand over her cheek. Her skin felt soft. So soft. "It's a hell of a long time to pretend to care about someone."

Tyler figured Lisa's two-year stretch had been pushing it. And she'd been damn good at pretending, too. She had him wanting things he'd never wanted until he'd met her. Like to give the whole domesticated life a try, even when the odds were he'd fail at it like his parents had. Shit! Why was he thinking about Lisa again?

"It's a hell of a big lie to cover up, too." She shook her head. "I'm sorry. What am I doing?" She rolled her eyes. "Bitching and whining when you're the one who should be furious. I could have gone by myself, you know. You shouldn't have had to face those...people. Though, I do have other names for them. He called *you* a fruitcake, and the man was wearing half his lunch on his tie."

He smiled and got that feeling again, the lightness in his chest. The best he could guess, and he was good at guessing, the sentiment had something to do with her defending him. "Actually, I'm glad I went." For the first time in a long time, Tyler actually believed he'd taken a step forward, away from something that had weighed him down for a long time. Hell, maybe his niece Anna had been right. He'd been a sad clown. All he'd needed was some time with a soft Alabama girl, with her sexy drawl and sweet body, to get him back on track.

"What's next?" she asked.

His mind was on finding a way to get her back on the sofa and in his lap, but he knew she didn't mean that. "Tomorrow, I'll call about the birth certificate."

"It's that easy? They can just tell you if it's real?"

"If it's real, they'll have it on file. I'm betting your parents had a false one made."

She blinked as if even that disturbed her. "What do we do then?"

"Then we're going to see about getting some DNA from Bradford. On the sly, of course. Rick works part-time doing security detail at the Bradford mansion. It won't be admissible in court, but we'll know the truth then."

"How long does that take?"

"For the tests, three or four days."

She nodded, and he could tell from her expression that she struggled hearing this.

Right before he turned on the engine, her cell phone rang. She looked at her purse and then shot him a panicked look. "It has to be him."

"Hand me the phone."

It was on the third ring before she got it out of her purse. Once she had it, she threw the phone at him as if it were hot. It hit him right in the crotch. He jolted and picked it up.

"Sorry," she said.

He looked at the small screen. "It's someone from the diner calling." The phone stopped ringing. He looked back at Zoe. "Probably Dixie; I went there before I went to your place. I needed your address, and she wasn't eager to give it to me. I told her I thought you were in trouble."

She frowned. "Did you tell her about the Bradfords?"

"No."

She stared at her phone. "Oh, shit. I have to work tomorrow."

"You can't," he said.

"But Dixie's counting on me. I'm on the schedule."

He frowned. "She can count on someone else. Call her back right now and let her know."

When Zoe looked about to argue, he added, "When I was at the diner, one of the waitresses said someone besides me had called looking for you there."

"Who?" she asked. "I don't know anyone here."

"I'm guessing it was the same person who used your apartment for target practice."

Her brow crinkled. "I didn't even stop to think. How could whoever did this know where I live? Or where I work?"

"I'm betting they've followed you from the mansion."

"You think...it's someone there?"

"That's the only thing that makes sense right now." He handed her the phone. "Call Dixie and let her know you won't be working."

"This sucks." She started punching in a number. "I hate letting people down."

"Getting shot... again... would suck more," he said.

Sleep hadn't come easy that night. And when it did, she was yanked back to the recurring nightmare she'd had for years when young. Locked in a dark closet, she had to use the bathroom. She didn't want to wet her pants—she was a big girl and had stopped doing that—but she didn't want to knock on that door and ask them to let her out. She knew whoever was out there wasn't nice.

Panic filled her lungs, then Lucky's comforting meow brought her out of it. She pushed her eyes open and sat up.

Lucky continued to paw at her face, seeking a bit of late-night TLC. She reached up to comply when suddenly nothing felt right. Not the bed. Not the blanket. Or the smells.

Where was she?

Everything came back. Safe house. Telling Dixie she couldn't come in for a few days. And... Tyler Lopez.

A vision of him filled her mind. Her heart did a little flip.

She remembered getting back to the apartment and dropping on the sofa, both mentally and physically exhausted. Tyler had offered to order some take-out food, but she'd told him she couldn't eat. He'd turned on the television and sat beside her, far enough on the end of the sofa that it didn't make her uncomfortable.

What had made her uncomfortable was the elephant sitting in the room. The kiss, the way she'd climbed on top of him. She needed to make it clear that it had been a mistake, that it shouldn't have happened. That it wouldn't happen again. But the right words never came.

She remembered him flipping through the channels and stopping on the History Channel. He'd looked at her as if asking if that was acceptable. She'd nodded, and within five minutes she'd started to nod off. He'd tried to get her to take the bedroom, but she'd woken enough to adamantly refuse. It was too early, plus she planned on taking the sofa.

The last thing she remembered was watching the Trojan horse being rolled into Troy. She must have fallen asleep.

God, she hoped she hadn't snored or anything.

She felt a blanket slip off her knees to land on the floor. There was a pillow there, too. Tyler had probably covered her and supplied her with a pillow. Nice guy. Good pep talk giver, too. Great kisser.

Don't go there!

Seeing her purse on the coffee table, she dug inside it until she found her phone and then hit a button to see the time—three a.m.

Realizing she had to pee, she tiptoed down the dark hall. Her pulse raced as she took steps into the darkness. Not a closet, she told herself. Just a hall.

She spotted a little sliver of light coming from under the bathroom door, and she could breathe again. Three minutes later, bladder happy, she stared at the toilet, debating to flush or not to flush. If she didn't flush, would he think she was gross? If she did flush, and woke him up, would he think of her as inconsiderate?

Inconsiderate won out over gross. She flushed, cringed when it seemed extra loud, gave her hands a quick rinse, and hurried out of the bathroom. Sitting on the sofa, she knew she needed to go back to sleep. The feel of her bra pulled across her shoulder, and she reached in, unfastened it, slipped it off, and put it on the sofa. Maybe if she had something to read...

She turned on the lamp. No books. She spotted a magazine on the second shelf of one of the end tables.

She pulled it out and frowned. A car magazine. Beggars couldn't be choosers. She flipped it open and started reading. The article on carburetor engines versus fuel-injected engines seemed just the thing to put her to sleep. Instead, her brain chewed on the info and stored it away. Like she really needed to know this.

But that was the thing with her brain. It loved information. Unlike both her parents, she had a ferocious hunger for knowledge. She read anything she got her hands on. Oh, her parents were happy for her, like when she got her SAT scores back, but her IQ was just another little difference between them. Maybe deep down, she'd always known they weren't her parents.

When her stomach growled, she remembered she hadn't eaten supper last night. She dropped the magazine and went into the kitchen. Opening the fridge, she found it empty with the exception of a pizza box and one beer.

Remembering her beggars-couldn't-be-choosers policy, she pulled out a slice of thin-crust pepperoni and eyed the beer. She didn't like beer. Then she remembered kissing Tyler and how he'd tasted. Malty, a little yeasty. Maybe she did like beer.

Setting the slice of pizza on the pizza box, she snagged the beer, opened it, and took a sip. Licking her lips, she let the taste tickle over her taste buds. "Not quite as good." But not bad. She snagged her pizza, took a bite, shut the fridge door with her knee, turned, and walked right into a warm wall of flesh named Tyler.

Make that a sleepy, completely shirtless warm wall of flesh named Tyler.

Eyeing the cold pizza she held out to the side, she sighed. Somehow she'd managed not to plaster the cold pizza to his chest. Considering he always ended up wearing food around her, he was lucky. "Isw ere ugree." She spoke around the pizza. If his puzzled look was any indication, the words were too mangled to make sense.

She swallowed and tried again. "I was hungry." And added, "I hope you don't mind."

"That's cold," he said.

"Me eating your pizza?" she asked. "I just..."

"No." He smiled.

She got entranced by his chocolate brown irises. This close, she could see tiny flecks of green. And he smelled like a sleepy man should smell—clean and freshly showered.

Showered. Something she hadn't done and wished she had. Another thought rained down on her. Had she even glanced at herself in the mirror? Checked to see the curl index of her hair? No. Odds were it was a mess.

"Then what am I being cold about?" she asked.

His grin widened. His hair wasn't perfect, either. But he looked totally adorable with his hair a little askew and his sleepy expression. He glanced down in that small little space between them. "You aren't acting cold. The beer's cold."

She looked down to where she had pressed the chilled beer to his bare, sculpted abdomen.

"Sorry." Her face grew hot. With a limp piece of pizza in one hand, a cold beer in the other, she slipped between him and the fridge, and moved to stand beside the sink, a spot that offered a bit more breathing room. But the air still smelled like him.

"Beer and cold pizza. Nothing tastes better in the middle of the night," he said.

He opened the fridge and looked inside. She used his diverted attention to look at him. The fridge's glow showcased him in the limelight. He wore his jeans, but the top button hadn't been fastened. The V of flesh showed no signs of underwear, either. As if he'd been sleeping in the nude and snagged on his jeans and got them only halfway on before he left the room. Or did he not wear underwear ever?

Now there was a thought.

He withdrew his own slice of pizza, looked at her, and frowned. "You'll have to share the beer."

He closed the fridge and took the beer from her hands. She watched the beer press against his lips as he drank. And again, she thought about his kiss earlier that had tasted so good.

"You having problems sleeping?" he asked.

"I wasn't. I mean, I slept. But I woke up. And couldn't fall back to sleep." Why was she having a hard time talking? The answer came hurling at her.

Because he was half-naked.

Again.

Last time she'd seen him with his undershirt. She hadn't thought that little piece of cotton had left anything to the imagination. She'd been wrong. Or at least, she hadn't imagined him looking this good. Sculpted abs, ripples of muscles, wrapped in naturally light olive-colored skin that begged to be touched. Did he work out twenty-four/seven to look like that?

She followed a line of dark hair meandering down his

chest, swirling around his inny navel, and disappearing behind his slightly opened zipper. Realizing she was staring at the bulge behind his zipper, her breath caught and she yanked her eyes upward.

He had the beer pressed to his lips again and wore a caught-ya grin. He set the beer on the counter and reached up and ran his finger over her bottom lip. “Tomato sauce.” He slipped his finger into his mouth.

She reached up, wiped her lip that tingled from his touch. Then she ran a hand through her unruly hair.

Her thoughts must have been readable. “It looks great.”

“Right,” she said in sarcasm, and stepped back.

He took a bite of his pizza, watching her. After he swallowed, he said, “It’s . . . sexy.” His eyes lowered to her chest, where her unsupported girls swayed slightly with her movement.

She sucked in a breath, and the air felt cold and light in her chest, yet she felt warm all over. Tingly. Sensitive. Her nipples tightened. Did he know she was turned on?

Warm, tense silence filled the room with a heavy awkwardness. “We should go to bed,” she said.

He arched an eyebrow in a playful manner.

“Separately,” she added.

He chuckled and handed her the beer. “You know, studies have concluded that sex is . . . a sleep aid.”

“I’ll just read,” she said.

His smile widened. “The study proved—”

“That’s okay.” She cut her eyes up at him, a look she shot her five-year-old students when she caught them picking their noses or doing something equally unappealing. “I’m finding an article on carbureted engines boring enough that it should do the trick.”

His grin widened. "Well, you're right, the sex wouldn't be boring. But it releases endorphins that help—"

"Seriously?" she asked.

"Seriously," he said. "It releases endorphins and—"

"No, I mean... You're seriously using that as a pick-up line?"

His grin widened. "Not working, huh?" His smile made the sexiness in his eyes intensify. "It was a shot in the dark. I've never been very good at it."

She suddenly found his humor contagious. "Never good at sex?"

He let loose of a laugh. It fell on her like a soft and welcome rain. She found herself wishing she'd met Tyler Lopez at a different time. A different place—like in Alabama when her life wasn't one big question mark hanging on by a thin thread.

When he sobered, he said, "Not good at pick-up lines." He moved in a few steps. "I'm actually really good at sex. I studied—"

"Enough," she said.

Still grinning, he brushed her hair from her shoulder. She felt his breath against her cheek, and his lips started moving lower.

"Really good at it," he whispered.

CHAPTER SIXTEEN

ZOE HAD NO DOUBT he was good at sex. And if he kissed her…

She could not let him kiss her.

"I think we should go to bed," she blurted out, and darted out of the kitchen.

"I'm supposing you still mean separately." Humor still played in his voice.

She went and dropped onto the sofa and grabbed her magazine. He stopped beside the sofa and put the last bite of pizza into his mouth.

She put her magazine down and rested her slice of cold pizza on top of it. While now might not be the best time to address this, she didn't have much of a choice. "I'm going back to Alabama in two weeks. It would be ridiculous to allow this to go anywhere."

He must have mistaken her dialogue as an invitation to join her, because he sat down.

Close enough that the dip in the sofa had her shoulder bumping into his. The brush of bare skin to bare skin sent a wave of pleasure running up her arm and filtering out all over her body. And the filtering felt nice. Sweet, erotic chills went places she hadn't felt tingling in a long time.

"So we have two weeks." Handing the beer back to her, he continued, "We could have a lot of fun in two weeks."

"And what about after that?" she asked.

He brushed the lip of the beer bottle over his chin. "We crucify ourselves between two thieves: regret for yesterday and fear of tomorrow. Fulton Oursler."

He reached over and picked up her pizza. "Then there's, 'Let us not look back in anger, nor forward in fear, but around in awareness.' By—"

"James Thurber," she said, and watched him take a bite of her pizza. "But then there's, 'You can't put the toothpaste back into the tube.' I think you said your sister gets credit for that well-said quote, and it's a good piece of wisdom to consider in this situation."

He pointed at her with what was left of the pizza slice. "Not fair using my own sister's quote on me."

"Why not? You used it on me." She frowned. "And it's a good analogy. With everything else I'm dealing with, I don't think I could handle a long-distance relationship. And the statistical data on them say they almost never work out."

"I wasn't suggesting..." He took another bite of pizza as if needing a diversion.

"You weren't suggesting a long-distance relationship?" She let that info bounce around her head. It continued to bounce until she felt it hit her heart, a heart still on the mend from her last relationship. A relationship with the last guy who made her feel all these wonderful feelings—tingly, safe, loved—only to leave her to crash and burn.

All her wound-up tension, sexual and otherwise, got twisted around in her gut and morphed into anger. "So what exactly are you suggesting?" she asked.

"Why can't we just enjoy the time we have?" He talked around the pizza in his mouth.

"Oh, so you just want to use me for a slip-and-slide bang toy while I'm here, huh?"

He must have been in midswallow, because he choked. For a second there, it sounded serious—some gasping and trying to swallow.

She prayed he would manage on his own, because she was too angry to save his life. Damn him! Damn all men!

When he caught his breath, he looked at her. "I didn't mean it like that." He went back to coughing.

She gave him about ten seconds. "Then explain to me how you meant it." The feeling swelling inside her reminded her of how she felt when Chris had told her he'd fallen in love with a stripper. It even reminded her how she felt toward her parents when she saw Nancy Bradford's picture.

Just because someone says they have your best intentions at heart, doesn't mean they won't break your heart in the end.

Her mom's words ran through her head. Zoe summed up her jumbled feelings in one word: betrayed. By him. By her parents. By whoever was shooting at her.

"Is this why you're helping me?" she asked.

He stood up. "No. I... Shit. Look, I did not mean to offend you," he said. "I'm not a womanizer. I thought we were two consenting adults who shared a mutual attraction. You overreacted to my suggestion."

His words, spoken so honestly and backed with what

he clearly considered logic, had her second-guessing herself. Then second-guessing went for thirds.

Had she overreacted? Was she wrong? Was she being a prude?

No. She'd slept with guys without knowing where the relationship was going. She just hadn't slept with guys when the option of a relationship had been taken off the table. And that somehow made it feel different. Like the difference between a sexy book and porn. The latter felt…cheap.

"You're right. I overreacted," she said. "I apologize. I'm aware that many adult women would jump at this opportunity. However, I'm afraid I'm not into sex for sex's sake."

"I didn't mean that, either," he said, sounding beyond frustrated. "I'm just…we're adults, and neither of us have someone else."

"How do you know I don't have someone else?" she asked.

He tightened his eyes. "Do you?"

"No, but that's not the point."

"Then why did you bring it up?"

She was trying to figure that one out herself.

"Look," he continued, "I was just saying that I really like you, but I'm not looking for—"

"Anything more than sex." He seemed to have a hard time saying it.

He opened his mouth to argue, and she held up her hand. "I get it. And I'm not saying anything is wrong with it. I'm just saying that I'm not interested."

She decided she needed to confirm something. "And if this was…in any way a part of the reason you offered to help me, then I will be more than willing to get my stuff and leave."

He raked a hand through his hair. "It's not the reason I offered to help." He clamped his jaw shut so tight it looked as if it would crack. She got the feeling she'd insulted him, and she was sorry for that, but she had needed to make sure.

"Fine then." She softened her voice. "So we can move forward as planned. You'll keep track of everything I owe you for your services, and then... when I get back on my feet, I'll reimburse you. Hopefully, this thing won't take very long and it won't be too terribly expensive."

He stood there staring at her as if trying to find something else to say. She decided to save him the trouble. Leaning forward, she picked up her magazine. "If you don't mind, I'm dying to get back to my article."

Muttering a curse that she thought was in Spanish, he turned around and shot down the hall.

She dropped the magazine into her lap and leaned against the sofa. Her chest ached with what felt like disappointment, but that would go away in time. Unlike with Chris, she didn't love Tyler.

The attraction issue was going to be uncomfortable, but now that she knew how incompatible they really were, that should fade.

Incompatible?

The word got hung up in her mind. Oddly enough, she had felt an almost instant kinship that in some ways was directly tied to her compatibility with Tyler. Well, not instant, not when he'd been dressed as a clown, but at the diner. She'd been drawn to his intellect, his wit, and his body.

Lucky jumped up on the sofa and rubbed his face against her arm. "You even like him, don't you?" For some reason, she'd been compelled to trust Tyler. But trusting someone to help her find answers wasn't the same as trusting someone with her heart. It all went to the lesson she seemed to be learning over and over again. Decent people, people you thought you could trust, could still hurt you.

She heard his footsteps coming down the hall. He stopped in front of her. She was hit again with how awesome he looked without a shirt.

"Here." He handed her his smartphone. "Order anything you want to read from Amazon." Lucky jumped down and started doing his figure-eights' dance around Tyler's ankles.

Zoe handed him back the phone. "I don't—"

"I saw the books by your bed at your apartment. I know you read when you can't sleep."

"But I imagine you do the same," she said, realizing another thing they had in common.

"I have a book." He took off.

Alone again her chest commenced aching. Lucky jumped up on her lap and meowed right in her face, as if defending Tyler.

"Sorry, buddy. I don't care what you say, we can't keep him."

Tyler gave up trying to sleep around six. He dressed, brushed his teeth, and started out of the bedroom. He told himself not to look at her. Pretend she wasn't there. He knew if he got one glance at her, he'd start coming up with even more questions. He'd already come up with about a dozen, all logged in his mental notepad. Some of them were about the case. Some of them about her—things he was curious about.

Did she always wake up in the middle of the night and go for a snack?

Did she always fall asleep early while watching television?

Did her hair always look that wild after she slept?

Would it look even wilder after he made love to her?

Then there were the questions about last night:

How had things gone so bad?

Why had her putting the brakes on a potential romance hurt so damn much?

He'd been turned down dozens of times. Well, not dozens, but enough that it shouldn't bother him.

It did.

He got halfway across the living room, a foot from the door, when he lost control. He looked over his shoulder.

And stopped dead in his tracks.

He'd been right. Looking at her was a catastrophic mistake. Her hair, locks of curly red strands, scattered all over the pillowcase. Resting on her side, her knees bent, she made the sofa look big. She had her hands tucked under one side of her cheek, looking... vulnerable. Asleep, she looked... younger. His mind brought up the image of her when she was four, the picture she'd shown him. She hadn't lost that innocent, precious look.

Oh, so you just want to use me for a slip-and-slide bang toy while I'm here, huh?

Her words rang in his head and felt like thorns raking over his conscience. They made him feel like some low-life, womanizing bastard who only wanted to use women.

In fact, the reason he didn't want a committed relationship was because, statistically, the odds were he might end up being just like his old man, who was a bastard. Then there was the time he'd attempted the whole hearth and home thing, and he'd been the one who ended up heartbroken.

All Tyler wanted was to share a pleasant couple of weeks with Zoe.

Yet, while tossing and turning in bed last night, he'd tried to see this whole argument from her point of view. Not because he thought she was right, but because the best defense was insight into your opponent. That way, he'd know how to explain to her how wrong she was when they talked about it. Consequently, after looking at this from her perspective, he realized it was true. He looked like a womanizing bastard. Did seeing a woman for mostly sexual reasons, when the woman was okay with the arrangement, make him a bastard? So maybe she wasn't okay with it, but how would he know if he didn't ask? Perhaps just asking a woman automatically made him a louse?

Damn it, he was overthinking things again. He swung around and left the apartment. He needed to spin his mental wheels coming up with questions that would help solve this case, not on questions about the ethics of sexual promiscuousness.

Once in the office, he made a pot of coffee. Considering how little sleep he'd gotten, he made it strong. Twenty minutes later, he was still mulling over their argument, unable to think about anything but Zoe. And not even thinking about things relating to the case, but personal stuff that he wanted to know about her. Finally, giving in, he pulled out a pen and paper and started writing down his questions.

Was she always so damn beautiful when she slept?

Did she always sleep on her side?

Was she grumpy when she first woke up in the morning?

Did she need coffee before she was sociable?

Shit. There wasn't any coffee in the apartment. He poured her a cup and gathered up some cream and sugar and a plastic spoon. He'd leave it on the coffee table. She could always heat it up when she woke up.

He eased open the apartment door. It didn't appear as if she'd even moved a muscle. He stood there, coffee in his hand, and watched her sleep. He remembered how he'd felt when she'd defended him to the asshole Thompson. The way she'd looked up at him with belief in him. Then he remembered how she looked when she'd been angry last night. His chest grew tight again.

But why was he letting this get to him? Hadn't life taught him to keep his emotional distance? Things never hurt as much if you didn't care.

He felt something at his feet. Lucky brushed up against his ankles. He set the coffee down on the coffee table. Steam rose from the cup. Kneeling, he gave the cat a rub behind his good ear. Damn, the thing was ugly. And yet, Zoe loved him. What kind of woman took in a mutilated cat? He mentally tagged that question to add to his written list.

But then an answer shot back at him. *The same kind of person who didn't go for short-time sexual flings with a possible womanizer.*

Frowning, he rose and started to walk out, but instead went to the kitchen where he'd seen a pad and pen. He scribbled a note.

Warm it in the microwave or there's more in the office. Come see me when you wake up. He tore off the sheet and set it down beside the coffee. He started to leave and stopped, knelt down, and reached for the note. He put the pen to the paper.

Sorry for...

What was he sorry for? He hesitated, the pen's tip still against the paper. Then, feeling a grimace all the way to his lower intestines, he finished the sentence.... *upsetting you.* He signed it with the letter *T* and stopped himself just before he added some Xs and Os.

He'd always added Xs and Os to the notes he'd written Lisa. When he'd first started dating her, he'd been working nights and he'd always leave a note on the bedside table. If something happened on the job, she'd always have his last note, letting her know he'd cared.

There it was again. The word *care.*

He stood and looked again at Zoe. Why was it that these last few days he thought more about Lisa than he had in the last year? Mentally, he tagged that one on to his personal list of questions, and then he left the room.

"Get that thing out of here!"

Tyler looked up from Lucky stretched out on his desk, his orange tail sweeping back and forth across his desk, to Austin standing in the doorway. Zoe was still sleeping when he went in to check on her for about the tenth time. This last time she had shifted slightly, and he spotted his phone tucked under the pillow. He'd almost tried to retrieve it, afraid someone might call, but at the last minute, he decided not to chance waking her up.

"He's just sitting here." Tyler looked to see the time: seven fifty-five. At eight on the dot, he was calling the Texas Department of State Health Services to see if Zoe's birth certificate was legit. His gut told him it wasn't, that the Adamses had someone make them up a fake certificate. Though he hadn't figured out why they would have done any of this. Did good people kidnap kids and then love them?

The whole thing was a puzzle, and he was itching to solve it—mostly for Zoe's peace of mind. And as soon as he proved the certificate was a forgery, he planned on giving Rick Clark a call and see about him getting him a little DNA from the old man.

Austin cleared his throat and motioned to the cat.

"He's not hurting anyone," Tyler said.

"It hurts me to look at him. She should at least buy him an eye patch."

Tyler frowned and eyed the time again. He'd already called Mr. Logan at Lab Inc. for some info. Unless Rick could actually get old man Bradford to open his lips and let him stick a swab in his mouth, any other retrieved item like a toothbrush was going to take a week.

"You're seriously not going to get rid of him?" Austin asked.

Tyler looked up. "You're seriously that afraid of a little cat?"

Austin laughed. "You're in a bad mood, which means you didn't get lucky."

Tyler reached for the phone. "Kicking someone's ass almost always helps my mood. Would you like to volunteer?"

"Where is she?" Austin looked down the hall as if he was half considering going to see her.

Tyler set the phone down. "She's still sleeping." He eyed Austin with a warning. It didn't matter that she'd shot Tyler's romantic attempt down. He wouldn't stand by and watch Austin try to make Zoe another notch on his bedpost. And the fact that Tyler saw that as so immoral, when it had been the same thing he'd wanted to do last night, sat on his conscience like a two-ton gorilla. Maybe he was a womanizer.

"You really are in a bad mood," Austin said.

"I need to make a call, so sit down and shut up."

Austin moved into the room...cautiously. "Fine, but I swear if that cats attacks me, I'll take off the tip of his other ear." He patted his gun under his shirt.

Tyler picked up the phone and dialed. Thanks to Pablo, his cousin with the Highway Patrol, he had the name and direct number. One of the investigative clerks had done some checking for him on a case a couple of months ago.

"Hi, Bee. It's Tyler Lopez, Pablo's cousin."

"You know, I could get in trouble doing this, right?" she asked.

"Yeah, but it's an easy one. Just need to verify a birth certificate."

"Give me just a minute," she said. "I just walked in. Let me pull up my T.E.R. program." Clicking of the keyboard filled the line. "Name and a date?"

"Zoe Adams. February twenty-sixth, eighty-four."

"Good year," she said. "My daughter was born then. What you got going, a fraud case?"

"Something like that." He held his breath and waited for her to say the record wasn't there. That there wasn't a Zoe Adams. Because why else would someone be taking potshots at her? What were the odds of her really looking that much like Nancy Bradford...

"Okay," she said. "Just one more button and we'll know if Zoe Adams even exists."

CHAPTER SEVENTEEN

"BORN AT SIX TEN A.M. in Shadows County at Main Street Hospital," Bee said.

"Are you sure?" Tyler asked.

"I'm reading it to you, aren't I?"

"And it's not tagged with a deceased flag?"

"Nope. But I'll cross-match it with my expired list."

"Thanks." Tyler picked up the pencil.

"What's wrong?" Austin asked.

Tyler held up one finger.

"Okay . . ." Bee said a second later. "There's no deceased record on a Zoe Adams. Miss Adams is still alive and kicking. Not that it means whoever you got claiming to be Zoe Adams is telling the truth. People will use anyone's name and Social Security."

Yeah, but it told him the most important thing. Namely, that a Zoe Adams had been born. Tyler said his thanks and hung up, feeling more confused than ever.

"Now are you going to tell me?" Austin asked.

He filled Austin in.

"So you think she's lying to you?"

"No," he said. "She's telling the truth. She was raised as Zoe Adams."

"Then maybe she *is* Zoe Adams," Austin said.

"No. She looks just like Nancy Bradford. And someone has attempted to kill her or at least try to run her off. There's a story here; I'm just not sure what it is."

His thoughts ran around in his head. To focus, he picked up his pad and flipped back a few pages to the questions he'd written about the case. One question stood out: "If Caroline Bradford was still alive, whose body was it that they found?"

"Shit. Maybe it was Zoe Adams's body that was found and mistaken for Caroline Bradford. Maybe something happened to her and the Adamses were either trying to cover up a murder or just wanted to replace her."

"Are they about the same age?" Austin asked.

Tyler pushed his papers back and went onto the computer to find the article on Caroline Bradford. "Caroline was nine months younger than Zoe. But they might have been the same size."

"Hey..." A female voice called from the doorway.

Tyler looked up, thinking it was Zoe, his gut tightened. He didn't know how to tell her about his discovery, but it wasn't her.

Ellen, the new receptionist, walked in looking a bit out of place. "I'm here and ready to work." Her gaze went to Lucky. The cat was still stretched out on Tyler's desk, appearing a little cautious of the new person in the room. Ellen's eyes widened.

"Oh, my," she said.

"See," Austin said. "I told you that thing was ugly."

* * *

The buzzing noise startled Zoe from a deep sleep. She shot up on the sofa, heart racing. The phone, Tyler's phone, went sailing to the floor.

"Hello?" came a feminine voice from the phone.

Zoe blinked. Did she accidentally answer the phone when she sent it sailing? She bent down and looked at the fancy piece of equipment.

She'd barely managed to find the books on the thing last night. His latest downloads on the psychology and social culture of Interpersonal Attraction had kept her up until almost four this morning. And much to her dismay, she concluded that she was the perfect case study of someone hot on the heels of some man.

"Tyler?" the voice asked.

"Shit." She had hit the Answer button. Still not fully awake, she grabbed the phone, looking for the Off button.

"Shit, what?" the voice came again.

"Shit," Zoe repeated, her voice hoarse from sleep, and she put the phone to her ear. "I'm sorry, I'll get... Tyler."

She jumped up and went down the hall and tapped on the bedroom door. "Tyler?"

"Hey, some Chica answered Tyler's phone," the voice on the line said, but Zoe knew she wasn't talking to her now.

"Who is this?" the voice on the phone asked, and this time she *was* talking to Zoe.

"No one." It sounded lame, but give her a break. She was still half-asleep.

"Hi, No One. My name is Sam. I'm Tyler's twin. Did you find Tyler?"

"Uh, I'm trying." She tapped on the door harder, and

when no one answered, she inched open the door. "He's not in bed," Zoe said, and realized how that sounded the moment she said it—which was a moment before Tyler's sister Sam yelled out, "He's sleeping with her."

"I'm not sleeping with him." Even to her ears it sounded like a lie.

Zoe shot back down the hall, her face hot from embarrassment.

"Did you check under the covers?" Sam chuckled.

"I'm not sleeping with him," Zoe repeated.

"Why not?" Sam asked.

"Because..."

"Are you married?" she asked.

"Yes," she said, thinking it was the easiest way to end this conversation. They'd think she was married and know she wasn't...

"He's sleeping with a married woman," Sam yelled.

"No," Zoe said. "He's not. I'm not—"

"Is this Lisa?" Sam asked.

"No." Zoe continued down the hall, stopping at the pink sofa.

"It sounds like Lisa," Sam yelled out, and Zoe heard all sorts of voices making comments in the background. Whoever this Lisa was, Tyler's family apparently didn't like her that much.

"I'm not Lisa." Zoe saw the cup and the note on the coffee table. She picked up the note.

The words, "Sorry I upset you," were underlined, and there were even a couple of Xs and Os beside the letter *T*. She got an achy feeling in her chest.

"You sound like Lisa," Sam said.

"I'm Zoe."

"Her name is Zoe," Sam yelled out, and then said, "My sister wants to talk to you."

"No," Zoe said, but it was too late.

"Hey, I'm Lola. Tyler's older sister. Is this Lisa?"

"No." Zoe grabbed the door and took off down the hall that led to the office.

"What are your intentions with my brother?" Lola asked.

"I don't have any intentions." Zoe walked into the office.

"So, you're just using him for his body, huh?" Lola chuckled.

Tyler looked up from his desk. His eyes went wide. "Hey."

He stood up, looking confused and apologetic. Probably about last night, she decided. But she hadn't had her coffee yet and didn't know if she was still mad at him or not. Just in case, she kept her expression neutral.

Before he could say anything else, she handed him his phone. "It's your sisters. They think we're sleeping together. They asked if I was married and I lied, I don't know why, it just popped out. Now they think I'm Lisa. And now they want to know what my intentions are with you. Can you clear that up?"

Tyler gaped at the phone. A male chuckle came from across the room. Zoe looked over at Austin, whom she'd met briefly yesterday afternoon when he popped in while she gave Tyler a lap dance. He was at his desk, laughing. Then she spotted Ellen, the receptionist, standing at the file cabinet in the back, also laughing. Zoe offered them one quick nod and then hotfooted it away.

"I'm sorry," Tyler said when he walked into the apartment three minutes later. He found Zoe in the kitchen pushing buttons on the microwave. No doubt attempting to heat the coffee.

"I can't figure out how to get this friggin' machine to work." She turned around frowning.

No anger in her blue eyes, but he said it again just in case. "I'm sorry."

"It's fine. I told you I overreacted. Let's forget it."

"I was talking about my sisters, but... I'm sorry about that, too. And like you've already established, I suck at apologies, so I'll just shut up now."

She pushed a hand through her hair. "I shouldn't have answered your phone. Well, I didn't really answer it. It woke me up, and the phone fell and must have hit the On button. I said something and they heard me and the next thing I know we're... having some insane conversation."

"It's not you, believe me. It's them. I told you they're crazy. At least sixty percent of all conversations with them are like that."

She looked back at the microwave. "Do you know how to work this thing?"

"Yeah, but the coffee's old by now. Let me grab you a fresh cup." He took off to the office and grabbed two cups and a plate with four donuts from the box Austin had gone after. Ellen and Austin were still laughing about Zoe and the phone call when he went back in, but he ignored them.

When Tyler came back to the apartment door, Lucky was standing there, meowing to get to Zoe. They walked in together. The sofa in the living room was empty. The tiny table in the adjoining dining room nook was empty. Tyler moved to the kitchen, thinking she'd be there, but nope. She'd disappeared. His gut started to panic, then he heard the bathroom sink running. He set the coffees on the coffee table and emptied his pockets of creamers and sugars next to the cups. Dropping on the sofa, he waited for her to come out.

He ran his fingers through his hair. He was going to have to tell her the news and his suspicions. It was bad enough to think the people who raised you kidnapped you, but to think they could have killed their own daughter, well that was tough to swallow.

He actually contemplated not telling her and then decided he had to.

She walked out of the bathroom and stopped when she saw him. She'd put her hair up, and he got a whiff of toothpaste.

"I brought coffee and donuts."

"Thanks."

She moved around to the chair as if she was afraid he'd try something. But how could he after she'd put him in his place like she had last night? He picked up his coffee and added a couple of creamers.

It was probably the Xs and Os he'd added to the note. He wasn't sure why he'd done it, but on one of the last trips he'd made to check on her, he'd remembered Lisa liking it, and before he'd thought it through... he'd scribbled them down on the note. And now regretted it.

He pushed the plate of donuts and the coffee over to her side of the coffee table.

She picked a creamer and added it to her coffee, gave it a couple of stirs, and then brought the cup to her lips. "Thanks."

"Eat." He motioned to the plate.

She picked up the chocolate-glazed and took a bite

out of it. A smear of icing was left on her bottom lip. He watched her tongue dip out to catch the sweetness. He remembered kissing her, and how she'd brushed her tongue over his. Hell, maybe it was a good idea that she'd sat in the chair.

"Have you called about the birth certificate yet?" she asked.

He set his coffee down and folded his hands between his knees. "Yeah."

He must have let something leak out in his tone because she leaned forward.

"And?" She set the donut down.

"The birth certificate is real."

Her face fell. "It can't be. I mean, I look just like Nancy Bradford and... and my memories. And—"

"I'm not saying you're Zoe Adams. I'm saying there is—or was—a Zoe Adams."

She shook her head. "But I don't understand." She set her coffee down beside the donut. "If they had their own kid, why would they have... You said *was*? Can't you check for death records?"

"I did," he said. "There was never a death filed."

"But there has to be. I mean..."

He gripped his hands together; he wasn't looking forward to saying this. "I'm just guessing here, but the body of the girl they thought was you... It could have been the real Zoe Adams."

She looked at him. "You think something happened to Zoe Adams and that's why... why they kidnapped me. To replace her."

Hurt sounded in her voice. "I'm saying it's a possibility."

She shook her head. "But I read that... that the body

was... burned and..." Tears filled her eyes, and Tyler had to force himself not to go to her and pull her into his arms.

"It doesn't mean they killed her." But it was hard-pressed not to believe it.

She shook her head. "They couldn't have. They could never have hurt a child. They never even spanked me. And there were times I deserved it."

But they hurt you, Tyler thought. Her "parents" had kidnapped her and kept secrets from her all her life. And right this moment Tyler wished he could get a pass to hell—because that's where he knew they were right now—to kick their asses. She didn't deserve to have to go through this.

"If we can prove that you are Caroline Bradford, I'm sure they will exhume the body."

She stared at the coffee cup. He saw a tear slip from her lashes to the cup.

"I want to take a shower." She popped up and so did Tyler.

Before she could walk away, he caught her arm. He just wanted to touch her, to let her know he cared. "Are you going to be okay?"

"I'm fine."

He expected her to pull away, but instead she fell against him. Her head pressed into the side of his shoulder. He debated putting his arms around her, and then, without giving it another thought, he did just that. He wrapped his arms around her, hoping he'd managed to do it in a totally nonsexual way.

He felt her reach up and take handfuls of his shirt in her fists, and she let go of a painful sob. "I know my parents kept secrets from me. I know they lied to me. I've accepted that. But they couldn't have killed their own child, Tyler. They just couldn't have."

He tightened his arms around her and held her against him.

CHAPTER EIGHTEEN

WHEN TYLER WALKED back into the office, Dallas was there, going over a few things with Ellen. Bud, Dallas's dog, was sniffing Ellen's leg. Tyler remembered Lucky and panicked for a second, then remembered seeing the cat in the leather chair in the apartment.

Everyone in the room looked at him.

Dallas smiled sheepishly, and Tyler knew he'd been told about his sisters' call. Problem was, Tyler wasn't in the mood to laugh about anything right now.

"I want answers, damn it," he started barking.

"But I thought..." Dallas hesitated. "Wasn't the birth certificate—"

"I don't give a rat's ass what they said. Zoe didn't make this shit up. Someone shot at her. There has to be a reason for that, and I don't think it's the lunch specials down at the diner. And right now the only thing that makes sense is that she's somehow tied to the Bradfords."

Dallas frowned. "But—"

"Did we question you when you believed Nikki was

innocent even after her ex ended up dead in her trunk after she told people she was going to kill him?"

Dallas's eyebrows shot up. He held out his hand. "I didn't realize that was what's going on."

Tyler didn't know exactly what Dallas implied, but he knew if he gave it some thought, he probably wouldn't like it. So he didn't think about it. At this point in time, he didn't care. He just wanted his partners behind him on this. He needed them.

It felt so damn right to have her believe in him at the station yesterday, and he was going to believe in her. She wanted answers, and by God, he was going to get them.

"Fine," Dallas said. "What do you want us to do?"

"Help me get to the bottom of this." Tyler's emotions and mind were running all over the place, and he couldn't seem to catch up with them.

Dallas held out his hand. "Where's your list of questions?"

Tyler went to his desk, picked up his pad, and dropped down in his chair.

"Read your questions," Dallas said, and went to his own desk.

Austin rolled his chair a little closer. Tyler looked down at the questions.

Why did making Zoe laugh feel so damn good?

Why was he thinking so damn much about Lisa?

Why had he written Xs and Os on the note, when his gut had told him not to?

All of a sudden, he added another question to the list. *Why after all the lessons he'd learned about caring too much from his dad, from Lisa, and from the police force, was he tempted to let down his guard with Zoe?*

The last question bothered him most of all. This was supposed to be just another case. Besides, she wasn't even going to stay here when the case was over.

"I think Dallas meant to read them aloud," Austin said, being a smartass.

Tyler scowled at Austin and then flipped the page to the list of questions involving the case. "Who was the dead girl they thought was Caroline Bradford?"

"Okay," Dallas said. "Let's start there. Since you're the best at researching on the Internet, why don't you go and find any missing children cases about that time? Also see what you can dig up on the Adams family and their daughter Zoe while they were in Texas. See if they have any connection to the Bradfords."

Tyler was usually the one referring the questions and giving advice on who should do what. What was it about this case that made him so crazy? The answer shot back. Zoe.

"What's the next question?" Dallas asked.

Tyler looked back at the list. "Why would Mildred and Ralph Adams kidnap a kid? Especially one so high profile if they didn't intend to get a ransom for her."

"You gave one possible answer to that earlier," Austin said. "If they murdered their own kid, they may have needed a replacement for her or they'd have gotten caught."

Tyler leaned back in his chair, which produced a loud groan of springs. He felt the sentiment echo in his chest. "Zoe doesn't believe they could have hurt a kid."

"So she wasn't abused in any way?" Ellen asked from the back of the room.

Tyler had forgotten she was there. So, it seemed, had Austin and Dallas. They all looked back at her at the same time. But her question ran around Tyler's head. Physically hurting a kid was only one type of abuse. His dad had managed to hurt his kids without ever raising a fist to them. Not that his mom had been so lucky.

"Uh, I'm sorry," Ellen said, obviously thinking she'd done something wrong. "I guess you just want me to file and keep my mouth shut. It'll be hard, but I can do that."

"No," Dallas said. "You're welcome to toss out ideas. This is how we work, put our heads together and come up with answers or at least leads to follow. However, this office is like Vegas—what happens here stays here."

"I pretty much figured that out all on my own."

"Ahh, good looking and smart," Austin said in his come-on tone, and he winked at Ellen.

"Thank you," she said in such a nonflirting manner that the message, "Not interested," was tacked onto the line loud and clear. Tyler even saw the look of surprise on Austin's face. And when Dallas turned away, a smile was pasted on his lips.

Tyler picked up a pencil. "I asked Zoe if they'd ever mistreated her. She insists they were never anything but upstanding parents."

Austin leaned his elbows on his knees. "It could have been an accident and they were afraid it might look intentional."

"That, and some kids block out the abuse," Ellen said. "Or they just don't want to talk about it."

"I know," Tyler said. There were a hell of a lot of things he preferred not to talk about. "But I don't think that's the case here."

"You're probably right," Dallas said. "But maybe she

might be more apt to tell another woman. Maybe Ellen could talk to her and just see if she gets anything."

"She talks to me," Tyler said, insulted they thought Zoe wouldn't tell him something. But then he remembered his sisters sharing things with each other before they came to one of their male siblings. "But I don't see how it would hurt," he amended.

He looked back at Austin. "But the whole accident angle... I don't think so. It just doesn't seem logical that they would go as far as kidnapping a high-profile child. Or any child to cover up an accident. Law-abiding citizens don't usually commit a crime without some serious motivation." He paused and realized an error in his thinking.

"But maybe they weren't law abiding," he said. "Maybe they were good parents but bad people. I need to get all the information I can on the Adamses."

"I'll take that one," Dallas said. "What county was Zoe Adams born in? I'll start looking there first. Maybe I can ask Tony or Rick to run a check and see if they were in any trouble with the law."

"Shadows County."

"Do we know who the officer was that headed the kidnapping case?" Austin asked.

"I have that." Tyler started looking through his notes. "A John Phillips. I read he retired shortly after the case went cold. If he's still alive, he'd be in his eighties now."

I'll see if I can run him down," Austin said. "If he's still breathing, maybe we can get something from him."

"Good idea." Bud came over and started sniffing on Tyler's leg where Lucky had rubbed against him. "Is Bud cat-friendly?" Tyler asked Dallas.

"The lady I got him from when he was a puppy had cats, but I don't think he's been around them since."

"Maybe we'll get lucky and he'll finish the poor thing off," Austin added.

Dallas looked at Tyler. "Is something wrong with the cat?"

"He was in an accident, but he's fine."

"He lost more parts than he kept," Austin said.

"He's fine." Tyler defended Zoe's cat. "But we should keep them apart." He refocused on the notes and started making a game plan for the day. And first on that list was stopping himself from making more out of this thing with Zoe than there was. He was a PI and she was a client. He had an obligation to solve her case.

Dallas's chair squeaked when he leaned back and cupped his hands behind his head. "Now that we all have our jobs on this case, how are we on the Drake and Smith cases?"

Tyler started to say he didn't give a damn about them but caught himself. They still had a business to run, so he dug through the files on his desk to find his written questions on those cases. Then he opened the computer to his case files where he'd started inputting the data electronically.

They discussed the two other cases: one a cheating spouse case and the other a missing person case. After a short discussion, Tyler assigned something for all of them to run down. Because Tyler wanted to stay close to Zoe, he agreed to do the Internet searches on the two cases. Austin was going to take over following Mr. Drake to see if his lunches with his secretary involved more than lunch. Last Friday, Tyler had done the honors, and it had been as boring as watching snails race. Dallas was going to visit the two clients and give them updates.

"Have we heard from Roberto yet?" Dallas asked.

"He's been calling in every Monday, but I haven't heard from him yet today. Which is odd." Tyler looked at the clock. "Usually he calls at eight o'clock on the dot."

Roberto Campo was their biggest informant, working the streets to get information on Rafael DeLuna, the low-life drug dealer who'd been responsible for framing the detectives for murder. Since the Feds had finally put the man on their wanted list, he'd slithered under some big rock. Although Tyler and the guys had managed to shut down several of his operations in the Houston area, all the leads had gone cold. Now they had Roberto looking into things in Dallas. Roberto hadn't found anything in Big D yet. *Yet* being the key word.

Dallas looked back at Ellen. "If a Roberto Campo calls in, you make sure he speaks to one of us."

"Roberto Campo," she repeated. "I got it."

"Have you given her all our info, cell numbers, home numbers?" Dallas asked Tyler.

"Not yet." Tyler looked up from rereading his list of questions. "But I finished the list on Friday, so I'll give it to her."

"Good." Dallas looked back at Ellen. "We have a desk, computer, and phone that's being delivered for you. Tyler will help you get the computer up and going."

"It may take a while to get everything set up," Tyler said, wanting to focus on Zoe's case.

Ellen looked down at the stacks of files around her feet and then up at the metal filing cabinets lining the back of the room. "I think I have plenty to keep me busy for a few days."

"My plan is to set you up in the entrance room," Dallas said. "We might have to lose the casket."

"Darn," Ellen said. "I was hoping to keep the casket. Makes for a good conversation piece."

"It makes a good doggy bed, too." Dallas patted Bud resting at his master's feet. Maybe we can just move things around. We'll see."

"I was joking," Ellen said.

"Yeah, but you're right," Dallas said. "It's sort of become our trademark. The other day I got a call from someone who wanted to know if we were the PIs who had the casket in their office. Hey, it's a gimmick, but if it works..."

Tyler leaned back in his chair again, only half listening to the conversation around him. When there was a pause, he spoke. "I'm getting with Rick and have him work on getting some DNA samples from Bradford."

"You don't want to wait and see what we get first?" Dallas asked.

"No, I don't want to wait," Tyler said matter-of-factly. "I want to get answers and put this case to bed."

"I don't think that's all you want to put to bed," Austin muttered, and shot him a shit-eating grin.

"Drop the wisecracks," Tyler snapped.

Austin glanced at Dallas. "See, I told you he was in a piss-poor, didn't-get-any mood."

Dallas wadded up a piece of paper and tossed it at Austin. "Now might not be the time to mess with him." But there was humor in Dallas's voice, too.

Tyler's phone rang. He checked caller ID and frowned. His older sister again. He'd told her that Zoe was someone he was working with on a case, but he knew his sister thought he was holding back. And her way of getting people to talk was to hound them to death.

She was good at it, too. He stood to go take the phone call in the conference room. Then he stopped and looked back at Ellen. "Can you do me a favor? Call Rick—his cell number is in my Contacts folder—and ask him if he can swing by if he gets a chance."

"Rick Clark?" she asked with some hesitancy he didn't quite understand.

He nodded and walked out to deal with the first hounding session by his sister.

Ellen sat down at Tyler's desk and accessed his electronic address book to find Rick's number. Her stomach fluttered at the thought of calling him. But she'd already told herself that she just needed to pull up her big girl panties and grow a pair. Well, she couldn't grow a pair, but she needed to just get over it. She worked here. Rick Clark was going to be in and out, and she'd have to deal with him.

She found his number and punched it in the phone. It rang once, twice. Maybe she'd get lucky and he wouldn't—

"Hey, how are they hanging?" His deep male voice flowed from the phone.

"Uh, they're not." She almost smiled, especially after having just told herself she needed to grow a pair.

"Sorry. I thought... Who is this?"

"Ellen Wise," she said.

"Usually it's Tyler who calls from there."

"I figured that." Ellen picked up a pencil. "I was just calling to—"

"To tell me you kicked the other guy to the curb and now you want to take me up on my dinner invitation," he said.

"No."

"A man can hope." He chuckled. "So you need for me to change another tire for you?" he teased.

"I don't think so," she said, and laughed.

"Right, but can I call you if I have transmission problems?"

"I'll give you the name of my dad's shop."

"Ouch," he said. "So what do you need Ellen I-can-roar Wise?"

She laughed again. What did she need? Suddenly, all sorts of erotic things ran through her mind, and her cheeks brightened. "*I* don't need anything."

"Damn, you really know how to hurt a man," he said.

She suddenly realized how much fun she was having talking to him. "Tyler—"

"What's this guy's name, anyway?"

"What guy?" she asked.

"The boyfriend."

She chewed on the question, and for the life of her she couldn't think of one man's name. Then she recalled the joke she'd told Nikki and LeAnn yesterday. "Bob," aka her battery-operated boyfriend.

"I already don't like him," Rick said.

"Tyler asked me to call you. He wants you to come by if you can today."

"I'm on duty today, but I have to run out after awhile. I'll stop by then."

"Fine. I'll tell Tyler. Bye." She started to hang up.

"Ellen?"

She bit down on her lip and put the phone back to her ear. "Yes?"

"I enjoyed talking to you," he said.

"Yeah. Me, too." And this time, she hung up faster and felt a tightening low in her belly, the one that usually happened with a certain type of wanting. Time to bring out Bob again.

She sat there, frowning at the phone. How could the man affect her just by talking?

"Everything okay?" A male voice piped up.

She looked over and saw both Dallas and Austin studying her. She'd forgotten they were in the room. She started going through everything she said and hoped it hadn't been anything too ridiculous.

"It's fine." She dropped the pencil. "He's working but will be out on errands and will stop by then."

"Good." Dallas continued to look at her as if they'd read every naughty and private thought that had swirled around her brain. "Did he say anything inappropriate?"

"No," she said... a little too loud.

"You sure? Because you're a really nice shade of pink right now."

She decided to rely on an old shut-a-man-up trick she'd learned in her serious dating years. "Oh, that's... hormones. Monthly cycle stuff that you don't want to know about."

"Okay then," Dallas said, and both men immediately commenced to working on their computers.

Good to know it still worked.

But still feeling antsy, Ellen popped up from Tyler's chair, shot to the back of the room, and commenced her filing. She picked up her first file and then mentally reached down, grabbed ahold of the elastic waistband of her big girl panties, and yanked them up to her chin.

By the time Tyler answered his phone, Lola had hung up. He debated not calling her back, then decided there would just be more hell to pay. So he popped into the conference room, sat down, and mentally prepared himself to be interrogated by one of the best.

"Hey, you called." He settled back in the chair.

"And *you* didn't answer."

He sighed. "I did answer, but you had already hung up."

"What, you too busy with Zoe to answer your phone?" There was a teasing tone to her voice, but he knew she was serious about pushing for information.

"I'm at work, Lola," he said, hoping to cut her off.

"Is she married?"

So much for that plan. "No, she's not married."

"Are you going to introduce us to her?"

"It's not like that."

"So you're just fucking her?"

He flinched at hearing his sister talk like that, then he flinched because while it had been different words, it was the same thing Zoe had accused him of wanting to do. "*Dios mio!* When did you start talking like that?"

"Since it seems to be your nephew's favorite word."

"Well, wash his mouth out with soap, the way Mom did us."

"I have," she said. "Today's soap must not taste as bad. He just keeps on doing it."

Lola's husband Roger was in the Marines and deployed overseas, which didn't give Roger Junior a strong male influence. "I'll talk to him," Tyler said.

"Thanks. But, I didn't call you to complain about my boy's potty mouth."

"I'm not sleeping with her," he ground out.

"Well, now, I'm curious about why you're not sleeping with her, but I didn't call you about your sex life, either." She sighed. "We got family problems. And I happened to find out you knew about them and didn't tell the rest of us the secret."

He knew immediately that she was talking about Sam, her black eye, and her asshole of a husband. "It wasn't my place to tell. And I took care of it." He looked down at his fist. It still was a little sore.

"You think just because you break the idiot's nose he's going to straighten out? It doesn't work that way. People don't always do what they're supposed to do."

"I know, which is why Sam should do what she needs to do."

"She's not you, Tyler. She listens to her heart, not her head."

"And her damn heart is getting her hurt over and over again!" Anger filled his chest. He stood up. "Did he lay another hand on her? I talked to her last night and she said everything was okay. I swear to God—"

"No, he hasn't hit her again. Not yet. But she said he went out drinking last night, and when he got home, he was combative. She's scared of him, Tyler."

"Shit! Tell her to leave his ass!"

"I wish it was that easy," Lola said. "She claims she still loves him. She had his baby, Tyler. And not only that, but the house is his. I told her she could live here, but she says with her, Anna, and the baby, it would be too crowded. She's right."

"I'll get her an apartment," he said. "Hell, I can call someone and rent one right now."

"She's not willing to leave him yet. She agreed to talk to him about therapy. She promised me that if he says no, she'll leave. So I'm just giving you the heads-up. Unlike what you did with me."

"Thanks," he said, and ignored her last dig.

"You're welcome. And bring Zoe over. We want to meet her. Maybe we can talk her into sleeping with you."

He rolled his eyes. "Don't do this."

"Do what?" she asked.

"Make more out of this than it is. She's a client."

"She's a woman and you're a man."

"Nothing is happening," he ground out.

"Why not?"

Because she doesn't want it to happen. "Because it doesn't make sense."

"Not everything has to make sense."

"It does to me," Tyler said.

"Dios!" she muttered. "Sometimes you just have to follow your heart."

"Like Sam? Because it's working out so well for her."

Lola let go of a groan. "Sure, she's made mistakes. But you're just as bad off as she is. Not everything is logical, Tyler. You're so smart, you try to analyze everything. But emotions can't be analyzed."

Which is why I try to stay away from them. "Bye, Sis." He shut off the phone and sat there for a good five minutes, trying to get his fury in check, both at Lola for her judgment of him but mostly at the thought of what Sam was going through. Was his sister destined to repeat their mother's mistakes over and over again? How could Sam be so blind? Hell, after several bad relationships and then her failed marriage, he'd even shown her the statistical data. Kids who grew up in the type of home they did were pretty much destined to repeat the same mistakes. And when Sam and he had been at the age where they were most impressionable, his parents' relationship went from bad to worse.

Sure, Tyler had still let himself try it. He handed over his heart on a silver platter to Lisa. She handed it back to him shredded in a hundred pieces.

He wouldn't make that mistake again. Letting people get too close could end badly. Especially when you were already a statistic waiting to happen. What the hell was it going to take for Sam to pull her head out of the emotional quicksand?

CHAPTER NINETEEN

As Ellen moved to the apartment door, balancing two cups of coffee in one hand, about to knock, Tyler walked out of the conference room. His gaze locked on hers.

"I thought I'd go chat with Zoe," Ellen said.

Tyler nodded. "Don't let the cat out. And don't push her too hard. She's had a rough few days. Seriously."

"I won't." Ellen remembered LeAnn saying Tyler had feelings for Zoe. The caring look in his eyes told Ellen they'd hit a bull's-eye on that one.

She knocked on the door and heard Zoe call out for her to come in. Ellen walked in and saw Zoe sitting on the sofa, her legs crossed underneath her with the television remote control in her hands. The TV was on, but she had placed it on mute.

"I thought you could use another cup of coffee," Ellen said.

"Yes!" Zoe met her halfway across the room and took one of the coffees. "I was about to go try to heat up the cold cup in the microwave."

"You should have just come in the office and gotten one."

Zoe shrugged. "After my last entrance, I wasn't sure I could top it."

Ellen laughed. She liked Zoe's honesty and her willingness to see the humor in things instead of getting angry. Ellen motioned to the sofa. "Do you mind? I've had just about as much testosterone as I can take for one morning."

"Please. I could use some company. *Judge Judy* reruns can only hold my interest for so long." Zoe joined Ellen on the sofa. "Nikki mentioned that this is your first day on the job?" Zoe said.

"Yeah," Ellen said. "And I'm wondering what I got myself into."

"They seem like nice guys," Zoe said. "Well, I really only know Tyler, but they seemed okay."

"They are," Ellen said. "Dallas is great to Nikki. But being in the room with three men at the same time is overkill. Seriously, there are clouds of testosterone floating above their heads."

"So you're not married?" Zoe asked with a chuckle.

Her laugh was honest and genuine. Ellen could understand why Tyler was so taken with her.

"Nah," Ellen answered. "Just me and my daughter. I like it that way, too." And she did, she told herself. Ultimately, it was her decision to stay single. If she met someone who really tempted her, she might reconsider. The thought hadn't cleared her head, when a vision of Rick took over. She pushed it away.

"How old is your daughter?" Zoe pulled her cup a little closer.

"Five, going on twenty." Ellen sipped her coffee. "She constantly amazes me."

"Oh, I love that age. I teach kindergarten. They are so

bright-eyed and bushy-tailed at five. Full of energy and a hunger for knowledge."

"She's a handful. But I found my true calling when I became a mom. Nothing I've ever done in my life felt so right." Ellen grinned. "You want kids?"

Zoe didn't hesitate. "Yeah, someday."

"You're from Alabama, right?"

"Yeah," Zoe said.

"Nobody special back home?" Ellen asked, easing into a more personal conversation. Considering she was a bit of a private person, she knew to tread cautiously.

The smile left Zoe's eyes. "I thought I was on the path to marriage and kids. But he had a change of heart."

"Cold feet?" Ellen hoped she wasn't being too pushy. "I mean, if you don't mind talking about it."

"No, it's fine," Zoe said. "But it wasn't so much cold feet. More like a stripper named Darlene." She chuckled, which told Ellen that Zoe was mostly over the pain. Ellen couldn't help but wonder if there'd be a day she could joke about her troubles with Noel.

"I hate it when that happens." Ellen grinned.

"Not this time." Zoe made a face. "I guess Darlene did me a favor. Better now than after we were married and I had a kid." Zoe's expression tightened. "I'm sorry, I didn't mean to imply that there's anything wrong with being a single parent."

"Don't worry," Ellen said. "Being a single parent wasn't my first choice, either. And it's not for the weak of heart. But my daughter's the light of my life. I wouldn't change a thing." And she wouldn't. Even dealing with Noel was worth having Britney snuggle up with her when they watched a Disney movie.

"You seem like you're doing well at it. Believe me, I see frazzled moms in my line of duty. They have this wired look in their eyes. You look okay."

"Thanks." Ellen decided to just plunge right in. "I heard about what's going on with you."

"You think I'm crazy?" Zoe asked.

Ellen could see the angst in Zoe's eyes and heard it in her voice. "No, I don't think that at all. I guess being a parent, my heart hurts thinking about a child having bad things happen to her."

Ellen noted that Zoe gripped her cup tighter. "Did they abuse you?" Ellen asked.

"Who?" She looked genuinely puzzled.

"The Adamses."

Zoe shook her head. "No." Her expression tightened. "Did Tyler send you to ask me questions?"

"No." Then Ellen decided to be honest. "It was Dallas. He said that maybe you might be more open to talking to another woman about these things." Ellen realized she'd omitted some of the facts. "He said that after I blurted out that sometimes people have a hard time talking about things like abuse." She met Zoe's eyes. "No one wants to admit to being a victim."

It didn't even matter if they were an adult, Ellen thought. She'd never told anyone but James about how Noel had completely fooled her.

"They didn't abuse me," Zoe said. "Not the Adamses."

Ellen's gaze locked with Zoe's. "But someone else did?"

"No. I mean, I don't remember. I only have short little snippets of early memories. A woman pushing me on a tire swing. Being read to by an older man in a room with books on all the shelves." She looked down at her cup. "Then there's the recurring nightmare I had for years. I don't know if it's real. Research says that recurring dreams might have bits of the truth in them, but they're not reliable. And even if they were, I never saw any of the faces of the people in the dream, and they didn't hurt me that I can remember. I was just scared."

"Have you told Tyler about the dreams?" Ellen asked.

"No. There's not much to tell. I'm locked in a closet, and I'm scared. I need to go to the bathroom, but I'm too afraid to ask."

Ellen bit down on her bottom lip. She could see Zoe's emotions. "Maybe you should tell him. It could help in some way that we might not think about."

Zoe nodded. "I will."

Ellen met Zoe's gaze. "I hope you're not upset with me for asking questions."

"No. I just...I've kept most of this to myself for so long, it's strange talking about it to someone."

"I know what you mean," Ellen said. "Some things are hard to share."

"You got your own demons?" Zoe asked, very observant.

"Don't we all?" Ellen said, trying to make light of it.

Ellen stood up. "Well, I'd best get back to work." She got all the way to the door before she looked back. "If *Judge Judy* really bores you, you can always come help me file."

Zoe smiled. "Seriously?" When Ellen nodded, Zoe's smile went wider. "I might just do that."

Rick had gone to interview a possible witness to a drive-by shooting, but unfortunately he hadn't been home.

So Rick headed to see Tyler instead, when he spotted a sign for a bookstore. It was the same one advertised on the bag Ellen had pulled out of the trunk of her car.

He took a sharp right into the parking lot.

Looking for the kiddy section, he found it by following the sound of kids' laughing. The shelves were lined with bright, colorful books. But what impressed him was the laughter. As he cut down another aisle, he saw a group of moms and kids, sitting in a circle.

The woman in the middle was reading to the kids. Her voice came out in high and low pitches. The kids sat mesmerized as she read from the book. Each time she read a different character's dialogue, she'd change her tone.

Rick tried to remember his mother ever reading to him, but he couldn't. Maybe moms didn't read to kids back then. He got a vision of Ellen reading to her little girl. He'd bet she was as good at reading aloud as the woman in the circle.

His gaze landed on a dark-haired little boy who was probably about the same age as Ricky. The boy stared in fascination. Rick's chest clutched, and he wondered if he'd ever get the chance to read to Ricky. He wanted that chance, damn it.

Moving closer to the group of kids, he listened.

"Can I help you?" a woman asked.

He looked down and saw a short, older woman staring up at him. She wore a T-shirt with the bookstore's emblem on it.

"No, I'm just watching." He looked back at the kids.

"Do you have a kid here?" She interrupted the best part of the story.

"No." He hardly looked at her, but he could feel her

looking at him. He finally glanced down. "Is something wrong?"

"Yeah," she said. "I don't...if you don't have a kid here, maybe you should go."

"Why?"

"It might make the moms uncomfortable," she said.

His brow wrinkled. "You think...Oh, hell. I'm just looking for a book," he ground out. Unfortunately, he said it a bit too loud, and several of the moms turned and looked his way with daggers in their eyes.

The salesclerk noticed, too. "If you don't leave, I'll call the cops."

"I am the cops." He snapped his badge off his belt and flashed it. "I was looking for a book for my kid."

She stared at his badge and blushed. "Oh, my. I'm... I'm sorry. I just—"

"Forget it. I'm out of here." He started walking toward the exit, and she followed.

"I'm sorry," she said. "We don't get a lot of daddies in here."

"Probably because you do the same thing to them as you did to me," he snarled.

"Please." She touched him on the arm. "Tell me what book you're looking for, and I'll find it and I'll give you a forty percent discount."

He almost continued on, but at the last moment, he decided he wanted the book more than he wanted to prove a point. Plus, if he considered the clerk's point of view, he supposed it could have looked strange. Why the hell did being a father have to be so damn hard?

He gave her the name of the book Ellen had recommended.

"That's a good one," the clerk said. "My grandson loved it."

Before he left, the clerk had sold him on three more books. When he got in his car, he debated if he wanted to mail the books to Ricky or wait until he saw him. If Candy didn't pull anything, he was supposed to go down in two weeks. He saw a vision of Ricky in his mind and smiled.

Maybe when he was there, he might try reading one of the books to his son. Though he wasn't so sure he could pull off the silly voices that the woman did. But he could try. The thought of making his son laugh sent a yearning to his gut.

He hadn't gotten his car started when his phone rang. "Candy again."

The temptation to answer it was great. He wanted to tell her he'd bought Ricky some books. He wanted to hear something about his son. Was he into books? Did he still love to play with the cars he'd sent him for his last birthday?

He could hear Jeff, his friend and lawyer, telling him not to take the call. And he hadn't been answering them, but what if something was wrong? Hitting the On button, he put it to his ear.

"Hello, Candy." He tried to keep emotion from his voice.

"Hi, Rick," she said.

"Is Ricky okay?" he asked.

"Yeah, he's fine." She paused, as if trying to find the words to ask something. Something that probably involved money.

"Do you ever read to him?" he blurted out.

"What?" she asked.

He frowned. "Read. You know, children's stories. Like bedtime stories. Someone told me if you read to them, they'll probably start reading early." An image of that someone—aka Ellen Wise—filled his head.

"He's only four," Candy said.

"He's five," Rick snapped, and closed his eyes. "You don't even know how old our son is."

"I just forgot."

"That's not something a mother should forget."

"I didn't call to get bitched at. I was hoping you might help me out again."

Fuck! "What is it this time, Candy? Drugs or booze?"

"Neither, you bastard," she snapped. "It's expensive raising a kid."

He shook his head. "Then give him to me so I can raise him."

"You just don't want to pay child support."

"Goddamn it, woman. Have I missed one payment? No. And why not? Because he's my son. I care about him. And damn it, but maybe I'd just like to know he's being raised right, by someone who loves him."

Rick heard the line go dead. "Motherfucker!" He slammed his palm on the steering wheel.

Furious, he picked up his phone and dialed Jeff's number. When Jeff answered, Rick didn't hesitate. "You got one more week. If I don't have my son away from her by then, I'll get him myself. They can have me arrested for kidnapping. I don't give a damn anymore." His gut knotted, remembering that Candy didn't even know how old Ricky was.

"Calm down. I was just about to call you. I've got a court date. Two weeks. Hang on that long."

"I want full custody," Rick said, not wanting to think about what his son was dealing with by living with a mom who didn't care.

"We can ask, but we'll probably only get joint. You'd better start looking around for child care and stuff like that. The judge will ask how you plan to take care of him."

"Okay," Rick said.

And right then, it hit him. He didn't have a clue how to do this. And he didn't just mean finding child care. He didn't know how to be a father.

His gut turned rock hard. He gripped the steering wheel and then recognized the emotion. Fear.

What if he screwed up? What if his kid didn't like him?

"Fuck," he said aloud. He ran a hand over his mouth. He'd have to stop using that language. He'd have to learn to read books in crazy voices. He'd have to learn to make peanut butter sandwiches and probably macaroni and cheese, and how to cut the crust off bread.

Yeah, he remembered his mom doing that for his lunches.

Too bad she'd been dead for over ten years.

He needed help. And he needed help fast.

One person came to mind.

He needed Ellen Wise.

Ellen was almost to her car when Rick's Malibu pulled up.

She gave her sagging mental panties a yank and hurried to her car. If she was lucky, by the time she got back from picking up the takeout for everyone's lunch, he'd be gone.

"Hey." He jumped out of his car in a hurry.

She waved and hopped into her car. She had just got the car started when he tapped on her window. Frowning, she hit the button to lower the window.

"I was hoping I could talk to you a minute," he said.

Damn, damn! She really didn't want to have to tell him no again. "I'm sorry. I can't. Gotta go."

"Can I buy you a cup of coffee this afternoon?" he asked.

"I'm sorry. I've already told you, I'm not available. Let's not make this harder than it already is."

"But..."

She started backing up. When she looked in the rearview mirror, he stood there looking miserable. Her first instinct was to put on the brakes, turn around, and apologize. She couldn't. No matter how much she might be attracted to him, she didn't need the complications right now.

CHAPTER TWENTY

TYLER SAT DOWN on the sofa and waited for Zoe to get ready. In the back of his mind, he recalled the sound of her laughter as she'd worked with Ellen. And damn, but she had a pretty laugh. Like bells. Nice bells, musical bells. He heard the shower cut off and envisioned her reaching into the cabinet for a towel. Inhaling, he could almost smell her—shampoo, soft skin. Naked skin. He tried not to imagine what she'd look like naked and wet. And willing.

He wanted her willing.

He picked up the magazine she'd been reading last night, hoping he'd find something to mentally chew on besides Zoe naked. But nothing held a candle to Zoe. Closing his eyes, he leaned his head back and inwardly groaned.

She'd been cordial all day, even helped Ellen do the filing. He caught her several times studying him—but she'd turn away as soon as he caught her, as if trying to put up barriers. He could accept it. She wasn't into fun...temporary flings. And he wasn't into...getting hurt again.

He'd go so far as to say that putting up walls was probably for the best. He had his own walls, and should be able to respect hers. But he didn't have to like it.

There wasn't much he liked about today. Sam's issues bit into his sanity. He'd talked to her but couldn't mention the call from Lola. So, he'd listened to her lie about how things were great.

He loved Sam. Before she'd gotten married the first time, he'd felt closer to her than anyone else.

It wasn't the marriage that came between them, either. He wanted her to be happy; it was just so damn hard to watch her make stupid choices that later hurt her. It started with a bad boyfriend. Then her first husband had cheated on her several times while they were dating, and yet she'd still married the bastard. When Tyler tried to talk to her, she'd accused him of being jealous that she still believed in love and he didn't.

It wasn't that he didn't believe in love. It was that he was probably preconditioned to fail at it. And maybe so was Sam. Why couldn't Sam learn from her mistakes? He sure as hell didn't need to be kicked in the gut again to realize the errors of his ways—caring too much should come with a warning label. He had his circle of people he looked after. His family, his partners. The smaller one's circle was, the less likely one would be disappointed…or disappoint others.

As if worrying about Zoe and about Sam wasn't enough, Tyler spent all day researching missing kids on the Internet. Not fun. There were more than he cared to count in the time period that Caroline Bradford had gone missing. Yet none of them could have passed for a four-year-old girl.

After that hideous job was done, he decided to help Dallas search the Adamses. He came up with nothing. Zilch. The same thing Dallas got. He decided to call the State Licensing Board. Zoe had said her dad had worked in construction and her mom had been a teacher. Finding out where they worked or maybe where they lived might be a starting point.

The bored clerk willingly looked up the information as long as Tyler entertained her with conversation. He'd been very entertaining. Mildred Adams had no licenses or permits to her name in the state of Texas. Later, Zoe told him that her mom hadn't gone back to school until she was in kindergarten, when they lived in Alabama, which explained that. However, Ralph Adams didn't have a contractor license. The helpful lady did a cross match on other licenses. She found one Ralph Adams who held a cosmetology license, one with a nursing license, and one who was a licensed mortician. Zoe said her father had been a contractor all his life, so none of those fit. Or at least didn't seem to.

Rick Clark was going to try to get some DNA from old man Bradford, but Bradford had him working out of the guesthouse. So figuring a way to get the old man's toothbrush or some other personal item was going to be tricky.

Rick also agreed to see what he could find on Zoe's parents through the Miller PD resources. But due to a personal emergency, he was taking the day off.

Tomorrow Tyler would call the Social Security Administration and try to bypass the open record forms, which could take weeks to get clearance. He also planned to call the county appraisal offices in the counties surrounding Shadows County, where the real Zoe Adams was born, to see if a Ralph Adams had ever bought or sold any property in those jurisdictions.

Austin had run down John Phillips, the retired detective who'd worked the Bradford case. He was alive, but he'd gone on a cruise and wouldn't be back for two days. Adding to the day's frustration was that Roberto hadn't checked in. He'd done this before, gotten caught up in something and forgot to touch base, and the next time Tyler spoke with him, he was going to address it.

So basically, nothing had gone right today. He knew that most of the jobs they worked were like this. You put in hours of research and feel as if you're getting nowhere and then stumble over some other new tidbit that makes it all make sense. It took patience. And Tyler was fresh out. Or maybe what patience he had was being spent to keep him from hauling Zoe back on the sofa and convincing her two weeks was better than nothing.

The sound of the bathroom door opening had him changing mental gears. He sat up, hungry to see her.

"I'm almost ready," she called out. "Just a few more minutes. I know guys hate waiting."

"Take your time." He frowned.

She'd agreed to go to dinner, then to run to his place to get some things from his apartment.

Finally, he heard her walking down the hall. He picked up the magazine, pretending to be occupied.

"Sorry," she said.

"No problem." He looked up and knew he was wrong. It was a problem. She'd left her hair down, swaying around her shoulders. His hands itched to touch it. Her lips were glossed with a color. But damn, her mouth was amazing. Whatever she'd done to her eyes made them more striking.

The problems didn't stop with her face, either.

The fitted green top accentuated her hourglass figure, and made him want to slip his hands in that sweet curve of her body that he'd found yesterday at the police station. The scooped neckline of the top hinted and teased at more cleavage than it showed, but the hint was enough to set a man's imagination on fire. He already had a heat-index code-red warning.

"Let me grab my purse." She headed for the kitchen, and his gaze followed her. Her jeans hugged every delectable inch of her lower body. Hugged it in a way that guaranteed his lower body wasn't going to be comfortable in his jeans.

His phone rang, forcing his attention from Zoe. Checking the caller ID, he saw the diner's number.

"Yes?" he answered.

"It's Dixie." The woman's Texas tone filled the line. "You said to call if anyone called and asked about Zoe."

"And?"

"Someone called. Wanted to know when she was scheduled to work."

"And what did you say?" He looked at Zoe, who seemed to know the call was about her.

"I told 'em what you told me to. That I didn't know 'cause she didn't show up for her shift today. Then I asked what they wanted with her."

"And?"

"He said he was with a collection agency. Lying piece of shit."

Zoe arched her brow in question.

Tyler held up a finger. "So no one came in and asked about her?"

"Nope," she said. "You gonna tell me what's up with that girl?"

"Did you check caller ID when he called?"

"It was listed as unknown," Dixie answered. "I care about that girl, Mr. Lopez."

I care about her, too. The truth of that thought sent a warning right to his gut. "I'm watching out for her. As soon as I can share things with you, I will. Thank you for calling."

He hung up and looked at Zoe. "Dixie. Someone called the diner looking for you."

"Who?" she asked.

"Said they were a collection agency."

"I don't owe anyone," she said.

"They're just checking to see if you've left town."

She folded her arms against her chest, as if feeling vulnerable. "And what do we do now?"

"We let them think that until we figure out who they are."

"And if we can't figure it out?" she asked.

"We have to."

When they left the apartment, he'd suggested Italian. She'd recommended a pizza joint.

He'd countered with a steak restaurant; she'd suggested a burger place.

He'd recommended a really nice Chinese place.

She insisted she knew a great Chinese restaurant and wanted him to try it. When he pulled up into the strip center in the run-down neighborhood close to her apartment, next to a pawnshop that he knew dealt with stolen merchandise, he reminded her he was paying for the dinner. She informed him that her meal should go on *her* bill. Then she'd teased him about being a snob.

"You can't judge a book by its cover," she'd said. "Seriously, it's great." She'd popped out of his car and headed to the restaurant.

He'd followed her. With jeans that fit like that, any man would have.

Zoe had been right. The mom-and-pop, hole-in-the-wall restaurant had the best cashew chicken and tempura shrimp he'd ever tasted. The entire meal cost less than fifteen dollars. Plus, Mom and Pop knew Zoe by name and served up eggrolls on the house.

Zoe asked them about their five-year-old grandson, whom she'd taught to write his name while eating here one night. He remembered Zoe claiming she didn't know anyone in town, yet it seemed everywhere she went she made friends—people at the diner, her neighbors, even Chinese restaurant owners.

Gazing up, he watched her chase a cashew around her plate with her fork. He liked how she ate. No picking at her food, no putting on airs as a lot of women did. She ate with appreciation.

"Okay, stick a fork in me." She pushed the plate aside.

"Good. I've been eyeing your last shrimp since I finished mine." He speared the shrimp and popped it in his mouth.

She laughed. "So you approve of my restaurant selection?"

"Oh, hell, yes." As he drank the last of his beer, he wondered if now was the best time to ask about the recurring nightmares that Ellen had mentioned to him.

Running his nail along the label of his beer, he asked, "Is there anything you remember when you were really young that might help figure out what happened?"

She inhaled. "Ellen told you?"

"She was just trying—"

"I know," she said. "I like Ellen; she reminds me of Tara."

"Who's Tara?" he asked.

"My friend who died in my senior year of high school."

She picked up a paper napkin and started folding it over and over again—a sure sign she was upset. He wondered if it was the question about her childhood or the memory of her friend that affected her.

Zoe looked up from her napkin. "Was Ellen really stabbed?"

"Yes." Was this Zoe's way of telling him she didn't want to talk about the nightmare? He decided not to push. "It was touch and go for a while, too. She was lucky."

Zoe frowned. "And I thought I had it bad."

"You got shot." He stacked his plate on top of hers.

"Scratched by a bullet," she said.

"It could have been so much worse." He'd concluded that the asshole who'd shot at her apartment hadn't been intending to kill her, but one of those ricocheting bullets could have gone awry. And he wanted to catch this idiot before he tried anything else.

"But it wasn't," she said.

He was about to suggest they ask for the check, when she picked up the napkin and started folding it again. "You know they say dreams aren't accurate."

So, she was going to tell him. He prepared himself not to like it. "I know. I took some classes in oneirology and read a couple of books on it. But there can be elements of truth there. And in some cases a lot of truth."

She started rolling the napkin into a long cylinder.

"The child psychologist told me it was just nightmares. That everyone had something they were afraid of. That the dreams were just my imagination pointing out my fears."

"What are you afraid of?" he asked.

She shrugged. "At first they suggested it was of the dark. But I didn't agree. I mean, I wasn't afraid of just the dark. It had to be in a small space."

"Claustrophobic?" he asked.

"Sort of, but not really. I mean, elevators, crowds, they never bother me, unless it's dark. It . . . it has to be a closet."

"Auchloclaustrophobia," he said. "It's a mix of—"

"I know," she said. She grinned, but it didn't look genuine. "I can spell it backwards, too. Having a name for my problem made me happy back then."

He heard so much in her tone—embarrassment, a little vulnerability. He waited to see if she'd continue. When she didn't, he asked, "Can you tell me about the nightmares?"

"There's not much to tell. I'm locked in a small closet. I'm there for a long time." She looked back down at the napkin, but he knew she wasn't seeing it but images from the dream. "I'm young. Petrified. I wet my pants. I wanted to ask someone to take me to the bathroom, but somehow I knew the person behind that door wasn't nice. So I curled up in a ball and tried not to cry too loud."

Tyler's chest grew heavy at the thought of how scared she must have felt. "How old were you when you started having the dreams?"

She shook her head. "I don't ever remember not having them."

"Do you still have them?"

"No." She said it quickly as if worried he'd judge her.

"Not like nightmares. Sometimes when I first wake up, if it's dark, I remember it. The feeling of being trapped." She unrolled the napkin. "When I was younger, I couldn't open a closet. It just freaked me out. But I got past that."

The need for revenge clamped down on his chest, and he dropped his hands in his lap so his tightened fists wouldn't give him away. He told himself she was lucky. He'd just spent the day reading about some kids who weren't, but he wasn't sitting across the table from those other kids. This was personal. It was Zoe.

"You don't remember a face, or you didn't hear voices?" he asked.

"No. I can't even remember how I got in the closet, or how I got out." She paused.

The silence grew loud. "Well." She sat up straighter as if she was accustomed to putting it out of her mind. "That's my emotional baggage in a nutshell. What's yours?"

CHAPTER TWENTY-ONE

HIS FIRST INSTINCT was to change the subject, but he realized how hard it had been for her to confide in him.

He turned the beer bottle in his hands. "You mean, you haven't figured that out yet?" He smiled to make light of it.

"Yeah, I got the whole 'convicted of a murder you didn't commit' thing going. But I meant childhood baggage?"

He dug deep. "My sisters used to put makeup on me and dress me in their nightgowns. I was supposed to be the princess."

She grinned. "Seriously?"

"Seriously," he said.

She giggled. "Well, after talking to your sisters on the phone, it doesn't surprise me."

He studied her smile. "I'm sorry about that. I told you they were crazy. But they're good people."

"I figured that," she said. "And honestly, I don't think their game damaged your masculinity."

"No, it hasn't." Seeing her eyes light up with humor after seeing the other emotions there felt damn good.

"What else? Besides being cajoled into cross-dressing."

"You need more?" he asked.

"I sense there's more." She took a sip of her water.

He tried not to frown, tried not to wonder what character flaw or trait of his helped her reach that conclusion. He started to come up with another story, but the painful truth slipped out. "I guess you could say my dad was a louse, and my mom's only flaw was she had a weakness for loving louses..."

"Was?" she asked.

"She died about four years ago. I still miss her."

"I know what you mean. I still miss..." Zoe didn't finish her sentence, but then she asked, "How bad of a louse was your dad?"

When he didn't answer, she held up her hand. "Sorry. You don't have to answer."

He did if he expected her to answer his questions. And he had a lot of them. "On a scale of one to ten, I'd say he was about a five."

"Abusive?" Zoe asked, frowning.

"Not to us kids. But to Mom, yes. Mostly when he was drunk—not that it excuses him."

"Is he still alive?"

"No. He died, liver disease, when I was nine."

"Sorry," she said.

"Don't be." He brought his beer to his lips even though he knew it was empty. "I'm not." He set the bottle down. For a second, he worried that he sounded too cold, but he didn't care. He hadn't loved his old man, why should he pretend?

She fiddled with her napkin for a second. "Is that why you became a cop?"

"Because my dad died?"

"No, because you grew up wanting to protect someone."

He considered what she said. "I've never looked at it like that, but I guess it could have influenced my decision. Mostly, I fell in love with the reruns of *Starsky & Hutch* when I was twelve. They got to shoot things, drive cars like maniacs, and always got the hot girls."

She grinned. "I'll bet they had sisters who dressed them up as little princesses."

He pointed at her. "Okay, I'm warning you, I haven't told a soul about that, so if I hear one thing about me having a cross-dressing stage, I'll know you told."

She placed her hand over her heart. "It'll go with me to my grave."

Mom, of the mom-and-pop-restaurant team, came over. "You enjoy? Yes?"

"It was great, as usual," Zoe said.

The woman looked from Zoe to Tyler. "I happy you find a good boy to eat with you. Not so lonely now, huh?"

"Uh, yeah." She shot him a cute embarrassed smile.

The woman dropped a small tray with two fortune cookies and the bill on the table.

Zoe held out the tray with the fortune cookies on them. "You choose."

"That's okay," he said.

"You have to; it has your fortune in it."

He smiled. "You believe in that?"

"A little bit," she said.

He grabbed one of the cookies. She waited for him to open it. Indulging her, he ripped opened the paper. "Are you supposed to read it out loud? Or are they like birthday wishes and you don't tell?"

"You can read it aloud if you wish."

"Never let the past stop you from making a future." He dropped the paper on the table and pretended as if it held no significance to him. "Your turn."

She opened it, put a piece of the cookie in her mouth, and then read it . . . silently.

"And?"

She looked down at the slip of paper. "It's profound."

"So read it." He leaned closer.

She focused on the tiny print. *"Be leery of men who cross-dressed in their youth."*

He laughed. "And I thought I could trust you."

She grinned and stood up. "Ladies' room."

He watched her walk away, then he noticed her fortune beside the half-eaten cookie. He reached for it.

Love is always a risk. But it's a risk worth taking.

Thirty minutes later, Zoe followed Tyler into his apartment. It wasn't your typical bachelor's apartment. There weren't take-out boxes, beer bottles, dirty socks, or magazines with half-naked women on the covers tossed around the room. There was a basket of folded clothes on the tan sofa, two pairs of shoes beside a leather recliner, and a stack of books on the coffee table: two old classics, a couple of biographies, and a copy of *Twilight.*

A smile curved her lips. She looked up at him. "Edward or Jacob fan?"

"Definitely Jacob. I'm rather upset with the outcome." He studied her, and when the pause grew a tad longer, he added, "Come on, I know you want to give me hell for reading it. Point out that it was due to my cross-dressing stage."

She laughed. "No, all I will say is that you have eclectic reading tastes."

"I could say the same of you." He pinched his brow at her. "Seriously, romance novels?"

"What do you think *Twilight* is?" She cut him an accusing look. "So you snooped around in my apartment?" She headed over to the TV stand where he had several framed photos.

"No more than you're doing to mine right now," he said.

She looked back at him. "Fair enough." She moved her gaze around. "The apartment's nice."

"It is," he said.

"A lot nicer than the apartment at the office. Why are you moving there?"

"The commute to work." He chuckled. "Seriously, Dallas and Nikki wanted to move out, and I spend so much time at the office I thought it would just be easier."

She refocused on the photos. "The crazy family?"

"That's them." He moved in beside her, his shoulder brushed against hers, and warm tingles shot down her arm from the quick touch. "That's Sam, my twin. The one standing next to her is Lola, my oldest sister. The ones you spoke with."

As he was listing off names of his other siblings and cousins, she saw the scratches on his knuckles and remembered meeting him in the clown costume with his hand bloody. Funny how she'd forgotten about that.

"And that's Anna, Sam's daughter." He picked up the picture, and Zoe sensed Anna was special to him.

She looked up at Tyler. "She looks like you."

"What's worse, she acts like me. Already has her nose buried in books."

"That's not a bad thing." Zoe met his gaze, remembering having her nose in books at the same age. "As long as she's not into cross-dressing, she's probably okay."

His grin came with sex appeal.

"So what is it you need to grab from here?" She remembered how good it had felt when he'd pulled her into his arms and she'd cried on his shoulder.

"Some kitchen supplies and clothes," he answered.

Her gaze shifted to the spot on his shoulder where she'd rested her head. She hadn't been held like that in… in a long time. Not that it had been sexual; it had been much more alluring than just that. It had been tender, caring.

And ultimately, that made it far more seductive than the kiss had been. Ever since then she'd been debating if saying yes to two weeks of wonderful pleasure, of bliss, was really such a bad deal.

And it didn't have anything to do with the fortune cookie, either. If she did take Tyler's offer, she'd have to accept it was not about finding happily ever after, it was about finding happy for two weeks.

"I'll do most of the moving later," he continued. "I have a lease on the place for another three months, so I don't have to hurry."

Her gaze went back to the photos of Tyler's family. She saw an older photo to the side that must have been of his mother. And Zoe ached a bit for the younger Tyler whose childhood must have been so chaotic. She couldn't help but wonder how much of that chaos was the reason he now avoided long-term relationships. And how much was about the mysterious Lisa.

Zoe's gaze went back to the large sofa and the books.

It was the perfect place to curl up and read. The perfect place to do a lot of things. Did Tyler bring a lot of women here to entertain?

Did he make love to them on the sofa? Or did he take them to . . .

"Hey, come into my bedroom. I have more books in there you might want to borrow."

He started moving.

She didn't.

Her feet felt as though they were sunk into concrete slabs on the wood floor. Not because she didn't want to go with him—she did want to go with him, right?

He got to the door and looked at her. A frown passed his lips. "I'm not trying anything here. You know that?"

Well, that was a disappointment. "Yeah," she said. Mentally, she pulled her feet out of the cement and followed him into the bedroom.

Pay dirt. Rick looked around to make sure the Bradford office was still empty, then he quickly pulled out the file that listed past employees beginning in the 1980s.

Taking the file to the desk, he flipped it open. Bradford had only seven employees at the time of the kidnapping, and that included yard people. There wasn't anyone with the name Adams, but Rick pulled out his pad and jotted down the info.

Tomorrow, he planned on seeing if he could find the cold-case file on the Bradford murder. But who knows if the cops back then had their facts right? Hell, who knew if he could find the damn file after so many years?

Writing the last names down, he felt antsy and hurried to replace the file. Getting caught snooping wouldn't be good. And around here, one never knew who was around. Bradford had more guards on duty than the damn president.

Sure the man had money, but Rick would bet the biggest source of thieves were the old man's family. When Tyler had first mentioned the job, he explained that the old man had always been a bit paranoid, but after his granddaughter had been kidnapped he went off the deep end.

Sitting back at the desk, Rick reached for a phone book and started making the list of day cares he'd call tomorrow.

He'd almost taken the night off. But he'd already taken the afternoon off at Miller PD to do his day care research. Besides, the day cares weren't open this late, and he might as well do something useful with himself instead of sitting at home fretting. Not that his afternoon off had proven to be that useful. He'd visited seven day cares, and not a one of them with openings offered the hours he needed. The ones that offered the right hours were filled and placed him on a waiting list.

Not that it helped. He possibly needed someone to watch Ricky in three weeks. Another thought hit: who could he get to watch Ricky for his night job? Were there nighttime day cares? Could he afford them? He wouldn't be paying child support, but they couldn't be cheap. Maybe he'd have to quit this gig.

He remembered being hauled back and forth from sitter to sitter while his mother worked her shifts as a nurse. Maybe quitting the night job was best. He didn't want Ricky to feel as if he didn't have a real home.

Rick's mind churned on the things he needed to do—childproof the house, buy the kid a new bed, maybe a bike.

Thank God, he already owned a gun safe. Could Ricky ride a bike yet? Or did he still need training wheels?

Earlier he'd gone by the grocery store and scouted out some kid-friendly foods: goldfish crackers, fruit snacks, and macaroni and cheese in fun shapes. What was considered junk food? What kind of food did Ellen feed her kid?

Jabbing his pencil at the phone book, he recalled how she'd nearly run over his foot to get away from him earlier. She'd totally misconstrued what he'd wanted to talk to her about. Pissed him off, too. He'd thought they'd gotten along when he'd changed her tire, and then when she'd called him to come by the office.

Leaning his head back, he wondered about this Bob she dated. Was he good to her? Did he know how to treat her in bed and out? What kind of men did a woman like Ellen go for? Someone who could show her a good time, but the kind she didn't mind hanging around her kid.

Somehow he suspected the latter was probably important to her.

The last woman he'd dated, which was too damn long ago, told him men like him were more of an acquired taste than every woman's dream. And that was fine, because most every woman's dream ended up being his nightmare. Between Sophie who'd stolen his car, or Vicki who lived with him for two years and maxed out his credit cards in the process, only to discover she'd been sleeping with her ex the whole time, and then . . . Candy.

Oddly enough, he didn't imagine Ellen doing any of those things. Maybe that made her too good for men who were an "acquired taste," but would it kill her to give him a few parenting tips?

"A penny for your thoughts."

Rick twisted in his chair to see Mrs. Daniels, Bradford's fifty-something daughter, standing in the doorway. She wore a tight red dress and a seductive cougar smile.

"Afraid my thoughts aren't worth that much." He stood up.

"Why? Are they naughty?"

Rick weighed his words. His gut warned him earlier that she was sizing him up for something other than a conversation. Frankly, he didn't enjoy her conversations, and the idea of more didn't stir his interest.

Then again, it had been a long time since he'd had sex. He weighed his decision before taking the option off the table.

"Not very naughty," he said.

Tyler's bedroom had dark oak furniture with accessories of different shades of taupe and red—masculine but classy. "Nice. Interior designer?" she asked.

"Cousin," he answered.

She found her gaze on the unmade king-size bed. "Hmm."

"Hmm, what?" he asked.

"You're the unmade-bed type."

"Your bed wasn't perfect," he said. "You tossed the covers over it."

"But that quick blanket toss says a lot."

He grinned. "It says you're a tad more of a neatnik than I am."

She laughed.

"The books are on the nightstand." He grabbed a bag out of his closet and started filling it with clothes.

She sat on the edge of the bed and stared at the books.

But her mind wasn't on the titles, rather on the feel of her hand pressing against the Egyptian cotton sheets and letting her mind wonder what it would feel like to lay on them naked.

Oh, hell, tonight in the shower hadn't she shaved her legs for this very reason? She looked back at Tyler.

"Find anything you like?" he asked.

You. "Yeah." She tried to find the right words. *I've changed my mind about the two weeks. You wanna prove how good at sex you really are? Come here, big boy, and let me show you a good time.*

None of the lines felt right. Did that mean this wasn't right? Oh, hell, was she making a mistake?

"You okay?" he asked when she continued to stare.

"Fine," she said. "I just—"

A chime rang in the apartment.

"My doorbell." He took one backward step toward the door, never taking his gaze off her, as if trying to read her. He grinned. "Don't snoop while I'm away."

"Wouldn't dream of it."

He walked out.

She sat there, wondering if the interruption had been divine intervention. A few minutes passed, and then she heard voices. And a crying infant.

Curious, she went to the door.

Tyler stood by two women; one of them held the noisy infant, and beside her was a little girl holding a...a carrier. A little meow came from the cage. It took Zoe a second to recognize them. Tyler turned as if he sensed her standing there. He wore a frown on his face as did his sisters.

"Zoe, these are my sisters, Sam and Lola. This is

Anna. And little squirt." He pointed to the infant. "Who isn't happy right now."

"Hi." Zoe took another step into the living room, hoping to distance herself from Tyler's bedroom. They already thought she was sleeping with him. The fact that she was considering it didn't make this *any* easier.

Sam and Lola didn't appear overly happy to meet her. Anna, however, offered Zoe a big smile. "Are you Tio Tyler's married girlfriend?"

CHAPTER TWENTY-TWO

"I'M NOT MARRIED." Zoe looked to Tyler for help.

"She's not married," Tyler said.

The baby screamed louder. "That's good." Sam bounced the baby in her arms. "Nice to meet you. I'm sorry, he's hungry. He cries when he's hungry."

Zoe couldn't help but wonder if Sam wasn't hungry, too. Her eyes looked red and puffy.

"I need to heat his bottle." Sam ran off into the kitchen.

"It's good to meet you, Zoe." Lola, the older sister, smiled.

Zoe saw Tyler glance at Lola with questions in his eyes. Lola glanced down at Anna.

Tyler looked at Zoe, and she guessed what he was thinking before he spoke. "Anna, why don't you take Zoe to my bedroom and show her your cat?"

Anna's brown eyes looked up at Zoe. "His name is Damien." She started toward the bedroom. Zoe followed.

Zoe shut the bedroom door and watched Anna kneel beside the cage and open the door. An orange kitten came swaggering out of the carrier.

"I have a red tabby cat, too." Zoe sat down on the bed.

"Where is he?" Anna looked around.

"He's at Tyler's office."

Anna picked up the cat. "Tyler gave him to me for an early birthday present. He saved him from being run over on the freeway. He said they both nearly became grease spots."

Zoe grinned. "Well, I'm glad they didn't."

"Me, too." She glanced at the door. "You know they wanted to get us out of the room so they could talk, don't you?"

"Do you think that was it?" Zoe asked, not sure what to say.

"Yeah, they do that all the time. Because I'm young. I don't know why they didn't want you not to hear."

Zoe scratched the kitten on his forehead. "Maybe it's private."

"Not really. It's about Mama getting another divorce." The child pulled the cat closer. "Not that I care. I don't like Leo." She looked at the door again. "Leo hit Mama. And then Tyler hit Leo. And now Leo's nose looks really funny."

Zoe remembered Tyler's bloody knuckles. "That's not good," she said, unsure if Sam would want Anna to spill the family secrets.

"I don't hit anyone." Anna shook her head.

"That's good." Zoe searched for a safer subject. "Tyler said you like to read."

"I just finished *Charlotte's Web*."

"Oh, I like that one." Zoe was impressed. Anna looked like a first grader. *Charlotte's Web* was way above her grade level.

"I didn't," Anna said. "Charlotte died."

"Yeah, it was a little sad." Zoe searched for a new topic. "Are you going to school yet?"

"I started first grade last week," she said. "But it's boring."

It would be for a gifted student, which Zoe suspected Anna was.

The kitten climbed up on the bed, and Zoe brushed her fingertips across his back.

Anna crawled up on the bed next to Damien. "Are you Tyler's girlfriend?"

Zoe hesitated before answering. "I'm his friend."

"So you don't kiss him and stuff?"

Zoe had to bite back a smile. "We mostly just talk."

"That's good." Anna shrugged. " 'Cause Tyler says he doesn't want to get married. Mama says it's because he still loves Lisa. But she fell in love with someone else."

Three hours later, Zoe walked out of the office apartment's bathroom, dressed in a pair of cotton shorts and a large T-shirt, her usual sleepwear. Tyler leaned against the hall wall. Lucky ran circles around his ankles.

They'd left Tyler's apartment and had gone to the grocery store. He'd been quiet the whole time, too. Oh, he'd thanked her for occupying Anna, and even explained that Sam had some marital issues and was going to be staying at his old apartment for a while. But gone was the playful mood they'd previously enjoyed.

Zoe figured out the reasons, too. No doubt, his sister's trauma brought back some of his childhood woes. Sort of how being in Texas brought out her own.

"It's all yours," she said, motioning to the bathroom door.

"You okay?" His gaze moved over her.

"Just dandy, and you?" She hadn't missed the haunted look in his eyes when he'd talked about his father. Tonight when they'd left his apartment, she'd spotted it again.

However, she couldn't blame the mood change all on him.

She didn't have a clue what it was that bothered her about Tyler currently being, or possibly having had been, in love with someone else, but it did bother her. For some reason, believing his past had left him incapable of getting involved with anyone was one thing. Yet knowing he was capable of it but just didn't want to get involved with her made it feel personal. As if she wasn't good enough for him to really care about.

But damn if her feelings weren't a jumbled mess.

"I wish you'd take the bed," he said.

"Sofa's fine." She started down the hall and then turned around. "I'm going to need some of my stuff from my place soon."

"I'll pick up a few things tomorrow. Alone. Just in case someone is watching the place."

She nodded.

He took a step closer. "I appreciate you occupying Anna while we dealt with that family stuff."

Zoe tried to push back the crazy feeling swirling inside her. "No problem. She's a smart girl."

"She is special," he said with pride.

They stared at each other for a long second. "I set the books on the coffee table, if you need something to read."

"Thanks." She started toward the living room.

"Zoe?"

She turned around but didn't say anything.

"Do you want me to leave the bathroom light on?"

She knew he was thinking about her phobia. Why did that suddenly annoy her? "That would be great."

He took a step closer. "I'm going to get to the bottom of this. I'm going to find out who tried to shoot you yesterday and who kidnapped you when you were a kid. I want to fix this for you."

"Who's going to fix you?" she countered before she could stop herself.

"Do I need fixing?" He looked perplexed.

"Nah, I'm sure you're perfect." She continued down the hall. And she'd bet Lisa thought so, too. Or had.

Right then, the most absurd realization struck. She was jealous. Jealous of a woman in Tyler's past. Now that didn't make a lick of sense! Heck, when she got back to Alabama she might need to go find herself another shrink.

"Hey," he said.

She looked back. "What?" A knot of complicated emotion formed in her throat.

"You can't just say something like that and walk away."

Yes I can. Watch me.

"Good night, Tyler." She moved into the living room and dropped down on the sofa. Lucky climbed up on the back of the sofa and started purring in her ear.

Zoe suddenly wanted to cry. Not too much of an uncommon thing lately. She'd cried more since she'd been in Texas than she had in five years. Well, with an exception of when her mother died.

But the heavy feeling knotting her emotions right now was different. She didn't want to cry because she lost her mother, or because her parents had lied to her. Not even because they might turn out to be murderers. The need for tears wasn't even because someone was trying to kill her.

She wanted to cry because she was starting to care about someone who didn't want to care about her. But given the chance, he'd love to fuck her. And she was actually considering letting him. She was that lonely, that pathetic.

Her need to cry increased with the vulgar thought bouncing around her head.

She heard him moving down the hall toward her. He dropped down beside her. His weight caused the cushions to shift and brought her shoulder flush with his. The oh-so-casual brush against him caused a sharp pain of longing to fill her chest.

And there was nothing casual about that pain... or the longing.

"What's wrong?" he asked.

Tears stung her sinuses. "I want to go back to Alabama. I just want to go home."

He frowned. "You can't," he said matter-of-factly. "Not yet."

"Why not?"

"Because... because there's a damn good chance that whoever tried to shoot you will try to find you in Alabama. And I did a little Google search on you today to see how easy that would be. I found your address, your telephone number, and your place of employment."

She pulled her legs up and dropped her forehead on her knees.

"Look," he said. "I know this is probably about last night. And you don't have to worry. I completely respect your decision. You have my word that I won't try anything. This is strictly business. I'm your PI and you're my client."

She raised her head and looked at him. Couldn't he have worked a little harder to persuade her? Was she that easy to forget about?

"Fine." She tightened her throat. "Now can I go to sleep?"

Ten o'clock the next morning, Tyler hung up the phone from talking with Roberto, disturbing Lucky from his morning nap. The feline seemed to think the clutter on Tyler's desk made the perfect sleeping spot.

"And?" Austin asked, his chair creaking as he leaned forward.

"He's pretty sure it's a DeLuna operation." Tyler smiled. "I think we'll be taking another chink out of that bastard's armor pretty soon. Roberto said he'd call us back next week. He's supposed to meet up with someone about possibly getting a position as a carrier for them. If he gets in, it could lead us to DeLuna."

"It's about fucking time," Austin said.

"Fucking time for what?" Dallas asked, stepping into the office and moving to his desk. He'd called earlier that morning saying he was going to stop in and see his brother and ask if he could pull some strings and see if they could get anything on Ralph and Mildred Adams. And then he had to take Bud to the vet to get his anal glands cleaned out. Something Tyler really could have gone without hearing about, too.

"Roberto called." Tyler gave Dallas the good news.

"You're right, it's fucking time." Dallas slapped a hand

on his desk. "Sooner or later, we're gonna get his ass." He reached his hand up over his head and stretched. "I knew it was going to be a damn good day after I got off the phone with Rick."

"He get something on the Adamses?" Tyler needed good news to give to Zoe. Wanted to find something to ease some of the tension that seemed to have surfaced since last night.

He wanted it before she did something stupid like go back to Alabama. He couldn't protect her in Alabama. And protecting her seemed to be all he could think about. And while his obsession over it might have concerned him, he told himself it was okay. That's what PIs did. Protect people. Which meant she was still just a case.

Dallas grinned. "First, Rick got us a list of names who worked at the mansion during the kidnapping." He pulled out a piece of paper. "And he figured out how he could get into the mansion." Dallas looked toward the door and lowered his voice. "Mrs. Daniels, the old man's daughter, has the hots for Rick."

"The same Mrs. Daniels we met?" Austin asked. "She's old."

"Supposedly, the woman likes tender meat."

Austin laughed. "I don't think there's anything tender about Rick Clark."

Dallas chuckled. "She invited him to the big house last night to eat some pound cake. The old man came down, but she mentioned a rain check." Dallas chuckled. "He said if he had to wrap his lips around anything other than cake, we were gonna pay."

"What else did he get?" Tyler asked, wanting to cut to the chase.

"He ran a check on both of them for warrants. Found nothing. Then he called Shadows County, where Zoe was born, and they did a local rundown. They found three unpaid tickets belonging to a Ralph Adams. It looks like they are two different guys. But one of them had a home address listed as Barker County. And I remember you mentioned something about one of the Ralph Adamses you ran across holding some sort of a state license in Barker."

"I think that was the one who held a cosmetology license," Tyler added.

"Right." Dallas continued. "Anyway, when I was telling Rick about Zoe's birth certificate, he asked if we'd had it cross-matched with death records."

"I did that," Tyler said.

"Yeah, but Rick remembered a case of his years ago about some guy from some small county in Texas who was running cons using names of deceased people who he knew hadn't been entered in the state's main system's death records."

"Why wouldn't they have been entered?" Tyler asked.

"Supposedly, some of the smaller counties either haven't gotten all that data on a computer or they just don't see the need to share the info. But that's not important." Dallas leaned both elbows on his desk. "What is important is that while Bud was getting his asshole cleaned out, I called Barker County to see if they could give me anything on Ralph, Mildred, or Zoe Adams."

Dallas, looking rather proud of himself, put his hands behind his neck. "Your girl was right."

Your girl. Tyler liked how that phrase felt rolling around in his eardrum. "Right about what?"

"Ralph and Mildred didn't kill their own child. Zoe Adams, the real Zoe Adams, died at four months old from lung complications. It was listed on Barker County's system. Death records should be faxed to us by lunchtime."

Zoe stood under the spray of warm water, hoping it would soothe the stress in her shoulders. She'd hardly slept the night before, agonizing over her attraction to Tyler and his new, strictly-business policy.

If he could completely disregard the attraction, so could she. She didn't need a man.

Yes you do! She was a normal, albeit a mite neurotic, twenty-six-year-old woman, who'd taken a hormonal vacation due to having her heart broken. It made complete sense that her sexual urges—which were a normal part of being human—would eventually return.

And now that they had, she'd deal with them. Just as soon as she got back to Alabama. There were plenty of men who'd made their interest known since Chris had taken up with the stripper. She just hadn't been interested in any of them.

Mentally, she envisioned the guys: Coach Bradley at school; Tim Hendricks, her neighbor's brother; her mom's lawyer who continued to call and just check to see if she needed any of his services. She tried to see herself with each of them. See herself wanting to run her hands over their abs the way she wanted to run her hands over Tyler's.

Okay, so maybe those men didn't have the right abs. Her heart clutched. She wanted Tyler. And honestly, was it so bad for her to have him?

No, it wasn't. Tyler was right. They were two consenting adults attracted to each other.

She cut the water off and pushed back the shower curtain. The loud barking put her on instant alert. But it was the loud cat screeching that shot her into action.

"Lucky!" She bolted out of the shower, slipped, and landed on her naked ass on the cold tile. But she didn't stay down. Bouncing up, she vaulted for the door, slung it open, did one quick glance to assure herself she was alone, and then followed the serious cat-and-dog-fight noises coming from the bedroom.

Lucky was on the bed. Bud bounced on and off the bed, barking and snapping his fat little jowls. To the dog's credit, he looked more like he was playing, but Zoe wasn't sure. And she sure as hell wasn't taking chances.

"Out!" She went after the dog.

Bud jumped up on the bed. And for a round, stumpy little fellow, he could really jump. He danced around the mattress, leaning down on his front paws and bouncing back up. Lucky, not enjoying his antics, stood up on his hind legs, hissing and swatting his paws like a champion feline boxer. His one eye shifted back and forth to keep track of the ping-ponging dog.

Zoe dove for the dog, missed, and landed facedown on the mattress. Popping up, she tried again, but Bud jumped down to the floor, ran around the bed, and leaped up on the other side. Zoe leaped up on the mattress and snatched Lucky in her arms.

Bud started hurdling up in the air like a dog after a flying Frisbee.

"Get out!" She started turning in circles.

Tyler heard the barking. Heard Zoe screaming. "Shit! Where's Bud?"

He bolted out of his chair, followed by Austin and Dallas, and all three went darting into the apartment.

"Bud, get your butt in here!" Dallas yelled behind Tyler.

"Bud!" Tyler cut the corner, and when his shoes hit a puddle of water on the wood floor, he nearly fell. "Shit," Dallas grunted behind him.

Tyler looked back and watched as Dallas landed on his butt. Then Austin cut the corner and fell over him and landed on his butt, too. Tyler started to ask if they were okay, but Zoe screamed again, the dog barked, the cat hissed. His partners were on their own. Tyler shot through the bedroom and...

And...

The moment his gaze landed on a naked Zoe jumping up and down on the bed, his mind couldn't think of anything else.

Well, until he heard Austin say, "Oh, my!"

And Dallas said, "Damn."

Zoe let out another ear-piercing scream.

Tyler pushed Austin and Dallas out of the bedroom and slammed the door shut. Then he swung back around.

Zoe had managed to snatch up a pillow, and she stood on the bed hugging it over her front with one arm while holding Lucky with the other. She danced from one foot to the other, struggling to keep the cat away from Bud, who soared up two to three feet into the air, barking with playful glee.

Zoe's pillow slipped down. Exposing her gorgeous breasts, which were jiggling up and down. She yanked the pillow up to cover her top half and exposed the red triangle of hair between her thighs.

"Stop," Tyler yelled at Bud.

The dog didn't obey.

"Do something!" Zoe screamed.

"I am." Then again, she probably meant do something more than stand there and enjoy the view. He bolted forward to grab Bud.

Bud shot across the bed. Zoe shot around to keep Lucky from him. With one knee on the mattress, Tyler got a close-up, fabulous view of Zoe's beautifully round and perfect ass.

She swung around, caught him entranced, and scowled. "Get the dog!"

"Do you need help?" Tyler heard Dallas call out between snorts of laughter. Damn, but Tyler had to fight not to laugh as well.

"No!" Tyler dove across the bed and grabbed Bud around his chest. Chancing it, he glanced up, finding the view from this angle amazing. Zoe, clutching her pillow, glared at him.

Hugging the squirming dog, Tyler backed off the bed, opened the door a crack, and pushed the dog out.

Then Tyler turned back around. Zoe still held on to Lucky and her pillow. She pulled the pillow up to cover her chest. Then, as if realizing what she was exposing at the bottom, she lowered it down. Personally, Tyler liked both views.

Right then he praised Dallas's choice of standard-size pillows in lieu of the queen size.

Lucky let out a pathetic meow.

"The cat okay?" Tyler asked, feeling the tightness in his lower body. If he stayed in here much longer, he was going to need his own pillow.

Zoe looked at the cat. "I think so." The cat squirmed loose, fell to the mattress, bounced off the bed, and darted under it.

Zoe froze, standing in the center of the bed, her pillow positioned in the optimum placement to hide all the best parts.

"Did you get hurt?" he asked.

"No." She clung to the pillow like it was her lifeline. "You can leave now."

He noticed her blush. Noticed it went all the way down her neck and behind the pillow.

"I could." He grinned.

"Don't you dare laugh!" Her eyes tightened, but it didn't look like anger. He could swear she looked about ready to laugh herself.

"Okay." He backed to the door, not wanting to waste one second of the view. Then, way sooner than he hoped, his butt hit the door. As he reached his hand back to find the knob, he continued to feast on the view in front of him. Even with optimum pillow placement, it was a sight to behold.

Her hair hung wet in ringlets down her shoulders. Her toes, with the nails painted a pink tint, curled into the down comforter. But holy hell, she stood there with nothing but a bag of duck feathers between him and every sweet wet inch of her naked skin.

He never hated duck feathers so much in his life.

"Leave!"

"Okay." He turned the knob, opened the door, and slipped out.

Austin and Dallas weren't in the hall. Smart men, he thought. He'd probably punch them if one of them had tried to get a second peek. Not that Dallas would, but Austin... maybe.

Tyler inhaled and took one step, but then he turned around and leaned his forehead against the door.

He stood there for all of sixty seconds, not sure what to say. Then, still clueless, he called out, "Zoe?"

"Yes," she answered with hesitancy.

"You're beautiful."

CHAPTER TWENTY-THREE

An hour later, with Austin and Dallas off on an investigation, Tyler sat alone in his office, trying to review Zoe's case file, unable to get the image of her bouncing up and down on the bed, naked except for a pillow, out of his mind.

Maybe thinking about it made him a pig, but he couldn't help it. Zoe had the kind of body that...that if he was a painter, he'd want to paint it. It was...perfect. Beautiful. The human body at its highest form. And sexy as hell was hot.

He tugged at his suddenly tight crotch and told himself it was enough. Time to get to work, damn it. Not only did he need to talk to Zoe about the implications of finding a death certificate for four-month-old Zoe Adams, he had errands to run. And he needed to check in on Sam.

He looked down at his notes on Zoe's case file. He'd done some more checks with Barker County and concluded that Ralph Adams, the man who'd raised Zoe, had indeed graduated from cosmetology school. Tyler also discovered the man had defaulted on his home loan the same year Zoe—or Caroline—had been kidnapped.

Tyler shifted the papers around and let his gaze move over them, taking in bits and pieces of each sheet. He always input everything into the computer, but he liked having a hard copy to stare at—he liked pairing things together to come up with more questions.

How did a guy who studied how to cut hair end up doing Sheetrock and roofing? And how did a male beautician end up raising the kidnapped daughter of a millionaire?

He shifted the papers and saw where he'd listed the other Ralph Adams. Maybe it was time to see if the hair-cutting Ralph had family. Tyler looked at the clock. But he would follow up on that later. He needed to talk to Zoe. He'd given her an hour to get over being angry or embarrassed at being seen naked by every member of the Only in Texas team.

As he walked out of his office, Ellen stepped out of the apartment. He waited for her to pass him in the hall.

"Is it safe for me to go in there?" he asked.

Ellen grinned. "She can only kill you once."

Zoe heard the door opening and looked up as Tyler walked in. He offered her one of his apologetic smiles. Funny how she could already read him. It had been months before she felt she had insight to what Chris had been feeling or thinking. And little did she know, she'd completely misread him. What she thought was frustration at his office turned out to be lust for a stripper. Maybe she was wrong about Tyler, too.

"You talking to me?" Tyler sat on the leather chair across from the sofa.

Funny thing about embarrassment, it could often be interpreted as anger, or it could easily lead to anger really quickly. Zoe generally worked at not letting her emotions take her places she didn't need to be.

"I suppose I can't really blame you," she said. "Except for the fact that you stayed in there."

"I was trying to help."

"And after you got rid of the dog?"

"I was worried you were hurt."

"And it had nothing to do with the fact that I didn't have my clothes on?"

He hesitated, as if weighing his words.

"Be honest." She cut him a sharp look that stemmed more from tease than temper.

"Maybe. Not that it's entirely my fault. It's a genetic defect in the male DNA. When male humans see a naked woman bouncing on a bed, walking away is completely out of our normal behavior patterns."

She almost smiled and then remembered. "And where does... strictly business fall into this?"

"Right after the male instinctual behavior." He held up his hand. "I got sidetracked in a very weak moment."

But damn, she wondered how she could create more weak moments. *"You're beautiful."* She remembered the last thing he'd said to her through the door. He'd taken possibly the most embarrassing moment in her life and made her feel sexy, appealing.

She wasn't mad, but she wasn't ready to completely let him off the hook, either. "Do you promise to try to fight the normal instincts of the weak male if you happen to find me jumping on the bed naked again?"

He hesitated. "I... can try." He looked perplexed.

Maybe it was a tiny bit evil of her, but what woman didn't want to keep a guy guessing?

His expression went from perplexed to suspicious. "Are you planning on getting naked and jumping on the bed again?"

She bit the inside of her cheek to stop from laughing. "I'll try to avoid that."

He grinned. "Not on my account, I hope."

She chuckled.

"Okay, now that we got that taken care of..." He grew quiet. The humor of the moment evaporated like a drop of water on a hot sidewalk. She recognized something in his posture, too. He had something else to tell her. And it wasn't good.

"What is it?" Zoe asked.

"We got more information in." He leaned forward and hesitated, as if searching for a way to put a good spin on whatever he had to say. "We found the death certificate for Zoe Adams."

Zoe's breath caught. "So, I'm dead." It was her bad attempt to make light of it.

"The child, Zoe Adams, the one Mildred Adams gave birth to on February twenty-sixth, is dead. She died at four months old from lung complications. The body they thought was Caroline Bradford wasn't the body of the first Zoe Adams."

Which was good news, she told herself. It meant Mildred and Ralph Adams hadn't killed their own child. But it didn't stop the swirl of emotion from swimming in her chest. Had all she'd ever been was a replacement? Breath held, she waited to see if there was more.

He continued, "They defaulted on a home loan the same year you were kidnapped."

"And?" she asked.

"Ralph Adams graduated from cosmetology school."

"You must have the wrong Ralph Adams. He never..." The realization hit that what she thought she knew was wrong. She didn't know the man she'd called Daddy. The man who'd called her princess. Lies. All of it.

"I know it's strange," he said softly.

"Strange?" She laughed, but not because it was funny. She tried to wrap her mind around it. "It's more than just strange. Did I ever really know either of them?" Her chest grew heavier. "My whole life down to its foundation is based on a lie. I don't know the people who raised me. Hell, it makes me wonder who I am."

"I can help you with that one." And before she realized it, he sat beside her on the sofa. The warmth of his shoulder pressed against hers, and it felt nice. So nice, an emotional jolt shot right to her heart.

"You're the girl who signed up for a pageant to be Miss Beaver knowing how ridiculous it was, but you did it because you cared about the mother of a friend who had recently died. You're the girl who visited an injured cat and took him in. You're the girl who teaches the grandchild of a Chinese restaurant owner how to write his name. That's who you are, and it doesn't matter if you call yourself Zoe or Caroline or something else."

He cupped her chin in his hand. "You're also smart, funny, and... in spite of being just a decent human being, you don't take shit from people. You're a tad stubborn, but can be reasoned with. Oh, and you're the girl who looks amazing naked jumping on a mattress."

She laughed, for real this time—even though she felt the tears rising in her throat. "You're doing it again."

"Doing what?" His fingers lingered on her face.

"Rocking at the whole pep talk thing."

He smiled. "I do rock at it, don't I?"

A warm feeling rushed through her, and she knew without question that she wanted two weeks of bliss with this man. Whatever the emotional fallout might be, she'd deal with it later.

Their eyes met. She could swear he was going to kiss her, and she had no intention of stopping him. None.

But he stopped.

He stood up. "I have errands. And I'm going to go to your place. Can you make a list of anything you want?"

Zoe had just sat down with a book when someone knocked on the door. "Yes?" she said.

Ellen popped her head in. "There's someone here to see you."

"Me?" she asked.

"Said her name was Dixie."

Zoe felt a smile move from her chest to her lips as she popped up from the sofa. She met Dixie in the entranceway and gave her a hug. A big one. It was crazy how quickly Zoe had attached herself to her boss, but crazy or not, right now it felt good.

Dixie hugged her back. When the hug ended, the older lady looked at the casket and then back at Zoe. "I don't know what is weirder, the casket or the dog *in* the casket."

Zoe chuckled and showed Dixie back to the apartment.

"I was gonna call before I came over," Dixie said. "But I was afraid that man of yours would have told me not to come."

Mixed emotions stirred in Zoe at the thought of Tyler being her man.

"I don't think he would have told you that you couldn't have come."

"Bull crappy. Since you spilled a couple of plates of food on him, he's acted as if he owns you. You should have seen him the day he came looking for you and you weren't there."

"I'm sorry. He was just... trying to protect me."

Dixie's wrinkles around her eyes and mouth deepened. "From what? Or who?"

Zoe frowned.

Dixie rolled her eyes. "Are you gonna tell me what's going on, girly?"

Zoe debated telling Dixie everything, but she couldn't completely keep her in the dark.

"I... uh... someone tried to shoot me."

"Who and why on earth would someone want to shoot you?"

"We're not sure, but Tyler's trying to find out."

"Oh, Lordie, young lady. Do you want to come stay at my place? Fred's got a whole cabinet of guns."

"Thanks, but I think I should probably stay here."

"You trust this Tyler fellow?"

Zoe took a deep breath. "Yes, I do." And right then Zoe realized how true it was. Somehow, someway, she trusted Tyler—with her life, anyway. Not so much with her heart.

Shortly after Zoe's friend Dixie left, Ellen said good-bye to Zoe and walked out of the office, content with her second day at work. She hadn't expected to enjoy it, but she did.

A foot out the door, she spotted Rick leaning against her car. Did the guy ever give up?

"Hey." He looked up from a book he held. "Have you read this one to your daughter?" He held up the book. "I—"

"You're kidding me, right? Do you think this is going to work?" She rolled her eyes. "You think buying my kid a book is going to win me over?"

"Oh," he said. "I didn't—"

"Move away from my car." She hated that she actually noticed how good he looked and how the color of his shirt brought out the green in his eyes.

"But—"

"No buts." She felt herself losing it. "Let me make it clear." She poked him in his chest. "I'm not going out with you. I'm not getting naked with you. We're not swapping bodily fluids, or dirtying up the sheets."

His eyes rounded. "I didn't—"

"You're attractive, okay. I'll admit it. You've got that whole bad boy image going for you. And I bet you're really good at all that. But it's not going to happen."

Now he was smiling, and he looked sexy doing it, too.

"I am good at it," he said. "But—"

"No buts!"

"Stop!" He put a finger to her lips. Warmth spread through her body, and all she could think about was getting naked with him.

"I heard you out; now hear me."

"Move your finger," she growled.

His smile widened. "Why? Do you bite?"

"Move your finger." She wasn't sure why she didn't just step back, but for some unknown reason, it was important he move it, and not her. And when he didn't, she did it.

She bit him.

"Ouch!" He jerked his finger from between her teeth, but laughed.

"Told you to move it." Suddenly, his humor was

contagious. A giggle spilled out of her lips, and she realized how incapable she was at dealing with him.

"I don't want to sleep with you," he blurted out. "Wait, that's not true." He grinned. "I would love to get naked and sweaty with you, but that's not why I'm here."

"Right." She arched a brow in total disbelief.

"And I didn't buy this book for your kid. I bought it for mine."

"You don't have a kid," she said.

"Yes, I do."

"Nikki said—"

"Well, Nikki's wrong. Ricky's five years old and he's been living with my ex, but I'm suing for custody. My lawyer said I needed to have things ready for him here. That's what I need to talk to you about." His expression darkened. "I don't know how to do this."

"Do what?" Ellen tried not to let her own issues with child custody cloud her judgment.

"Everything. How do I find a day care? I've tried, and either they're filled up or their hours won't work for me. And what do kids eat? I looked it up online and I'm more confused. Is macaroni and cheese considered a starch or a protein? Do I need to get him a doctor now? Or wait until he breaks something?"

The emotion in Rick's voice kept her standing there. "Has he always lived with your ex?"

"Yes," he said.

A little of her own judgment snuck in. "Then why would you do this? Why would you uproot him like that?"

"Because I'm pretty damn sure she's back to using drugs again. It's either that or alcohol. She got clean when she was pregnant, and even when Ricky was little, she was okay. But just in the last month or so she's acting different. Asking for more money every week or so. She called once at three in the morning, and I don't think she even knew what time it was. As a cop, I see it all the time. I don't want my kid to be around that."

Desperation filled his eyes. And she felt it for him, too.

"Believe me," he said. "I know I'm gonna suck at this. But I'll suck less than Candy does when she's doing drugs. And I'm not stupid. I can learn how to do it. I just need some help."

Her heart sank. "Don't you have a mother who could—"

"She's dead."

"Family?"

"I'm an only child."

Ellen frowned. "Girlfriend?"

He shook his head. "That's why I'm coming to you. You're a mother, and I can tell you're good at it. I just want some advice. Please."

His green eyes met hers with conviction. Conviction for a child, the one thing she couldn't say no to.

"Strictly business," Tyler repeated for about the hundredth time since he'd left Zoe on the sofa. What was it about her that sent self-control packing? She'd turned him down. That should be it. Only, he knew she didn't want to turn him down. She was attracted to him.

She just wanted more. More than he was willing to give. More than he *could* give.

He'd left her on the sofa at the office apartment and gone to check on Sam. Ramon, his brother, and Lola had been there. When Sam left to put the baby down, they'd given him the scoop—some of which he'd gotten last night. Sam had told Leo he either went to therapy or she was leaving. He'd told her he wasn't going to sit with any shrink and talk about his fucking feelings.

So Sam had packed up the kids and left. She'd sworn to Tyler that she wasn't going to take advantage of him. He'd just looked at her and told her that she wasn't taking advantage of him. But if she loved her kids, she'd straighten herself up before what their own parents had done to them was passed down.

Thirty minutes later, he was at Zoe's apartment. He opened the top dresser drawer and stared down at her silky underwear. Pink seemed to be her favorite panty color. His mind created an image of her wearing them, then stripped them off and had her standing in the middle of the bed, wet and hugging a pillow.

Strictly business.

He'd given her his word and intended to keep it. Unless she changed her mind. And then... Then what?

He'd use her for a slip-and-slide bang toy?

He gritted his teeth. It wouldn't be like that. He really liked Zoe. Anything they shared would be special. Temporary, but special.

Didn't that make it different?

He wanted to believe it did.

He was about to shut the drawer when he heard the front door open. Listening, he tried to figure out who'd walk into Zoe's apartment without knocking.

The answer shot back. *No one.*

No one with good intentions.

He heard footsteps coming down the hall. Heavy footfalls told him the intruder was either a large woman, or a man.

He suspected a man.

He reached for his gun and backed up behind the door.

The figure appeared in the doorway. Definitely a man, and one who probably outweighed Tyler by fifty pounds.

Tyler held up his gun. "Don't move."

The man came at Tyler so fast it reminded him of his linebacker days in high school football. It wasn't just the guy's size, it was how he hit. His shoulder knocked Tyler against the wall. He hit so hard, and so fast, Tyler's gun flew to the dingy carpet with a loud *thump*.

As the guy pulled away, Tyler grabbed his hair and ears. He pulled the guy's face down and his knee up.

The painful grunt told Tyler he'd done well, but before he was able to enjoy that fact the big ox pulled away and threw his right fist, catching Tyler on the chin.

It jarred his bone and brain. Thoroughly pissed, and ready to get serious, he threw a right hook to the guy's jaw.

The sound was nasty. Tyler hoped it was Bozo's nose. Holy hell, this guy's nose was a lot harder than Leo's. Tyler's knuckles started to throb.

The man stumbled and fell against the dresser; Tyler's gaze cut to his gun. But the two-ton intruder grabbed a lamp off the dresser and swung it like a club at Tyler's head.

CHAPTER TWENTY-FOUR

ZOE TOLD HERSELF she had no reason to worry. Tyler hadn't said when he'd be back. But it had been four hours. She'd made herself a sandwich and tried not to think about him out dining with... Lisa.

Strictly business. He'd said it, and she'd wanted it that way... until she'd been ready to throw in the towel along with her bra and panties. And yet, he'd been the one to pull back from what felt like a potential kiss.

Maybe he'd changed his mind. Decided she wasn't really his type. He had, after all, seen the merchandise.

But he'd appeared to like what he saw. Hadn't he?

She remembered the way he'd looked at her. She'd seen his gaze fill with delight as his eyes traveled up and down, depending on the area with less coverage and more exposure.

So if he wasn't out hitting on some other woman, maybe he was with his sisters. The sisters who thought she was married, who were probably warning him about her intentions.

Or maybe someone started taking potshots at him?

And God knows he didn't believe in staying out of sight. She'd already gotten shot trying to protect him. Who knows, the bullet that got her could have hit him. Hell, she might have saved his life.

And she wasn't there to do it again.

Her heart knotted at the idea of Tyler possibly being hurt. Of getting shot. Of getting himself killed.

Tyler jerked to the right, but the lamp caught him in the shoulder and knocked him down. Madder than the devil now, he grabbed his gun, rolled over, and pointed his Glock at the guy holding the lamp above his head.

"I hate to resort to movie quotes, but... this one is just so damn appropriate. 'Go ahead,'" Tyler seethed, "'make my day!'"

Bozo took a small step back. Tyler stared the man in the eyes as he slowly got to his feet, his finger still on the trigger.

"Fuck." The man dropped the lamp.

It landed on the carpet with a loud *thud*. Tyler could only imagine how it would have sounded against his head.

The man scowled. "I'm not dying over this."

"I think that's my decision now." Tyler spat out some blood.

"It wasn't personal. I'm just a dick making a living like you."

Another P.I.? Tyler looked at the man again, but no signs of recognition came. Then again, the guy could have known him. Tyler's face had been plastered all over the news.

"PI?" Tyler asked.

The man nodded. "Like I said, it's not personal."

"It felt personal."

"You gave as good as you got." The man wiped blood from his nose.

"Who are you working for?"

The man hesitated.

And that *really* pissed Tyler off. "Do you not see my fucking gun?"

The man scowled. "It's the same fucking guy you're working for. Thomas Bradford."

Ellen agreed to meet Rick at a diner close to her house while Britney played with a neighbor. The restaurant was empty except for him sitting alone in the booth reading a children's book. Ellen couldn't help but smile. As soon as the smile hit, she bit it back. She had an hour to give Rick some parenting advice, wish him luck, and send him packing.

"Hey." She slipped into the seat across from him.

"Hi." He closed the book. "I figured I should practice."

"Reading?"

He made a funny face. "When I bought the books, there was a lady reading to the kids. She had this singsong voice that all the kids loved." He frowned. "I'm not sure I can pull that off."

Ellen smiled. "You'll learn."

"I hope so." He pulled a notepad out. "It's a lot to deal with. I don't know where to start. Child care, pediatricians, nutrition."

"Yeah, it is," she said. "But kids are so resilient. They were created to survive until we get our shit together and figure out how to be a parent."

His green eyes tightened. "I'm probably being biased, but I think it's easier for women."

"You're right," she said.

"So you admit it's easier?"

"No, I meant you're right about being biased." She laughed. "Some women can change tires, and some men are super dads."

He shrugged. "But you didn't get accused of being a pervert because you watched a woman read books."

He told her what happened at the bookstore.

Ellen laughed. "I'm sorry; it's not funny, but it is. Okay, I'll concede, maybe it is a little harder for men."

"Thank you." He handed her a menu. "They have sandwiches."

She placed the menu down. "Just coffee. Britney's at the neighbors, and I shouldn't stay long."

He nodded. "Bob isn't going to get mad, is he?"

"Bob?" she asked.

"Your boyfriend." His right eyebrow arched. "The guy you do get hot and sweaty with."

She swallowed. "No, he's not the jealous type."

He studied her. "You don't have a boyfriend, do you?"

She hesitated. "No," she confessed. "But we're not here to discuss that."

He continued to stare at her, and she knew he wanted to push it but held back.

Smart man.

She pulled a book from her bag. "Here. It's the best parenting book I know of. As you can tell, it's well read." She flipped through the pages. "There's a whole chapter on nutrition, on getting your kid to eat, and a list of healthy recipes. There's even a section on single parenting. The author is a single parent, and I like her no-nonsense style."

She handed him the book. He flipped through the pages. Then he reached for his pad. "I'll just write the name down and pick up my own copy."

"You can keep it," she said. "I thought I lost my copy and bought another one before I found it."

"Thank you." He smiled sincerely. "I knew you were the person who could help me."

"Now about child care. I have a list of places I checked when I was looking for child care a year ago. These are individuals who just take care of a few kids. I didn't want to put Britney into regular day care. All the stories of neglect scared me too much." She pulled out the list and handed it to him. "They all came highly recommended by other mothers. At the time they all had openings, but I don't know about now."

He looked at the list and then at her. "Wow, this is great. Is Britney at any of these?"

"Mrs. Franks," she said, and wished she'd left that one off the list. The less she had to see this man, the better.

The waitress, a pretty brunette teen, came over. "Are you sure you don't want something to eat?" Rick asked. "Come on. Let me buy you a burger. It's not a date, just a thank-you."

"I'd take him up on it," the waitress said, grinning. "He's kind of cute. I'd even date him if he wasn't so old."

"I'm not old," Rick said.

Ellen laughed and relented. They ordered burgers and coffee, and the waitress walked away. "So"—he motioned to the book and paper on the table—"how long before all this gets easy?"

She made a face. "Wouldn't know. I haven't got there yet."

"Jeez, make me feel good, won't you?"

"Sorry," she said. "But seriously, it's hard. You worry all the time. You feel as if you've gotten a part of parenting down, and then they're out of that stage and in another one. But it's worth it. Sometimes at night, I'll sneak into her room and watch her sleep. She's so beautiful, so innocent. I just want to do right by her."

"Something tells me you are," he said.

The waitress dropped off their coffees. Ellen pulled her coffee cup closer. Her curiosity got the best of her. "So, you and your son's mother, were you married?"

He nodded. "Yeah. A year."

"What happened?" She emptied cream into her coffee.

He stared down at his coffee. She thought he wasn't going to answer her. "Don't know exactly." He looked up. "I thought we were doing okay. I mean, we were both sleep-deprived."

Guilt filled his eyes. "Looking back, I guess I didn't do my share. I was working two jobs to pay for all the baby expenses. I tried to help, but I didn't know how. He had that acid reflux and cried all the time. About the only time he didn't cry was when she was breast-feeding him. So when he'd cry, I'd bring him to her. She would get furious, but what did she expect me to do? Grow breasts?"

"It might have helped." Ellen tried for humor.

He set his coffee down. "I came home from work one day, and they were gone. I found her at her mom's, and she said married life wasn't for her. Within a month, I was signing my divorce papers. I begged her to come back. Told her I'd do anything, but she wouldn't have it."

"Did you get him for weekends?" she asked.

"Once, but the kid cried nonstop. I thought he was

sick. He wouldn't take his bottle, so I took him back early. She told me I had to pay more child support if I wasn't going to watch him. So I paid another hundred a month. I'd go see the kid once a week; half the time she wouldn't let me in."

"Did you complain to her lawyer? I mean legally, she can't do that."

"Legally, she didn't give a fuck." He ran a hand over his face. "Sorry," he said. "I threatened to go to the lawyer. She claimed that wouldn't get me shit, that when she told them I hadn't even taken Ricky on my weekends, that they'd take all my rights away. I felt she sort of had me over the barrel."

Ellen could relate to having someone making threats.

"When he was two, I started my weekends again, but after one weekend, she moved to Louisiana. I started driving up once a month. I'd tell her I was coming, but half the time she wouldn't be there and I didn't even get to see the kid. Even after all this time, Ricky cries if I ask him to go anywhere with me. The kid's scared to death of me. So I end up visiting him a couple of hours and leaving. The times I do get to see him, I feel like I'm a chore he has to do. He hardly talks to me. It's as if he's angry, and I don't know what for and I don't know how to talk to a kid."

He looked at Ellen. "You think I'm a terrible father, don't you?" Emotion laced his voice.

"I think you made some mistakes," she said honestly. *As we all have.*

"Yeah, thinking I could save Candy from her lifestyle was one of them. She started dancing at clubs again, and, while I can't prove it, I think she's using again. She's always hit me up for a couple hundred every other month or so, but I never doubted it was really to help pay the rent or something. Now, she's called like six times these last few months asking for cash, saying Ricky needed something. I ended up sending it. I can't stand thinking what the kid must be going through."

"I don't blame you," Ellen said.

The waitress dropped off their burgers. As soon as she left, Rick looked up. "I'm sorry. I didn't mean to unload on you."

Ellen smiled. "It's okay."

They both dressed their burgers. Rick glanced up. "So, how did you end up being a single parent?"

"Wrong guy and a faulty condom," Ellen said, hoping that would put the subject to bed.

"Is he still in the picture?" he asked.

She looked down at her burger. "Very little, when it's convenient for him."

"Is he an asshole?"

She picked up her burger. "He wouldn't win a father of the year award."

He popped a French fry into his mouth and studied her. "I unloaded on you, so if you want to bitch, go for it."

She grinned. "But I bit you earlier, so I figure we're even."

He laughed. "I guess that's fair." He popped another fry into his mouth and just stared at her.

"What?" she asked when it got uncomfortable.

"You're easy."

She chuckled. "Easy?"

"I mean, you're easy to talk to. Easy to like."

She swallowed and stared at her plate. Almost as if he knew that line of conversation made her uncomfortable, Rick chose another topic. He talked about the things he planned to buy for his son. Ellen saw the spark of excitement in his eyes as he talked for fifteen minutes about the places he wanted to take the boy—places he remembered his dad taking him before he died.

"How old were you?"

"Six," he said. "I don't have a lot of memories of him, but what I do remember is that I liked hanging with him."

She knew he was wishing he could find that same connection with his son. "Your mom remarry?"

"Nah. I think it took everything she had to work and take care of me." They continued to chat while they ate.

When she pushed her plate away, Rick smiled. "Thank you so much for meeting me. I feel better about everything."

She looked at him, knowing Rick wanted to do right by his son. "You're going to be fine," she said. "You'll get the daddy thing down."

He grinned. "I hope so."

Checking her watch, she moaned. "I'm late." She tried to pay for her food, but he wouldn't hear of it. He left a twenty and followed her out.

While she went through her purse, he leaned against her car door. "Can I ask you something?"

She knew what it was. "No." *Where were her keys?*

"It doesn't have anything to do with getting hot and sweaty."

She looked up.

He grinned. "Okay, maybe it does. Why are you so adamant about not liking me?"

"I never said I didn't like you." Lord, help her, right now she couldn't find one thing about him she didn't like. The way his shoulders looked a mile wide. The way his biceps bulged under the green shirt. The way the dress pants fit across the front of his thighs. She even liked him. The way he cared about his son. The way he admitted his mistakes and tried to do better.

Damn, if she didn't like that confident twinkle in his eye. She even liked his persistence. A woman had to respect a guy who didn't give up easily.

"I do like you." She dug into her supersized purse for her keys.

"That's why I'm having a problem with this," he said.

She looked up again.

He arched his eyebrows. "I feel a spark here. I haven't..." He hesitated. "I haven't really enjoyed talking to a woman like this in... a long time. Maybe we just got off on the wrong foot. Maybe we—"

"Not happening." She tried not to breathe, because she could smell him—a spicy scent, probably a mix of after-shave and pheromones. And those pheromones were at this moment making her dizzy with desire.

"Okay. But why are your eyes saying something else right now?"

"What are my eyes saying?"

"They're saying, 'kiss me.'"

She squinted at him. "Remember, I bite."

"Oh, I haven't forgotten." He grinned. "That's why I'm going to let *you* kiss *me*."

She leaned closer, telling herself she planned to get nose to nose and demand he give up.

Instead, she pressed her lips against his. And it was like magic. No, better. His mouth fit perfectly against hers. His tongue slipped inside, and she told herself she had to stop this. But he pulled her even closer. He was solid, everywhere her body touched his. And she hadn't felt this kind of solid in a long time. She missed this. Missed having someone to lean on. Someone to…

She felt the kiss coming to an end but wasn't ready. She was going to give herself hell for doing this, so she'd better make it worth it.

Wrapping her hands around his neck, she gave him everything she had. Her skin hummed with pleasure, her limbs felt weak, but that was okay, because his arms were around her.

"Excuse me," a familiar female voice said.

Ellen jerked back and stared at the young brunette waitress.

The girl smiled. "I think these are your keys." She leaned in. "Told you he was hot."

Ellen took the keys. And only when she saw the girl walk back inside did she meet Rick's eyes. They were bright with desire—probably like her own.

"That was a mistake." Tears stung her eyes.

"Why?" he asked. "It didn't feel like a mistake to me."

"I can't do this, Rick. Please."

"I didn't—"

"I know it's my fault. But do me a huge favor. The next time my eyes say kiss me, tell me to go to hell."

Two hours later, almost nine o'clock, Zoe sat on the large pink leather sofa with her phone in her hand. She'd called Tyler twice. It went straight to voice mail. She hung up. What was she going to say, even if she reached him?

Just wondering if you were alive.

Wondering if you were out seeing Lisa.

Wondered if you wanted to come back and start working on our two weeks of wonderful.

Yes, she'd probably regret it. But after the withdrawal period, and she suspected there would be withdrawals, she would have the memories. And unlike with Chris, since she went into this with no expectations, maybe those memories could be stored away in a secret little place where she could pull them out and sift through them on lonely Sunday afternoons.

She heard a door close somewhere in the office. Was it Tyler? She listened as footsteps came down the hall. The door opened, and he walked in.

Something was wrong. It registered in her mind before she realized what it was. She saw the blood on his light blue shirt. Then she saw the bruise on the side of his face.

"What happened?" She jumped up and went to him.

"I ran into some trouble."

She touched his jaw. The raspy feel of his stubble on her fingertips sent a jolt of emotion running into her hand that hit her chest hard. "What kind of trouble?"

"The three-hundred-pound kind."

Her breath caught. "Are you hurt anywhere else?" She stepped back and gave him the head-to-toe check. Her gaze stopped on his right hand; his knuckles were swollen and blue.

"Oh, Lordie." She reached for his hand.

"I'm fine." His dark brown eyes met hers, and she felt her heart skip a beat.

"No, you're not. You should get it x-rayed. I'll get my purse." She turned to find it. "I'll drive you to—"

He caught her with his left hand. His touch was light, and his thumb brushed back and forth over her skin. "It's not broken." He held up his right hand and opened and closed his fist.

"It could be fractured," she said.

"It's not."

"It could be."

He shook his head. "I've broken it before. I know what a break feels like. I'm fine, Zoe." He brushed a strand of hair from her cheek with his left hand. For a second, she thought he was going to lean in and kiss her, but he didn't. That disappointed her, too. And then she saw it, that look in his eyes. He had something to tell her.

"Who was the three-hundred-pound guy?"

"I was getting your things from your apartment, and he broke in."

"Did he get away?" she asked. "Did you get a look at his face?"

"He was another PI."

"I didn't hire anyone else," she said.

Tyler frowned. "He was hired by Thomas Bradford."

She shook her head. "Why?" Questions started zipping through her mind. "My own grandfather is trying to kill me?"

"We don't know that. The PI insisted he didn't have anything to do with the shooting."

She sat there, her mind racing. "But would he admit to the shooting if he did it? And…does this mean that Thomas Bradford believes I'm his granddaughter? Why would he check me out unless he knows something?"

"It could be because you were hanging out at his place."

"So you haven't talked to Mr. Bradford?"

"He left this morning for LA for some cancer treatments. I tried to reach him, but the hospital won't put him through on the phone."

She breathed in a big gulp of emotion-filled air and

tried to figure out how that information made her feel. "How bad is the cancer? Is he going to die?"

Tyler frowned. "I don't know."

He followed her to the sofa and sat beside her. His shoulder brushed against hers. "You okay?"

She looked up. "Yeah. I guess. Oh, hell, I don't know. I'm just . . . I feel as if I opened a can of worms, and now I'm not so sure I want to go fishing. My real grandfather might be trying to kill me, but he also might be dying. Should I be afraid of him or feel sorry for him? What should I feel? I'm so confused." She paused. "You know him. Do you think he could really be the one doing this?"

He sighed. "I wish . . . He's a new client. And we've mostly dealt with his security guy. So I don't know what he's capable of doing." He studied her with sympathy. "If you need to cry, I still have one good shoulder."

His words ran inside her head. "You hurt your shoulder, too?"

"He got me with a lamp. Not that I didn't get a few good ones in, too."

"Are you sure you shouldn't go to the hospital?"

"I'm sure." His face was so close to hers.

She stared at his jaw. He was going to have a doozy of a bruise. She got up from the sofa and walked into the kitchen, opened the freezer, and found a bag of corn. She dug deeper until she found a bag of peas. When she turned around, he was standing at the kitchen door.

He stared at the frozen veggies in her hand. "You hungry?"

"No, these are for your face and your hand."

She moved in, dropped the corn in his hand, and then held the peas to his cheek.

"That's cold," he said.

"That's the point."

She could swear he moved an inch closer. Or maybe she had. Her breasts were touching his chest. She felt the swirl of desire rush through her.

"Did you eat dinner?" He leaned his forehead down and rested it against hers.

She cut her eyes up at him, and their gazes locked. His left hand slipped into the curve of her waist.

"I made a sandwich." Butterflies swirled in her stomach, and she took a slight step back. She wanted this, didn't she? Why was she stepping away when she wanted to get closer? Two weeks, that's what she wanted. Fear filled her heart. She trusted him with her life, so why was it so hard to give him two weeks? Oh, yeah, because it wasn't just her life in jeopardy, but her heart. But he wasn't asking for her heart, and all she had to do was make sure she didn't offer it.

She closed her eyes.

"I'm sorry," he said.

She looked up. He ran his uninjured hand through his hair.

I want this. I take the deal. "Did you eat?"

"No, but—"

"Go sit down and ice your hand and jaw, and I'll make you a sandwich."

"You don't have to do that."

"Don't be silly. You got beat up trying to solve my case. I think I can fix you a sandwich. Do you like—"

"Whatever you had is fine." The words came out tight, as if he was suddenly frustrated.

"But—"

"I'm not picky, Zoe." He walked out.

CHAPTER TWENTY-FIVE

"YOU OKAY, MAMA?"

Ellen, stretched out on the sofa, looked over at Britney, who sat in her beanbag chair. "I'm fine, honey."

Britney frowned. "You look sad."

"No." She forced a smile on her lips.

"Did you go see Daddy?"

"No, I ran errands."

"You always look sad when you see Daddy."

"Why would he make me sad?"

"Because he talks mean to you."

Ellen flinched and tried to remember when Britney could have heard them arguing. She tried not to let her see the animosity between them. It wasn't fair to Britney.

"When did he talk mean to me?" She sat up.

Britney shrugged. "All the time. He's never nice like Suzie's daddy is to Suzie's mom."

Ellen went over and kissed her daughter's brow. "That's because your daddy and I aren't a couple anymore. But that doesn't mean we both don't love you. Things are fine, baby doll."

Ellen moved to the kitchen.

"Daddy was here this evening," she said.

Ellen looked back. "You saw him?"

"I saw his car out of Suzie's window."

"And you didn't come out and see him?"

"Suzie and I were playing." She looked back at the TV.

Ellen bit down on her lip. Britney had always been excited to see Noel before. Hey, he usually brought her gifts—a new doll, a new book. But apparently, Noel's disappearing act lately had cost him some of his daughter's affection.

She almost scolded Britney and told her she should have come and spoken with him but decided that it wasn't fair. A child's love should be earned, not forced.

"Did he stay here long?" He'd probably raise hell because this was the second time he'd come and she hadn't been home. She remembered that she hadn't checked her messages. He'd probably left about a dozen.

Not that she cared, or that she'd stop doing what she wanted because he might find an hour to visit his daughter. When he'd told her he would be here on Sunday afternoons, she always made sure Britney was here. And if he wanted to set a regular visitation time, she'd work with him.

Her mind shot to Rick and his ex keeping his son away from him. He'd regularly driven to another state to see his son. Noel couldn't drive across town.

"You want some popcorn?" She moved into the kitchen and pretended everything was fine. And they would be fine, Ellen told herself. But she didn't need to rock the boat by getting involved with Rick. They kissed and it had been one hell of kiss, but it had to end. Especially since he was known to be a player. Okay, he might not be all bad as LeAnn thought, but nevertheless, with her record of picking men, it would surely be a disaster. Even if the whole Noel issue didn't exist, her heart couldn't handle another heartbreak.

Tyler dropped onto the sofa, tossed the two bags of frozen vegetables beside him, and raked himself over the coals for doing it again. He heard her moving around the kitchen preparing him a sandwich and he inwardly moaned. He had zero willpower where she was concerned. Zilch!

Less than five minutes in the room with her, and he found himself trying to get closer, and then...touching her. Why? Logic said to pull back. He'd made up his mind that it was the best thing for both of them. Damn, maybe he couldn't do this. Lucky landed in his lap. Tyler looked at the cat and gave the animal a scratch under the chin.

Maybe he should call Austin, have him take over. As soon as the thought flipped through his brain, he rejected it with a big, "Hell, no!" He wasn't putting her in the hands of Mr. Playboy. The man didn't even like her cat.

Tyler stared Lucky in his one good eye. "You got an opinion?"

Lucky meowed and jumped off the sofa.

Tyler leaned his head back, closed his eyes.

She'd said "no," so he didn't get why he continued to make advances. In the past, when he made up his mind to do something, he did it. Make a plan and stick to it. What was different this time? That's when it hit him. It wasn't *all* his fault. She sent him mixed messages—those sweet smiles, the teasing remarks, the way she moved up close to put a bag of frozen peas on his cheek. Not that she did it on purpose. She was just instinctively nice. Sweet. Sexy. He remembered how she'd moved so close and held the peas to his face, how her breasts felt against his chest. He felt her nipples tighten, then saw her eyes widen as if realizing their proximity. Obviously, she had as hard of a time not touching him as he had not touching her.

So what did that mean?

It meant if he persisted, he might end up getting what he wanted. Her naked in bed. Him naked with her. His mind created the image of her jumping on the bed wet and nude. Moaning aloud, he reached for the frozen vegetables and dropped them on top of his stiffening crotch.

He didn't want this to be something she'd do and regret.

"Here," she said.

His eyes shot open. She held out a plate with a sandwich neatly cut into halves.

"Those veggies aren't going to do any good in your lap," she said.

They might. He took the plate and set it on his lap before she made him move the cold compress from between his legs. Unsure what to say, he grabbed half of the sandwich.

His teeth sank into the soft white bread, then tasted… Not ham, or cheese, or turkey. What the hell was it?

He cut his eyes up, moving the hearty bite of bread and something unidentifiable and gooey into his cheek. "What kind of sandwich is this?"

"Banana and mayo," she answered. "You don't like it?" A frown pulled at her mouth.

"No, it's… fine." He couldn't seem to bring the lump of food out from his cheek.

"I tried to ask, but you said you weren't picky."

"I'm not." He told his taste buds to stop rebelling. He liked bananas and didn't hate mayo on a normal sandwich. But who the hell ate banana sandwiches?

"It might be an Alabama thing." She answered his question without his even asking it. "You don't have to eat it."

"No, it's good." He managed to chew the bite and swallow it. Hurting her feelings held less appeal than eating the nasty fruit sandwich.

She grinned. "You don't like it."

"It's not that. I just... never ate one before."

She chuckled. "Eating should not be a painful experience. And you looked as if you were in pain."

"Not pain. It's just an acquired taste, and I'm acquiring it." He raised the sandwich.

"Please." She grabbed the plate.

He frowned. "Give it back."

"No." She laughed. She tried to take the piece of sandwich between his fingers, but he stuffed it in his mouth.

She laughed, moved in front of him, and put the plate under his face. "Just spit it out."

He met her laughing blue eyes and felt something twist in his gut. Why did she have to be so damn pretty, so damn refreshing?

"Spit!" she said.

He grinned, shook his head, and tried to shut off his tastes buds.

"You're crazy, you know that?" she said.

Yeah, he was. He was loco over her. And he didn't do crazy. Where was the logical Tyler Lopez?

"Not everything is logical, Tyler. You're so smart, you try to analyze everything. But emotions can't be

analyzed." His sister's words rang through his head. And went straight to his solar plexus.

But then Zoe's grin widened and her eyes glittered with humor, and he made up his mind. He'd get himself in check later; now he just wanted to see her smile.

"Fine, punish yourself and eat it. But it's not going to matter a hill of beans either way."

At that point it didn't matter what it meant to her; he did it to make her smile. It replaced the shadows of hurt he'd seen in her eyes five minutes ago with laughter. Sweet-to-the-soul kind of laughter. Hell, she could make him another one and he'd choke it down.

She took the plate with the other half of the sandwich on it and went into the kitchen, but she was chuckling the whole way. And he watched that beautiful backside sway side to side with each step. The memory of her bare bottom when she'd turned to ward off Bud rushed back. He tucked the frozen vegetables deeper into his lap.

A minute later, before the cold had taken the edge off his hard-on in the making, she came to the doorway of the kitchen. "Will a ham sandwich be better?"

"I'm fine."

"You afraid you won't like it, either?" She giggled.

He grinned. "Fine, make the sandwich." And right after he ate it, he was going to take a cold shower.

Shortly later, Zoe sat beside Tyler on the sofa as he ate the sandwich with obvious pleasure. She tucked away the info that Tyler didn't like banana sandwiches. Then it hit. She didn't need to collect data on him, because he wasn't going to be around that long. But they had two weeks, give or take a few days. And she wanted them.

All she had to do was figure out how to move things along in that direction. She really shouldn't have backed away from him in the kitchen, and she wouldn't next time. While she told herself she should be able to just come out and say, "Let's have sex," she couldn't see herself being that bold.

He set the plate on the coffee table. "Thank you."

"You're welcome." She leaned a bit closer and remembered what she'd told herself she needed to tell him—something safer than having sex. "Uh, Dixie came to see me today."

"Did someone else call or come looking for you?"

"No. She just wanted to stop in and make sure I was okay."

He frowned. "She doesn't like me."

"She doesn't know you like I do," Zoe said.

Her words seemed to cause him to flinch.

"You tell her everything, did you?"

Zoe explained exactly what she told Dixie, and when she finished, he leaned forward.

"Good." His gaze met hers, and he said, "I think I'll call it a night." He popped up.

"But it's early," she said.

"I think I'll read."

"Why don't... we could play Scrabble."

His gaze tightened. "Scrabble?"

"I saw the game in the hall closet."

His brow creased with a frown that didn't quite go to his lips. "I'm not the best person to play Scrabble with."

"Why, you're not any good at it?" she baited him.

"No. I'm good, it's just..."

She recalled what else he'd said he was good at. "Super, I'm pretty good at it, too."

His brows tightened again. "People hate playing word games with me."

"Why, because you're too smart?" She arched an eyebrow.

"Yeah." He looked uncomfortable admitting it. She knew exactly how he felt, too. And she realized another thing they had in common. "What was your score?"

"At Scrabble?" he asked.

"No, IQ."

He hesitated. "A hundred and eighty."

"Hmm, then maybe you don't want to play with me." She saw doubt in his eyes.

"What was your score?" he asked.

She decided not to lie. "Officially, it was a hundred and seventy, but—"

"I'm impressed," he said.

"But I purposely missed several questions."

He reared back on the heels of his shoes and studied her.

She retrieved the Scrabble game from the closet.

"Why?" He watched her open the box. When she set aside the black cloth bag that held the letters, she met his gaze. He stepped closer. "Was it because you didn't want people to treat you like a freak?"

She pulled out the board. She considered just agreeing with him because he was partially correct—she had learned early on that being smart set her apart from most of the other kids. But that wasn't the whole story.

She took in a breath. "That and because I didn't want to be that different from my parents." She realized how that might have sounded, and she added, "They weren't slow, they were normal. I already had so many differences from them. My hair, my eye color, my body structure."

She sat down on the sofa and unfolded the board. "I think, deep down, I already knew all this and didn't want any more evidence thrown in my face." When she looked up, she saw the serious expression on his face and didn't want the mood to go there.

She slapped her hand on top of her knees. "What do you say? One game?" And a little more time to convince him to make a move on her.

She saw the answer flash in his eyes. He was going to turn her down. Her chest ached, and she knew if he walked away from her now, she wouldn't get the courage to do this. She'd talk herself out of it.

"We could make it interesting...put a wager on the table." She smiled.

"I thought you were broke."

Her gut tightened. "Okay, let's make it really interesting." She saw puzzlement in his eyes. Before she realized what she intended to say, she'd said it. "Let's wager our clothes." Feeling her cheeks grow hot, she looked down and fiddled with the wooden shelves that held the letters. She could feel him staring. What the hell had she done?

She waited for him to laugh at her.

"Strip Scrabble?" His voice sounded deeper than before.

"Yup." Still not looking up, the embarrassment spread all the way to her toes.

She heard him mutter something under his breath. He sat in the leather chair across the coffee table. "I did warn you that I'm good at it, right?"

She forced herself to look up. "As did I."

Their eyes met, her heart raced, and she offered him the black bag. "Let's see who goes first."

CHAPTER TWENTY-SIX

"HELP A GUY OUT. Give me her number," Rick said into his cell phone as he sat on his bed. He couldn't stop thinking about Ellen. He went back and forth between the kiss to the tears in her eyes when she drove off.

"My wife will kill me," Tony said. "She wants you to stay away from Ellen."

"Why would she . . . ?" Was that why Ellen was so adamant about not going out with him? Tony's wife was bad-mouthing him. "What did she tell Ellen about me?"

"Hell, I don't know. But you can't blame LeAnn. You don't have a good record."

"It's my fault that women treat me like shit? That Candy took my kid away?"

"No, but it's your fault for picking the wrong women. The only women you've ever brought around LeAnn have either been strippers or dressed like they were. What the hell does that say about you? And when you're not dating some skank, you're bad-mouthing women in general. You come off like a bastard."

"She took my kid."

"Yeah, and it's a raw deal. But can't you see that if you'd found someone halfway decent to have a kid with, this wouldn't have happened?"

"I wanted to help her." Rick rubbed his forehead. For all Candy's flaws, he'd loved her.

"I know. That's your problem. You've got a thing for women in trouble. And if they're a little slutty, you fall twice as hard. Not that slutty is all bad, but you know what I mean." Tony chuckled as if to make light of the situation.

But there was nothing light about it. "Okay, fine. You're right. I've got a problem picking women. And hell, maybe LeAnn was right to warn Ellen about me, but this isn't about a hookup." Then he remembered the kiss and how soft she'd felt in his arms. But he didn't want to call Ellen to talk about the kiss; he wanted to apologize. Ellen knew all about being a parent, and he needed someone he could go to. He was afraid he might have ruined that.

"I'm not stupid, Rick."

"It's about Ricky." He hadn't mentioned any of this to Tony, because he was scared Tony would say that it was his fault, just like he'd always done. And hell, maybe Tony was right, but damn it, Rick was trying to do the right thing now.

It wasn't too late. Hopefully.

"What about Ricky?" Tony asked.

"I got a court date next week for full custody. My lawyer said I needed to show the judge I was serious. I need help, Tony. And Ellen's a mom. She met me for dinner tonight, helping me figure out the whole parenting thing."

"Why didn't you ask for LeAnn's help?"

He almost said because she didn't have kids, but Rick

remembered that LeAnn and Tony had lost their baby. LeAnn probably knew a thing or two, but... "She doesn't like me, Tony. I'm not saying I blame her, but it's the truth. Help me out here."

"You're my best friend, and my partner, I'd take a bullet for you, but what you're asking will get my ass in trouble with my wife."

"If the question comes up about where I got her number, I'll tell her that I'm a cop and can get anything. Come on, do me this one favor."

Tyler reached into the bag to grab a letter. What kind of game was she playing? And he didn't mean Strip Scrabble. He meant the game she was playing with him. Was this her way of saying yes to his two-week proposal? He almost said, let's skip the game and go to the bedroom. But he spotted a flicker of nervousness in her gaze. If this was how she wanted it to go... Hell, Strip Scrabble had to be fun.

He pulled out an *H*. Eight out of twenty-five, the odds were in his favor for being first. He'd have her naked and in his arms before she could say double-word score.

She slipped her hand into the bag and pulled out a *C*.

"I guess you're lucky," he said.

She smiled but still looked nervous. "That's what keeps the game interesting. Luck." She looked at his swollen hand. "You sure you don't need to keep those on ice?"

"I'm sure." He hadn't thought about his hand since she'd mentioning stripping. "So how does this work?"

"I think I'll take a glass of wine." She stood up.

"Nervous?" He grinned at her, not to tease her but hoping to soothe her.

"A little," she confessed. "Then again, I think you saw everything earlier."

He laughed. "Pretty much."

Her cheeks grew slightly rosy. "You want some wine?" She started for the kitchen.

"Yes." And this time he didn't stop himself from enjoying the way her butt moved. But holy hell, he wanted her naked and in his arms.

He stood up and tugged on his jeans, knowing things were going to get interesting, and tight. Not that he planned on trying to hide anything. He couldn't. She'd see it all when he lost his jeans. Having forgotten underwear both times he'd gone to his place, he was going commando. Not that he was into underwear all that much when he was at home.

A smile brushed his lips when he thought about her learning that little fact.

He'd settled back down when she came in with two glasses of red wine and passed him one. "We'll use the point system," she said. "Twenty points equals an article of clothing."

He wondered if she'd played this game before and wanted to believe she hadn't. Then he wondered about her romantic past. Considering she didn't take sex lightly, he figured she didn't have a long list of former lovers. He liked thinking that, too.

He pulled out her seven letters. "So what does the winner get, besides keeping their clothes?"

She hesitated as she lined up her tiles on the wooden base. "I don't know; I've never played this before."

A lightness filled his chest. "How about breakfast in bed tomorrow?"

She cut her baby blues up and grinned. "I make a mean banana sandwich."

He laughed. "I think the winner sets the menu."

Before Tyler had lined up his tiles, he had six possible words. Unfortunately, none were going to get him a piece of clothing, unless he landed on one of the double-word squares.

He watched her study her letters and smile. "You look confident."

He loved the humor in her eyes. "I am," she said. "You do know that the first person who plays earns a double-word score?"

"Really?"

"Really. Would you like to see the Scrabble rules?" She picked up the rule pamphlet.

"I trust you." And even if he didn't, he wanted to get to the part where they took off their clothes. Things were already tight in his jeans.

She set out her first word—*zephyr.* She looked up. "It means—"

"I know what it means." He smiled and then calculated her score. The *E* landed on the double letter. With the double-word square added in, she'd earned fifty points. And he'd lost two articles of clothing.

She looked up with a wicked smile.

He countered that smile with one of his own because he'd just figured out his word, and Zoe was about to lose two articles of clothing herself.

Just to make it more fun, he stood and unbuttoned his shirt. Slowly. He stared right at her when he did it, too. By God, he wanted her to enjoy it. Plus, if he set the bar in the presentation of the clothes removed, hopefully, she'd follow his path and put on a show as well. He opened the shirt, one side at a time, giving her a look at his T-shirt-covered abs. Then winking at her, he slipped his long-sleeve shirt off his shoulders.

He gave the shirt a few swings in the air and then tossed it on the sofa.

She laughed at his little performance. While he contemplated which garment should go next, he ran his hand down his chest to the clasp of his jeans, and then up again. He honestly didn't know what constituted sexy for a woman, but he knew what he liked when watching a woman take off her clothes, and he wasn't above playing the game.

Her eyes followed his hand up and then down. His gut tightened with desire to get this game moving along, but teasing her was fun. Dropping back in the chair, he removed his tennis shoes.

She looked at him in puzzlement, but she didn't say anything.

"You can hold the applause," he said. "But you can stick bills in my socks anytime." He held up his socked foot.

"Too bad I'm broke." She rolled her eyes and then reached into the black velvet bag.

When he started putting down his tiles, she said, "Let me finish. No reason to hurry."

Except that she was going to be taking off her clothes.

He waited, impatiently, for her to replace her tiles. Finally, she looked up, and he took his turn. He used her *H* in *zephyr*, and laid out the word *hazards*. With the double-word score, that gave him two pieces of clothing.

He smiled. "Would you like my suggestions on what should go first?"

She scowled, but he could see the tease twinkling in her blue eyes. She pulled her legs up on the sofa and slowly unlaced her shoe. When she got one off, she lifted it up. "One." As she started to work on the other, she added, "And this one will be two."

"No," he said. "I counted my shoes as one. They come in a pair."

She grinned like a little vixen. "Which was an unfortunate mistake on your part. Is a shoe not an article of clothing?"

He studied her suspiciously. "So this is how you're going to play it."

"Just playing by the rules." Then she shrugged oh so innocently.

"And who wrote these rules?"

"I did, of course." She bent down to finish unlacing her other shoe.

"Come on," he said. "At least give me your shirt."

She continued to work on her laces. "Sorry, the participant removing the clothes gets to choose the article." She took off her other shoe.

He studied the sexy, flirty way she held her shoulders and tilted her head. She was having fun. So was he.

He smiled. "You do know that's just going to make me work harder." *And get harder.*

"One would hope," she teased. "For someone with a hundred and eighty IQ, you're not looking so good."

He laughed. "We just got started."

While he drew out his tiles, she refocused on the board. Then using his *R*, she finished her turn with the word *frisky.*

"Hmm. Interesting word choice." He went to work

figuring out how many clothes she'd earned. With the double-word square, it gave her twenty, with the double letter she made it up to thirty. With her ten in reserve, she'd earned herself two more articles of clothing.

He tried to decide the best move—or he should say, the best removal. He could shock her and remove his pants, which would definitely up the tension, or he could tease her more.

He propped up his right ankle on his left thigh and made a production out of removing his sock. Tossing it with the shirt, he stood up, reached for his fly, undid the button, took the zipper down just a bit, and then pulled it back up.

She watched him, unable to hide the touch of embarrassment that had her cheeks getting red. He decided he enjoyed teasing her. Then he reached into the waistband of his jeans and pulled out the hem of his tee. Slowly, swaying and flexing his muscles as he did it, he pulled the shirt over his head.

She'd seen him without a shirt on last night, and he knew she enjoyed it, too.

"Meet your approval?" he asked.

Her face brightened. "It's okay."

"Just okay?" He put his hand over his heart. "I'm crushed."

She grinned. "It's nice."

"Better. But I was hoping for more." He sat down and refocused on the game.

He gave his word choices another quick check. The best option was the word *query*. It would give him a triple-word score and earn him fifty-one points and two articles of clothing.

He placed his letters, grinning the whole time. "Take it off," he said when he finished. "And let's make it interesting this time."

She grinned and reached for the button on the top of her blouse.

He rubbed his hands together. "Oh, yeah, good choice."

She rolled her eyes. "But I'm kidding." She pulled her foot up and lowered her sock.

"Now that's just mean."

She added a little seductive smile as she slowly pulled the sock off. After removing the second sock, she held both her feet up in the air and wiggled her naked toes.

"Damn, you're cute," he said.

"Hmm. Cute. I was hoping for something more."

"Give me more than socks, and you might get more than cute."

Giggling, she lowered her feet, and he said, "Hey, keep your naked feet where I can see them. I should have some thrill since I'm sitting here without my shirt."

She laughed. "Foot fetish, huh? I've heard about your kind." She propped her feet up on the coffee table beside the game board.

He adjusted his chair and put his own bare foot beside hers. The sides of their feet brushed against each other. She had tiny feet, feminine, with light pink–painted toenails. He ran his big toe up to her ankle and back down again. It felt good. Maybe he did have a foot fetish.

When he looked up, she was staring at their feet, too. Her expression told him she liked it as much as he did. And if she liked that, wait until he got his hands on her body.

She glanced back at the board. After studying her letters, she went with the word *suave.* It got her eighteen points, and with her seven points left over it got her one article of clothing.

She looked up with a glint of challenge in her eyes. He ran his big toe down the side of her foot again. How quickly could he get this game to the good level? He decided not to push his luck. Best to get her partially naked first. Bending at the waist, he pulled off his other sock.

He sat his right foot on the table, next to hers. "Mine aren't as pretty as yours, but my second toe is longer than my first, and you do know what that means, right?"

She checked out his feet again and reached for her wine. "I don't know what that means, but I'll bet it's sexual."

He laughed. "Would it be worth mentioning if it weren't?" He picked up his glass and took a sip. They stared at each other over their glasses. The look was long and heated.

Then, eager to get more of her clothes off, he focused on the game. He found one twenty-point word using her *Y,* and it fell on a double-word square. He lined up the word *jewelry.* Grinning, he wiggled his brows at her. "Now, it's going to get interesting. Two articles, baby."

She sent him another mock frown. "Are you looking at the tiles when you get them?"

"No, I'm lucky," he said. "I met you, didn't I?" And the truth of those words hit his heart. He continued to watch her, waiting for her to take something off.

She took a sip of her wine, stood up, and reached for her blouse.

He leaned back. The first button came loose, and then the second. He got a peek at her bra, a white lacy piece of satin that hugged the sweet mounds of flesh. His jeans got tighter, and he knew the bulge was visible, but he no longer cared.

She slipped the shirt off her shoulders.

"Happy?" She looked adorable with her shy smile, wearing just a pair of jeans and a bra.

"Oh, yeah. But not happy enough to forget that you owe me two pieces of clothing." Damn, he wanted to go to her and pull her against him and help her decide what she lost next. Though in all honesty, he didn't know which item he wanted her to lose next—the jeans or the bra. His mind brought up an image of her breasts with their rose-colored nipples with a pillow playing peek-a-boo over them. Okay... he'd vote for the bra to go for now.

He waited to see her choice. She reached for her jeans, and he watched as she slipped them down carefully so as not to take the silky pink panties with them.

Pink, like most of her panties in her drawer.

His breath caught when he saw the little triangle of fabric covering what he knew was a patch of red hair, and he decided this choice wasn't bad, either.

He got a vision of him removing those panties with his teeth. Things got painfully crowded in his jeans, and more than anything, he wanted to lose his pants. He wanted to hold her against him, to rock her in his arms, laugh with her, feel her smile against his chest.

Their eyes met. "I need another glass of wine." A touch of insecurity laced her voice, but the smile was confident. So he told himself not to worry.

He watched her walk away, her round backside shifting

beneath the pink panties as she moved. His gaze moved up to the hourglass curve of her waist. He remembered how perfectly the palms of his hands fit there. A second image filled his mind. Her on top of him, him buried up to her navel inside her as he held her waist and set the rhythm of their lovemaking.

That image had him standing up and readjusting things in his jeans to prevent zipper burns. The temptation to follow her into the kitchen, remove the wine from her hands, and lead her into the bedroom was strong.

But she'd started this game, and he decided to let her finish it. He could be patient for a little while longer. He had a feeling it was going to be worth the wait.

Ellen had gotten Britney in bed, showered, and had just crawled into bed herself when she listened to Noel's messages. Each one got more irate. Why hadn't she been home? Maybe because he hadn't told her he was coming!

Her phone rang, and ready to give him hell right back, she took the call.

"If you'd told me you were coming, I'd have been here."

"Excuse me?" The male voice coming from the phone wasn't Noel's.

It took about a second to recognize it. "Rick?"

"You okay?" he asked.

"Yeah, I... I thought you were someone else. I should have checked the number, sorry." Then it hit her. "How did you get my cell number?"

He hesitated. "I'm a cop, Ellen. I pretty much can get whatever info I want."

"Right," she said.

"Look, I know it's late. I just wanted to call and say I'm sorry. I didn't mean for any of that to happen today."

She bit down on her lip. "I think I kissed you."

"Yeah, but it upset you, and while you were the one to do it, I initiated it."

"You did do that." He gained a point for honesty.

"And that's why I'm apologizing. You looked upset when you left. I'd hate to think our kiss upset you so much that you won't help me get ready for Ricky's arrival."

She curled a handful of blanket in her hand. "You really don't have anyone else?"

"I swear."

She hesitated. "Fine."

"Thank you." Relief sounded in his voice. "And if you need anything from me. Maybe not changing tires, since you can do that, but anything else, I'm your man."

All sorts of images filled her mind. She cleared her throat. "I thought we weren't going there."

"I wasn't." He sounded just as sincere as before. "I swear it. I was thinking more about parking tickets. And now I'm going to hang up before you assume I'm saying something else that I'm not saying."

She laughed. And it felt good laughing, too.

"Good night, Ellen," he said.

"Good night, Rick."

"Thanks again," he said.

"You're welcome." There was a pause. "Are you going to hang up?"

"I was waiting for you to."

She laughed again. "How did you really get my number?"

"I told you, I'm a cop." His tone went high again.

"Dallas gave it to you."

"No, I swear."

She heard the honesty again. "What about Tony?"

"No. I'm a cop."

"A cop who can't lie worth a damn."

He went quiet. "Please don't tell LeAnn. Tony told me under duress. I begged him for Ricky's sake. And he swore he'd shoot me in the kneecaps if LeAnn found out."

"I won't tell." Her curiosity hit again. "Why doesn't LeAnn like you?"

"Because I'm a no-good son of a bitch."

She considered her next words carefully. The last thing she wanted to do was give this guy hope, because the odds of anything happening between them was hopeless, but she wanted to know. "I'm not sure she's right about that. So why does she think it?"

She heard him exhale. "According to Tony, I date the wrong type of women."

"That's all?"

"And maybe I'm a little bitter that I've had some bad relationships. But as Tony points out, it's probably my own fault because I'm attracted to the wrong type of women."

"And what kind is that?" She ran her fingers up and down the blanket.

"The kind that need saving. I like riding up on my white horse and saving them from the ugliness of the world. It's why I'm a cop."

"Interesting. So why are you attracted to me?"

His pause said so much.

"Don't worry," she told him. "I asked."

He exhaled again. "I don't know. Do you need saving?"

CHAPTER TWENTY-SEVEN

ZOE LEANED AGAINST the kitchen counter and tried to get her racing heart under control. Insecurities threatened to rob her of the joy filling her chest. She wanted this. When was the last time she'd had so much fun? Felt so alive.

She wanted to have hot sex with Tyler Lopez. He wanted the same thing. That much was evident in how he kept pulling at the legs of his jeans. A smile brushed her lips, remembering how he'd watched her remove her shirt.

So what was the problem?

The problem was that the whole "removing of the clothes" thing suddenly made her remember Chris and his stripper. Remembering Chris made her remember how much it hurt losing someone.

But this was different. She didn't love Tyler.

Are you sure?

The question bounced around her knotted stomach. The truth hit her full force. She was a breath away from falling in love with someone who only wanted two weeks.

How did that happen? How could it have happened so fast?

She remembered reading once that people in intense situations were more likely to connect emotionally. For sure, things had been pretty intense. And they were about to get more intense. And intimate. And wonderful.

Which she wanted. Squaring her shoulders, she told herself she'd just have to go into this with her eyes wide open. She had to accept that there was a damn good chance she wouldn't walk away from this unscathed. But maybe, just maybe, if she just kept telling herself it was temporary, she could minimize the damage.

Grabbing the bottle of liquid courage, she moved back into the living room. "You need a refill?" He stood beside his chair.

"Sure." She saw his eyes move down her body. She liked how he looked at her. Boldly, but in a way that made her feel beautiful. He didn't leer like many men did.

She set her glass down on the coffee table beside the game board and reached for his glass.

He took a step closer, bringing that wonderful bare chest and sexy abs with him, and brushed a strand of hair from her cheek. She looked up; their eyes met again.

She smiled and handed him his wine. "You ready to lose your pants?"

"Only after you lose that bra and panties," he said. "I'm looking forward to you serving me breakfast."

She moved around and sat on the sofa and studied the board. Her next word only brought her ten points, and not having enough points in reserve, it meant he kept his jeans.

He played next, only earning seven points, but with his points in reserve, he earned another article of clothing. In spite of wanting this, and even enjoying it, she felt her face heat up when she reached back to remove her bra.

His eyes widened, and she could swear his brown eyes darkened. Desire, heat, need. She saw them all. She felt the same thing. And it gave her the confidence she needed to smile as her bra strap slipped off her shoulder.

He smiled and she saw him inhale, his nostrils flared. "You are so damn beautiful."

She bit her lip. Her nipples tightened from his gaze. She looked down at the board, feeling the butterflies in her stomach and the moisture collect between her legs.

She looked at the game board and found it hard to think of letters, much less words. Finally, her mind cleared, and she was able to see her options. It only gave her twenty-two points, but at least then they'd be neck and neck, each down to one article of clothing.

After placing her tiles on the board, she looked up. He was still looking at her. At her breasts. She grabbed a pillow and tossed it at him. "Hey, we're playing a game."

"What game?" he asked in a teasing voice that came out deep and masculine.

She pointed to the board. "Give me your jeans, big boy."

He looked at the board, grinned, and then stood up. "Looks like I'll be the one serving you breakfast."

She watched his hand go to his zipper, and only then did she realize what he'd said.

"You don't wear—"

"Sometimes I do. Sometimes I don't."

He'd unzipped his jeans and pushed the Levis over his hips. His sex, hard, thick, and long, bounced up and almost touched his navel.

"Oh, my!" A giggle escaped her before she could stop it. "I guess I won." She cut her gaze to his face, because looking below was...hard.

He grinned. Not an ounce of embarrassment in his eyes, just pride. Just like a man. Though she didn't begrudge him. He had a reason to be proud. Her eyes shot to his erection.

He started moving toward her. She stood up because it would have been too awkward to remain sitting with his arousal right in her face.

He reached out and gently pulled her against him. She felt his sex, hot and long against her bare stomach. It sent a jolt of excitement through her, and an achy sensation formed between her thighs.

He lowered his mouth and kissed her, gently, letting her know he wasn't in a hurry. His hands moved over her naked back, leaving a trail of tingles in their wake. He might not be in a hurry, but she didn't want to wait all night. The thought embarrassed her, but she didn't care.

She wanted Tyler Lopez to make love to her.

So she took his hand and walked to the bedroom.

He turned the light on. She turned it off.

A grin filled his eyes. "I've already seen everything."

"I still like the lights out."

"Let's compromise." He turned the dimmer switch on.

She nodded, then reached down to pull off her panties. He caught her hand.

"No, leave them on," he said in a deep voice. He backed her up until her legs hit the edge of the bed, and he lowered her down... and stretched out beside her.

Tyler brushed her hair from her eyes. She was so damn readable, and right now, he wanted to read her. He wanted to get this right.

Propping up on his elbow, he studied her face. He saw

a little embarrassment, a lot of passion, and only a touch of insecurity. Dipping his head down, he kissed her. Slow, easy.

His goal was to get her so damn ready that when he entered her, she'd be as motivated as he was to find that little slice of heaven. She slipped her right hand behind his neck.

His dick pressed against her pelvic bone. The brush of her skin against his shaft caused a sweet friction that had him shifting his hips oh so lightly.

She must have sensed it because her left hand shifted down his chest, down to his abs, and found the length of him. Her palm wrapped around him, tight, and then tighter.

He moaned and pushed himself inside her hand twice. The last thing he wanted was to come inside her palm.

He caught her hand and lifted it above her head. "Slow and easy."

She smiled.

He leaned down and kissed her lips, then he moved to her chin, her neck. When he closed his lips around her nipple, she moaned, a sweet little sound.

He smiled against her nipple. "You like this?"

"Yeah." She moved her hip up slightly, telling him she was ready. But he needed more than ready.

He slid his hand down to her navel, then over the top of her pink panties, letting his touch go deeper into the cleft of her mound. The wetness that met his fingers had him getting harder. She raised her hips to meet his touch.

"Somebody is wet." He met her gaze.

She blushed, which made him grin. He waited to see how low the blush would go. "Damn, this is fun." He slipped his fingers inside the elastic band, and more sweet moisture met his fingers. He sank his index finger into her center.

She moaned again. And he wondered if she'd get louder when he got serious. He remembered his fantasy of removing the panties with his teeth, and he started inching downward, kissing her soft skin as he went.

He buried his face into the pink silk and inhaled her scent. Her hips shifted up again, and the moisture on the panties pressed against his lips and he tasted her. And it left him so hungry. He caught the edge of her panties and pulled them slightly to the side and ran his tongue from her center up. He heard a sharp breath when he touched her clitoris.

"Slow down. We got a long way to go." Teasing her was more fun than he'd imagined.

"Why slow down," she muttered. She reached down to pull off her panties, and he caught her hand. "No, I told you, leave these."

She tilted her head. Her eyes were bright with desire. "You can move a little faster."

He laughed. "I could. But I think I like playing with you."

She frowned. "You do know paybacks are hell, right?"

"Is that a threat or a promise?"

"Both." She shifted her hips up again.

"Well, if you weren't talking so much, I might be doing this." He lowered his mouth and caught the top of her panties with his teeth and started pulling them down. She lifted her hips to assist him. And that was just fine. It freed up his fingers to find that wetness again.

He kissed the side of her thighs as he moved past.

Suddenly, she moaned and shot up. She nearly caught him in the eye with her knee when she reached down and pulled her panties off.

"Now, can we get busy?"

He laughed again. "Forceful little vixen, aren't you?"

She came at him, pushed him down on his back, and then climbed on top of him. He felt her moist center land low on his belly. "So you like being on top? I got that from the other day."

She eyed him with a devilish grin. "Payback."

She started slipping down. A part of him didn't want to stop her; another part knew if she pressed her wet lips against his dick, it was all over.

He caught her under her arms and flipped her back over. "Sorry. But I'd kind of like to do it this way."

His tip lay right at her center. Everything in him said to lift his hips and slip inside the waiting wetness. But a voice screamed in his head to stop and grab a condom from the bedside table.

But first, he really wanted to finish what he'd started earlier. He pushed up on his elbow and met her wide blue eyes. "Give me two minutes down there, and then we'll get busy."

She blinked, but didn't answer.

"Deal?"

She nodded. He inched down her body, loving how her skin felt against his. He nudged her legs apart a little bit more. Then he pressed his lips against her mound and slowly moved his hand up. His fist felt tight, bruised, but he ignored it. He had a mission.

She flinched when he slipped his finger inside her. "Okay?" he asked.

She muttered something that he thought was yes, and

while he moved his finger inside her, he used his tongue to bring her the *big O.* Her hips moved up and down, and before he was ready, he heard her squeal. She tightened her thighs around his head. Pressing his tongue against the sweet swollen flesh, he felt the quiver of her orgasm. He didn't think he'd ever felt anything so wonderful.

He wiped her moisture from his lips. "It didn't take two minutes." He slid up to steal a kiss and then grabbed a condom.

Sitting on the side of the bed, trying to open the foil package, he felt her shift, and before he knew what she intended, her hand had moved between his legs. She didn't circle him with her palm, but she oh so gently touched the tip of his dick. He looked down and saw he had moisture collected there, and she rubbed it around his head.

Growling and holding himself in check, he finally used his teeth to open the package. And in seconds, he'd moved her hand, slipped on the rubber, flipped her on her back, and moved on top of her.

Her hair was in her eyes, and he moved it away. And then with one quick adjustment of his hips, he was inside her.

She was tighter than he'd imagined. While everything in him wanted to push, go deep, and fast, he feared she might not be ready. So slowly, inch by sweet inch, he moved inside her, pulling out and pushing in. She raised her hips to meet his. He let her set the rhythm and waited to know she was there before he moved faster.

Her hips came faster against his, and he didn't hesitate. She closed her eyes, leaned her head back, and while his balls were tight, his dick about to explode, for just a second all he wanted to do was watch her.

She gasped, made that sweet little squeal again, and he knew the second she came from her expression, even before he felt her wall of muscles start contracting, milking his seed.

He rose up on his elbows and moved faster, deeper, and before he was ready, he felt the sweet throbbing explode into something so wonderful, so beautiful, that it took his breath.

This time he was the one making noises. When the wave of pleasure passed, he remembered not to fall on top of her. He reached around her, pulled her against him, and fell to his side, holding her butt against him because he didn't want to leave her body just yet.

When he could talk, he whispered in her ear. "That was amazing."

Her face was pillowed on his chest, and he felt her nod.

Wrapping his arms tight around her, he searched for something else to say to try to communicate how awesome he really thought it was, but the words weren't there. He wasn't sure they existed. But he'd search for them later, when his mind was fresh.

Suddenly, he heard a quick intake of air, and fear shot to his gut when he recognized that sound. Zoe Adams was crying. But why?

He pulled back, brushed her hair from her face, and sure as hell, her eyes were wet.

"Did I do something wrong?"

She shook her head. "No." She touched his face. "I always cry when I... have an orgasm."

He studied her closer. "Good tears?" He remembered reading that some women did this.

She nodded.

He brushed a few wet streaks from her cheeks. "Okay."

She grinned at him, teary-eyed and all. It was so precious that his heart folded over onto itself.

They stared at each other, and again he felt the crazy need to say something. But what? When the words *I love you* formed in his head and shot to the tip of his tongue, he bit them back. He couldn't say them. He couldn't feel this.

It wasn't...logical. It wasn't part of his plan. This was...temporary.

He rolled all the way on his back and brought her with him, wrapping his arms around her, holding her tight against him. He felt his sex slip out of her. He closed his eyes, missing that connection of being in her body.

He brushed his hand over her back, still not able to talk.

She lifted her head, resting her chin on the center of his chest and met his gaze. "It's going to be a very short two weeks."

He nodded, not knowing how she'd somehow read his mind. Then his chest tightened to the point of real pain. Two weeks weren't enough. He needed more.

Zoe awoke to pitch blackness. Her breath caught. Her mind put her back in the closet. She was hungry, dirty. She wanted her mama.

"You okay?" a deep male voice asked. And just like that, it all went away. The fear, the panic. Her head was on his chest. His arms were around her. Solid, strong.

"Fine," she said.

"You had the dream, didn't you?"

She closed her eyes. "No, I just remembered."

His arms tightened. He ran his hand up her back. "Do you want to talk about it?"

"Not about that." Realizing he sounded wide awake, she cut her eyes to where she knew the window was. No light peered around the edges. "What time is it?"

"A little after one," he said.

"You haven't slept?"

"Not yet."

She tried to pull away, and he caught her. "Is it because of me? I can sleep on the sofa."

"*Dios*, no. It's not you. Sometimes I can't sleep. This feels good."

It was the first time she'd heard him say a Spanish word, other than to curse. "You can read if you want. The light doesn't bother me. I sleep with the light on most of the time."

"I'm going to catch who did this, Zoe." His voice sounded angry. "If they're still alive, they're going to pay."

She let his words run around her head, bumping into all sorts of emotions. "I know this sounds crazy. I don't care so much about catching anyone. I just want to know for sure. I want answers." She buried her head back on his chest. "I want to know why my parents... why the Adamses did this."

He got quiet. "You do realize that if we prove you are Caroline Bradford, then there will be an inheritance. A lot of money."

She bit down on her lip. "Now I know you are going to think I'm crazy. But I don't want the money. Because if I take it, then people everywhere will think that's what this was all about. And it wasn't. Never has been."

"Yeah, but the money could make things easier for you. You could take some time off from work."

"I don't want to take any more time off. I love my job. It kills me that I'm missing the first month. That's when the kids bond with you."

He got quiet for a few minutes. "Why did you become a teacher?"

"My mom would take me with her sometimes to watch her teach, and she was so good at it. She loved it, and I knew that I wanted to be just like her." Her chest hurt remembering how much she'd loved this woman. "Sometimes I want to stop loving them. But I can't."

His arms tightened around her. "Then quit trying." She closed her eyes and just breathed. The room smelled like sex, and it made her remember how good it had been. She'd cried. And she'd lied to him about it. She didn't always cry when she came. She'd only cried because she realized she was in love with him. Another pain hit her chest; Tyler Lopez was somebody else she was going to have to try to stop loving.

Her throat tightened. She'd gone into this knowing it could happen. She just had to enjoy the next two weeks and worry about picking up the pieces later.

They lay in the dark, not talking. She knew he was still awake; she could feel it in the way he breathed. A few minutes later, she pulled away and sat up.

"Where are you going?" he asked.

"I think I'll take a shower."

"Wait."

The light came on. She looked back at him. She felt naked, a tad vulnerable. But the insecurities faded when she saw the way his eyes moved over her. Or was it how he looked in bed, his naked chest glowing in the lamplight, his hair mussed, the sheet resting low on his waist.

"You want company?" he asked.

She noticed the tent in the sheet.

Just enjoy it, deal with the fallout later. "As long as you don't hog the soap," she said.

CHAPTER TWENTY-EIGHT

RICK ROLLED OUT of bed at six with his usual morning hard-on. But this morning instead of just muttering he needed to get laid, he thought of Ellen. Getting naked and sweaty, and doing all the things she'd said they were never going to do.

He remembered their conversation on the phone.

"Then why are you attracted to me?"

"I don't know. Do you need saving?"

He also recalled how she'd answered the phone, thinking he was someone else. But damn, his gut told him she did need saving from something, or someone.

Not that he was going there. He needed her right now, and his gut also told him that if he pushed for more, she'd pull back. He wasn't pushing. If she needed him—for dirtying up the sheets, or whatever—he'd be there. But he wasn't going to risk pissing her off. From now on, he was on his best behavior.

At ten o'clock, he had to appear in court to testify on a murder case that should have been put to bed a year ago. A no-good bastard had killed his mom.

Donning his suit pants and a white button-down, he

slung his tie over his suit coat. No way would he wear it until he had to.

Going to the kitchen to pour himself a cup, he checked his messages on his cell. He had ten voice mails from Candy. Fuck!

His doorbell rang. Dropping his phone beside his coffee, he went to see who the hell it was at this ungodly hour. Looking through the peephole, he saw an older woman. It took a second to recognize her. Candy's mom.

His gut knotted, thinking something might be wrong with Ricky; his hands shook as he unbolted the door.

He yanked open the door. "What's wrong?" The words barely left his mouth, when he saw his son beside her.

"Hey, Ricky." He tried to get the panic out of his voice. Then he met the woman's eyes. "Come in."

She shook her head. "I don't know how to put this, but things are bad with Candy. She doesn't want the kid. She dropped him off a week ago. But I have to work." She held out a suitcase. "This ain't much, but Candy didn't bring much."

Rick took the suitcase, his eyes still on the tears in his son's big green eyes. He gripped his hand tighter around the suitcase's handle. It took everything he had not to slug the woman for her brutal words.

Instead, he knelt down and touched his son's shoulder. "Hey, it's gonna be okay. I swear it."

The boy wouldn't look at him. That hurt. Rick stood, and for the kid's sake, he forced himself to say the right thing. "Thank you for bringing him."

She nodded. He reached for Ricky with his free hand and pulled him inside, wanting the woman gone before she said something else that hurt his son. He started to shut the door.

She put out her hand. "I had to pay a babysitter a couple of times. Could you . . . ?"

Gritting his teeth so hard it hurt, he reached for his wallet. He handed her a couple of twenties and then shut the door.

He breathed in and out, trying to hide the fury. Then he looked at his son, and his chest grew heavy with emotion.

"Hey, Ricky. You hungry?"

He shook his head.

"I make a mean pancake." Were pancakes okay to feed kids? "Or an egg and toast?"

Ricky shook his head again and went over and sat on the sofa without talking.

When Zoe woke up the next morning, it was almost nine and she was alone. But on the bedside table was a plate with a banana sandwich and a note. She laughed and picked up the note.

Hey beautiful,

I didn't want to wake you, but I didn't forget our deal. Not knowing what you liked, I did the best I could. I didn't want to leave you, but . . . Dallas and Austin would start asking questions if I didn't show up in the office. Come see me when you wake up. I miss you already,

XOXO,
T.

Zoe pulled the letter to her chest and started crying.

* * *

A little after ten, Ellen stood from her desk, walked back to the office, and stuck her head in the door. "The printer still won't print," she told Tyler, who'd cleaned off all the papers on his desk.

"Really?" He smiled. "Must be a loose wire. Easy fix." He popped up, looking extra cheery. He glanced at the paper he had in his hands, wadded it up, and tossed it into Dallas's trash can. "Two points." He walked out.

Ellen looked up at Dallas and Austin, who both wore smirks on their faces. She knew exactly what they were thinking, too. "Looks like somebody had a good night."

Dallas and Austin burst out laughing. "He hasn't stopped grinning since he got here," Austin said.

A bell rang. Ellen looked toward the front office. "Hey, the bell's working now." Tyler must have also connected the chime. Now when someone walked in, it would ring, letting her know they had company.

She took off toward the front to greet the visitors.

When she cut the corner, she came to a quick stop. Rick stood whispering to Tyler beside her desk. A young boy stood nearby petting Bud, who had his head hanging out over the edge of the casket. Just one look at the boy's dark hair and bright green eyes, and she knew he was Rick's son. The boy glanced at her and then shifted his gaze back to Bud.

"So you met Bud?" Ellen moved to the boy.

Rick and Tyler looked up. "Hey." Rick nodded at Ellen. "Ellen Wise, this is my son, Ricky."

"Nice to meet you, Ricky," Ellen said.

The boy looked up but didn't stop petting Bud. "Is that his name? Bud?"

"Yup."

Rick stared at the kid with a look of relief that she didn't quite understand.

"He's an English bulldog," Rick said.

The boy shot Rick a quick glance. Rick looked back at Tyler. "Well?"

Tyler shrugged. "It's fine with me. If she doesn't mind."

"Mind what?" Ellen asked.

Rick moved in and motioned toward the hall. Tyler walked over to the boy. "Do you want to see Bud do his tricks?"

Ricky nodded.

Ellen noticed Rick looking back at his son. Then he glanced back at her, and she followed him down the hall.

"Hey, Rick," Dallas said. "What's up?"

Rick ran his hand through his hair and looked back at her. "I came by to ask a big favor of Ellen and you guys."

Dallas exchanged a glance with Austin. "What is it?"

"My kid." Rick glanced at her. "My ex's mother just dropped him off at my place this morning."

"I didn't know you had a kid," Dallas said.

"Yeah. He's been with his mother in Louisiana. I've been trying to get custody, so this is a good thing, but I'm in a jam. I took the day off to try to take care of things, but I've got a court appearance, a murder case; I can't miss it." Rick looked at Ellen with pleading in his eyes. "I've got to testify, and I was hoping that maybe Ellen could just keep an eye on him here for an hour or two."

Ellen saw the confusion in Dallas's eyes.

"I can do it." Ellen spoke at the same time another voice said the same thing.

Ellen looked at the door where Zoe stood.

"I don't have anything else to do," Zoe said.

"It's fine with me." Ellen looked back at Rick. "Between Zoe and me, we'll manage."

Relief washed over Rick's face. "Thank you." He looked at his watch and then the door. "I should check on him."

Ellen walked out behind him. "Is everything okay?" she asked.

Rick shook his head. "Hell, no! Right in front of the boy, Candy's mom told me Candy didn't want him anymore. I swear to God I almost hit her."

"Oh, my!" She motioned Rick to move into the conference room and closed the door behind them. "I'm so sorry." She touched his arm. "How is Ricky taking it?"

"I don't know. The first word he said all day was to you. I couldn't get him to eat anything, either. I'm so fucked, Ellen."

"No, you're not. It'll be fine. He's scared and needs some time to adjust."

He grimaced. "I called the lady who babysits your daughter, and she said she could take Ricky next week. I've already told my lieutenant that I'm taking the rest of the week off to try to figure everything out."

She nodded. "It will be fine," she told him again.

He looked at her. "I'm so scared, I'm shaking. I don't know where to start. Should I take him to the doctor?"

"Is he hurt?" Her gut tightened.

"Not that I know of, but there's no telling what he's been through." He raked his hand through his hair again. "I should be shot for letting this happen!"

"You were trying to get custody," she told him, feeling his pain.

"I should have done it years ago." He closed his eyes, and when he opened them, she saw the moisture there. "I swear to God, if Ricky's messed up because I screwed up, I'm never going to forgive myself."

He inhaled deeply, held the air a moment, and then blew it back out.

She moved her hand from his arm and touched his chest. "Don't borrow problems. Take it one step at a time. Kids are so resilient."

He placed his hand over hers. "Thank you. You have no idea how much I appreciate this." Frowning, he looked at his watch. "I gotta go. I swear, I'll come right back here when it's over." He started out, then turned around. "I don't know the redhead. Do you think she's okay to watch him?"

The fact that he wasn't willing to leave Ricky with a stranger gave her perception of him another boost. "It's okay. She's a kindergarten teacher. But I'll be here, too."

He walked out.

Ellen followed him into the front office. Zoe and Tyler stood beside Ricky. The fact that Tyler had his arm around Zoe's waist told Ellen they'd been right about Tyler's good night.

"Roll over," Tyler said. But the dog kept raising his paw.

Ricky chuckled. "He doesn't want to," the boy said.

Ellen saw a smile brighten Rick's face when he heard his son laugh. Rick walked up to his son and knelt down. "I'm gonna have to go for a few hours, but I'll be back. I promise."

The boy nodded but didn't speak. Ellen saw the disappointment in Rick's expression as he ruffled his son's hair. Her heart ached for Rick, and for Ricky.

"Be good," Rick said. Then he looked back at Ellen, nodded, and walked out.

Ellen brought a chair for Ricky over to her desk, and Tyler loaned the kid his laptop to play games. She told him all about Britney, and an hour or so later, he started opening up. Ellen got the feeling that the kid was going to be okay.

"Where is your little girl?" he asked.

"She's at school and then she goes to the sitter. I think your dad said it will be the same place you'll be staying."

He frowned and looked at the door as if worried his dad might walk through it.

"I've only known your dad awhile, but since I met him, he's been talking about you."

He looked up, uncertainty flashing in his green eyes. "My mom said he wouldn't take care of me when I was little. I don't think he wants me, either."

Ellen swallowed a lump of emotion. "Sometimes mommies and daddies get mad at each other and they say things that aren't true."

He looked back at the computer. "Do you get mad at Britney's daddy?"

"Yes. And I try not to say things, but it's hard. I think your daddy is a nice guy."

"He yelled at Mama sometimes. I heard him in the other room."

"He probably shouldn't have done that, but I'll bet he's sorry."

Tyler listened to the phone ring for the hundredth time. Frustrated at not getting anywhere on Zoe's case, the calls to the government officials were getting him nowhere.

Everyone was too busy to help out a PI. He'd even had his cousin run down the list of employees who had worked for Bradford during the kidnapping. One had a criminal past, and Tyler got excited until he found out the guy had died five years ago. That would make it kind of hard for him to be behind the shooting.

Finally, Tyler decided to follow another lead with less potential. He called the Tourist Bureau for Shadows County and asked for the telephone number of any historian in the area.

He was given the name Burnett Bankhead, who was supposed to be older than dirt, but who loved to chat about his town and the townsfolk and had even written a book on the subject. Unfortunately, Burnett was either not home, deceased, or hard of hearing, because he didn't answer his phone. And he didn't have an answering machine. Tyler hung up the phone in disgust.

Austin leaned back in his chair. "I just got a call from that retired detective Phillips, who worked the Bradford case. He said he'd rather come in and talk, but he can't come until tomorrow."

Tyler rubbed a hand over his face. "Great. Maybe that will pan out. I'm going to check on Zoe, and then I'm going to head over to the Bradford place and talk to Bradford's security guy, Randall Windsor, and Mrs. Daniels." He also wanted to go check on Sam.

Dallas looked up from his desk. "I thought you didn't want to talk to the family yet."

"That changed when I found Bradford's PI at Zoe's apartment."

Dallas nodded. "I'm surprised Windsor hasn't called to give us hell. He was chapped when Bradford hired us."

Tyler looked at his list of questions. "And Windsor worked for the old man when the kidnapping took place."

Dallas frowned. "You think he's behind it?"

"He could be," Tyler said. "Okay, I'm checking on Zoe and heading out."

Austin's chair squeaked as he leaned forward. "Try not to bang the headboard into the wall this time. It was distracting the last time you checked on her."

Tyler scowled. The guys had given him hell all day. While he hadn't admitted anything, they'd figured out he'd had sex with Zoe. He almost denied it but decided not to bother. He was sleeping with Zoe, and it was freaking amazing. Every other second, he was thinking about how good it had been. Mentally, he'd compiled a list of all the ways he wanted to pleasure her tonight. And if he could just stop thinking about her leaving in two weeks, he'd be on top of the world.

"Do me a favor and one of you stay here until I get back. It should be before five, but just in case I get hung up. I don't want her to be by herself."

Dallas looked up. "I'll be here. I spoke with Tony about digging up the Bradford case files. He won't give it to us outright, but if there's something he thinks could be useful, he might help us out. You do realize that the statute of limitations on kidnapping has passed. If we find out who did this, they'll be going after a murder charge for the kid in the casket?"

Tyler sighed. "I know. But we'll get him on attempted murder for shooting at Zoe."

Tyler walked out. He found Zoe in the kitchen, bent over, pulling their sheets out of the dryer.

"Hey." He studied her butt. She wore her jeans again, the ones that fit so damn well.

She stood up and turned around. "Hey." She wrapped her arms around his neck and kissed him.

"I don't know why you're washing them," he said when the kiss ended. "We're just going to dirty them up again tonight."

She rolled her eyes. "You're that confident?"

"Oh, yes. I've already come up with my plan of seduction."

"And what's that?"

"I bought a book on Amazon about erotic massages."

"You did not." She poked him in the stomach.

"I did." He leaned close. "They mention a lot of interesting pressure points."

She laughed, and he ran his hand down her back. "I'm going to run out for a while. I shouldn't be long, five at the latest, but Dallas is going to stay until I get back."

"I don't need babysitting."

He frowned. "If the PI tells the family I caught him going through your apartment, then they might suspect you're here."

The humor in her eyes faded. "Have you gotten in touch with Mr. Bradford yet?"

"No, they won't let him on the phone. I've tried, but I was told he's being discharged in two days."

"You think someone in the family is behind trying to kill me?"

He hated admitting it, but he did. "I haven't ruled it out yet."

Her frown deepened. "Then I don't want you going over there alone."

"I'll be fine." He gave her a quick kiss and started out.

"If someone shoots at you, duck and stay down."

"Got it," he tossed over his shoulder, and had to force himself to leave. Because what he really wanted to do was to drag her to the bedroom and try out a few pressure points.

Ellen knocked on the apartment door right at lunch. Zoe, still feeling overwhelmed at her night with Tyler, was pretty much hiding out.

"I was thinking of grabbing some burgers for the guys and Rick's son Ricky, and wondered if you wanted one."

"Nah, I had a banana sandwich a bit ago."

"A what?" Ellen asked.

"A banana sandwich." When Ellen made a face, Zoe added, "I think it's an Alabama thing." Then she couldn't help but smile, remembering Tyler trying the delicacy.

Ellen stared at her for a few minutes, then she arched an eyebrow. "Hmm?"

"Hmm, what?" Zoe asked.

"You and Tyler both have that same look about you."

"What look?" Zoe asked, but she suspected she knew what Ellen was talking about. It was the oh-God-I-had-fabulous-sex look. And it had been fabulous. But it had also been confusing. Oh, heck, she was so damn confused right now.

Ellen chuckled. "It's okay. You don't have to say a thing."

Zoe pushed her own issue aside and remembered earlier when Rick had shown up. She arched her own brow at Ellen. "Fine. I won't say a word. Just like you don't have to explain the look you got on your face when Rick was here."

"I was...I did not look any different," Ellen said, and

then guilt followed by relief flashed and she chuckled. "Okay, why don't we both plead the fifth?"

"Sounds good," Zoe said, but something about just chatting with Ellen about not talking about it felt right. But damn, when she left, she was going to miss more than just Tyler.

Tyler had to wait for the guard to check before he'd let him through. Did Bradford think this was Fort Knox?

Finally, the guard opened his bulletproof window. "Mr. Windsor is going to meet you at the entrance."

Tyler drove up to the house and eyed the grounds. He couldn't help but imagine Zoe running around the yard. Then he wondered if she'd be the same person she is now if the Bradfords had raised her instead of the Adamses. Generally speaking, Tyler didn't care too much for people who came from old money. Considering Zoe's giving personality, he had to admit the Adamses had done a damn good job with her.

As Tyler got out of his car, he gave the grounds another glance, and a more dismal thought ran through his mind. Was this where the abduction took place? According to the press, the mother said Caroline had gone outside to play, and when she'd checked on the child a short time later, she was gone.

Good to his word, Mr. Windsor appeared around the corner. When Tyler got a good look at the man, he got a sneaking suspicion that this visit wasn't going to go well.

"I was wondering when one of you guys would show up and fess up," Windsor said.

"And we were wondering why you didn't come to see us earlier." The older man started walking toward the house, and Tyler followed. They entered the first room on the right, an office.

"Mr. Bradford isn't here, but I almost guarantee that the first order of business when he does arrive will be to fire your asses."

"Really? What for? Taking a case? How did we know your guys were involved?" It was a lie, but it sounded good.

"You nearly killed someone who was working for us."

"Bullshit. We fought a little. And we wouldn't have done that if you had come to us in the beginning to do your checking."

"You do the hiring for security, that's all. This was a private matter."

"What kind of a private matter?"

"Not that it's any of your business, but the chick was hanging out here. Following the boss's limo."

"So you hire a PI to check into anyone who has an interest in the famous Bradford family? Isn't that a bit much?"

"The old man's a bit paranoid. So yeah, we do."

"Do you also shoot up these women's places and try to scare them off?"

"We didn't do that."

Tyler studied him and couldn't tell if the old man was lying. "What about Mrs. Daniels?"

"What the hell does she have to do with this?"

Tyler couldn't tell him what he knew, so he skirted the truth. "I figure she's looking out for her old man, too."

"She's looking out for her next liposuction, or some young stud who'll tell her she looks twenty-nine. She doesn't have shit to do with security."

Interesting, Tyler thought.

"So what do you know about this chick?" Windsor asked, and Tyler got a feeling he might be hiding something.

"I know someone has been leaving her threatening phone calls and that they shot up her apartment."

"That's why she hired you?" he asked.

"What other reason could there be?" Tyler asked.

"Don't know, but I thought maybe you could tell me why she was snooping around the place, besides the obvious."

"Obvious?"

"Just tell me the girl left and went back to Alabama and won't be wagging her little ass around here hoping to get the old man in bed and land herself a quick million."

Tyler's insides tightened. "Why don't you ask your PI what happens when people piss me off?" he growled. "Tell Mr. Bradford to contact us when he gets back."

CHAPTER TWENTY-NINE

SOMEONE KNOCKED ON the apartment door. Before Zoe got it open, she heard a baby crying and pretty much suspected who was on the other side. Had Tyler's sisters come back to ask about her intentions? And just what would she tell them now, *Don't worry I'm only going to take advantage of him for two weeks*? Her chest hurt thinking about it.

Zoe opened the door to a very worried-looking Sam holding a crying baby. Her daughter, Anna, stood at her side.

"Come in." Zoe smiled, and Anna stepped inside.

"Is Tyler here?" Sam asked.

"Is your cat here?" Anna asked.

"Tyler went to run some errands." She looked down at Anna. "Yes, Lucky is here."

"Can I see him?" Anna asked.

"He's kind of shy." Zoe wasn't sure how Anna would take Lucky's appearance.

"That's okay," Anna said. "All cats love me."

Zoe grinned.

Sam frowned. "Why is it that I have seven siblings, and when I need one, not one is available?"

"Have you called his cell?"

"I got voice mail."

Zoe looked at her watch. "He said he'd be back by five. That's less than two hours. Why don't you come in and wait?"

When Tyler got to his apartment, Sam wasn't there. He tried calling her, but she didn't answer. He decided to wait awhile, and, not wanting to waste time, he grabbed his phone to call the historian at Shadows County, hoping to get him this time. He saw he had a message. Someone must have called when he was meeting with Windsor.

It was Sam, asking him to come by.

He tried calling her back, but got her voice mail again. "Where are you, Sis?"

Then he dialed Burnett Bankhead. The old man answered this time, and Tyler had to remember his approach. Unfortunately, lying seemed the best bet.

"Mr. Bankhead, my name is Tyler Lopez; I'm a fellow history lover, and I'm helping a friend do some family research. Shadows County is always popping up. I was told by several people at the courthouse that you were the go-to guy."

Tyler didn't know what questions he might ask that would give him something useful, so he decided to ask a bunch of them.

For fifteen minutes, Tyler listened to the old man's stories. Finally, Tyler got a word in and mentioned the Adams name.

"Yup, we had some Adamses here. One of them really hung their hat in Barker County."

"Yeah, Barker came up, too," Tyler said, hopeful.

"What was their first name?"

Burnett paused. "Ralph Adams. Father and son."

"Father and son?" Tyler said. "I don't remember there being a Junior on the name."

"All I know is that they were father and son."

Tyler started running everything he'd learned about the other Ralph Adams. And suddenly something clicked—something that could answer a hell of a lot of questions, too. But just to be sure, Tyler asked one more question. "The father, didn't he own a funeral home?"

"Yup, he did."

Before Tyler hung up with the old man, he'd turned on his home computer to see if his theory washed out.

Tyler had fifteen minutes before heading back to his office. But he'd wanted to stop by Tony's office and see if he'd found the Bradford file. Tyler needed to confirm his suspicions.

"Hey." Tony looked up from the file on his desk. "I was about to call you." He motioned for Tyler to shut the door.

"You found it?" Tyler closed the office door.

Tony frowned. "It's ugly. But at least now I understand how they misidentified the body."

Tyler sighed. "The body was missing the head."

Tony's eyes widened. "How did you know? I don't think they ever let that leak out."

Tyler debated sharing what he knew, but maybe if he gave Tony what he knew, Tony would reciprocate. "Ralph Adams's father ran a funeral home."

Tony leaned in. "And?"

"A week after Caroline Bradford was kidnapped, a

mother and a five-year-old girl were killed in a head-on collision with an eighteen-wheeler. The papers stated the victims were decapitated and burned."

Tony looked disgusted. "Ralph Adams stole a body from his dad's funeral home and made it look like Caroline Bradford?"

Tyler nodded. "It explains why no one reported another child missing. The mother and daughter would have had a closed casket. I'm betting the girl's casket was empty."

"But why?" Tony asked.

"I haven't figured that out yet. But it means it wasn't planned. Adams couldn't have known that a child's body would show up. I know this sounds crazy, but considering that Zoe was never mistreated growing up, I can't help but believe that he did it to try to help Zoe."

"Wait," Tony said. "The body wasn't found until weeks later."

"Considering he worked in a funeral home, he probably knew how long to wait for the body to decompose enough that very little information could be learned. How was the body located?"

Tony pursed his lips. "An anonymous caller said his dog kept going over there and he'd smelled something really bad."

"He wanted them to find it."

"But why?" Tony asked.

"Because he wanted someone to think Zoe... Caroline was dead."

"The cops?"

"No, I think he wanted to convince the kidnappers that she was dead."

Tony shook his head. "But how would he have stumbled

across a kidnapped kid? And if he had stumbled across the kid, why wouldn't he have gone to the cops?"

"Maybe he was part of it in the beginning, and when it got ugly, he couldn't go through with it. Or..." Tyler decided to toss out his less likely theory. "Maybe there was a cop involved in the kidnapping."

"Come on, Tyler. You're pushing it now."

"I'm just thinking out loud. The lead detective, a Sergeant Phillips, retired right after the case. And he wasn't retirement age yet. He's coming by to talk to me tomorrow."

"After a case like this, a lot of cops throw in the towel."

"Maybe." Tyler looked down at the file. "Who were they looking at for the crime?"

"All the employees were questioned. One of the lawn workers, Frank Campbell, had a record, but they could never find any proof of his involvement."

"I don't think that fits. He died five years ago. So it would've been hard for him to be taking potshots at Zoe." Tyler raked a hand over his face. "Is there anything else in there that wasn't leaked to the press?"

"One thing," Tony said. "The day the kid came up missing, they found a clown mask in the weeds."

Tyler's gut tightened.

Tyler was five minutes late getting back. He'd made a quick stop to grab a bottle of massage oil. He stuck his head into the office to see Dallas. "Hey, I'm back. Did Tony call you and fill you in?"

"How did you know?" Dallas asked.

"I figured he would. Anything on this end?" Tyler asked, eager to go see Zoe.

"Nothing, but Austin put the Drake case to bed.

Finally got an image of the husband taking his assistant to the hotel."

"But isn't the assistant—?"

"A guy? Yup. Guess Mrs. Drake was wrong about him being a no-good womanizer."

Tyler looked down the hall toward the apartment. "I'm going to—"

"Yeah, go to your girl. She might need your help."

Tyler turned back. "Help with what?"

"All I can say is if we don't make it in the PI business, we can always open up a day care."

Tyler took off to see what the hell Dallas was talking about.

Zoe sat on the sofa and looked up when Tyler walked in. "Hey," she said.

She had a baby carrier on the sofa beside her.

Suddenly, Anna came marching from the kitchen with Lucky in her arms.

"Hi, *Tio.* Did you know that Zoe's cat only has one eye and three feet?"

"Yeah, I did." Tyler looked at Zoe in puzzlement. "Where's Sam?"

"She didn't really tell me where she was going. Just that she really needed to be somewhere and wanted you to watch the kids."

"She went to see Leo," Anna said.

"Shit!" Tyler exclaimed.

"Tyler!" Zoe shook her head.

Anna giggled. "Oh, Mama will get mad at you for saying the *S* word!"

Tyler sat down beside Zoe, on the other side of his nephew. "How did this happen?"

Zoe frowned. "She looked desperate."

Tyler grabbed his phone and dialed Sam's number. It went to voice mail.

"Did you find out anything?" she asked, trying to distract him.

"Not about the Bradfords, but I did come across something." He glanced at Anna. "Can it wait?"

Zoe nodded.

Thirty minutes later, he was pacing in the kitchen with a screaming baby in his arms while Zoe heated up a bottle. She looked up at him and smiled. "Nothing is sexier than a man holding a baby."

He growled. "Don't mention sex to me right now. I had a completely different plan for this evening."

She moved in and kissed him. When the kiss ended, he juggled the baby to one arm and dialed Sam again. Still no answer.

"You worried?" Zoe asked.

"I always worry." His sister never thought things out. For just a second, he remembered thinking he'd been doing the same thing with Zoe. But the difference was, Zoe was leaving and all of it would come to an end. As bad as it hurt to think about it, it gave him some reprieve from beating himself up for what he was feeling.

"I'm sorry. I didn't know it was wrong to offer—"

"It's not your fault," he told her, talking over the sound of the baby's screams. He remembered all the things he needed to tell her about her case. He looked out to make sure Anna was watching the television.

She put a top on the baby bottle and handed it to him. He stuck the bottle in the kid's mouth, and the baby quieted down. *"Gracias a Dios,"* he muttered, and then sat at the tiny two-seat table in the corner of the kitchen to feed the child.

She moved in close. "What did you find out?"

He sighed, not sure if now was the right time to talk about it.

"Tell me," she insisted.

But damn, he wouldn't want to wait, either. "We think we know the real identity of the kid they passed off as Caroline Bradford."

"Who?"

He read the ambivalence in her eyes. She needed to know, but didn't want to know.

"It was someone who had died in a car crash."

"But how...?"

"Ralph Adams worked at his father's funeral home. That's why he went to get his cosmetology license."

"Why would he steal the child's body?"

"We don't know. But we're going to find out."

She bit down on her lip. And if he didn't have Leo Junior in his hands he'd have reached for her to hold her. She looked up. "How did you find this out?"

"I spoke with a town historian over at Shadows County, where I learned about the funeral home. Then I did a search to see if there were any deceased kids around the time you were kidnapped. Plus, Tony finally got his hands on the Bradford case file. The pieces fit."

"What else did the case file give you? Did they ever suspect Mr. Bradford of doing this? Or his daughter?"

"No. They were looking at one of the lawn people, but they could never get any proof."

She nodded.

He had to ask. "Do you remember anything about… being abducted?"

"No. All I remember is the closet. That's it. I swear."

He debated telling her the other thing; he wasn't sure why, but he suspected it would upset her.

"Why?" she asked as if she could read his mind.

"The day you went missing they found a clown mask in the adjacent property."

He saw the pain flash in her eyes.

"I should have guessed, huh?" Her voice was laced with pain.

"No." He stood up, with the baby still sucking on the bottle, and pressed a kiss on her brow. "It's going to be okay."

Then he told himself the same thing. Because like it or not, he had a feeling of impending doom. And it wasn't just about the case, or about Sam. It was about…Zoe and the fact that he'd lost his ability to think logically anymore.

"You didn't have to do this," Rick said, helping Ellen load the dishes, but he was so friggin' glad she had. He wondered if she knew how much it meant to him. He wondered if she minded if they made this a regular gig. Once, twice, hell, maybe seven times a week. But damn, he liked being with her. There was something…easy about her. No big fuss. He liked the way she did things. From how she prepared a meal to the way she decorated her place. She kept things mostly simple. He could really use some simple in his life, too.

When he'd picked up Ricky this morning, she had asked if they wanted to come over for dinner.

"Ricky asked to meet Britney," Ellen said.

"I could tell he was excited to come." Rick leaned over the sink to see Ricky and Britney playing outside. He felt Ellen lean in beside him.

Ricky, running after a ball, fell. "Ouch! You sure we shouldn't be out there?"

She laughed. "You are acting like a brand-new parent."

"I am a brand-new parent. Much to my shame."

She went to the table to get the dirty glasses. "So how was he this afternoon?"

Rick frowned. "He finally spoke to me, I think it was six, no seven words."

"It'll get easier," she said. "He's scared right now."

Rick peered out the window again, and he saw Ricky look at him and frown. "He's scared of me, isn't he?"

"Yeah."

His gut clenched. "What do I do?"

"You be patient. You love him. He'll learn."

He looked back outside. "Shit! Where are they?"

The back door opened, and the two kids walked inside.

He heard Ellen chuckle, and she leaned in. "You need to relax." She looked back at the kids. "Do you guys want some ice cream?"

That got two loud yeses. So ice cream was okay; Rick stored that away in his mind. So were hamburgers, fries, and carrot sticks. He had a lot to learn, and he planned to be an A plus student.

In a few minutes, Britney and Ricky had left to play in the other room. "You want a beer?" She started for the fridge.

"I would love one." His gaze shifted to the soft sway of her backside. And he reprimanded himself.

"You make it look easy." There it was, that word again—*easy*. He sat on the edge of the sofa.

She came back and handed him a beer and then settled down beside him. Not close, but close enough he could swear he could smell her skin, and it did crazy things to his libido.

Her phone on the coffee table rang. She picked it up, checked the number, and then set it back down. A tight frown appeared in her eyes. That was the fifth time she'd done that tonight.

"If you need to get that," he said. "I..."

"No."

The next second, it was his phone that rang. He pulled it out of his jeans. He looked at Ellen. "It's Candy. I should..." He stood up and walked into the kitchen. He didn't fancy talking to her, but he knew, sooner or later, they would have to discuss Ricky and the papers she would need to sign. Plus she might be concerned. At least, he damn well hoped she would.

"Hello, Candy," he said, trying hard to keep the anger from his tone.

"Hi, Rick," she said. "Look, I know you've helped me out a lot, but Ricky's sick and I need to take him to the doctor."

Fury burned in his gut. "Really, Candy? Ricky's sick?"

"Yes. I'm sure it's not anything serious, but it could be. I need a couple hundred."

"You really are one piece of low-life shit!"

"You won't even pay for your son to go to the doctor, and you call me a piece of shit?"

"Ricky's not sick, Candy, and do you want to know how I know it? Because he's with me."

"What did you do?" she asked. "He's supposed to be with my mom."

"Yeah, well, your mom doesn't want him. And from what your mom said, neither do you."

"That's enough!" Ellen snapped from behind him, and she yanked the phone from his hands, jabbing buttons.

"What?" he growled at Ellen.

She motioned to the door behind her and frowned.

Ricky stood there, staring up at him.

"Fuck!" Then he almost said it again before he realized what he'd done.

"Britney, why don't you and Ricky go back to your room," Ellen said.

Britney reached out and took Ricky by his hand. "Come on. I think your daddy is in trouble."

Ellen handed Rick his phone back, but he could tell from the fire shooting at him from her blue eyes that she wasn't finished with him. Britney was right. He was in trouble.

"She tried to tell me Ricky was sick so I would send her some money. She doesn't even know Ricky's with me."

Ellen scowled at him. "It doesn't matter. Rule number one is that you don't talk bad about his mother, or to his mother, in front of him."

Rick raked a hand through his hair. "I didn't know he was there."

"You always assume they are," she scolded again. "And frankly, you don't talk to *anyone* like that in front of him. Do you want him to grow up and talk to people like that? Is that what you want to teach your son?"

His fury at Candy and maybe at himself bellowed up again. "You don't understand what I've been through."

"Please." She looked back as if to make sure the kids

weren't there and lowered her voice. "I don't care how bad Candy is. The asshole I have to put up with certainly isn't a bed of roses. But I do it, Rick. I suck it up, and I do it for my daughter."

He stood there and let her words roll over him as he pushed his own issues aside. "What does he do?"

"It doesn't matter."

"The hell it doesn't," he said. "Is that why you don't want to have anything to do with me? Because you're afraid of him?"

"I think it's time for you to go."

"Really? So you can point out my mistakes, and tell me how I'm screwing up, but no one can tell you."

"I'm not screwing up."

"You are if you're letting some asshole control your life. Is that the reason you aren't dating anyone? Because he has you under his thumb?"

"This isn't any of your business. And for the record, you asked me for help. I didn't ask you."

"Well, excuse me for caring."

He stood there looking at her and suddenly realized he'd probably screwed things up with the one person who would help him with Ricky. And yet, his gut told him he was right.

"I'm sorry," he said. "And you are correct, I did ask you for help and you didn't ask me. But I'm going to say one more thing, and then I'll get Ricky and leave because I know I've outworn my welcome. And just in case you miss it, it's the same message that you just told me, and you were right." He paused. "Do you want Britney to grow up and let people treat her the way you're letting her father treat you? Is that what you want to teach your daughter?"

He saw her spine stiffen. “You don’t understand.”

“I’m sure I don’t. But I think you just told me it didn’t matter.” He started out, and then he turned around. “Again, I’m sorry that I got upset and upset Britney and Ricky. And if you don’t want to ever do this again, I’ll accept it. I hope like hell that’s not the case, because... as you can see, and as you pointed out, I need a lot of help. And maybe, just maybe, if you’d give me a chance, we might be able to help each other.”

He started off and then turned back around again. “I didn’t mean to imply that I don’t think you’re a good parent. You’re awesome. And I want to learn from you. You’ve already helped me more than I would have imagined possible.” He paused to see if maybe she might say something. But she didn’t. Great. He’d really messed up this time.

He turned and took two steps out of the kitchen, his chest heavy. Then he swung back around. “I didn’t say all this to get you to date me. I’m completely fine with just being friends.”

He took one step back. “I’m leaving now.”

This time he got halfway across the living room before turning and going back into the kitchen. “And while I’m fine with being your friend, it won’t be easy. The kiss you gave me was amazing.” He paused. “I didn’t want you to think that I wasn’t attracted to you. I am. I’m just saying that if friendship is all you want, then—”

She finally held up her hand, and she walked toward him. He didn’t know if it was to slap him. He deserved it, so he stood there willing to take it.

Instead, she got within a foot of him and stopped. “Do you ever shut up?”

"Not when I feel like I screwed up and this might be my last chance to make it right. Am I forgiven?" His chest hurt.

She nodded. "Yes, you are forgiven."

He smiled. "Thank you."

She stepped closer. Her blue gaze locked with his.

He swallowed. "Your eyes are telling me to kiss you again like when we were at the restaurant. Do you still want me to tell you to go to hell?"

She laughed.

"Are you finished fighting?" Britney asked from behind them.

"Yes, we are," Ellen said.

"But I need to apologize," Rick said. "I was upset at Ricky's mother and said things I shouldn't have. It was bad of me, and Ellen was right to correct me. I'm really sorry, son." He watched Ricky's face, not sure he was old enough to understand an apology.

Britney smiled. "She's almost always right."

"I'll bet she is." Rick grinned, even though he noted that Ricky wasn't smiling, and he could kick himself for making things even harder for him. He'd done the same damn thing to Ricky that his grandmother had done, and he'd wanted to shoot her. Now he was the one who deserved to be shot.

CHAPTER THIRTY

"A Mr. John Phillips is here," Ellen announced on the phone's intercom the next morning.

"Send him back," Dallas answered, touching a button.

Tyler was just finishing his fifth cup of coffee. For the second night in a row, he had gotten maybe thirty minutes of sleep. His mind chewed on problems—Zoe Adams leaving, finding the lowlife who kidnapped her and tried to shoot her, Sam and her relentless need to make things right with Leo. His twin had gotten back about seven last light, teary-eyed, saying Leo still refused to see a counselor.

This kind of obsessive worrying wasn't like Tyler. He normally approached his problems with logic. He threw enough questions at a problem until he found a resolution and then set out to fix it. And yeah, he'd tried doing the same with these issues, but he couldn't find a resolution.

Not that all he'd done was obsess. When he wasn't chewing on problems, he was having sex. Or he was contemplating the sex. Good sex. A lot of it. The massage idea was a hit. A big one. The memory wiggled through his mind like a breath of fresh air, and his chest expanded with a feeling he could only define as...happiness. Because he hadn't felt it in so damn long, he realized his family had been right all along. He'd been one damn sad clown lately.

Problem was, the thing that was making him happy was about to leave.

His phone dinged with an incoming text. He picked it up and looked at the sender. Zoe. He read the message. *Miss you.*

Footsteps moving toward the office brought Tyler's head up.

"Have a seat," Tyler said when John Phillips walked in, carrying a briefcase. He wasn't as old as Tyler thought he'd be. Maybe sixty.

"Something funny?" the old man asked.

"No, why?" Tyler asked.

"You got this big grin on your face."

Tyler heard Austin and Dallas cough, covering up their laughter. Was that what he was doing all the time? And how they knew...?

"Just in a good mood," Tyler said.

"Got lucky last night, did you?" Phillips asked.

This time Dallas and Austin didn't even try to hide their laughter. Tyler grinned.

A few minutes later, when Tyler asked him about the case, all traces of humor had faded from his eyes.

"I guess we all have them, don't we?"

"Have what?" Tyler asked.

"Cases that haunt us."

"Yeah," Tyler said, and he knew that Zoe's case would be one of his. Not because he wouldn't solve it but because solving it meant losing her. But damn, that thought hurt.

"About every six months or so," Phillips motioned to

his briefcase, "I'll go through my notes, thinking I'll see something I missed."

"You brought them with you?" Tyler asked.

"Sure did."

"You wouldn't mind sharing them with us, would you?" Dallas asked.

"We'd be quite grateful," Austin added.

Phillips leaned back. "That depends on why you want to know. You guys don't look like the type to chase a cold case for the fun of it. Tell me what's up, and if I agree with what you're doing, I might be persuaded to let you guys make some copies of what's in this here briefcase."

Tyler laced his hands together. "That sounds fair, but before we show our cards, would you mind answering a few questions?"

"Ask away." Phillips reared back in his seat and crossed his arms over his barrel chest. "If I don't like 'em, I won't answer 'em."

"Who did you really suspect for the kidnapping?"

The man rested his hands palms down on his knees. "My gut told me it was one of the lawn guys, Campbell. I just couldn't prove it. And the week before the body was found, we actually put a tail on him. Forensics were certain that the body had only been in the new site for a few days. He couldn't have moved that body."

Tyler nodded. "Do you think he was alone in the kidnapping?"

"I never knew for sure. But I danced a jig when I found out Campbell died."

Tyler leaned his elbows on the desk. "Why did you retire? You were young."

Phillips crossed his arms over his chest again. "You're

barking up the wrong tree, buddy. Don't get me wrong. I respect you asking, but I'm telling you, that case ripped my heart out. That and losing my partner; it took a toll. I couldn't face it."

"You lost your partner?" Tyler's curiosity was piqued. "Did he work on this case?"

"He assisted some in the very beginning, but it was my case."

"What happened to him?" Tyler asked.

"It wasn't related to the case. He was on vacation, doing some fishing, and someone robbed and shot him."

"What was your partner's name?" Tyler asked.

"Now don't you go trying to find shit on a marble floor. Marcus Dean was a good man."

Tyler leaned back and decided to follow this lead on his own. "Did you ever suspect any of the family in the kidnapping?"

"I know everyone wanted it to be that way. Rich family kills their own daughter, but I didn't buy that. That girl's mama, she was broken. A good woman. Not uppity like the rest of them. Honestly, when her plane went down right after that, I almost thought she wanted it that way. Losing that little girl ripped her heart out."

"And Mr. Bradford's daughter, did you ever feel . . . ?"

"Never cared for that cold woman. She actually hit on my partner. Her niece was missing and she's trying to get laid. But I don't think she could have killed that child."

"But do you think she might have been involved in the kidnapping?"

Phillips settled back in his chair. "You know what I find interesting?"

"What's that?" Tyler asked.

"Why you keep talking about the kidnapping and don't seem to give a rat's ass that the girl was murdered. Maybe you don't know how sick it was, but—"

"Hey," Zoe said from the doorway. "Can I steal a cup of coffee?"

Tyler frowned.

John Phillips looked back at Zoe, and his face went instantly pale. He blinked, looked back at Tyler, and said, "Okay, this just got screwy, because I don't believe in ghosts. So I think I'm done yapping my jaws until I get some explanations."

Zoe awoke with a start. She reached for Tyler, but he wasn't there. She looked at the clock. 3:33 a.m. "Tyler?" When he didn't answer and she didn't hear any bathroom noises, she slipped out of bed, naked. She spotted Tyler's shirt on the dresser and slipped it on. The realization hit that in ten days, she'd be back in Alabama and sleeping alone. The thought grew heavy and landed with a thump in her chest.

She had accepted that she was in love with Tyler Lopez. She had also accepted that it probably wouldn't go anywhere. Funny how she'd added the word *probably* to the sentence. She just kept hoping that maybe when it came time to leave, Tyler would suggest they rethink the whole long-distance relationship thing. But she vowed she wouldn't be the one to bring it up. He'd made his position clear in the beginning, and she wouldn't pressure him.

He wasn't in the living room or the kitchen, so she opened the door that led to the business. Light spilled out of the office. Her bare feet barely made a sound as she moved to the door.

Tyler sat at his desk, one hand on Lucky's back moving his fingers over his fur as he read from the open file on his desk. She stood there for several minutes, savoring the view of him shirtless and so intense.

He must have sensed her because he looked up. "Hey, what are you doing up?"

"Looking for you." She moved in and sat on the edge of his desk. "What are you doing?"

"Reading over Phillips's notes again."

She frowned. "Do you really think his partner's death was related to my case?"

"Yeah, I do. It's too much of a coincidence. He was killed in Barker County."

"But that doesn't mean my dad killed him." Zoe had given up trying not to refer to the Adamses as her parents. They had raised her, loved her. And as hard as it was to accept they were behind any of this, she couldn't stop loving them. "He was a gentle man, Tyler."

Tyler's expression filled with empathy. He slid his hand over her knee. "If your dad had anything to do with it, I bet it was to protect you." He shook his head. "Whether we like it or not, we are products of our parents and our upbringing. Our flaws, even our good traits, are due to our circumstances. You are incredible, and that has to mean they were incredible parents."

She smiled. "Thank you."

His expression went from empathetic to sexy. "And you look a hell of a lot better in my shirt than I do." He reached and touched the hem of the shirt to raise it.

She slapped his hand and giggled. He grinned sheepishly and ran his hand up and down her calf.

"Can't you sleep?" she asked.

"My brain is too busy chewing on things. The case, Sam, and...sex." He slowly moved his hand up to her thigh. The sweet sensation of his touch had her catching her breath, and when he slipped under the shirt, she didn't stop him this time.

When his fingers moved higher between her thighs, she didn't stop him, either.

"You're going to end up with a wet spot on your desk." She giggled.

"Well, damn," he said, and laughed. And then he brushed all the paperwork off his desk. "I knew there was a reason I cleaned off my desk."

Friday morning, hyped up on caffeine and sex, Tyler sat at his desk and wondered how long he could go without sleeping. He'd usually get by with five hours a night, but he was down to one or two. He didn't know what was wrong with him.

That wasn't true.

He knew.

He just didn't want to think about it too much.

"Did you ever hear from Mrs. Drake?" Dallas asked Austin.

Tyler ignored their conversation and focused on his shit.

He'd recalled a psychology book he'd read a couple of years back. It had covered how the brain worked in different phases of one's life. One of the side effects of being in love was the inability to sleep. Others were an intense sex drive, a sense of euphoria, and the inability to stop thinking about the person with whom you were enamored. Symptoms he had. Not that he was in love. He just was on the road to being there.

His ability to sleep had vanished. In three days, they'd gone through a twelve-pack of condoms. If he hadn't been worried about chafing, he would have used twice that many. He was happy for the first time in...a long time. And there wasn't a second that Zoe didn't pop into his mind.

And she was leaving.

That bit down on his sense of euphoria like a hungry dog. And yet, seeing how Sam let herself be abused because of their flawed upbringing sent up red flags for Tyler. She was a walking example of the old adage: Insanity is doing the same thing over and over and expecting different results. And damn it, if he didn't watch out, he was going to find himself in that same boat.

In spite of believing from the start that he was preconditioned to fail at marriage, he'd pushed his logic aside to believe in Lisa. To believe he could have what his older brother and his older sister had with their spouses. He'd thought he had it, too. And then he'd been accused of murder, of being a dirty cop. He could have handled the betrayal of the force; sure, it would have hurt, but he could have gotten through that. But when Lisa stopped believing in him, Tyler realized how stupid he'd been to let down his guard.

In the back of his mind, he could hear the words Lisa had thrown at him after he'd been arrested. "I don't know what I believe, Tyler. They have your prints."

How could she think he could butcher a man and his wife? *Dios*, she'd ripped his heart out that day. And down deep, he knew it shouldn't matter, but it still did. He didn't want to be hurt like that again. Losing Zoe was going to hurt like hell, but it would hurt twice as much if he started believing again. What he had to do was just enjoy it while it lasted. Let her walk away and know that while it hurt, it would only hurt more if he tried to hold on.

"Hey." Zoe bolted into the office. "Where's Lucky? The apartment door was left open."

"I must have..." Realizing he'd been the last one out of the apartment, he popped up. He looked back at Dallas. "Where's Bud?"

"Bud?" Dallas shot up from his chair.

"Shh!" Ellen appeared in the door of the office. "You guys gotta come see this."

Tyler wrapped his arm around Zoe and followed Ellen. Dallas and Austin came behind them.

Ellen motioned to the casket. Tyler eased in, Zoe at his side. Bud and Lucky were curled up together, practically spooning in the casket. Everyone laughed. The dog and cat stirred. Two big canine bug eyes and one feline eye stared up at them, but the animals were too comfortable to move.

"Traitor," Austin said to Bud, and everyone laughed.

"That's sweeter than apple pie," Zoe said, and leaned against Tyler.

Sweet was having her next to him, Tyler thought. *Enjoy it while it lasts*, he told himself. But his time was ticking away.

Tyler was back at his desk about an hour later when he heard the bell chime, telling him someone had just come in, and then, "Sir, you don't go back there until I..." Ellen's voice rose from the front room.

"What now?" Dallas muttered.

"If it's another cheating-spouse case, I say we take it,"

Austin said. "I just invested in a watch camera, and I can take pictures anywhere now without being seen."

Tyler stood to check on Ellen.

He hadn't gotten a foot from his desk when he saw the old man walking through the doorway.

"Mr. Bradford," Tyler said, trying not to show his surprise.

Bradford stared at Tyler. "Would you like to explain why you attacked my hired help?"

Hired help? Was that what he called PIs? Tyler asked himself, somehow feeling insulted. "Well, sir, your *hired help* broke into our client's apartment."

"She was snooping around my mansion. I sent him to get some answers."

"Problem is someone sent a thug to kill her, too."

"That wasn't me! And thanks to you, my man came back empty-handed, so do you mind telling me why this client of yours was snooping around my place?"

Tyler looked at Dallas. "Can you make sure we're not disturbed?" The last thing he wanted now was for Zoe to walk in.

Dallas stood. "I'm on it."

Tyler motioned to a chair. "Have a seat."

As Tyler settled back in his chair, he tried to decide which approach he'd take. He'd had several different approaches planned but hadn't decided the best tactic yet.

While Tyler found it hard to believe Bradford was behind the kidnapping, or had someone try to run her out of town, it was evident that someone at the mansion had recognized Zoe and wanted her gone.

Tyler cupped his hands together. "It's a long story."

"Well, make it short. I don't have much time. Matter of

fact, I'm told I have six months. So I don't intend to waste any more than I have to by dealing with this."

Tyler leaned back in his chair. "I'm sorry."

"Don't put on airs for me. Just answer my question."

"Her name is Zoe Adams." Tyler waited for the old man to respond to it.

He didn't.

"I had her name," Bradford snapped.

"That's right, you had one of your security officers pull her over and give her a ticket while he was on duty for the Glencoe PD."

"I did no such thing," Bradford said. "I hired a PI to find out what she was up to. That's all. What I want to know is what she's looking to steal or take from me. I'm tired of people taking things. I've had too many things taken from me in my life."

Tyler got the feeling he wasn't talking monetary things. "She doesn't want anything. Have you had the pleasure of seeing Zoe Adams?"

"Seeing her?" Bradford looked confused. "She followed my limo. And I was told she was hanging out at the front gate."

So the old man hadn't really gotten a good look at Zoe. Tyler worried the truth would be too much for a dying old man. "Are you aware of the broadcast of *Unsolved Mystery Hunters* that featured the Bradford kidnapping?"

"Aware of it? I filed a civil suit against them. Bringing up family matters like that just to help their ratings is a crime." He frowned. "Is that who she is? Someone from that show?"

"No." He folded his hands together. "I don't know how to say this without it sounding crazy. But *we* think that Zoe Adams is Caroline Bradford."

The old man looked stunned, then he stiffened. "Do I look like a fool? What kind of PIs are you if you believe some nonsense like that. My granddaughter was murdered."

"Actually, according to the police records, her body was never officially identified." Tyler saw no reason to point out why.

"But..." The old man sputtered. "She had on the same clothes she was taken in. They were burned, but we knew they were hers because her name had been sewn into the tags. And there was her stuffed dog."

"I know. But we think someone wanted everyone to believe she was killed."

"Why?"

"We don't have those answers yet."

Bradford shook his head. "My granddaughter's dead."

Tyler opened his desk and found the copy of the picture he had of Zoe in first grade. He pushed it across the desk. "Do you recognize this little girl?"

Shock entered his faded blue eyes. "There are programs that can alter photos."

"This one wasn't altered. And neither is this one." He clicked his mouse to bring up his screen saver, which was a shot he'd taken of Zoe with his cell phone. "It was taken two days ago." Tyler turned his laptop around.

The old man gasped. Tyler knew in his gut that Bradford wasn't that good of an actor. He hadn't known who Zoe was and therefore didn't have a reason to shoot at her. But someone else had.

"She looks just like my daughter-in-law," the old man said.

Tyler nodded. "I know."

"I don't understand. How could...? Where's she been? Why did she wait so long to come back?"

"She didn't remember. She had one or two vague memories of her childhood. When she saw the show, some of the things she had remembered all her life made sense."

"Where is she? I need to see her. I'll need DNA tests."

"DNA is fine. I'll check with Zoe about meeting you. But there's a problem." He leaned in. "Someone has tried to kill Zoe, and the only thing that makes sense is that it's someone at your mansion. And the only reason that someone would want her dead is because they were behind the kidnapping."

"That's ridiculous. My hired help are trustworthy."

"What about your family?"

CHAPTER THIRTY-ONE

"IS BRITNEY HERE?" Ricky asked when they pulled up at the Only in Texas office. His three words came out with more excitement than Rick had heard from him all day.

"No. But Ellen is." And Rick was eager to see her, too. He'd thought so much about her that he'd driven himself crazy. His litany for the last few days was... What would Ellen do? Not that he didn't think about her outside of parenting. He couldn't stop thinking about their kiss—or about how, when she laughed, her eyes twinkled like Christmas lights. And that's how she made him feel. Like a kid at Christmas.

He'd needed to talk to Tyler, but Rick could have done it over the phone. He pulled on the rearview mirror. He ran his hand through his hair and then popped a mint in his mouth.

"Is she your girlfriend?" Ricky asked.

Rick flinched. "Uh, just friends."

"She's pretty."

"Yeah, she is." And she was smart and so easy to be around. She was... perfect. Simple and yet nice. She...

"Are we going to just sit here, or are we going inside?" Ricky asked.

Rick flinched again, realizing how easy it was to just get lost in his thoughts when Ellen was the subject. "Let's go inside." He ushered his son out of the car and into the PI firm.

Ellen looked up when they walked in. "Hello."

The first thing he noticed was her smile. Genuine, as if she was happy to see him. Then he noticed she was looking at Ricky and not him. Oh, well. It still felt good.

Ricky ran up to her desk. "Can I play with Tyler's computer again?"

Rick made a note to get some kid games on his old laptop.

"I can ask," Ellen said.

"Is Bud here?" Ricky asked.

"Yup, he's in the office. Why don't you go on back? I'll follow in a few."

Ricky took off, and finally, she looked at Rick. While her smile wasn't quite as vibrant, it wasn't forced. "How are things?" she asked.

"We're managing."

"I expected to get a lot of calls from you," she said.

"I didn't know if you really wanted to deal with me."

She looked puzzled. "I told you everything was fine."

"Yeah, but I guess I was still insecure."

"Don't be."

"In that case, do you think maybe I could buy you and Britney dinner tonight for cooking for us?" His gut knotted, waiting for her reply.

"I cooked hamburgers and oven-baked fries."

"Yeah, but they were really good. And the company was... great."

She smiled. "We'd love to have dinner. I was actually thinking of suggesting you take Ricky over to the sitters today and let him meet her, so it won't be so new to him on Monday."

Rick frowned. "Damn, why didn't I think of that? Should I call her?"

"Just tell her you want to drop by. As a matter of fact, we could meet up there and then go to dinner."

"Yeah, that sounds great."

"Good," she said.

And it was, but for the life of him he didn't know where things were going between them.

They walked back to find Ricky. He was on the floor petting Bud, and Tyler was pulling another laptop from his desk. "I was just about to call you," Tyler said, and then handed the laptop to Ellen. "Here. He asked if he could play with it."

"Thanks," Rick told him. And then he looked at Ricky. "Can you tell him thanks?" Rick actually felt proud of himself for thinking to remind Ricky. Parenting stuff kept you on your toes. But the book Ellen had given him was a saving grace.

"Thanks," Ricky said.

When Ricky and Ellen walked out, Rick dropped down in the chair across from Tyler. "I'm sorry about not being available tomorrow to go to the Bradfords, but I need to get things situated with Ricky. I came here to tell you that I don't think I can work next weekend, either. It might be best to find a replacement."

"I get it. The kid's more important. That's not why I wanted to talk to you. Tony told me you're friends with Stan Martin, the Glencoe cop who retired a couple of years back."

"Yeah, I partnered with him when I first came on. Why?"

Tyler filled him in on what they'd learned about the Bradford case, from the old man coming into the office to the death of the retired detective's partner. "Officer Dean was murdered in the same county where Zoe's parents had lived."

"You really think Dean was behind the kidnapping?" Accusing a fellow officer didn't sit well with him.

"I'm just asking questions. But John Phillips has a high opinion of Marcus Dean. I'd like a second opinion, and Martin worked with Dean for a while."

"I'll call him this afternoon," Rick said.

"We'll compensate you," Tyler said.

"We're talking about a phone call."

"One other thing," Tyler said. "What was your impression of Mrs. Daniels?"

Ricky knew what Tyler was thinking. Someone at the Bradfords' did the shooting. "She's always talking about going to a shooting range. I don't see her pulling the trigger, but she might hire someone to do it."

"What about Windsor? What does your gut say about him?"

Rick considered the question. "I think he looks out for number one. If he thought Zoe could finger him for a crime, I wouldn't put it past him."

Tyler frowned. "I'm taking Zoe to the mansion for dinner Sunday night."

"And you don't like it," Rick said.

"And I don't like it," Tyler confirmed.

Friday afternoon, Zoe was vacuuming the living room and worrying about her upcoming dinner with the

Bradfords. She had no idea what to expect. Would they like her? Resent her? Could someone in the family really be the person wanting to kill her? If so, why? When she heard a knock on the apartment door, she turned around.

"Dixie!" Zoe ran past Tyler to hug her boss. Or her ex-boss. Chances were, she'd be going home and never work at the diner again. No more Dixie. No more being one of Dixie's girls. No more Tyler, either, and all his friends. Her throat suddenly grew tight.

When Zoe pulled back, Dixie stared at her almost as if she was reading her mind. "You okay, girly?"

"I'm fine. You?" Zoe said, talking around the lump in her throat.

"I miss seeing your smiling face across the counter." She patted Zoe's cheek like a concerned mama. And the touch increased the size of the knot in Zoe's throat and brought tears to her eyes. She blinked them away.

"I'm sorry. He wouldn't let me come back to work." She pointed at Tyler and forced a grin.

"I figured as much." Dixie frowned at Tyler. "It's always a man's fault," she said in her teasing voice.

"Because someone tried to shoot her," Tyler snapped as if not realizing Dixie was joking.

"I know. Which brings me to the question. Have you found out who?"

"I'm working on it," Tyler said, obviously not wanting to go into anything with Dixie. "I think I'll just go back to my office." Tyler moved in, studied her eyes as if noting her pain, then he leaned in and kissed her.

When he left, Dixie set her big canvas bag on the coffee table. "I knew that man had his sights on you."

"Sit down," Zoe said, and attempted another smile.

"I brought you some supper." She waved at the bag.

"Chicken and dumplings?" Zoe asked.

"And squash casserole."

"I love you," Zoe said, but it wasn't because of the food. It was because she had so few people who really cared about her.

Dixie sighed. "What's going on, Zoe? Who's trying to hurt you?"

Zoe took a deep breath to fight back the tears, and for the next thirty minutes, she told Dixie the truth.

"Listen to them laugh," Rick told Ellen that Friday evening.

They had gone out for pizza. While Ricky and Britney had played video games in the restaurant's game room, Rick and Ellen had talked about baseball. Who would have ever thought she knew a lick about baseball—but considering she could change out a transmission, he probably should have guessed. Not that they agreed on their favorite teams. He went for the Astros, and she was a Dodger fan. But just sitting there chatting, debating with her on the best team, was... well, fun. More fun than he'd had in a hell of a long time.

Then because Ricky had wanted to show Britney his new race-car bed, they'd come back to his place. When he first got home, he went to the gun safe and locked up his weapon. Ellen watched him.

"What?" he asked when she continued to stare.

"Nothing, I'm just glad you do that. Lock it up right away. I... don't like guns around kids."

"Don't worry. I would never leave it out." They sat on the sofa, and he loved having her beside him.

In spite of having the kids less than thirty feet away, all he could think about was showing Ellen his own bed.

"They get along really well," she said.

"Yep."

There was a lapse of silence. "He was married," she blurted out.

It took him only a second to understand that she was talking about Britney's father.

"I swear I didn't know he was married," she went on. "He had an apartment downtown. We met at a coffee shop. He's a high-powered lawyer at Baker and Quarles. I was enamored. I was a fool."

She didn't look at him. Rick put his hand on top of hers. The pain in her voice was palpable.

"When I found out I was pregnant, Noel told me he was married and offered to pay for an abortion. I hated him for that, but I wanted to keep the baby. So I packed up and moved to Florida. Three years later, Dad started having health issues and I had to come back." She paused. "One day Noel ran into Britney and me, and he knew. He was angry at first, then he said he was glad. Then... then things got bad."

Rick stroked his thumb over her hand but didn't say anything.

"It started when I met James. He was a plumber. A nice guy. Noel didn't approve. He threatened to sue me for custody. I didn't believe him at first, then he had someone follow me, hoping I'd do something stupid." She paused. "And I did. James and I had sex in my hot tub. Britney was at my mom's." She swallowed. "His guy got some pictures, and then Noel threatened that if I didn't break it off with James, he'd use the picture to prove I was an unfit mom. He reminded me what a big-shot attorney he was."

Rick felt violated for her. "Just because you have a relationship with someone doesn't make you a bad mom."

"I was furious. I had to tell James, and then he got furious."

"Of course, he would." Rick couldn't help but wonder where nice-guy James was now.

She glanced at Rick. "James was furious at me for not telling him the whole story about Noel. He didn't believe I didn't know Noel was married."

"Then both of them are assholes."

She turned her hand over and laced her fingers through his. "I went to see a lawyer, just to see where I stood legally. I was told that with Noel having the pull he does in courts, there was a slight chance Noel could actually take Britney."

"That's bullshit," Rick said.

"Half of life is bullshit."

"Wait," Rick said. "You told me he doesn't even see her on regular visits, didn't you?"

She nodded.

"So his wife doesn't know about Britney?"

"He said he told her."

"That's more bullshit. If he'd told her, he'd have a regular visitation schedule."

"Maybe she just doesn't want him to see Britney." Ellen met his gaze again. Tears welled in her eyes. "I'm scared, Rick."

Those tears had his heart doubling over. "Can I talk to him?" *Teach the asshole a lesson.*

"No. I need to do this myself."

He nodded but didn't like it. He looked at their locked hands. "Where does this leave us?"

"Is it too much to ask for a little time?"

He brought her hand to his lips. "Good things are worth waiting for."

She leaned in and kissed him, but it ended way too soon. "Good things are hard to wait for." Her smile was so sexy, his gut clenched. "And on that note, I should go."

"Are you going to the paint party tomorrow at Dallas and Nikki's house?" The idea of seeing her again so soon thrilled him.

"If I can get my mom to watch Britney." She grinned. "I thought that was really clever, throw a party and hand everyone a paint brush when they come in the door."

"Why don't you bring Britney? I'm bringing Ricky."

Ellen bit down on her lip, and he figured he knew why. "You haven't told Nikki or LeAnn about helping me out, have you?"

"Not yet. They—"

"They aren't big fans of mine," Rick said. "To be fair, I see why they feel that way."

"I don't care what they think. I'll see you tomorrow."

"You know, if you don't want to tell them—"

Ellen squeezed his hand. "Of course, I'm going to tell them."

For some reason, that squeeze, and her words, felt pretty damn good. They walked down the hall. The kids were on the car bed, and Britney was reading aloud.

"No," Ricky said. "Not like that. You have to make the funny voices like my dad does."

Emotion swelled in his chest, and his throat tightened.

Ellen smiled and whispered, "Told you you'd do fine."

* * *

"Do you think it's too purple?" Nikki asked Zoe Saturday afternoon.

"No, I love it." Zoe re-dipped her brush into the paint can.

"Good. Dallas thinks I'm crazy! But who wants to live with white walls?"

Zoe and Tyler had come to Nikki's new house for their paint party. Funny how these people had intimidated her so much earlier, and now Zoe found them…refreshing. When she got back to Alabama, she hoped to reacquaint herself with some of her old friends. Taking care of her mom, during those last six months, had cut her off from everyone but Chris. Then after Chris left, she'd become a hermit. But she was going to change that.

Just as soon as she got over losing Tyler. The thought sent a pain right to her heart. She looked back and saw him chatting with Rick. She sensed they were talking about her. She knew Tyler cared about her. She just didn't know if that caring meant anything. Part of her was holding her breath, waiting for him to make some declaration of his feelings. The other part was prepared to have her heart shattered into a million, un-put-backable pieces.

LeAnn, who'd just arrived with her husband, Tony, walked up.

"Where's your brush?" Nikki asked.

LeAnn frowned. "Sorry. I can't stay and help. I have errands. But I told Tony to put on the burgers. I'm starved. I'll help with lunch and—"

Nikki looked at LeAnn oddly. "You said you were queasy this morning."

"It passed," LeAnn said.

Nikki's eyes widened. "Oh, my God! Are you—"

"Shh!" LeAnn said.

Zoe got the clues and grinned. "Congrats."

LeAnn beamed. "I'm not sure. I'm just a week late. I haven't even told Tony yet."

"Told Tony what?" Ellen walked up.

Nikki made a ball shape in front of her belly and pointed to LeAnn.

"Ahh!" Ellen hugged LeAnn.

"Shh," LeAnn said. "Tony will die if he finds out you guys knew before him."

"We won't say a word."

"Good," LeAnn said. "That's why I can't stay. The paint fumes—"

"Oh, God, get out of here," Nikki said.

"I'm going to sit outside until lunch." LeAnn looked over at Ellen. "But first, we need to talk. You're dating Rick, aren't you?"

"What?" Nikki asked.

Ellen held up her hand. "We're not dating. Yet."

Zoe noticed the firm tone Ellen added to the *yet.* One more reason she liked Ellen—she wasn't a pushover.

"Right now, I'm just helping him adapt to being a parent," Ellen said.

"Right now?" LeAnn piped in.

Ellen didn't answer.

LeAnn sighed. "I have to admit, he wins some points stepping up to the plate for his son."

Ellen looked at Rick. Zoe saw the smile in Ellen's eyes. "He's not a bad guy."

Nikki frowned. "I'll get Dallas to kill him if he hurts you." Nikki looked at LeAnn. "You get away from the paint fumes."

Nikki and LeAnn walked off. Zoe saw again the way Ellen looked at Rick. And her heart ached knowing that was the way she looked at Tyler. The only difference was, Ellen had a possible future with Rick.

Five minutes later, Ellen left to check on the kids. Zoe concentrated on the back and forth of the purple paint she brushed on the wall. She thought about her upcoming dinner with the Bradfords tomorrow night.

"Hey."

So deep in thought Zoe jumped and swung around. Then she burst out laughing when she saw the four-inch purple stripe she'd just painted across Tyler's face. He laughed back and then kissed her and got purple all over her face.

They may not have a future, but what they had right now was damn near perfect.

Saturday night, Rick had just fallen asleep when his ringing cell phone awoke him with a start. He almost didn't reach for it, thinking it was Candy. She hadn't called him back since the other day. For Ricky's sake, he hoped she pulled herself together and got help, but he'd be damned if he'd let her continue to use him, or hurt their son.

He switched on the lamp. When he saw the name on this phone his heart lunched. Ellen. Was something wrong?

"Is everything okay?" he asked. They'd had a blast at Dallas's. The kids had played while they'd painted. While he hadn't gotten nearly as close to her as he would have liked, she'd never shied away from him. He got the feeling she'd told LeAnn and Nikki about them, too.

"Were you sleeping?" she asked.

"No," he lied, and sat up a little.

"I was just... wondering how heavy of a sleeper Ricky is."

He ran a hand over his face. "What?"

"Is Ricky a light sleeper?" she asked.

"No... why?" That's when the possibility of what she might mean had him sitting the rest of the way up. "He sleeps like a rock." He pressed a hand to his bare chest.

"Then would you like some company?"

"Hell, yeah!" His smile came all the way from his gut. "What about Britney?"

"She's at my mom's."

"I'm really liking this idea," he said.

"Then would you mind opening your front door? It's lonely out here."

He laughed. "Seriously? You're here?"

"Yes."

"One second, I need to get some clothes on."

"Oh, that's all right," she said. "I'm not wearing much, either."

Rick shot out of bed and couldn't get to the door fast enough.

"Where the hell did you find her?" Tyler's older brother asked Tyler during their mandatory Lopez family Sunday breakfast. Tyler looked up and watched Anna lead Zoe by the hand into the kitchen with all the females.

Tyler had spent the last two days deliberating whether he should bring Zoe or not. He'd decided to just miss it. But Lola and Sam had called and insisted he bring Zoe. Then Anna had called and pleaded. He cratered. He could never say no to Anna.

"Would you believe under my desk?" he said, not thinking.

Ramon's eyes widened.

"Not like that," Tyler said.

Ramon laughed. "Is it serious?"

As a heart attack. "No," Tyler lied. Luckily, his phone rang, saving him from being quizzed for details. It was Rick, and Tyler had been hoping he'd call. "Excuse me." He moved to the corner of the room.

"What's up?"

As of yesterday, Rick hadn't been able to get hold of his old buddy, the retired cop who'd worked with Officer Dean. Tyler would bet his right ball that Dean had been in on the Bradford kidnapping.

"Got Martin this morning. You were right, he doesn't have the same high opinion of Officer Dean as Phillips does. I took the liberty of asking about Phillips, too. But Martin said Phillips was a good man. A little too soft for the job, but good people."

When Tyler hung up, he went to find Zoe, hoping to save her from his sister's wrath. Anna stepped in front of the door. "I'm supposed to stop you from coming inside."

Right then he wondered if bringing Zoe here hadn't been a mistake.

When he darted around the gatekeeper and into the kitchen, Zoe was laughing with Lola. They had taken out the photo album. He knew what photos they were showing her, too. "I already told her what you guys did to me."

Lola chuckled. "He was such a cute princess."

Zoe grinned up at him. Her smile sliced through him. How the hell was he going to let her go?

Breakfast was like it always was—loud, with a lot

of laughter. In honor of Zoe, they all told Tyler stories. Before the plates had been cleared, Zoe knew every embarrassing thing he'd ever done. From his mom finding a stack of *Playboy* magazines in Tyler's room, to the time his science experiment blew up the garage when he was ten.

Everyone loved Zoe. Then again, how could they not? She even surprised him by speaking Spanish. "You didn't tell me you knew Spanish," he said as they helped Lola collect the dishes.

"You didn't tell me you built bombs, either."

Everyone laughed. Everyone but Sam. She seemed more worried about her cell not ringing than anything else. Tyler knew she was hoping Leo would call. It stung to watch her do this to herself.

When he caught Zoe alone in the kitchen refilling her coffee, she looked at him, and her big blue eyes filled with gratitude. "Thank you."

"For what?"

"For sharing your family with me. Yesterday at Nikki's and now this. It's just what I needed."

Tonight was the dinner at the Bradfords', and Tyler knew she'd been more than ambivalent about meeting everyone. So was he, but for different reasons. Bradford had informed him that his family would all be there. And Tyler had checked to see which guards were on duty then. Windsor was on the list. So his two suspects would be there.

It was hard to believe someone might try something at a family dinner, but desperate people did desperate things. He knew because he was feeling desperate himself. His two weeks had dwindled down to a week. And while he had some answers, he didn't have all of them. Namely, who had taken potshots at Zoe? And how the hell was he going to breathe when she left him?

When they joined everyone back in the living room, there was a lull of silence, and Tyler knew they'd been talking about them.

Lola finally spoke up. "In three weeks, it's Ramon's birthday. We're going all out. Tyler, you will bring Zoe."

Zoe stiffened beside him. "I'm sorry, I won't be here then."

"Where will you be?" Anna asked.

"I have to go home to Alabama."

Anna grimaced. "Is it because Tyler told Ramon that he wasn't serious about you?"

Tyler's gut clenched.

"Anna!" scolded Sam and Lola at the same time.

Tyler opened his mouth to say something but didn't have a clue what it might be.

"It's okay," Zoe said, but Tyler didn't miss the flash of hurt in her eyes.

CHAPTER THIRTY-TWO

WE AREN'T SERIOUS. Zoe felt the sting as she got in Tyler's car to leave his sisters.

Oh, no. Zoe'd just been his sex toy this past week. She plastered a smile on her face. She had sworn to keep her composure. But on the inside, she was a puddle of emotional goo. And somewhere in that goo was some good, old-fashioned redheaded ire waiting to bubble to the surface. Not that she planned to let it leak out.

"I'm sorry about that," he said as he settled in the driver's seat.

"Not an issue," she said. *But hey, would you like my liver to slice and dice next, because you did a fine job on my heart?*

She pushed her fury to the side. He'd told her this was how it was going to be. She'd gone into this knowing, and she couldn't start wallowing in self-pity now.

She could wait until she got back to Alabama for that. Then she could fall apart.

"Look," he said. "I didn't mean—"

"It's fine. You never lied to me. We are exactly what

you proposed we would be. Two adults, attracted to each other, and enjoying two weeks."

It was what she'd agreed to from the start. But now, well, she just might have to cut those two weeks short.

At six o'clock Sunday evening, Zoe stood next to Tyler in front of the Bradford home. She wore the one nice outfit she'd brought with her, a fitted green dress with tan flowers. She hadn't questioned her choice, or felt the least bit insecure until the man wearing a tux opened the door.

As the gentleman led the way, she leaned in and whispered to Tyler, "Did he say anything about this being formal attire?"

"No," he whispered back. "You look great. Relax." He'd worn a pair of navy trousers and a buttoned-down light blue shirt. She'd watched him get dressed. T-shirt, shoulder holster, gun, and pants. Only a couple of times had she seen him wear boxers.

She watched him look around as if he expected someone might jump out at them.

"I could tell you the same thing." She continued walking down the hall, her gaze shifting about the home that smelled of furniture polish and floor wax. The smell called to her like a familiar scent.

"Right here," the tux-wearing doorman said. But at that second, Zoe's attention became riveted on a winding staircase. Dark wooden banisters swept up to the second floor. Déjà vu hit hard. She'd been here.

Driving up the driveway, she'd felt some of this, but the staircase brought it on stronger. She saw her younger self running down the stairs and being scolded by a woman in a maid's uniform.

"Don't run, sweetheart." The voice from the past came from the top of the stairs, and she looked up and in her mind's eye saw the redheaded woman.

Zoe felt Tyler's hand fit into the curve of her waist. "You okay?"

She turned to see the opening of a large sitting room. A room filled with people who stared at her. Someone gasped as if in disbelief.

Zoe recognized some of them from her Internet searches. The woman was Amy Daniels, Mr. Bradford's daughter. The two teenage girls must be her children. There were a couple of men, two older women, and Mr. Bradford. All of them stared at her. All of them looked as if they were about to attend a prom. Or a funeral. They all wore dark, brooding colors. Suddenly, her twenty-nine-ninety-nine splurge at the discount outlet felt less than perfect.

No one spoke.

"Come in, dear." Mr. Bradford motioned her closer. Closer when all Zoe could think about was running. Her heart thumped in her throat. Her palms sweat.

"She does look like our dead aunt," one of the brunette teens said.

"She could have had facial reconstruction," said the other. "I saw it on *CSI*."

She felt Tyler stiffen and she touched his arm, hoping he understood that she wanted to take care of this herself.

"I didn't," she said, keeping her voice steady.

"Don't pay any heed to them," Mr. Bradford said. "Come, let me get you a drink. We have a lot to talk about. I hope you don't mind, but I asked my lawyers to be present."

Lawyers? When he introduced the guys in the suits, Zoe nodded and felt Mrs. Daniels's cold gaze.

"It is amazing," said one of the older women. "I'm your great-aunt Sylvia. Do you remember me?"

Zoe looked at her. "I'm sorry, I don't."

"We don't know for sure if she's Caroline." Mrs. Daniels pulled a glass with amber-colored liquid to her lips.

"We will as soon as the DNA test comes back," Mr. Bradford said. "But I admit you bear a striking resemblance to my late daughter-in-law."

"But Stacy's right," Mrs. Daniels said. "She could've had plastic surgery."

"Why would I do that?" Zoe asked.

"For a piece of the Bradford fortune? Why else?" Mrs. Daniels snapped.

Zoe wasn't sure what she'd expected. Maybe shock, a lot of awkwardness, but she hadn't expected the open hostility. "I meant, why would I do that if I knew you'd do a DNA test."

"Maybe you hoped we'd take your word."

Zoe looked to the other people in the room, thinking one of them would have called the woman on her rudeness, but they didn't. Was this how these people were? She met Mr. Bradford's gaze. She saw the need for answers in his eyes. But what she didn't see was love or affection. The truth stabbed her like a knife in the gut. She'd said all she'd wanted was answers, but she'd been lying to herself. A ball of hurt swelled in her chest.

She'd wanted them to love her. The grief of losing her father, her best friend, and the months of caring for her mother while cancer ate away at her bones, as well as the final straw of Chris's betrayal, had all left her feeling lost.

She'd wanted to belong to someone, to matter to someone. Her throat tightened, but she refused to cry.

"I think getting a facial reconstruction in the hopes you wouldn't need proof is a bit much, isn't it?" she countered.

"Fine, but if you are Caroline, why wait to come forward?"

"She didn't remember," Tyler bit out, his tone taunt with anger.

"But she conveniently remembered when you heard the moneybag of the family had terminal cancer," Mrs. Daniels snapped. "I hope you've heard that he lost his ass in the stock market and his last two business ventures were failures."

Zoe emotionally flinched at the abruptness in which the woman had said those words, as if her father wasn't in the room. As if his dying was nothing that caused her the least of concern. Zoe looked at Mr. Bradford, thinking she would see emotion in his eyes that told her he'd been affected by the crudeness of his own daughter's words. But Zoe saw nothing. As if he was immune. Did these people even have feelings?

"I came because I saw my picture in the *Unsolved Mystery* show." *I came because I'd lost everyone I cared about.*

Her gaze cut to Tyler. She'd wanted to belong to someone, and all she'd found in Texas was a bitter and miserable family and a man who couldn't love her back. Tears stung her sinuses. More than ever, she wanted to leave Texas.

"It's time for dinner," a man, dressed in a white uniform, announced from the doorway. "I have the first course waiting, sir."

"Then let's eat," said Mr. Bradford. "Chef Morris is a five-star chef."

Zoe stared in shock. How could they eat with so much hostility clogging up the air? Was this normal for these people?

"I'm sorry," Zoe said. "But I don't...I don't belong here."

She turned around and walked out with Tyler fast behind her. Her heels made popping sounds on the marble floor.

Don't run, sweetheart, she heard the voice from the past say again, but that was exactly what she was doing. She was running, and she wasn't going to stop until she got back to Alabama.

Suddenly, Tyler's laugh spilled out into the big entranceway and seemed to echo. "I'm so fucking proud of you."

Fifteen minutes later, Tyler pulled up in the Only in Texas parking lot and eased to a stop in the parking area around back. "How about I order some food in?" he said. The sun was setting and cast a gold hue on Zoe's face. She looked so damn sad that he wanted to just hold her. But holy hell, he'd never been so proud of someone in all his life.

"Shit," Zoe blurted out.

"What?" He followed her gaze to her car. "Damn!" Her windshield was shattered. Spray-painted on the passenger side door were obscenities.

He reached for his gun. His gaze shifted around to make sure the person responsible was gone.

Ten minutes later, Tyler called the cops just so he'd

have this on record. They sent someone over to make a report, but he didn't expect them to do shit about it. And since he really couldn't tell them why or who he suspected had done this, it was little help.

After the cops left, Tyler went into the office and called Mr. Bradford. The man started giving him hell for taking Zoe away from his house. Tyler interrupted the old man. "Is Windsor still working tonight?"

"Why?"

"Just answer me!"

"He didn't come in tonight. Why? You don't think… Is Caroline okay?"

He almost bit out that her name was Zoe. "She's fine." He hung up. Tomorrow morning Tyler and Windsor were going to have a long chat.

Going back into the apartment, he pulled her against him. "I'll have it fixed tomorrow."

"I have insurance." Her head rested on his chest.

They ordered Chinese food and ate on the sofa with the television on. Zoe barely talked or ate. He pulled her against him again. "Need a shoulder?"

She smiled. "I think I'd better go it on my own."

He wasn't sure what that meant, but he didn't like it.

When they went to bed, Tyler decided sex was out of the picture, so he'd been surprised when Zoe crawled into the bed and kissed him in a suggestive way.

He pulled back and brushed her hair from her face. "You sure?"

"Yes." When she ran her hand down his chest, there was something slightly different in her touch. A desperation. The feeling seeped into his chest as he made love to her. This time, there was no playfulness, no talking. But there wasn't a spot on her body that he didn't pass his lips over, either.

She reached for the condom and slid it over him. Then she crawled on top and with a slowness that left him breathless, she lowered herself on top of him.

She gazed into his eyes while moving up and down, easy strokes until he couldn't stand it anymore. He placed his hands on her waist and encouraged a faster pace. She obliged. Afterward, he bundled her up in his arms and held her while she cried.

Happy tears she'd told him. But they didn't feel happy.

Tyler lay awake watching Zoe sleep, his mind going over and over what he planned to say to her. How was he going to convince her to stay in Texas? How could he do it without making promises he swore he'd never make? Startling him, his phone rang. Looking at the time, almost midnight, he hurried to get it. His first thought was Sam. He prayed he was wrong.

He wasn't.

"Tio?" Anna's scared voice came through the line.

"What's wrong, Anna?" he asked, and saw Zoe sit up.

"Leo's here and he's being mean. Can you come hit him in the nose again?"

Tyler grabbed his jeans, his stomach in knots. "I'm on the way. You stay in the room. Okay? Promise me."

By the time he'd gotten off his phone and grabbed his gun, Zoe was dressed.

"Don't take the gun," Zoe said.

Tyler frowned. "I'm not going there to shoot him. I'll get much more pleasure beating his ass to a pulp if he laid a finger on her."

"I'm coming with you."

"No, you're not."

"Someone needs to watch the kids," Zoe said.

She had a point. "Fine, but you stay in the car until I say you can come in."

"Stay here," Tyler told Zoe ten minutes later as he pulled into the parking lot in front of his apartment. He heard Leo yelling when he stepped out of his car. He ran to the door and let himself in.

Leo had Sam against the wall. Tyler saw the blood on her mouth. "Take your hands off her!" he growled.

Leo stumbled back. Sam slid to the floor and started to cry. Leo was so drunk, he swayed. It took Tyler back to his childhood so fast it made him dizzy. Leo came at Tyler. And Tyler realized the difference from now and back then. He wasn't six years old. He knew how to fight. When Leo swung, Tyler swung back with everything he had.

He gave him one right in his mouth. The man fell over the sofa and landed on the floor. But he got up and came back at Tyler.

"Stop it!" Sam yelled.

Tyler ducked Leo's fist and swung again. The man fell. "Did I tell you what would happen if you laid another hand on her?" Leo got to his feet and took another swing. Tyler grabbed the man by the shirt.

"Stop it!" Zoe yelled from the doorway. Tyler looked back at the door and saw Zoe staring at him in something akin to fear. And for some crazy reason, he remembered Lisa staring at him when she'd told him it was over.

He shoved Leo down on the sofa and looked at Sam. "Are you okay?"

"Yes. I'm sorry," she sobbed. "You were right. I brought this on myself. I can't do this to my kids. Now all I have to figure out is how to stop loving him." She glared at Leo. "But I will. I will stop."

Zoe walked past Tyler and knelt down beside Sam. "Come on," she said. "Let's go in the kitchen and let me make sure you're okay."

It was after four that morning before Tyler returned to the Only in Texas office. Zoe had hardly said two words to him. He'd hardly said two words to her.

Hell, he couldn't even look at her.

When they got to the apartment, she headed straight for the kitchen. He dropped on the sofa. When she came out, she reached for his hand and put the bag of frozen peas on it.

"I don't need that," he said.

"Yes, you do." She held on to his forearm.

He gave up and let her hold the cold bag to his hand.

"You didn't do anything wrong tonight, Tyler," she said.

When had she gotten so damn good at reading him? "You were afraid tonight; I saw it in your eyes."

"I was afraid of someone really getting hurt. Not that that jerk wouldn't have deserved it, but..." She paused. "But I wasn't afraid of you."

He inhaled. "I hate getting that angry."

"Everyone does," she said.

Emotion knotted his throat, and he couldn't answer. After a few minutes, she got up and went to bed. And he let her go.

Tyler stayed on the sofa until the sun was up. He might have dozed off, but mostly he thought about Sam, and about how he loved Zoe with the same desperation that

Sam loved Leo. He'd been fooling himself to believe he wasn't in love. So now the question was, what the hell did he plan on doing about it? Logic told him to let her go. That the longer he held her, the harder he'd fall. And yet…Oh, hell, he couldn't lose her. Was this what Sam felt? And if he was so sure that Sam was making a terrible mistake, was he doing the same? Then again, he could be worried about nothing. He didn't even know if she would consider making this into something permanent.

However, she knew all his flaws, every single one of them. How he made lists to the point of being compulsive, how he was a bit of a nerd, how he had a whacky family that occasionally made his life hell. She'd seen him at his worst, when he was angry. And she'd stood up for him at the police station that day. So what would she say to him if he told her he loved her? Would she take a chance on him? Did he deserve her? Would she end up walking away from him like Lisa had?

The first thing Tyler did after sunrise was to call someone to come out and replace Zoe's windshield. The second thing he did was to inform Dallas about Windsor. Austin hadn't arrived yet.

"I'm going over there now," Tyler added.

"I'll go with you," Dallas said.

"No." Tyler put his gun in his holster.

Dallas looked at him. "I hate to say this, but you look like shit. I heard what happened. Is your sister okay?"

No, he thought. She was in love. And love was killing her. Just like it was killing him. "Yeah, it sucks."

"I think I should tag along."

"I'm fine. Stay here and watch Zoe. Even if Windsor tries anything, he's fat and slow, I think I can take him."

"Even fat old men can pull a trigger."

"He's right." Austin appeared at the doorway. "About both things. You look like shit and you're not going alone."

Zoe was still sleeping when Tyler went to check on her the last time. He left her a note on the bedside table. *Got someone working on your windshield. Need to run out. Be back soon. We need to talk. I'm sorry.* He put a couple of Xs and Os and then drew a heart. He hoped that would be her first clue as to what he wanted to talk to her about. But damn, it wasn't going to be easy.

Dallas followed Tyler to Windsor's home, a not-so-good house, in a not-so-good subdivision. The house, like the neighborhood, was run-down. No one answered the door, and his car wasn't in the garage. They hung out for an hour before deciding to go to the Bradford mansion to see if he'd gone in. He wasn't there, either.

But Mrs. Daniels was in. Tyler questioned her about why she'd sent one of the security guards to warn off Zoe. She claimed she'd heard her father chatting with the PI about checking the redhead out, and she worried her father might be involved with a young bimbo like he had been several years ago. So when she saw Zoe following the limo, she'd thought she could take care of it herself. Sadly, he believed her. Especially when he realized she hadn't been looking out for her father, but his money.

Tyler left there to take Sam to the police station to take out a restraining order against Leo. He wasn't certain, but his gut said that Sam might mean it this time. She even told him she was going in for counseling.

He'd tried to call Zoe, but she hadn't picked up. Was she angry? Or maybe just visiting with Ellen?

It was after one when Tyler got back to the office. He wanted to make sure the repair guys did a good job on Zoe's car, but it wasn't there.

His breath caught. As he ran inside to find her, he told himself to relax. Zoe probably had someone take the car in to get the graffiti removed.

Ellen wasn't at the front desk. Relieved that he wouldn't have to make polite conversation, Tyler headed into the apartment. The knot of worry in his stomach would dissolve as soon as he saw her. But she wasn't in the living room. She wasn't in the kitchen, the bathroom, or the bedroom. Heart in his throat, he looked in the corner of the bedroom where she'd set up the litter box.

It was gone.

He saw a note on the bedside table. Chest hurting, he picked it up. *Thanks. You were right, it was fun. Make sure you send me the bill.*

She'd left. Left him. "Fuck," he said when he realized that the reason he couldn't find Windsor was because the asshole might be following Zoe right now.

Tyler picked up the phone and dialed her number. He wasn't surprised when she didn't pick up. He just hoped like hell it was because she was mad at him and not because Windsor had gotten to her first.

CHAPTER THIRTY-THREE

Zoe had cried as she drove out of the Only in Texas parking lot. She was also crying when she passed a sign welcoming her to Louisiana three hours later, and still crying when she hit the Mississippi line. She finally got herself under control around Hattiesburg.

Lucky meowed, and at the next rest stop, Zoe pulled over, filled the small litter box with litter, and let Lucky out of his carrier.

Giving him some privacy, she got back in the front seat. He climbed over the seat, put his paws on her chest, and rubbed his chin against hers. She started crying again.

After a few minutes of sobbing, she looked at her phone. She had sixteen voice mails. She could guess who they were from, too. She still checked.

Much to her surprise, one wasn't from Tyler. She listened to it. It was her school principal. Zoe played the message.

"Just wanted to call and check in. Also, a Mrs. Matthews called looking for you. Her mom was a teacher

here for years and she was friends with your mom. Anyway, her mom passed away a few months ago."

Zoe remembered. She hadn't been told in time to make the funeral, but she'd sent a card and some flowers.

"Anyway, she said she was cleaning out her mom's things and found something that she thinks belongs to you."

Zoe couldn't guess what it was, not that she cared. Unless it happened to be an extra heart, because hers was completely broken.

The second the message ended, her phone rang. Closing her eyes, she debated the wisdom of talking to him. She supposed she had to sooner or later.

"Hello," she said.

"Where are you?" He sounded panicked. "Are you okay?"

Hearing his voice, her eyes filled with more tears.

"I'm fine."

"Where are you?"

"Mississippi. Halfway home."

"Christ. Zoe. Look, Windsor is missing. He could be following you right now!"

Still parked at the rest stop, Zoe's heart jerked. She looked in the rearview mirror.

"What kind of car does he drive?"

"A red Honda." He rattled off a license plate.

Zoe looked back. Cars zipped past. "He's not following me."

"You don't know for sure."

"He's not here, Tyler. I'm looking."

He sighed. "Okay, I just crossed over the Louisiana line."

"You're where?"

"Louisiana. I want you to turn around and drive toward me. And we'll find a spot to meet in the middle."

"Why?"

"Because Windsor might be following you."

"I told you, he's not following me." She looked again to be sure.

"Christ! There's my phone. It's Dallas. He might have news. I'll call you right back. Will you pick up?"

She hesitated. "Yeah."

He clicked off. Zoe put Lucky up, and with one tear-filled eye on the road, and one on her rearview mirror, she continued toward Alabama.

"What you got?" Tyler asked.

"We found Windsor," Dallas said.

"What did that bastard say?"

"Nothing. He ate his gun. Left a note."

Tyler couldn't say he was sorry. "Did he confess?"

"Yeah. I haven't read it, but Tony and Rick were called to the scene. Officer Dean and another cop as well as Ralph Adams's names were mentioned."

"Fuck." He'd hoped Zoe's dad wouldn't have anything to do with this. "Okay, I've got to call Zoe."

"Has she answered her phone?"

"Just now."

"Is she headed home like you thought?"

"Yes," Tyler said.

"What are you going to do?" Dallas asked.

"I don't know."

Tyler called Zoe back. She answered on the second ring. "Did he have news?"

"Yes," he said. "Windsor killed himself."

"Oh, God!" she said.

"He left a note confessing."

He heard her catch her breath. "What all did he say?"

"I don't have the details." He hesitated to tell her, but he knew she wanted the truth. "But Tony told Dallas that his letter mentioned Officer Dean, the cop who was murdered, another cop, and your dad."

"My dad was part of the kidnapping?"

"I don't know, Zoe. That's all I know."

She hiccupped again.

"I'm Googling a meeting place now."

"Why?" The word came out low.

"You're upset."

"I'll be fine," she said.

"We need to talk," he countered.

"About what?"

His gut twisted. "You didn't even say good-bye." Neither had Lisa. He'd come home from the first day of the trial and she'd moved out. He'd had to chase her down to find out why. And now he was chasing Zoe.

"Good-bye," Zoe said.

"Zoe... please."

She hung up. When he called back, she didn't answer.

Tyler drove all the way to Mississippi until he realized he was a fool. Zoe had left. Why the hell was he doing this?

On Wednesday Tyler called, and Zoe let it go to voice mail. She did listen to it, and God help her, she'd hoped he might say something crazy about how he loved her and couldn't live without her. Instead, he told her the DNA test came back. She was Caroline Bradford. Zoe cried. He told her about the note. Her dad hadn't been involved in the kidnapping, but Windsor suspected he'd killed Dean, probably to save her. And the other cop who'd been involved had died several years back.

Later that day, she went to school and told her boss she could start the next day. She needed to do something besides cry. And the only thing she could think she wanted to do was walk into a schoolroom and have sixteen five-year-olds who would look up with adoration.

Before she left, her principal asked if she'd called Helen Matthews. "She called two more times."

Now curious, Zoe called her and then drove straight to her house.

Helen handed Zoe a metal box. On it was her mom's name and a note that said, "Give to Zoe."

"I don't understand," Zoe said.

"I found it under Mom's bed when I was cleaning out the house. I tried opening it, but it has a combination lock. It doesn't feel as if much is in there, but it felt important."

"How long has she had it?" Zoe asked, suspicious that in the box were answers she'd thought she'd never have.

"I don't know, but my mom's been suffering from Alzheimer's for years. It was slow coming on, but we've known about it for a long time. I'm assuming that your mom gave it to her before she died. Unfortunately, Mom's memory was already going downhill then."

Zoe hugged the box and started for the door. "Thank you."

Helen smiled. "You're welcome. When you get it open, tell me what's there. I'm curious."

Zoe nodded, but she didn't promise. She wasn't sure

she wanted to taint her mom's reputation. As crazy as it sounded, Zoe didn't care what she learned. As far as she was concerned, her mom and dad had done her a huge favor by taking her away from the Bradfords.

Thursday afternoon, Rick tossed a load of whites into the machine; both he and Ricky were out of underwear. The last four days had been crazy. A good crazy. Things with Ellen were fantastic. They were meeting back at his place every day at lunch and feeding on each other instead of fast food. Things with his son were better, but not great. Ricky still didn't laugh when he read to him, and getting him to talk was like pulling teeth. But every day was a little bit better.

In addition, he'd had two new homicides and had called Ellen twice to beg her to pick up Ricky for him until he could get away. He didn't know what he would do without her. Frankly, he didn't want to find out. He knew he was falling in love with her, but it was happening so fast it was scary. And with her unresolved issues with Britney's father, nothing felt solid.

When Rick walked out of the kitchen, Ricky wasn't on the sofa watching television anymore. "Ricky?"

The boy mumbled something from his room, so Rick started for the sofa to veg before packing Ricky's lunch for tomorrow. Being a parent wasn't for wimps.

He'd just about landed on his butt when he spotted the dining room chair in front of the bookshelf. Had Ricky gotten a book? His gut clenched when he remembered what else was on that shelf. The key to his gun safe.

His gaze went to the safe. The door wasn't open. He

still popped up to check. He passed his hand over the spot, and the key wasn't there.

His gaze shot to the safe again, and from this angle he could see the door was ajar.

"Christ!" He started running toward Ricky's room, and that's when the gun went off.

CHAPTER THIRTY-FOUR

RICK'S HEART STOPPED BEATING. Tears filled his eyes as he pushed open the door. Ricky sat on the bed.

Rick lunged at Ricky and ran his hands up and down the kid's body looking for blood. "Are you okay? Are you okay?"

"I'm sorry, I'm sorry," the boy screamed, and tried to pull away.

Rick didn't stop until he convinced himself Ricky wasn't hit. At first he didn't see the boy's tears. Rick didn't realize he was crying, either, until he felt the wetness on his face.

"I'm sorry. I'm sorry," his son sobbed.

Rick sat on the bed and picked the boy up and wrapped him in his arms. "It's okay." And then Rick started sobbing with his son.

The boy stopped screaming, and Rick realized his son was hugging him around his neck. Finally, the kid pulled away and stared up. "Are you crying because you're mad at me?"

"No, son. I'm crying because I love you so much, and if you'd gotten hurt, I couldn't have lived with myself."

His bottom lip quivered. "I just wanted to help Ellen."

Rick wiped his cheeks. "Help Ellen what?"

"If she had a gun, then maybe Britney's father wouldn't be so mean to her. Britney says he's always like that to her. That he never says nice things to her like you do. And she was right, he wasn't nice."

"What? Did you see Britney's father?"

He nodded. "Yeah, he came to see Britney, and when he went to leave, he and Ellen walked outside. We hid under the living room window and heard him talking to Ellen. He treated her like the bad men who always yelled at Mom. She told him to just leave. But he told her he had a right to be there with his daughter. He said an ugly word, too. And he didn't even apologize like you did."

When Ricky fell asleep, Rick paced his apartment until he decided he had to do it. Not him personally, but it had to be done. He snatched up his cell phone and called Tyler. "What do you need?" Tyler asked, sounding even more miserable than he'd sounded these last few days.

Rick dropped down in a chair. "You know how you kept trying to pay me for things?"

"You need some money?"

"No, I need a job done. I'd do it myself, but with Ricky and work, I'm booked. And it might take some time."

Zoe set the box on her kitchen table and got a knife to pry it open. Then setting the knife down, she punched the date of her birthday into the combination. It opened. Inside she found several newspaper clippings about the kidnapping—the one with her picture on the tire swing—and about her real parents' plane crash. Beneath that was a letter. She recognized her mother's handwriting. Zoe's chest grew heavy.

Dear Zoe,

I'm a coward, or I would have told you this myself. Your father had planned to tell you when you were eighteen. But when I lost him, I just couldn't imagine losing you, and I was afraid if you learned the truth, you'd hate me.

But how do I tell you that you are not my daughter when in my heart, you are. You are the most precious gift I've ever known, and I have loved you like my own. But the truth is that you are not my biological child. Even as I write this now, my heart is breaking in fear that you will not understand. That you will blame me and your father. Please, baby, let me explain before you toss away the love you hold for us.

Our little girl, Zoe Adams, died at four months old. We had resigned ourselves to not having any more children. And it was not easy for us, because having children had been a dream for both of us. Then one day your dad brought home a very scared little redheaded girl and a story that was almost too hard to believe.

His cousin, Marcus Dean, had become a cop and moved to Miller, Texas. Another of your dad's friends, Randall Windsor, moved up there as well. Both these men, in spite of his cousin being a cop, were not good men. Your father would still meet them and their friends once a year to fish or hunt. On one trip, they were drunk and came to your father with a crazy idea for a get-rich plan. They wanted to kidnap a little girl and get the ransom money.

Your father thought they were just drunk. But a few months later, he read in the paper about a kidnapping. He didn't want to call the police in case it was just a weird coincidence. So he tried to call his cousin. He never answered. He finally reached Marcus's girlfriend who told him that Dean was in Barker, at the family's lake house.

Your dad found his cousin drunk and talking out of his head. He said things had gone bad, that you had seen someone's face, and they were going to have to take care of the problem. He said Windsor had gotten cold feet and just wanted to let you go, but the other guy involved insisted they had to kill you or they'd all go to prison.

Your dad couldn't let him do that. They argued and Marcus pulled a gun. They fought and he accidentally killed his own cousin.

Your dad was a good man, Zoe. He would never have hurt anyone. He was so scared because Dean was a cop. He called Windsor panicking, thinking since Windsor had wanted to put a stop to it, he might help. But instead he told your dad that there was another cop involved and he was on the way up there now to finish the job. He told your dad to keep quiet or they'd pin everything on him since he'd been with them on that fishing trip a few months back.

He got you out of that closet, and brought you home. You were in shock and dehydrated. We took care of you. We don't know how long you were in that closet. You didn't talk for a week. Your dad didn't know what to do. Windsor called him furious asking where you were; your dad lied and said when he found you in the closet you were already dead and he took you out and buried you.

We decided to wait awhile until we got enough money to leave town, a week, maybe two, and then we'd drop you at a police station. But Windsor kept calling saying the other kidnapper, the other cop, didn't believe you were dead. Then a little girl about your size died in our town. Your dad worked at his father's funeral home, and he had a crazy idea. He fixed it so they would stop looking for you. And as soon as we sold the house, and had enough money to run, we planned to drop you off at a police station. But right after that your real parents were killed in a plane crash.

By then, we both loved you so much, but I wanted to do the right thing. So I went to see the Bradfords. Mrs. Daniels met me at the door and wouldn't let me in. I told her I had news about you, but she didn't believe me, and on top of that she didn't even seem to care. She threatened to call the police if I ever came back. Oh, Zoe, she was so cold, I simply could not see taking you to her. So we walked away from everything, our families, our friends, and the house, and we moved to Alabama. And we lied. We lied to you. We lied to everyone.

> We were going to tell you when you were eighteen, but your father died and I was so afraid if I told you the truth that you'd hate me. So I took this lie to my grave with me. I hope someday when you have a child of your own, you realize how easy it would be to live a lie for fear of losing that child.

Zoe left the letter on the table and went into her room and cried some more.

When she woke up in the middle of the night, she scanned the letter and sent a copy to Tyler's e-mail. She was about to go to bed when she got an e-mail back from him. What was he doing up at this hour? The same reasons she was, heartbroken and couldn't sleep? As she clicked the mouse to open the e-mail, she held her breath, hoping for a sign that told her he cared.

He replied with three words. *Are you okay?*

Not I miss you. Or, I can't stand to be without you.

She answered back with two words. *I'm fine.*

Then she went back to bed and cried some more.

When Zoe got home from school on Friday, she was exhausted. But being at work helped. She only thought about Tyler every fifteen seconds instead of every three. Zoe heard a knock. Her heart jumped in her throat. Tyler? It wasn't him. But they were from Texas. Mr. Bradford and another man stood outside her door.

The stranger was a big man, and his two black eyes told Zoe that he'd been the man who'd broken into her apartment.

"May we come in?" Mr. Bradford asked.

"Why?" Zoe asked.

"To talk," he said.

She looked at the big man and back to Mr. Bradford. "You can come in, but he can't. He broke into my apartment."

Mr. Bradford moved in and sat on the sofa, while the big guy waited outside. The old man looked uncomfortable, and Zoe worried he was in pain. "Do you need something to drink?"

"No, I'm fine. I realize that my family behaved badly. I guess I didn't behave much better by not stopping it." He paused.

"If you are waiting for me to disagree with you, you'll be disappointed."

He smiled at her. "You've got your mom's wit, you know?"

Zoe hesitated. "No, I wasn't being funny, just blunt, and that came from my dad, Ralph Adams."

"Didn't Tyler contact you? The DNA test proved you are my granddaughter."

"I know," Zoe said. "But Ralph and Mildred Adams were my parents. They raised me. Loved me. Spoiled me a little bit, but they taught me right from wrong, and more importantly they taught me how to treat people. It's something your family knows nothing about."

He frowned. "We lost so much. First my wife in a car accident, then you, and then your parents. Somewhere along the way, we got bitter. But you are still a part of us. You belong with us." When she shook her head, he added, "There's money that should be yours."

"I don't want it," Zoe said. "I know you find that hard to believe. But money doesn't make people happy. That family of yours is the most miserable bunch I've ever met."

He laughed. "You do tell it like it is, don't you?"

"Pretty much."

He paused. "I'm dying."

Zoe's heart ached for him. "I know. And I'm really sorry about that. And if we lived close, I'd visit you. But we don't. I'll call if it will make things better for you."

He sighed. "I'm leaving you the money; you can do with it what you want. Give it to charity if you want."

Zoe sighed. "What kind of cancer do you have?"

"Liver."

"Then I'll leave it to the cancer foundation that researches liver cancer."

Saturday night, Tyler called Rick and told him to come over. He handed him a brown envelope. "Austin said it was the easiest job he's ever done. One day and the bastard showed his true colors. Get this, the guy went to lunch at a strip club. Took a girl into the back room. Then met his too-young intern at a hotel after work."

"I figured as much," Rick said.

"And we did some checking. Did you know his father-in-law is Mr. Quarles, meaning it's his father-in-law's law practice?"

"Just gets better and better," Rick said.

"What are you going to do with the photos?" Tyler asked.

"I'd love to take them over to his law office and post them on the reception room walls. But that's not my place. I'm giving them to Ellen; if she needs to use them, she can. Or she can burn them. I just wanted her to have a little ammunition."

Tyler nodded. "You do know that we consider her part

of this family, and if you hurt her, all three of us will be on you like stink on shit."

"Don't worry, you won't need to." Rick looked at Tyler. "How are you doing?"

"How do I look?" Tyler asked.

"Like something a dog wouldn't eat."

"That's how I feel."

Sunday morning, Tyler showed up for the family breakfast under duress. He'd been called by each of his siblings, and by Anna, and told if he wasn't there, they'd come get him.

Breakfast was good. Lola made French toast, and Tyler ate more than he'd eaten in the last five days.

No one mentioned Zoe; he figured they had discussed it and decided against it. But Ramon never was one to follow rules.

"Why the hell did you let her get away?" Ramon asked when he walked Tyler back to his car a little after nine that morning.

"She left," Tyler said.

"Then go get her and bring her back. She loves you; you could see it in the way she looked at you."

He shook his head. "I'm not like you. I'm not good at this."

"Not good at what?"

"Relationships. Statistically, I'm preconditioned to screw them up." He rubbed his fist, still bruised from where he'd hit Leo, and the PI, and then Leo again.

Ramon saw Tyler's reflex. "You think..." He paused. "Unless you're keeping something from me, the only time you've ever raised your fist at someone was to protect yourself or someone you love. And if you think that that makes you like our old man, you're giving him way too much credit. Hell, if I'd been the one to find Leo with Sam the other night, I'd beat the *hombre* within an inch of his life." Ramon shook his head.

"It's not just that. I wouldn't hit a woman, but I still screw up."

"How?"

"Statistically..."

"Don't go jabbering about statistical crap and logic, Tyler. We all know you're smart. But let me tell you something, brother, being smart doesn't mean you got a lick of common sense. And right now your lack of it is showing big-time."

"Both Sam and I—"

"I know you guys were young, and Lola and I were already leaving the house to avoid the crap that you and Sam witnessed. Perhaps we were wrong, but we were too young to realize things. And yes, Dad was a piece of shit. But that old man is dead now. Been dead a long time. Why don't you try burying him?"

Tyler shook his head. "It's better this way. It will just hurt more if she leaves later." Though he didn't think it really could hurt more.

Ramon scratched his head. "*Dios!* This isn't about dear old Dad. It's about Lisa."

"Not true," Tyler growled.

"You just said, she'd leave you later. You're just scared. All these years, I admired you going into the police force and doing all this tough-guy stuff—my brother, the big bad guy who wasn't afraid of anything. Who knew you were just a scared wimp? Your sisters had it right, dressing you up as a little girl."

Tyler bristled. "I'm not scared." But even as he said it, he knew he was lying. He hadn't wanted to care about anyone since the force and then Lisa. Because caring about people meant you could be hurt.

"Then go take a chance, damn it. Quit being afraid of losing something you don't have, and something you won't have if you don't grow a pair of *cojones*."

Ramon walked away. Tyler muttered curses and got in his car. He'd started back to the office when he saw the sign for the I-10 East. It was crazy, but it wasn't. He took the exit and started to Alabama.

Rick asked LeAnn to watch Ricky for a couple of hours. She said she was happy to do it. And when Tony walked him out to the car, he told him that LeAnn was pregnant. Rick had never seen Tony so happy. Rick gave the lucky man a hug.

When Rick pulled up in Ellen's driveway, he didn't see the Porsche parked in front of the house until he cut off his engine. He knew who owned the car. He was about to leave because he didn't think Ellen wanted him here, but Ellen and Noel walked out.

Shit!

They hadn't seen him yet but would if he started the car.

Noel turned and waved his hands in anger at Ellen. Rick couldn't make out the angry words, but if the look on her face was any indication, it hadn't been nice.

Rick couldn't stop himself then. He got out of the car. Hearing Noel say the word *bitch* had Rick slamming his car door shut.

Both Ellen and Noel turned toward him.

He walked up, eyed Noel coldly, and stood by Ellen.

"So this is him, the guy you're spending all your time with instead of our daughter," Noel sneered.

Rick smiled, thrilled that Ellen had told this asshole about him.

"What's so damn funny?" Noel asked.

"Not a damn thing," Rick said. "I'm just happy to be here. I'm a lucky man." He wrapped his arm around Ellen's waist. "Did you know that Mr. Quarles of this guy's law firm is his father-in-law?"

Ellen looked puzzled.

"Are you having me investigated? Who the hell do you think you are?" Noel asked.

Rick bit back his smile. "I'm the man you're going to see a lot of around here."

This wasn't the way he wanted to play this, but what the hell. He handed Ellen the brown envelope. "Got you a little gift."

She looked confused, and he motioned for her to open it.

"Couldn't you wait until I left?" Noel asked.

Ellen looked from Rick to Noel, and, stepping back a few steps, she pulled out the photos and held them close. At first she didn't understand. She shifted the photos. Her eyes widened, probably getting to the image of Noel sticking money in a stripper's panties. He held his breath, praying she wasn't going to be angry at him for having it done.

"What the hell is that?" Noel asked.

Ellen looped her arm with Rick's and started walking to the door. "Good-bye, Noel."

"You're not planning on sharing your gift with him?" Rick said.

"If I have to, I will. Did you take these?"

"The Only in Texas team did." He frowned. "I asked them to check into it."

She shook her head. "His father-in-law really owns the firm?"

"Yup. And I'm assuming his father-in-law wouldn't be happy to learn his daughter's husband was a rounder. I don't think the jerk ever told his wife about Britney."

"I think you're probably right." She leaned against his arm as they walked to the front porch. "Where's Ricky?"

"LeAnn is watching him for a bit." He heard Noel's Porsche drive off. "I'm in love with you, by the way. And it's not because of Ricky. I mean, I love that you helped me, but…it's you. Everything about you. The way you approach life. I want you in my life."

She gazed up at him with a smile that warmed his heart. "I come with a kid."

He grinned. "So do I."

Tyler stopped three times. Twice for gas and a bathroom. When about an hour outside of Zoe's town, he stopped for a clean shirt and some deodorant at Walmart. While looking for the men's department, he ran across the toy department and found one other item he had to have. Then as he went to payout, he passed the grocery store department and filled his cart with a few other items.

At 9:45 p.m., he parked in front of Zoe's apartment. Her lights were still on. As he made his way to the door, his heart did a bad rendition of the theme song from *Jaws*. Ramon was right. He was scared. Scared she'd reject him the way Lisa had rejected him. But Zoe was so much more important to him than Lisa had ever been.

He knocked on the door. And he heard Lucky meowing. At least he knew someone was excited to see him.

He saw the peephole go black. And could swear he heard her gasp.

The door opened, and when his eyes lit on her, his heart felt like it took flight. She had on pajamas, pink ones. Seeing her made his chest swell with emotion. Happiness and then fear.

"What are you doing here?" she asked.

He held out the game. "I lost my partner at Strip Scrabble."

She didn't smile, and he realized how that might have sounded. That this was all about sex. And it wasn't.

"I miss you," he blurted out. "And I realized that I might have screwed up the best thing that ever happened to me because I didn't tell you how I felt. And I was going to tell you, but I got scared, and then you left and I really got scared."

She bit down on her lip and looked like she was going to cry.

He didn't know if that was good or bad, so he figured he'd better talk fast. "Seeing my parents' dysfunctional relationship left me feeling impaired, but I moved past it. Then between the force accusing me of being a corrupt cop and Lisa walking out...I put up barriers. It seemed logical that if I didn't want to feel that way, all I had to do was not let people get close. You managed to break through those barriers. And now I love you. You know all my flaws. You get along with my crazy family. Both my real family and the friends. You make me laugh and..." Lucky started doing circles around his ankles. "And I love your cat, too."

When she didn't say anything, he asked, "Can I come in?"

She stepped back.

He and Lucky walked inside.

"Can you say that again?" she asked.

"Can I come in?" He grinned, knowing that wasn't what she meant, but he was just so happy to see her and she'd let him in, which meant he might just have a chance.

"I don't mean that."

Hope filled his chest. "Would it be the part about how I loved your cat?"

She arched one brow and looked at him. "You think you can just waltz in here and tell me you love me and that'll make everything hunky-dory."

Was that humor in her voice? Or was he just wanting it to be? "That was my first plan," he said, his hope dwindling because he wasn't completely sure if she was joking.

"And your second one?"

"I'm working on it right now. Usually, I always have a backup plan, but... lately, and only with you, I don't have a backup plan. I mean, I always follow logic, but logic wasn't any help at all. So I took a chance and followed my heart, and that's why I'm here."

"Your heart?"

"Yup." He hesitated and then handed her the bag of grocery items. She looked into the bag of bananas, white bread, and mayonnaise, and then back up at him in puzzlement. "I know it's stupid. I don't even know why I bought them. I saw bananas, and all I could think of was you and your sandwiches and how much I wanted you back." He paused. "I do not like banana sandwiches. To be honest, I really don't like them, but I'll eat them for the rest of my life if you'll make them for me. I love you, Zoe."

She moved in. "You realize that once you say something like that, you can't take it back."

He fit his hands in the curve of her waist. Touching her sent waves of sweet pain running through him. "Yeah, it's like toothpaste. You can't put the toothpaste back in the tube. Lola Lopez."

"She's a smart woman," Zoe said.

"That she is, but more important is how you feel about her brother." He arched a brow.

She smiled and leaned in closer, her lips a whisper from his. "You mean the guy who hates banana sandwiches but will eat them for me?"

"Yeah, that would be him."

"I'm crazy about him."

"Crazy enough to follow him back to Texas?"

"Yup, that crazy."

She wrapped her arms around his waist and rested her chin on his chest while her blue eyes gazed up at him. "I love you, Tyler Lopez."

He laughed and picked her up. "And you can't take it back."

"Never," she said, and kissed him.

PI Austin Brook
seeks vengeance against
a deadly criminal.
But the temptation of a
beautiful girl may
be even more dangerous…

Please turn this page
for a preview of

TEXAS HOLD 'EM

CHAPTER ONE

Austin Brook opened his front door and stared at his two PI partners standing shoulder to shoulder on his front porch. They looked pissed enough to chew glass. He knew why they were here. He even knew why they were pissed. Still, he decided the best approach would be to take a page from his dating manual and do the same thing he always did when he got in trouble with a woman. Namely, feign ignorance and pretend everything was just fine.

"Hey," he said. "What brings you guys by?"

"What the hell do you think you're doing?" Dallas O'Connor snapped.

Austin grinned. "Well, I was thinking about taking a piss when someone started pounding on my door."

Bud, Dallas's dog, nosed his way between his owner's legs and stared up at Austin with the same bulldog face as Austin's partners.

The fact that Bud was an English bulldog made his look understandable. Not that Austin didn't understand his partners' dire expressions. He knew they'd attempt to derail his plan.

"I thought you guys were in Galveston." And he was supposed to be gone when they got back. Austin raised his boot and scratched the dog's neck between the folds of loose canine skin.

"We came back early. Roberto called us." Dallas, a big man carrying a bad attitude, pushed inside, and Tyler, slightly less bulky but equally tall, joined him. Bud, snorting and probably farting, followed at their heels.

Austin shut the door and then regretted it when, sure as heck, the strong odor of doggie gas hit him square in the face. As if instinctual, all three of them waved a hand to clear the air.

Tyler's gaze, his eyes as dark as his black hair, shifted to Austin's suitcases sitting beside the bar. "I thought we decided to let Roberto handle this."

Roberto was the undercover man they had digging up info on the SOB DeLuna who'd framed them. And while Austin liked Roberto, the guy was taking too damn long to get the job done.

"No, you two decided that," Austin said, letting the bitterness shine through in his voice. "I distinctly remember telling you that I was tired of handing everything over to Roberto and getting handed back shit. It's been six months since he's given us a solid lead on DeLuna." That meant it was time for one of them to intervene. And since both of his partners now had wives to consider, he figured it was up to him to do it.

And that was just fine with him.

"My bet is by now all of DeLuna's men know our faces," Dallas said. "You go through with this, and we'll be buying your casket in a matter of weeks."

Austin sat down on his favorite armchair and stretched

out his cowboy-boot-clad feet. "Just use the one we keep in the entranceway of the office and save yourself some money." The damn casket had been left by the previous owners of the building, which had been a funeral home. Now it was sort of their icon.

"He's serious," Tyler said, using his calm voice that always reminded Austin of a damn therapist. Not that Austin had gone to one in a hell of a long time. Well, not since he was thirteen and decided that being a ward of the state didn't mean he had to follow their damn rules.

"So am I," Austin said. And he was. His mind was made up.

"What brought this on?" Tyler asked. "Is this about your—?"

"Stop! Quit trying to get in my head." Austin felt his anger surface. But it was directed more at the stranger who'd shown up at the agency and spilled her dirty laundry right in front of everyone than at his two partners. Still, that didn't mean he had to discuss it with them.

"You want to know what brought this on?" he asked. "It was the year and a half I was fucking locked up in prison. Or have both of you forgotten about that?"

It seemed to him they had. Okay, maybe they hadn't forgotten it, exactly, but they'd somehow gotten past it. And while Austin was friggin' happy for them that they'd been able to do that, and he'd danced a jig at both their weddings in the last two months, he couldn't get past it. He wouldn't until DeLuna was behind bars.

Or dead.

Tyler exhaled. "I just think—"

"Then stop thinking!" Austin moaned. The last damn thing he wanted was to have anyone rummaging through his mental closet. There were just too many damn skeletons, too many nailed-shut trunks of emotional crap, that he didn't want to think about it.

"Damn it, Austin," Dallas snapped. "This is shit. We need to stick to our plan."

"What plan?" Austin asked. "We don't seem to have a plan anymore."

Dallas's shoulders tightened. "The plan hasn't changed. We keep picking apart his organization until we force DeLuna to come out of whatever hole he's taken cover in to face us. Use your brain for once. You know as well as I do that we lose every advantage by going to him instead of having him come to us."

"Look, nothing personal, but you two have other priorities right now. As in wives. And I get it. But what he did still eats away at my gut. I want my pound of flesh."

"Roberto is working it," Dallas said. "If you go in now, you'll probably get him killed. Can you live with that?"

Austin raked a hand over his face. When he opened his eyes, he found himself staring at his partners' concerned faces. Real concern. Damn it to hell, he knew they were here because they cared. And yes, he felt the same way about them. If anything, the bond he had with these two were the closest thing he'd ever come to having a family, but...

"I don't know what Roberto told you," he said, speaking calmer. "But I've already worked this out with him. I'm not even going to Fort Worth. I'm checking the other lead that—"

"Which lead?" Dallas asked.

"The sister."

"Half sister," Tyler corrected.

"Whatever," Austin said. "They're Latin, and you"—he pointed to Tyler—"know how important family is in that culture."

"She's half-Latin," Tyler corrected again. "And stop stereotyping."

"It's a good stereotype," Austin said.

"Roberto watched her for a month and found no connection to DeLuna," Dallas added.

"Yeah," Austin replied, "but I'll bet my left nut she knows what rock he's hiding under."

"You could lose more than your left nut. And even if she knows, why would she tell you?" Dallas asked. "Plus, Roberto tried connecting with her, and it didn't work."

Austin smiled. "I'm not Roberto. I'm charming. Women like me. It's a natural gift."

He was just like his biological father...or so his "mother," aka the woman who'd given birth to him, raised him for a few years, and then abandoned him had said. The brief conversation they'd shared came back to haunt him, but he pushed it aside. He wasn't going to think about that. Nope. So he shoved the memory back into his mental closet.

Only it kept falling out. She'd come looking for peace of mind and ruined his in the process.

"We know the type of women who find you charming," Tyler said. "Leah Reece is educated, and she's part Latin, which means she's too smart to fall in bed with you."

"Now who's stereotyping?" Austin asked. "Besides, I didn't say I was going to sleep with her. I said I was going to charm her. Get her to trust me enough to confide in me. And actually, her being Latin works in my favor." He grinned. "We've discussed this before. I go for blondes. Of all the brunette Victoria's Secret models, there's only one brunette I'd pick before I'd sleep with their whole list of blond models."

"How the hell does Victoria's Secret models come into this?" Dallas ranted.

"Anytime you can bring them into the conversation, it's a good thing." Austin grinned. "Besides, I've already worked out a plan. Roberto rented me the apartment next to hers. She's a vet, and I've been thinking about getting a dog, so I'll buy one and pop in to see her and say... 'Hey, aren't we neighbors?' And, *voilà*! Instant connection."

"Right," Tyler said. "Once again, you didn't do your research. Leah Reece isn't a regular vet; she's a specialty vet."

"Like a gynecologist?" Austin grinned again.

Tyler smirked. "Like a Feline Specialist. Feline as in cats." He laughed. "I'd pay to be a fly on the wall. You, an ailurophobe, are going to try to charm a Feline Specialist. I'll bet she's got at least two or maybe three cats living with her."

People really had three cats? "I'm not scared of cats."

Okay, maybe he was a little. "So, the vet angle won't work," he said. "I'll find a different way." Somehow, someway, he'd win Leah Reece over enough that she'd confide in him about her brother. How hard could it be? She was, according to Roberto, a petite little thing with a soft spot for animals.

"I still don't like it," Dallas said.

"Me, either," Austin admitted, still thinking about the cats. "But I'm doing it."

The way he saw it, he had no choice.

* * *

Monday morning, Leah Reece was busy doing one of the things she did best.

"I swear, you enjoy this, don't you?" Sara, her vet assistant and good friend, asked in a teasing voice, and stroked the anesthetized cat on the table.

"Can't you see the satisfaction in her eyes?" Evelyn, the office manager of Purrfect Veterinarian Clinic, added from the doorway.

Leah grinned but didn't look up until she removed the second testicle from the tiny incision and dropped it into the metal container. It landed with a tiny *thud* in the pan beside its brother ball. "I was just thinking that I'm good at it, but it doesn't bring me the type of joy you two are insinuating. Now if Spooky here walked on two legs, thought he was God's gift to women, and spewed out come-on lines instead of purring, then it would do my heart good."

Sara laughed and so did Evelyn. Then Evelyn cleared her throat in that kind of way she did when she was about to offer some advice that she knew going in wouldn't be well received. "It's been two years. I think it's time you stop dreaming of castrating them all, and remember what a man can do for you."

"Oh, you mean like cheating on you with your cousin and running up your credit cards by having phone sex with strangers?" They all laughed. Sometimes even the truth was funny. Or it could be after two years.

Still in the doorway, Evelyn gave Leah her I'm-serious look. Leah adored Evelyn; she'd been the first employee Leah hired three years ago when she'd started the practice.

She'd known Evelyn was the right fit when Leah asked

her if she had any prior office management experience and the fifty-five-year-old answered, "Nope, but I managed to keep a household afloat, take in over ten cats, clothe and feed three boys, get two through college on my husband's car salesman income. If you need someone who can run a tight ship, balance a budget, knows how to get stains out of men's underwear, and doesn't mind picking up hair-balls, I'm your woman. Besides, with the economy down, and one boy still in college, I could really use a job."

Evelyn cleared her throat again, pulling Leah back to the present. "Carl was an idiot."

And managed to make her feel like one, too. "But he was so good at it." Leah checked Spooky's scrotum one more time.

Sara laughed again. "I think both of us would have helped you castrate Carl. But Evelyn's right—not all men are scum."

No, Leah thought. Some of them were even worse. Carl was just the last in a long line of men in her life to disappoint her. First had been her father. Then her half brother. And a few boyfriends along the way, who'd lied and cheated as easily as they drew in air. If she didn't have Luis, her younger brother, she'd have given up on the whole male species. But as it was, she would be hard-pressed to trust another man. And the only kind she'd let get close were the feline variety that she'd previously neutered.

"Don't you miss it, just a little bit?" Evelyn asked.

"Miss what?" Leah moved Spooky into the kennel cage and placed him on a soft mat where he would wake up. She gave the unconscious feline an ear rub. Hopefully now that he was fixed, she could find him a home. But Lordie, she was such a sucker for a stray.

If she didn't already have four fur babies at home, she'd add him to her collection.

"A man's touch," Sara answered for Evelyn, and her voice went dreamy. "The way the palm of his hand moves over your skin or fits just so in the curve of your waist. The way seeing him look at you like you are eye candy makes your skin get ultrasensitive. Those sexy bedroom smiles that make you want to squeeze your thighs together a little tighter. Oh, and that moment when he's naked between the sheets and—"

"Oh, my." Evelyn started fanning herself. "I'm gonna go call my hubby and tell him to come home early." She walked out, her step a little peppier than when she'd walked in.

"Well?" Sara asked.

"Well, what?" Leah barely got the two words out. Her mind felt like mush, and her body ached for something she didn't think she could ever allow herself to have again. She'd tried it. And as wonderful as it all was in the beginning, it cost too damn much. Both emotionally, and monetarily. Phone sex didn't come cheap.

"Do you miss it?" Sara asked.

"Not at all," Leah lied, and looked down at the testicles she'd just removed.

"Hey, Leah." Evelyn appeared in the doorway again. "You have a phone call. He says it's your brother, but it doesn't sound like Luis."

THE DISH

Where authors give you the inside scoop!

♥ ♥ ♥ ♥ ♥ ♥ ♥ ♥ ♥ ♥ ♥ ♥ ♥ ♥ ♥

From the desk of Rochelle Alers

Dear Reader,

I would like to thank everyone who told me they couldn't wait to return to Cavanaugh Island. And like the genie in the bottle I'm going to grant your wish.

You will get to revisit people and places on the idyllic island, while being introduced to others who will make you laugh, cry—and even a few you'd rather avoid. It is a place where newcomers are viewed with suspicion, family secrets are whispered about, and where old-timers are reluctant to let go of their past. Most inhabitants believe what happens in Sanctuary Cove, Angels Landing, or Haven Creek stays in Cavanaugh Island. Angels Landing—or "the Landing," as the locals refer to it—takes its name from the antebellum mansion and surrounding property that was and will again become a crown jewel on the National Register of Historic Places.

In ANGELS LANDING you will meet newcomer Kara Newell, a transplanted New York social worker who inherits a neglected plantation and a house filled with long-forgotten treasures and family secrets spanning centuries. Kara finds herself totally unprepared to step into her role as landed gentry, and even more unprepared for the island's hunky sheriff. Her southern roots help her adjust to the slower way of Lowcountry life, but she finds herself in a quandary when developers concoct elaborate schemes to force Kara into selling what folks refer to as her birthright. Then there's hostility from newfound family members, as well as her growing feelings for Sheriff Jeffrey Hamilton.

Jeff has returned to Cavanaugh Island to look after his ailing grandmother and to assume the duties as sheriff. His transition from military to civilian life is smooth because, as "Corrine Hamilton's grandbaby boy," he's gained the respect of everyone through his fair, no-nonsense approach to upholding the law. However, his predictable lifestyle is shaken when he's asked to look after Kara when veiled threats are made against her life. When Jeff realizes his role as protector shifts from professional to personal, he is faced with the choice of whether to make Kara a part of his future or lose her like he has other women in his past.

So come on back and reunite with folks with whom you're familiar and new characters you'd want to see time and time again. You will also get a glimpse of Haven Creek, where artisans still practice customs passed down from their African ancestors. Make certain to read the teaser chapter from *Haven Creek* for the next installment in the Cavanaugh Island series.

Read, enjoy, and do let me hear from you!!!

Rochelle Alers

ralersbooks@aol.com

www.rochellealers.org

♥ ♥ ♥ ♥ ♥ ♥ ♥ ♥ ♥ ♥ ♥ ♥ ♥ ♥ ♥

From the desk of Christie Craig

Dear Reader,

Have you ever stared in the mirror and had yourself a mini identity crisis? Felt unsure of who you really were? I have, and that was the inspiration for BLAME IT ON TEXAS. But for my heroine, Zoe Adams, her identity crisis isn't so mini.

Imagine seeing a childhood picture of yourself splashed across the TV screen on an unsolved mystery show, which claims you were kidnapped from some highfalutin' Texas millionaire family. Imagine learning that your corpse was supposedly discovered shortly after you were kidnapped. Imagine it, when all your life you've had some strange memories that didn't make sense.

With Zoe's parents—or people she thought were her parents—deceased, she's certain of only one thing: She's not dead. (Although, after her fiancé ran off with another woman, taking her heart with him, she hasn't felt too alive.) So Zoe does the only thing she can: She takes a leave of absence from her job as a kindergarten teacher, packs up the only thing that matters in her life—her handicapped cat—and hightails it from Alabama to the Lone Star State.

Her search for answers lands her in a whole lot of trouble, too. When someone starts taking pot shots at her, she winds up under the protective arm of a sexy commitment-phobic PI who is more than willing to play bodyguard. Between Tyler Lopez, his family and friends, and all the zany characters she meets while working at Cookie's Diner, Zoe learns that who you are isn't so much about your birth name or who your parents were. It's about whom you let into your life and whom you love.

From Texas-sized flying cockroaches and ticked-off clowns, to games of strip Scrabble, writing the story of Zoe and Tyler was the most fun I've had doing something that wouldn't get me arrested. The chemistry between these two characters lit up the page from the moment she drops three plates of food on him. Hot grits and sunny-side up eggs never looked so good. I hope you enjoy the story of two people stumbling their way through life's bumpy roads and landing smack-dab in the lap of love.

I love hearing from readers, so please come visit me at www.christie-craig.com; find me on Facebook at https://www.facebook.com/christiecraigfans; or follow me on Twitter at @Christie_Craig.

Laugh, Love, Read.

Christie Craig

♥ ♥ ♥ ♥ ♥ ♥ ♥ ♥ ♥ ♥ ♥ ♥ ♥ ♥ ♥

From the desk of Nina Rowan

Dear Reader,

Confession #1: I'm terrified of math. I have been a math-o-phobe since first grade, when we learned basic addition and I had to count on my fingers to make sure I was getting the answers right. Confession #2: I still count on my fingers. Confession #3: I'm way, way beyond first grade.

Math and I have never found a groove. I'm okay with some numbers (2 and 5 are polite acquaintances of mine, if not exactly friends), but others make me nervous (7 is somewhat flinty, and 9 is plain evil). I never memorized the multiplication tables. I still can't do long division. My son is now a first-grader and completes his math homework faster than I can check it.

So what provoked me to create a heroine who is a brilliant mathematician? Lunacy, of course, and maybe a little bit of "Ha! I will confront you, Math, even though you scare me." At least in writing about a mathematician, I could channel my fear into creating a hopefully unique and memorable heroine.

If there is one thing Lydia Kellaway, the heroine of A STUDY IN SEDUCTION, does not fear, it's numbers. Equations comfort her. She enjoys theorems, series, postulates. She understands them. They understand her. And I loved the idea of a Victorian woman who has a harmonious relationship with math and who is renowned for her extraordinary intelligence.

The seed of Lydia's character came while I was researching nineteenth-century Russia and discovered information about Sofia Kovalevskaya (1850–1891), a prominent Russian mathematician who made major contributions to the field.

Despite the barriers she encountered in academia, Sofia earned a doctorate *summa cum laude* from the University of Gottingen, becoming the first woman in Europe to hold that degree. Personal and professional struggles did not prevent Sofia's success, as she soon became the first woman in Northern Europe to hold a full professorship at the University of Stockholm. She published numerous papers, edited a mathematical journal, and received the competitive Prix Bordin from the French Academy of Sciences.

While Sofia Kovalevskaya inspired my idea of a heroine who is a mathematician, I wanted Lydia to be a unique character in her own right. I loved that she could immerse herself in numbers and find comfort in equations, but what did that mean for the other parts of her life? What would happen if Lydia had spent her childhood in lonely isolation, with only numbers as her faithful companions, and then was suddenly forced to confront the exact opposite of intellect—the pull of lust?

After her destructive early experiences, Lydia lives in safe comfort inside her head...until Alexander comes along to wreak havoc with all his hot, Russian sexiness. He is fascinated not only by her body, but also by her brilliant mind. Writing about how Lydia's affinity with math affects and changes their relationship was both a challenge and a pleasure.

Confession #4: I'll never overcome my fear of math. Words I love, but numbers I'll merely tolerate. I'll always carry my portable calculator, and when my son's math homework gets beyond me (which it soon will), I'll either study with him or recruit someone else to be the homework helper. I'll keep working at multiplication, especially the 7s and 9s, but in the meantime I take a small measure of comfort in Sofia Kovalevskaya's remark to one of her teachers: "I was unfortunately weak in the multiplication table."

Happy Reading!

Nina Rowan

Find out more about Forever Romance!

Visit us at
www.hachettebookgroup.com/publishing_forever.aspx

Find us on Facebook
http://www.facebook.com/ForeverRomance

Follow us on Twitter
http://twitter.com/ForeverRomance

NEW AND UPCOMING TITLES

Each month we feature our new titles and reader favorites.

CONTESTS AND GIVEAWAYS

We give away galleys, autographed copies, and all kinds of exclusive items.

AUTHOR INFO

You'll find bios, articles, and links to personal websites for all your favorite authors—and so much more.

GET SOCIAL

Connect with your favorite authors, editors, and other Forever fans, and share what's important to you.

THE BUZZ

Sign up for our monthly romance newsletter, and be the first to read all about it.